Invizibles II

Provocation

E S Carpenter

Published by Quesylis P H

Cover by Morgan Wermuth

Dedicated to those who continue to try, even in the face of certain defeat.

Chapter One
Round Two

Ben knocked before opening the Ferguson's front door. "I'm here."

"I'll be down in a minute."

Kye walked from the family room toward his friend and playfully smirked when they made eye contact. "Is that it? You traded me in for my sister?"

He dropped his soccer backpack next to the door. "Stop. You know we're just practicing."

"Every day?" He led Ben to the family room.

"I have to if I'm gonna make the team. Tryouts start in a week." He eyed Kye. "Besides …you can come to the field with us."

"So I can be your ball-boy and chase your bad shots?"

"You can get the good shots too."

Kye stopped and turned as he fought his grin. "Very funny."

"Just come." Ben plopped on the loveseat. "And stop your jealous whining."

"Hey!"

Jaime turned the hallway corner, and came into view, wearing soccer shorts and a t-shirt that read; Girls kick A …and soccer balls. "What are you two whispering?"

"Ben is trying to recruit your ball chaser."

"You got something better to do?" She turned into the kitchen.

"I need a lazier best friend." Kye headed toward the stairs. "Let me get my sneakers."

Faith approached the soccer field an hour later, and they joined her at the goal line, then casually sat and joked until Kye laid back with his hands under his head and stared at the blue summer sky. "The more days that pass, the harder it is to believe we rescued aliens."

"But we'll always have proof." Ben reached for a soccer ball.

Faith sat between Jaime and Kye. "I really like not hearing from those military guys anymore."

"We gave them a sandbox. What more could they want?"

"Do you think they'll come around looking for gel?" Ben glanced at Kye as he patted his pocket.

Faith frowned at her brother. "I can't wait till years pass and we don't have to think about them anymore."

"Have any of you thought of any ideas we can use the gel for?" Jaime eyed them while fixing her ponytail.

Kye fought his grin as he raised a finger. "I want to fight social injustice."

"Yeah. We should think of a way to use it to fight for things like fairness and equality."

"I think he was joking, little brother."

Jaime glanced at Ben and smiled. "And I don't think invisibility helps win those fights."

"Maybe there's corruption we can expose."

Faith eyed him. "Political corruption?"

Kye frowned. "Is it possible to separate those two words?"

"Wow." Ben swatted at the bugs hovering nearby. "I can't believe we're having trouble thinking of how we can use the stuff."

"How about, investigating international kidnapping rings? Stop human trafficking?"

Kye turned toward Faith. "Yeah. I'd like to fix some of the things adults can't."

Jaime nodded. "That list is longer than we can handle."

"Let's just save it until we think of something real." Ben stood and toed a ball away from the group. "We don't have to use it right now, just because we have it."

Faith extended her open hand. "Wait. Are you saying you're thinking about using it for the rest of your life?"

"Not just me …us." Ben's voice softened. "We're a team …aren't we?"

"Well, what do I do when I get married and have a baby?"

"One of our parents will watch it." Kye stood and brushed his pants.

Jaime watched Faith's eyes widen, then refocused on her brother. "Kye!"

"What?" He pointed at Faith and grinned. "She's the one who asked."

Faith fought her grin. "Asked what?"

"What we should do with the kid when we have an assignment after we're married."

Faith extended both open hands as her back arched in playful adamancy. "I did no such thing!"

Kye smirked. "Yeah …that isn't what you meant."

She stood. "It isn't!"

"Fine." He raised his nose and shut his eyes. "Then I take my acceptance back, especially since there's no ring."

She leaned toward him grinning, with her fists clenched. "I didn't ask!"

"She didn't." Ben shrugged as they eyed him. "It sounded more like she's just assuming." Ben smiled as Kye fist-bumped him.

"Just ignore them." Jaime frowned before motioning to her brother. "Ben's right though. We have it and when something happens where we can help by using it, then let's use it."

"And in the meantime, let's keep it hidden and not waste any." Ben spun and kicked his ball into the net.

Faith looked up. "We should hide it somewhere safer though."

Ben shrugged. "I think our hiding place is good."

Kye smiled. "How 'bout a safe deposit box? The word safe is in the name."

Jaime shook her head. "They cost money."

"Not a lot."

"Do you think we should still keep a small drop in our pocket, just in case?" Ben toed another ball backward and practiced his footwork.

"I think we should … at least for a while."

He stared at the sky. "I just want to work as a team again. I thought we were great together."

Jaime smiled. "We were, weren't we."

Kye stole Ben's ball and passed it to Faith. "Hell yeah."

She kicked it, then watched it dribble toward the net. "Yeah we were."

Jaime's phone signaled a group text. *Friends and teammates meeting at the practice soccer field for a pick-up game in a half hr if interested*

She hit reply and began typing. "Guys, there's a pickup soccer game here in half an hour."

"Our friends?" Faith ran and tapped the ball into the net as Ben raced to intercept it.

She nodded. "Friends and teammates."

"Yes!" Ben raised both arms. "I love this place."

~*~

The last scientist walked into the laboratory's adjacent conference room, then sat and opened his laptop. He nodded toward Doctor Farris before making eye contact with his other colleagues. "Sorry I delayed the meeting, but I couldn't abort the thermal conduction imaging process."

"Understood, Doctor Eryn. That machine has been temperamental since day one." Doctor Farris adjusted her notebook and lifted her pen. "Is there any change in the latest readings for our remaining sample?"

"Preliminary images show varying degrees of microscopic inconsistency at multiple grid coordinates for the visible samples, but the invisible piece still remains undetectable."

"What molecular magnification range are you using?"

"In twenty micron intervals capping at two hundred and fifty microns." He inhaled. "The thermal equilibrium may be inhibiting the detection process, but the molded plastic isn't conducive to a change in thermal conductivity."

Doctor Farris turned to Doctor Lee. "Might a pressure differential circumvent the problem?"

The scientist shook his head. "The thermal dynamic would compromise the plastic's integrity."

She faced Doctor Diomari. "And how are your electron microscopy experiments proceeding?"

"No discernable data, and we've completed scanning a focal range from one centimeter to five microns, with a magnification to thirty thousand through the spatial resolutions."

She turned to Doctor Reese "And the optical micro-fields experiment?"

"We've extended the 4Pi STED diffraction to thirty nanometers, with no discernable reading."

She faced Doctor Amadu.

"The radiometric measurement is immediately negative infinity."

She penned a checkmark before referencing the next line. "Any energy transfer?"

"None."

"Magnetic measurements?"

"Still zero."

"Hyperspectral imaging analysis?"

"Nothing."

Doctor Farris glanced at her list. "Did I miss anyone?" She paused after acknowledging everyone's nonresponse, then placed her elbows on the cherrywood conference table and folded her hands. "The halving process has proven highly beneficial for location refinement, and though we're now working with less than five percent of the original object, all indications confirm we must continue our current process." She eyed her associates. "Agreed?"

Nine affirmations followed, and she smiled. "Then we'll proceed after lunch."

An hour later, the team filed into the laboratory, still discussing the clandestine facility's surprisingly pleasant lunch accommodations. Doctor Farris diverted from her intended path and walked to the reconstructed plastic toy spaceship as other associates gathered around it. She smiled before shaking her head. "Are any of you equally perplexed by the object we've been studying?"

"A scientifically undetectable toy is an interesting enigma." Doctor Sayf scratched his unkempt hair. "And it's definitely been identified as nothing more than a reworked toy sandbox, available for online purchase?"

Doctor Eryn displayed his phone. "I saved the website if you'd like to see it in its unmodified form."

Doctor Sayf smiled. "Thank you, Marquise, but that's unnecessary."

"We've also purchased one, and it should arrive any day." Doctor Farris shared an inviting smile. "In the meantime, would anyone currently not busy like to assist me as I continue the dissection process?"

"I'd be honored, Bria."

"Oh, excellent Tianya."

Twenty minutes later, Doctor Farris handed the newly sliced, visible half-sample to Doctor Kardelen, and held the remaining invisible piece between her glove-covered finger and thumb. "How about diagonal cuts to differentiate the remainder?"

Tianya raised her safety shield and smiled. "Why not?"

Doctor Farris loosened the two L-shaped clamps on the hold-down, and slid the remaining one and a quarter by two and a half inch block of invisible material under the device before gently hand-tightening the guide.

"Preparing dissection thirteen." She adjusted her safety shield before pressing the red power button, and the blue cobalt beam instantly appeared. She eased the guide toward the hand-made mark referencing the edge of the material, and paused before carefully engaging the invisible object, then jumped as the cold laser cutter unexpectedly disappeared.

"Help!" She froze, still gripping the invisible guide clamp as the fine cobalt beam emanated without a visible source. "Kill the power!"

An associate quickly pressed the emergency button on the workroom wall, initiating a reverberating siren as the room dimmed, while two other scientists ran to her as lab motors changed pitch from the power loss. "Are you alright?" … "What happened?"

"Don't step close! I'm not sure what happened, but I guess we hit paydirt."

"Are you harmed?"

"I'm perfectly fine, but our quest for the true point source of invisibility may have just been breached and scattered with the cut, so do not approach."

"Someone flip the breaker on this machine so we can turn on the power."

Chrystal called out from a distance after gaining a sightline. "An emergency crew will be here within minutes."

They heard another associate shout from the direction of the electric service panel. "Machine four breaker is off. It's safe to reengage power."

"Reengaging."

The main breaker reset with a loud click, and lights immediately brightened as electronics restarted and machine motors re-amplified in pitch and volume.

"Command rescue ma'am; Lieutenant Jaggar. Do you need our assistance?"

Doctor Farris eyed the stranger, dressed in a florescent yellow protective suit. "Why yes, Lieutenant. Please kindly extricate me from my current predicament without touching anything between us." She twisted and faced her colleagues without moving her feet. "We have to swab the area and the sample; the invisibility source must have contaminated the machine, and we must attempt scientific recovery."

"Understood, Doctor."

"We've all just become janitors."

An unidentified voice grumbled, "…With tweezers."

"Commander Lacey is on the phone, Doctor. Would you like me to connect him through the laboratory speaker system?"

Bria nodded. "Please, Chrystal."

She stepped out of sight, and a moment later, spoke to the ceiling as she came into view. "You're connected, sir."

"Hello, Doctor Farris."

"Hello, Commander."

"Is anyone harmed?"

The frozen scientist raised her head after scanning the room. "No, Commander."

"Excellent. May I ask what happened?"

"We're assuming we breached the invisibility source, but in doing so, our primary directive has changed to one of tedious recovery."

"We're accessing the video, Doctor. Lieutenant Jaggar, are you in complete control of the situation?"

"Yes, Commander."

"You have my authority to accommodate Doctor Farris's requests as quickly and efficiently as possible."

"Yes, Commander."

"In the meantime, I'll be reviewing video of the incident."

Doctor Farris looked past the still-invisible cobalt cutter, and into an adjoining office. "I can see three from our team doing the same, from where I stand."

"I assumed. Chrystal, dial me direct for any need or status change, until our situation has returned to normal."

"Yes, Commander."

The call-ending click prompted everyone's refocus, and two yellow-suited rescuers moved quickly toward the giant overhead crane parked high against a far back wall.

"Do you have a fear of heights, Doctor?"

"No, Lieutenant."

"Then we'll have you removed within minutes."

"Thank you, Lieutenant." Doctor Farris refocused on Chrystal. "Please project a numbered three inch by three inch computer grid with X and Y axes, to cover this section of the laboratory."

"Yes, ma'am."

~*~

Charlie knocked as he entered Mitch's office. "I'm bored."

Mitch laughed after glancing at him, then refocused on his computer screen. "Is that a sign of the apocalypse? I never heard you say that."

"I can't believe how interesting the Fallwater incident was, and how much I miss the activity." He placed his mug on Mitch's desk and plopped in his usual chair.

Mitch shook his head before continuing his report.

"Aw, c'mon. I go stir crazy sometimes, staring at these walls. Don't tell me you don't too."

"Speak for yourself."

He sat back and smiled. "At least you got a promotion out of it."

"Yeah, but you know the baggage that comes with." Mitch continued typing.

"Do you mean in general, or the incident."

Mitch smiled as he glanced from his computer. "Yeah."

"Speaking of the incident; when do you think this case will be reopened?" Charlie's eyes narrowed. "Have you heard anything?"

Mitch inhaled, then spun in his chair and leaned on his desk. "Every time I open my email, I expect to read it's re-opened, and I really don't feel like starting another battle with those kids. I get the feeling it won't end as well as the last time."

He chuckled. "They kicked our ass, the last time."

"Very funny, but you know what I mean."

"But it isn't your or my choice. The General was pretty adamant about pursuing the invisibility quotient."

"I know, but why are you reminding me?" Mitch frowned as he looked in his empty coffee mug. "Are you just torturing me?"

"Hell no." Charlie laughed. "All that does is cost me beers."

He pointed. "And we're playing dumb if the colonel questions anything not currently recorded."

"Of course." Charlie shrugged. "Maybe we won't even be part of battle two."

"That may not be better than being a part of it."

"But at least we won't be disobeying direct orders if we're not." Charlie's brows rose. "Are we on that same page?"

Mitch shook his head. "Battle two will cost everyone too much."

"What battle doesn't cost too much?" Charlie's breathing quickened. "But we'll have less information if we're not involved."

"Why are you drudging this up?"

"Because we have to prepare for the next battle."

Mitch's voice lowered. "And how are we supposed to do that?"

"You're supposed to figure that out. You're the new captain. My job is just to present the military problem."

Mitch leaned back, fighting his smirk. "You're my military problem."

He lowered his chin as he stared. "I'm your secret weapon."

~*~

"I cannot believe we've been kneeling for days." Doctor Dahmir lifted his knees and placed his kneeling pad at the edge of the next computer-generated three inch laboratory grid line.

"Keep concentrating on the compensation, Sakib."

He laughed as he tweezed the top of the polished gray epoxy floor. "Well put, Lena. That does help."

"Not completely. I spent an hour in the sauna after dinner last night, just so I could lay flat. I haven't knelt this long…ever."

"I was thinking about doing that, but opted for a bottle of wine instead."

"Did it work, Sharae?"

She chuckled. "Surprisingly well."

Doctor Lee eyed the void the invisible cobalt cutter occupied. "We're not working until we finish, are we?"

Bria folded her hands on her lap as she knelt. "We're getting closer, Adriana, but we have no deadline and must continue being meticulously thorough."

"Our team will continue, with your permission, Doctor Farris."

Bria eyed the newly acquainted head of the military forensics team. "Do any members of my team have a reason why our new partners shouldn't continue our quest after we retire for the evening?"

"None here."

"Anyone?" She paused through the silence before smiling at Captain Devereux. "You have our permission, Captain, as long as you notify us immediately, upon any discovery."

"Of course, Doctor." The captain scanned the remaining grid squares before resuming his tedious recovery effort.

Bria's voice rose. "And with notification, we will reconvene here, immediately."

Nine affirmations followed.

A loud shriek broke the next extended silence.

"Freeze! Everyone freeze!" Doctor Eryn stared at the empty space where Doctor Summer knelt moments before. "Bonnie, are you alright?"

A voice emanated from the void. "I'm fine."

"Did you freeze?"

"Yes."

"Do not move!"

"Is something happening?"

"Yes! Stay frozen!"

"Please tell me what's going on!"

"You're invisible!"

"Are you serious?"

"Very serious! Don't move!" Doctor Farris raised her voice. "Chrystal! Can you hear me?!"

"Coming." Chrystal stood at a distance as she came into view. "What do you need, Doctor?"

"Commander Lacy's presence."

"I can't stay like this for long."

Everyone stared at the voice's location as Captain Devereux moved toward it. "Doctor Summer, are you still kneeling?"

"Yes."

"Where are your hands?"

"My left hand is resting on my left knee and my right hand is squeezing tweezers, roughly two inches in front of, and almost directly between my closed knees."

"Are your knees behind X-axis gridline fifty-eight? Can you see and differentiate gridline fifty-eight?"

"Yes, Captain. I can see just as well as I could before the incident. Better in fact, I see the luminescent droplets I believe we're searching for."

"What gridlines are your tweezers between?"

"Between *X*-axis fifty-seven and fifty-six. *Y*-axis *CH* and *CI* …roughly an inch from charlie hotel and two from charlie indigo."

He moved behind the invisible doctor.

"May I touch, then follow your right shoulder down to your hand?"

"Please, Captain. My thumb is starting to cramp."

He touched her shoulder, then quickly traced down her arm until his hand rested an inch from the grid coordinates she identified. "I'm going to take the tweezers from you. Continue squeezing them until I do."

"I can see you perfectly, Captain."

"Good. I'm going to trace your hand until I grip the tweezers. Help me not release anything it might be holding."

Doctor Summer suddenly reappeared, then Captain Devereux took a petri dish from his associate before holding it under his opposite hand.

"What do you have, Captain?"

"Commander, we believe we may have identified an invisibility particle. I am squeezing invisible tweezers."

Doctor Kardelen displayed a small lab clamp. "Shall we clamp the tweezers in their current position?"

"Not yet, Doctor." The captain eyed the previously invisible scientist. "Did you say you could see unseen droplets of material while you were invisible?"

"Yes, Captain."

Captain Devereux and the petri dish suddenly disappeared.

"Are you alright, Captain?"

"Yes, Commander. Code Omega."

"Do you need our assistance, sir?"

A calm voice emanated from the invisible captain. "My team …esteemed doctors, please suspend recovery, after identifying and recording current grid points."

Commander Lacey smiled at Doctor Farris, after appearing beside a massive machine. "Shall we adjourn to the conference room?"

"Absolutely, Commander." Bria glanced in the direction of the still-invisible captain before raising her voice. "Science team eight; conference room meeting after marking your grid location. Bring your notes and work logs."

Commander Lacy sat back after the last three scientists took their places around the conference table. "Besides Doctor Farris, how many of you have family?" He watched all but two hands politely indicate inclusion, then smiled. "Well, I have good news. Your time with us has concluded and the facility will be making your departure arrangements. You will be leaving on Wednesday, which gives you two and a half days to conclude last-minute reports and logs, and hopefully, we'll have you home for a leisurely weekend with your families and friends. It has been wonderful hosting you, and we're grateful for all your work. Your hospitality liaisons will contact you shortly with more specific departure information and coordination."

He stood and straightened his uniform. "In the meantime, please use the facility in a more leisurely manner. You've earned it."

He walked to the conference room door, then turned to the group. "Oh, your exit briefings will commence tomorrow morning in conference room *D* one zero three, at nine hundred hours. You no longer report to this laboratory suite." He nodded, then immediately exited.

"Well, that was unexpected and unceremonious." Doctor Amadu scratched his nose as he closed his computer.

Adriana inhaled. "Not rude, but rather abrupt."

"A military goodbye."

"Initiated by a rather uncreative *code omega*?" Bria chuckled.

"I guess they have their prize and our method of discovery."

"To argue their side; we really didn't produce much."

"It isn't like we didn't try, Tianya." Doctor Farris's hand wave dismissed the commander's departure speech. "We did just fine and I'd like to add, it's been an absolute pleasure working with all of you, and I hope I get the pleasure again."

"So I guess this is it?" Doctor Summer leaned forward. "Anyone care to join for dinner and a few drinks this evening?"

Doctor Sayf closed his laptop. "An excellent suggestion, Bonnie. I'd be honored."

"Shall we say seven …at the Italian Bistro?"

"Definitely. Anyone care to join us?"

"Count me in." Doctor Eryn smiled.

"Gladly."

"I think I'll nap first, but join after if you don't mind a tardy arrival."

"Oh …fashionably late, Adriana?"

Sharae snickered. "Not a bad idea, and then I'll join too."

"Shall we meet at the bar?"

Doctor Sayf stood. "See you there."

Lena clapped lightly. "Oh, I'm looking forward to this."

"Is it a ticket if you drive a golf cart drunk?"

Tianya chuckled. "Why worry about it. Let's call for golf cart taxis. We all live in the same neighborhood."

Doctor Farris shut her computer. "…Until Wednesday."

~*~

Kye followed Ben into the house through the inside garage door, then around the family room and up the stairs. "I can't believe you made the freshman soccer team."

"Did I do alright?"

"You did fine for your first game ever."

"Thanks." Ben frowned. "I can't believe how hard soccer is, and how easy Jaime makes it look."

Kye grabbed a game controller. "She should be decent. She's been playing since she was four."

"She's a whole lot better than decent." Ben glanced twice then narrowed his eyes as he stared at his model shelf. "Hey." He inhaled as he stepped toward the shelf. "Hey."

"What?"

Ben held his finger to his lips before turning music on, then motioned Kye closer and cupped his hand to Kye's ear. "My models are moved."

Kye stepped back and sneered. "So?"

Ben shook his head then leaned close. "You don't understand. I have a deal with my mom. I don't want her breaking anything…" Ben scanned the room before removing his phone, and typed. *..so I clean this shelf myself …and they've been moved*

Kye lowered his voice. "By who?"

He pressed keys before turning the phone. *No one in my family*

Kye scratched his head before opening his phone and typing. *R U positive?*

Very

"Damn. Who else would…"

Ben stared at the shelf, "Exactly." then pointed to the closet before quickly moving around the room, waving his spread arms. Kye took his prompt and felt inside the closet. "…You sure?"

He nodded, then displayed his phone after keying another message. *Do you have gel on you?*

Ben raised a finger as Kye started talking, then pointed to his phone, and Kye sighed before typing. *How do you know?*

I know. Inviz first ..Explain later

Kye opened Ben's closet and removed the two bats from Ben's baseball backpack, then passed one before reaching in his pocket for his gel bag, and both silently disappeared.

Ben pointed invisible fingers to his eyes and then around the room, and Kye shared another text. *What are we looking for?*

Ben peered out his back bedroom window, then turned as he typed. *Anything or anyone*

"Okay. Together." Kye inhaled before stepping toward the door.

Ben led him from the room, and they carefully searched the house before facing each other in the family room. Kye pressed phone buttons as he squeezed the bat under his arm. *R we searching outside?*

Ben nodded and keyed a message. *Look for anything unusual Both yards...but not inviz*

But we can't see them if ... U think they hav some?

Yeah its been at A51 how long? Ben erased the message before typing another. *look out windows- inviz first ...if theyr there... theyll kno we have more if they spot us*

Kye nodded before looking down and typing. *Should we tell S and D?*

We'll txt them and Aunt Kitt after we search outside. If we spot something ..we ll share.

They peeked out every window before turning visible, then examined Ben's yard before heading to Kye's.

"What are you two doing?" The squeaky screen door diverted their attention as they examined the ground.

"Oh good. You're home."

"Why? What's going on?"

Ben interrupted Kye and focused on Jaime. "How was your game?"

"One one tie but we should've won." Her voice brightened. "How'd you do?"

"We lost two to one."

Her chin dropped as she stared at him. "No. I meant, how'd *you* do?"

Ben squinted. "I think I did alright."

Kye continued examining the ground. "He did good for his first game."

Her eyes narrowed as she waved a finger at their feet. "What are you doing now?"

Kye motioned her closer, then put his finger to his lips and pointed to a specific footprint before typing. *Look like anyone's?*

She studied the partial boot-print, then keyed a reply. *You don't think*

Ben held his phone toward her. *There s more*

She stared at him, and he raised his finger before typing. *NOT HERE*

She inhaled after scanning the yard. "Let's see if Faith can borrow the car." She sent a quick message.

Kye nodded. "Good idea"

They met Faith as she pulled into the drive. "Hurry. I have ten minutes to get mom."

"Where were you?"

"At the dance studio. The rest of you were doing something." She glanced at them as she backed into the street. "What's going on?"

Jaime gestured to the back seat. "They think we've had visitors."

Ben leaned forward. "I know we did. My models were moved."

"Why do you think they were moved?"

"The fighter jets were switched."

Kye squinted. "They're the exact same model."

"Not the pilots. One pilot has your color hair and one mine …and I always keep you off my right wing. They were perfectly in line, but switched. And nobody in our family would touch them."

"Don't they have helmets on?"

"Yep." Ben nodded. "Then the footprints."

Faith glanced at Jaime before looking through the rearview mirror. "Footprint?"

Ben pulled on the front passenger seat. "More than one."

"But the one in our yard is by the tree …right where... It's a boot print and none of us wear boots."

"Dad wears boots, idiot."

"Dad's boots are old and have no tread. These were deep tread boots."

She turned into the elementary school parking lot. "This conversation ends when we see mom."

"Okay, but take a look at the footprint when we get home, and dad's boots when he gets home."

"Sure."

"And if they're different, can we call Becca and Steve?"

Faith shut off the car after stopping by the school's front walkway. "Sure."

Jaime turned toward Kye. "Did you check and see if the gel is still where we hid it?"

Faith glanced at her watch, then dialed her phone and the call went to voicemail. She waited for the beep. "Mom. We're here."

"No. Even if they looked there, they wouldn't see anything."

Faith dialed again after checking the time, and the call went to voicemail. She hung up and eyed the building. "Ben, go knock."

"Sure." He ran up the walkway to the school's main entrance and pressed the intercom. Moments later a woman opened the door, and after a brief conversation, he sprinted to the car. "Mom isn't here. They said two guys in strange police uniforms came for her this morning, and took her away."

Faith's eyes widened. "That's not funny."

"I'm serious."

"No!" Faith exited the car and jogged to the entrance.

"You two stay here." Jaime opened her door and quickly followed.

Kye and Ben watched Faith cover her mouth as the lady shut the school door, and Jaime held her close as they walked back to the car.

Ben shuddered as Jaime opened her door. "Is it true?"

She nodded.

Ben quickly dialed, and they heard his father's voicemail message. "Dad! Dad, please pick up!" He waited. "Call as soon as you get this!"

"Holy shit." Kye pressed his fingers through his short hair. "I'm texting mom and dad."

"About what? You're not telling them what's going on, are you?"

"I'll ask them what we're having for dinner." He smirked. "That sounds pretty normal for me, don't you think?"

Jaime reached for Faith's hand after she buckled in. "Are you alright to drive?"

Kye pulled on the driver seat. "I will if you can't"

Jaime watched her sit, frozen, then scanned the parking lot. "But we need to move. We need to not be parked here."

Faith wiped her eyes, then started the car. "I can't believe this."

"We shouldn't jump to conclusions." Kye leaned forward and touched her shoulder. "But whatever it is, we'll take care of it."

"I guess that confirms the footprints and models." Ben's breathing intensified as he leaned against the back door.

"It's a good thing we know a few superheroes." Kye's phone beeped twice and he read each text. "Ask mom." … "Why? Do you want something special?"

"Your mom and dad?"

He nodded, "Sounds normal." then his eyes narrowed. "Why weren't they taken?"

Ben frowned at Kye. "They found it in our yard?"

"Why can't they leave us alone?" Faith sighed as they stopped at a traffic light.

Ben raised his pant leg and removed the second phone from his sock, then smiled at Jaime. "Time to call Aunt Becca?"

"Cause we have something they want."

Ben nodded at Kye, then typed a quick message. "I hope she still carries it."

"Are we driving to Becca now?" Faith hesitated as she drove through the intersection.

"I'm thinking we shouldn't be home. Besides, what's our choice?"

Jaime's statement silenced the car, and they drove quietly until Ben's second phone beeped.

"Yes!" He quickly dialed Aunt Kitt's secret phone and she responded immediately. "Is something wrong?"

"I'm so glad you kept the phone." He put her on speaker.

"I told you I'd always be here for you."

"Mom's school just told us two strange police took mom away this morning."

Faith glanced back. "And dad isn't answering his phone."

Ben leaned forward. "Something's wrong. Can we come over?"

"No. They know I'm involved and may be waiting. Let's meet in the place you took us, that doesn't exist."

"Perfect!" Kye lowered his head after eyeing Faith. "Sorry."

"How soon?"

Faith glanced at the phone. "Soon?"

"Have you talked to Uncle Steve today?"

"No, but let me call him and I'll text you a time."

"Okay." Ben ended the call.

"What do we do now?"

"I swear if they hurt your mom, I'm gonna declare war."

Jaime shook her head at Kye. "Let's not go there yet." Her eyes widened as everyone stared at her, and she tilted her head. "Considering that's what the other side does for a living?"

Ben's second phone rang and he read the ID before swiping the screen. "Hi, Aunt Becca."

"Steve isn't answering his phone."

"You're kidding."

"I wish I was."

Jaime wrapped her arm around the back of her seat. "Nobody came for you today?"

"I haven't been at the office today. I've been showing houses."

"Do you think they took Uncle Steve from his office?"

"Let me call his work friend. Call you right back."

Faith peered through the rearview mirror. "Where am I driving to?"

Jaime slid her fingers through her hair. "We'll figure that out after Becca calls back."

Ben swiped the screen after the first ring, then pressed the speaker button and held the phone between the front seats. "Hi."

"He's not in the office and Dylan hasn't seen him all day."

Faith glanced back. "Are we in trouble?"

"Should we tell our mom and dad?" Jaime stared at the phone.

"Tell them their parents are gone, or tell them everything?"

Ben shook his head. "We were told not to."

Kye sat up. "By who; the people who arrested your mom and dad?"

"They're probably not arrested." Jaime's eyes widened as she shook her head. "They didn't do anything illegal."

Faith glanced at her. "Then what would you call it?"

"Interrogation?" Ben eyed his sister.

Jaime covered her eyes with her forearm as she slouched in the seat. "Oh that sounds much better."

"Let's call the lieutenant!" Kye motioned to the phone.

"Good idea, but I have to go home for the number."

Faith refocused on the road after glancing at the phone. "Then we're going to your house?"

"…If we want to call the lieutenant, but I'm not sure my house is safe."

Kye stared at Ben's phone. "Then we should all go in together, after getting invisible somewhere down the street."

"Good idea. Let's meet in the apartment complex behind my house and walk into the back yard from there. Do you know where the Stone Point apartment complex is on Alina Avenue near my house?"

"No, but we'll find it."

"After you turn into the complex, make the first left and drive the parking lot all the way behind building *E* as in Edward and park by the dumpster. I'll meet you there."

Jaime lowered her window as Faith parked, and Becca pointed to the gray block dumpster enclosure before holding up a plastic bag.

Kye tapped the back window. "That's perfect."

Their invisible forms followed Becca into her yard and they spread out, searching for signs of intruders before silently following her to the back door. She unlocked it quietly, but before entering, Kye placed his hand on her arm, then motioned to the group to let him lead and he searched the house before waving them in.

"This is eerie." Becca locked the back door.

"But we're getting good at being stealth." Kye offered a joking shrug as Jaime shook her head.

She pointed around the room. "Is anything out of place? Can you tell if anyone's been here?"

"Look for boot prints."

Becca scanned the room. "I don't see anything, but I can't think of anything specific to look for."

"It's okay." Ben rubbed her back. "Where's the lieutenant's number?"

"In the middle drawer of the foyer cabinet." She hurried toward the front door, then held the card up after identifying it.

Jaime waved as Becca rejoined them. "Okay. Let's get out of here, just in case anyone's listening."

They hurried to the door, then remained silent until reaching their cars.

~*~

Mitch lifted the office phone receiver without turning from the computer. "Captain Cooper."

"Good afternoon. It's Rebecca DiMarcantonio. We met in the parking lot at Storyland Amusement Park a few weeks ago?"

"Yeah. Hi. What can I do for you?"

"My nephew informed me, their mother...my sister, was taken from work this morning by unusually dressed police, and their father isn't answering his phone. Do you have any idea what's going on?"

Mitch sighed. "No, but let me make some calls, and you'll get a call back from a different number."

"This number is untraceable."

"Thank you." Mitch ended the call, then pressed the control room direct line. "Time for lunch."

Charlie chuckled. "It's almost time to go home."

"Then let's take a quick walk next door and get a coffee."

"Seriously?"

"I need coffee. Care to join me?"

Charlie paused. "…Sure."

Mitch met him outside the control room but didn't speak until they shut the outer door. "Fallwater battle two has begun."

"What did you hear?"

"Nothing from our side, but do you remember the aunt and uncle?"

Charlie chuckled. "I'll never forget him berating Cowboy at the amusement park." Charlie stopped as they passed the corner of their fenced-in lot. "What about them?"

"She just called. The kids just informed her, unusually dressed police took their mother from work this morning, and they can't reach their father."

"Wonderful." Charlie rubbed his face then inhaled as he slid his fingers through his hair. "Did she mention anything else?"

"No, but if it's true, I'm thinking the re-engagement has begun."

Charlie walked past the restaurant door. "Are we on the same page, regarding where everyone stands?"

"Ben mentioning the C-130 makes me believe the teenagers were at the airport. The idea we no longer have the original item, and the replacement was invisible…"

Charlie frowned. "Why did they replace the thing. Nobody would have questioned anything if the box was empty after it arrived."

"Maybe they were worried we'd open the box before shipping it."

Charlie stepped further from the door. "It's going to be difficult finding out where the parents are."

"I'll call the colonel."

"I doubt he knows."

Mitch's eyes narrowed. "Why do you say that?"

Charlie inhaled as he turned away from the restaurant window. "There's something about me I don't share, but it's time for a slight reveal."

"Okay."

"Special Op's is more extensive than even some military think."

Mitch grinned. "You were Air Force."

"Do you realize they're the only military without an elite ground force? Yet they know the inside…even the floor depth, of what they're targeting? Do you think that precision is lucky guesses?"

Mitch sighed as he watched a car enter the restaurant's lot. "The military doesn't guess."

"No, they don't."

Mitch motioned with his head, then started walking. "Let's go make the call."

"I'm listening, right?" Charlie shared an awkward smile.

"I'd mind if you didn't."

Charlie broke the next momentary silence as they walked toward their building. "We also need more information from the others. Agreed?"

Mitch nodded. "It's time. Nothing traceable."

His voice lowered as he reached for the door. "I'm the go-between."

"Thanks." Mitch pressed his fingers through his hair. "The peace lasted longer than expected."

"Yeah, but it's never long enough."

They walked in silence to Mitch's office, and he pressed two phone buttons after turning to a blank notepad page.

"Good afternoon, Mitch. What's going on?"

"Good afternoon, Colonel." He glanced at Charlie, then adjusted his seat. "I was wondering about the aftermath of the Fallwater incident, and the general's intel orders. Is there anything we can assist with? …Anything our team can do to help facilitate successful completion?"

"Not at the moment, but I'll request your assistance if needed."

"Is there anything we can do with regard to the families involved? Would you like us to search the location again? Any preliminary work?"

"We're good right now, Mitch, but I'll keep you informed. In the meantime, just continue to search for new treasures."

"Always, Colonel."

The call ended, and Charlie smirked. "*I'll keep you informed* is military speak for, *Even if I know, I ain't sharing.*"

"Nothing." His eyes narrowed as he unlocked his computer. "This is going to be fun."

"Like abscessed teeth." Charlie inhaled as he straightened in his chair. "Time to establish communication."

Mitch opened the desk drawer and handed Charlie a note. "The aunt called from an untraceable phone."

He read the number. "I'll reconnect with a few old contacts. Maybe we can get some info on our end too."

"Are you alright with any initial cost?"

Charlie nodded. "Mind if I leave a few minutes early?"

Mitch waved his hand. "Be careful."

"You don't reach military retirement without learning that trick." He inhaled as he stood. "But thanks for the sentiment."

~*~

Becca's phone vibrated, and she read the screen. "It's Steve!" She raised the volume. "Honey, are you alright?"

"Yeah. What did you need?"

"Where were you? Are you safe?"

"I was at a client's working on a program, and I couldn't answer. You know there's times I can't"

She leaned against her car. "Nobody came for you? Nothing unusual happened today?"

"No. Why? What's going on?"

"Taylor was taken from work this morning, by strangely dressed police."

"You're kidding. Who told you?"

She eyed the four as they stood together by her SUV. "The kids."

"Where are they?"

She smiled at Faith. "Here with me."

"Where?"

"The apartment complex parking lot. Are you on your way home?"

"Yeah."

"Meet us at Taylor's instead."

Becca parked in the drive as Faith pulled into their garage, and they greeted Steve before entering the house through the inside door.

"Have either of you tried calling your mom or dad again?"

Faith glanced at Ben, then nodded at Becca. "We've been trying all day."

Steve eyed Ben after checking his watch. "Keep trying."

He pressed the speed-dial and Taylor immediately answered. "Benny! I was just about to call you!"

"Mom!?" He sat up.

Faith ran to his phone. "Mom! Are you with dad?"

"Yeah, love. Are you two alright?"

She leaned toward Ben's hand. "Yeah! Are you?"

"We've been better."

"Where are you?" She reached for his phone. "Are you on your way home?"

"We should be home in about forty-five minutes."

"Okay. Be careful."

"See you both in a bit."

Ben ended the call as Faith hugged Becca. "Thank god they're alright!"

"Quick meeting before they get here?" Steve motioned toward the family room, then lowered his voice after everyone sat. "What are you telling them when they come in asking what they're going to ask?"

Kye's eyes widened. "Should we tell them everything?"

"I still vote no."

Jaime stared at Ben. "Me too."

"Why not?"

Faith sat up. "Yeah. Why not?"

Jaime shook her head. "We're going to have to give up the stuff if we admit we have it."

"Can't we just tell them everything else?"

"How are we going to share any part of what happened, without sharing that?"

Ben gestured to Jaime. "She's right. Why not continue playing dumb?"

Kye snickered, "Because of the meeting with Mitch and Charlie, and the pictures on the garage."

"I don't see a way to avoid telling them, now that they've been interrogated." Faith folded her arms around a pillow.

"How about you don't share anything more than they know?"

Ben pointed to Becca. "I vote for that."

Steve nodded. "As long as we're on the same page with what gets shared and what doesn't."

"But what do they know?"

"I'm sure they'll tell you." Becca smiled at Faith. "Parents usually do."

Jaime reached for Faith's hand. "And let's not share more than we have to."

"Can we order pizza? I'm hungry."

Jaime frowned at her brother. "You're always hungry."

"Are we telling them about the footprints, or that we think someone was in our house?"

"Not yet." Steve glanced at Faith before acknowledging Ben. "There's nothing they can do about it, so why upset them?"

Becca's second phone rang and she looked at the unrecognized number. "Be quiet a second." She extended her hand then accepted the call. "Hello?"

"Ms. DiMarcantonio?"

She increased the speaker volume. "May I ask who's calling?"

"This is the call you were promised, from a friend you called earlier, and this is our secured line."

"Hi. Ours is too."

"Perfect. That friend and I are your allies and wish to assist you with your new concerns. Please share our existence with your five associates."

"They're sitting here with me."

Ben knelt near Becca and leaned on the coffee table. "Did you ever visit the four of us?"

"Yeah. Someone mentioned a C-130 during the visit."

"That would be me." Ben smiled. "I'm *W* for wired guy."

"Then everyone is identified?"

Kye scooted next to Ben. "Yeah. You're *C* for contact. Your friend is *A* for ally. We are *D* for dancer, *S* for soccer, *B* for baseball, *P* for pool lady, and *G* for gray."

Steve pointed at Kye and playfully frowned. "Very funny."

Kye shrugged. "It was all I could think of."

Faith sat forward. "Our parents will be home any minute."

"They're released?"

"Yeah."

"We need to get together."

"When? Where?"

"We'll figure that out. In the meantime, promise me you'll continue following the advice shared during our visit."

"But how? Aren't our parents going to question us tonight?"

"Ask questions as if you know less than them. Extract information. Give none." The call disconnected.

Faith pressed her fingers through her hair. "That's easier said than done."

"Why? We don't know anything." Ben extended his hands. "Aren't we curious why everyone thinks we know stuff?"

"Everyone knows we know more than we're saying." Jaime pointed to Becca's phone. "He actually told our parents we know more than we're saying."

Kye smirked. "Then I guess he was wrong too."

Ben jumped up. "The Invizibles are back in business!"

"Wonderful." Faith placed her hand on her forehead. "Wired guy is wired."

The inside garage door opened.

"Mom!" Faith jumped up and ran to her with open arms.

"Hi, love" She glanced around the room. "Hello."

"Dad!"

Cal wrapped his arms around Faith as everyone rose to greet them. "Hi, sweetheart."

"I've never been more happy to see you." She kissed and hugged him.

"It's good to see all of you."

"Yeah…" Taylor eyed them. "…but why are you all here?"

"Because we got scared when you weren't at school and Miss D'Nashia said strange police took you away, so we called the people we love and trust?" Ben motioned to Becca and Steve after kissing her.

"No other reason?" Taylor's gaze narrowed as the room went silent. "But I'm glad you're all here." She inhaled. "We have questions for all of you."

"And we have a thousand for you!"

Taylor squinted at Faith's reply, and Jaime leaned away after kissing her. "Yeah. What happened today?"

"Two guys in very plain, black, almost unidentifiable police uniforms came to the school, and I was called into the principle's office and after calls verifying their authority, was asked to go with them."

"What authority?" Steve sat forward. "Who did they say they were?"

"Homeland Security."

"They arrested you?"

She turned to Becca. "I asked them if I was being arrested, and they said, no."

"You couldn't refuse to go with them?"

"That was my next question, and they said, no."

Ben eyed his father. "Did they come for you too?"

Cal shook his head. "No. Mom called me."

"Where did they take you?" Kye sat on the floor next to Ben.

"An unmarked office building in Tancil and we spent hours answering questions. Constant questions that we didn't know how to answer, and we need answers." She frowned. "They said, what they found in our yard and what they now have, are distinctly different, and in order to not take further action, we need to tell them the details leading to this difference."

Cal inhaled. "And if we don't find out and tell them, they're going to get the information from you."

"Mom, we really don't know what you're talking about."

"If I remember correctly, the two gentlemen who visited, said you do know what we're talking about, and it's time to stop playing this game."

Faith's voice softened. "We don't know why those two thought we knew something."

Cal shook his head. "Don't give us that BS."

"Dad, we swear."

His brows rose as he faced Ben. "You swear?"

Taylor placed her hand on her head as she eyed Cal. "The pictures on the garage wall. How could I forget?"

"You didn't tell them, did you?"

"Please stop."

Everyone quieted as Steve stood and leaned on the back of the loveseat, facing both parents. "You're being played. They're playing your love for your kids, against you."

"Well it's working. I don't want them in trouble. Especially with the people we talked to." Taylor shuddered. "They were so cold and calculating."

Becca's head shook softly. "They're not in trouble."

"That's not what it seems like to me."

"Because they're professionals, and know how to play you for the love you have for them." Steve pointed to Faith and Ben. "And the only way they're in trouble is if you get them in trouble."

Taylor's brows rose as she motioned to Cal. "Us?"

Becca nodded softly. "Yeah."

Taylor squinted as she eyed her older sister. "Then what are we supposed to do?"

"Act as dumb as us, Mom."

Cal's voice deepened. "But we're getting the idea you aren't dumb at all."

Kye energized. "We are too! Just dumb teenagers."

Jaime shrugged. "At least, he is."

Faith giggled. "Yeah, but he's funny."

Kye pointed at her. "Don't forget my cute butt."

Taylor sat up. "What?"

"Nothing, Mom."

Ben knelt as he pointed to his sister. "She thinks he has a cute butt."

"Shut up, twerp."

He sneered. "You love me."

Cal studied Becca then shook his head. "We're not getting answers, are we."

She offered a silent apologetic smirk.

Chapter Two
Voluntary Demarcation

Mitch lifted the turn-signal lever, then dialed his phone after moving into the right lane. "Hey, Charlie."

"Wassup?"

He turned onto the highway onramp. "I have orders to attend a meeting in Tancil this morning."

"Okay. No problem." Charlie paused. "What the hell's in Tancil?"

"No idea."

"What's it about?"

"They asked me to bring my Fallwater reports."

Charlie's exhale came through the phone. "Alright. I got the fort."

"I'll let you know as soon as I can whether I'll be back in the office today."

"Let the phone ring, just in case I'm concentrating with my eyes shut."

"Wonderful." Mitch caught himself smiling as he ended the call, and he drove another fifty minutes in silence before turning into the unmarked office building's almost vacant parking lot. He removed his leather briefcase from the back seat, then silently confirmed the location, using the multiple government license plates on the nearby cars. The stagnant lobby air caught his attention as he entered the building, and he noted the lack of a business directory as he waited for the elevator.

He followed the narrow third-floor hallway as directed, until he identified the door marked with the instructed dark blue block letters, then pressed the beige button on the doorjamb.

"May I help you?"

"Captain Cooper." He searched for the intercom.

"Please enter and have a seat." The door buzzed and he quickly grabbed the handle.

He sat in one of the metal folding chairs lining the temporary cloth entry partition, then silenced his phone before studying the room. He felt his breathing change as the knowledge of the previous day's events and unusual meeting request, sent adrenaline through his system.

"Captain Cooper." A gentleman in a pristine black jump-suit and perfectly shined jump boots suddenly appeared. "Follow me."

He continued studying his surroundings as he walked the narrow hall. The lack of basic accompaniments gave all indication, the office was temporary, and the lone centered table and three folding chairs in his assigned room, confirmed his growing unease. The gentleman closed the door behind him without entering, and he sat uncomfortably.

He rose as the door reopened, and the first gentleman motioned toward his chair. "At ease, Captain."

A second gentleman placed a stack of manila folders on the table, as the first sat. "You will be recorded as you share all aspects of the Fallwater event, from the initial moment, through and including exit sessions."

"What are you looking for?"

"Answers." The man's eyes narrowed as he stared.

He controlled his breathing as he studied the unmarked gear each man wore. "Are you military?"

"Did you receive your orders from your superior?"

"Yes."

The second gentleman opened a notebook and placed a pen on its first page. "Jot down a timeline to help organize your dissertation."

He glanced at the empty page. "Everything?"

The gentleman stood. "Do not use previously written notes. Begin talking when the timeline is finished. You're free to stop intermittently to gather your thoughts. You're free to backtrack if you feel you've missed something important. Continue until you've shared all you recall without reference, but be thorough."

The second gentleman stood, then gathered his folders. "Would you like me to take your briefcase?"

He lifted the pen and stared at the notebook. "No."

The second gentleman nodded, then both left the room.

He thought about scanning the ceiling and walls for surveillance devices as he stared at the blank page, but realized the futility. They just openly declared the room, wired.

After an extended period writing notes and breaking down the incidents by timeline, he began; carefully comprising all perspectives, including Cowboy's. He looked up after finishing, "That is my recollection, without notes." then folded his hands and patiently waited.

The two gentlemen re-entered the room after an extended interval, and the lead person sat and leaned forward. "We would now like to discuss your reports. Did you bring them as directed?"

"Yes." He removed his folders and placed them on the table.

"Are there any reports in your possession, not forwarded to your superiors?"

"No."

The lead gentleman sat back and rubbed his face. "There are discrepancies between your and your associates' recollections, we would like to discuss in detail."

The second gentleman opened a file, traced a line with his finger, then raised his stare. "You're aware, the item captured and the item now in our possession are not the same."

"I have not verified that assumption, nor have I had it verified."

"We have." The gentleman inhaled and exhaled slowly. "You may now assume our confirmation."

"Until I know on whose authority you speak, I have not confirmed."

The second man tilted his notepad and began writing. "Why do you de-emphasize the role of the adolescents in your failure to complete your mission?"

"They're insignificant."

"That's an erroneous assumption."

"I've confirmed that they're typical young law-abiding citizens whose only fault or complicity was their proximity to the event." Mitch folded his hands on the table and smiled. "Why do you think our operation wasn't perfectly executed?"

The first gentleman breathed noticeably. "We have evidence discrediting that scenario. Why is there a difference in your and your associates' perception of the role the adolescents played?"

"Associates as in more than one?"

"Answer the question."

"Because I ran the operation and know the execution was flawless."

The second gentleman pointed to the open folder. "You failed to accomplish your objective."

Mitch motioned to the folders. "I disagree unless you can show me where I failed. Be specific."

The lead gentleman balled a fist as it rested on the table. "Please lose your adversarial attitude."

"My adversarial attitude?" He sat forward and stared at the lead interrogator. "You two haven't even offered me the respect of my rank, by even sharing your names."

"Would you like us to adjust your rank?"

Mitch joined his hands, then held them in front of his closed lips, and smiled.

The gentleman sat back and raised his chin. "Please share the thought."

Mitch inhaled, then softened his tone. "As I mentioned in my soliloquy, upon discovery, we enforced a continual guard around the object. Not one set of eyes; multiple eyes. Not civilian eyes; military eyes. What is in our possession, is what we captured and shipped."

"We have documents disputing that assessment, and verbal indication, the adolescents were instrumental in your failure to complete that objective."

"Teenagers took offense, uninvited adults were intruding in their lives and hassling a few of their friends, and decided to fling shit back? How unusual."

"Teenagers didn't just take offense, Captain. They thwarted our mission objective, and we have statements confirming their admission."

"Statements from who …the adolescents? Because I personally took statements from the adolescents, affirming they have no clue what was found in their vicinity." Mitch paused, then broke the uncomfortable silence. "Your claim of their participation and proof of their participation look like two different things."

"Are you stating you believe the teenagers had nothing to do with your mission's failure?"

"I'm stating I have no proof we failed, let alone proof any teenagers interfered with our mission."

The second gentleman continued writing. "That's a hedged answer, Captain, which means you believe the teenagers may have interfered with our mission."

The lead gentleman smiled. "Why do you believe they may have interfered, Captain?"

He glanced between both as their interrogating replies came in quick succession. "Because I'm human, and events, no matter how meticulously planned, can and do go awry, which may be beyond my or any associates' vigilance." Mitch leaned forward and rested his forearms on the table. "But that doesn't mean my team failed. My team executed brilliantly, seamlessly, and flawlessly."

The second gentleman patted his folder pile. "We have contrary opinions."

Mitch faced the gentleman. "Talk to me when you have contrary proof."

"We will talk to you before that, Captain. Be here for a polygraph test tomorrow at oh-eight-hundred." The first gentleman stood as the second gathered his folders, then both quickly exited the room.

Mitch sat an extended moment, then lifted his hat and tucked it under his arm before retracing his path toward the building's exit. He drove until the building disappeared from view, then lifted his phone and dialed. "You up for a beer?"

"Sure." Charlie glanced at the clock. "You're about an hour and a half away?"

"Roughly."

"Let me call Joel and tell him I'll be late. Usual spot?"

"No. Where the four of us last went."

"I'll see you there."

"Before you leave, call Alex and confirm that he dismantled all audio-surveillance in Fallwater and the uncle's neighborhood. If he hasn't, make it his assignment for tomorrow."

"Will do."

Charlie exited his car as Mitch turned into the parking lot, and they walked in silence to the building. Charlie held the door, and let Mitch lead to the bar, then raised two fingers and smiled at the barmaid. "Light beers."

She smiled. "Short or tall?"

Charlie's grin widened. "Do you have extra tall, or wide and tall?"

"No." She smiled.

"Extra deep?"

"No." Her smile increased.

He playfully frowned. "Tall."

She walked away after placing their glasses, then Charlie lifted his. "To future endeavors."

They gently touched glasses.

Charlie lowered his beer after a refreshing sip and inhaled slowly. "I never saw you so quiet. Are you sharing?"

Mitch slid his fingers through his hair. "I'm still trying to process everything."

"Did they threaten you?"

Mitch centered his glass on the coaster. "Hell yeah, including my rank and I'm scheduled for a polygraph tomorrow morning, and there's no way in hell I'm passing."

"So?"

"They threatened to bust me."

Charlie lowered his beer. "They love to threaten. It's their *M O*."

"Well, I don't appreciate them threatening my rank."

"Mess with me any way to the middle, but don't mess with the food on my table." Charlie inhaled. "One of my dad's sayings, growing up."

"Do they have the power?"

"Do you want me to lie, and tell you everything will be alright?"

Mitch turned from his beer. "Why am I friends with you?"

"We're not friends." Charlie lifted his glass. "We're brothers."

"Well what do you suggest I do, dear brother?"

"Ride the storm." Charlie finished his beer, then smiled at the server as he pushed the glass away. "But not to worry. You won't do it alone."

"I'll be alone tomorrow morning." Mitch pushed his empty glass away.

"Stick to your story. You did nothing wrong. Missions fail. You aren't the first commanding officer whose mission failed. They don't bust officers for executing flawlessly, just because the mission failed. If you concentrate on nothing else. Concentrate on that."

"We did execute flawlessly."

"Yep." Charlie smirked as he lifted his new beer. "We were just outwitted."

"Did you ever contact them?"

Charlie's smile disappeared as he nodded.

"What did you tell them?"

"Keep to our advice."

"Are we setting something up?"

Charlie nodded again. "Tonight. You're not invited."

"What are your thoughts about what's next?"

"You know the rules of engagement. One side attacks, then the other counterattacks."

Mitch's eyes narrowed. "Are you planning a counterattack?"

"Not yet. I'm more concerned with trying to read their next move."

"Any ideas?"

Charlie lifted his beer. "More than I want."

Mitch raised his. "I don't see them breaking pursuit until they reach their goal."

"Me either, and that's how I'm preparing." Charlie glanced at the TV and inhaled. "It's the rules of engagement. Who are we to not follow rules."

Mitch playfully choked on his sip.

~*~

Ben's second phone vibrated, and he pulled it from his sock as he walked home. *Special pool party here tonite. U4 go for icecream or school clothes shoppng and come over here tonite if Faith can borrow the car. Tomorrow nite if she cant. Let me know ASAP.*

Ben quickly opened his other phone and typed. *Guys we have a special meeting at G+P's tonite. Can we say we're going school shopping at the mall? Faith ask mom for the car.*

He entered the family room through the garage. "Hi."

Taylor turned from the stove. "Hi, love."

Faith fluffed her sofa pillow as she glanced at him. "Jaime and I are going shopping at the mall after dinner. You and Kye wanna come?"

"I'll text him."

His phone beeped moments later, and he looked up after reading. "We're going."

Faith faked a smile. "Good."

Taylor motioned from the kitchen, with the wooden spoon in her hand. "I don't want you out late, understand?"

"Yeah, Mom."

"Do you want us to go now and eat when we get home?"

She motioned to the pans. "Dinner's almost ready."

They ate in near silence until Faith finished and sat back. "May I be excused?"

Taylor eyed her plate. "Yes."

She glanced at Ben as she carried her dish to the sink. "I'll be right down. Text Kye when you're done."

Ben stood when Faith came into view, then both gave Taylor a kiss as she continued cleaning up. "Bye, mom."

"Be careful, and don't be late."

Faith held the inside garage door for Ben. "We won't"

Ben glanced at her after texting Kye. "You know we're probably gonna be late."

She sighed as she spotted Jaime and Kye walking toward the car. "I know."

They pulled into the apartment complex behind Becca and Steve's house, a half-hour later.

"Are we?" Kye raised his sealed plastic bag.

Jaime shrugged. "I think we should."

Ben texted Becca after disappearing, then followed the others into the yard, and the back door opened as Faith reached the patio. "Hi."

Becca smiled as she held the door. "It's still strange."

Kye's invisible hand caressed her arm, and she stiffened. "It's only us."

"Hi *G*."

Steve slid his hand along the side of his graying hair. "I want a new letter."

Charlie pointed in the direction of the invisible voice. "Wow."

"Hi *C*." Jaime suddenly appeared.

Charlie raised his hand to his mouth. "Wow."

Kye suddenly appeared with his hand extended toward Charlie. "Hi *C*. I'm *B*."

Charlie jumped back and Faith giggled as she appeared.

"Jesus!" He pointed to Kye before tentatively shaking his hand.

Becca tilted her head. "W?"

Ben suddenly appeared behind everyone, on one knee with his elbow on his other, and fist under his chin. "Yes?"

Charlie spun, then raised both hands to his hair. "Oh my god!"

Faith eyed Becca. "Music please."

"No old stuff." Kye pointed at her as she walked to the stereo.

She pointed back. "Be nice to me. I already owe you one ass smacking."

He arched his hips. "Can I have it now, please?"

Jaime pointed at Faith. "Don't laugh."

Charlie stood with his mouth open, then scratched his head. "You guys can do that whenever you want?"

Steve extended his open hand. "Do we have to watch our words?"

"Is there another radio or stereo?"

"Sure." Becca reached for the TV remote.

Kye grinned. "We have to build a cone of silence."

Steve chuckled. "How do you even know about the cone of silence?"

Becca shook her head as she accessed a radio channel. "They made it a movie."

"Oh! We should have numbers, like eighty-six and ninety-nine."

"I like our letters."

Steve frowned at Faith. "I don't like mine."

"Mine is worse."

Kye pointed to Becca. "*P!*"

Faith giggled, then shrugged at Jaime.

Ben eyed Charlie. "Where's *A*?"

Everyone quieted as Charlie motioned to the kitchen table. "No *A* ...*ever*. ...Can't."

Jaime raised a finger, then displayed her phone. "We type, then backspace erase after passing them around. Don't hit send."

"Brilliant." Charlie smiled as he displayed his second phone and began typing, then passed the phone. *A can't meet. Too much to lose. He ll know everything.*

He typed again when his phone returned, then passed it. *Share what you want?*

Jaime's voice softened. "How much do you want to know?"

His brows rose after placing both hands on the table. "As much as you want to share."

Faith quickly typed. *You told us not to share – even wth u I did But things are changing.* He frowned.

Becca leaned forward. "Can we whisper instead of typing?"

Ben nodded. "Or we'll be here all night."

Faith lifted her phone. "We can type once in a while."

"Agreed."

Becca waved a finger. "Who's starting?"

Jaime raised her hand. "I will since it started with me."

"We actually never heard the story."

"Superheroes only tell sidekicks on a need to know basis."

Becca playfully smacked Kye's shoulder. "Wiseass."

"Guys."

They glanced at Ben, then focused on Jaime.

She leaned forward and whispered, "A week before school ended, I was talking to her," She pointed to Faith. "when I heard a loud thud in our back yard."

Kye motioned between him and Ben. "We heard it too."

Jaime nodded before refocusing on Charlie. "We thought the dog did something, but when I checked, we found something way crazier."

Charlie extended his hand. "I saw pictures."

"But it wasn't invisible when we found it."

Ben sat up. "And that's when you were able to detect it."

She leaned forward and whispered, "Kye went to lift it and accidentally stepped in something it spilled."

Faith removed a plastic bag from her pocket, then opened it and reached inside before holding her hand toward Charlie.

His eyes narrowed before reaching for her empty hand, and grinned as he felt an invisible plastic bag. "Is there some inside?"

All four nodded. "We all carry one, in case your friends hassle us."

"My friends don't hassle my friends."

Ben hopped in his seat. "Cool."

Jaime leaned further forward. "Anyway, we quickly figured out we needed to hide it and protect it." She waved her hand, demonstrating flight.

"And we almost didn't make it."

"We made it." Faith eyed Ben, then refocused on Charlie. "But then people came with that dust…"

"You were supposed to bring it over here that day."

Kye nodded at Becca. "I forgot about that."

Ben leaned forward. "Another hour and it would've been gone."

Faith motioned to Becca. "We told her the day before and made plans to bring it here."

"Instead, it went to where you were."

Charlie's head tilted as he eyed Jaime. "How do you know where it went?"

"We went with it." Ben waved his plastic bag.

Jaime smiled. "We like the hidden office."

"And you're missing a few blankets."

Charlie shook his head as his breathing increased. "Amazing."

"It gets better." Kye grinned.

Charlie squinted. "Did the other side ever have it?"

"Yeah."

"The airport." Ben tapped Kye's shoulder. "That's where we stole it back."

Kye shook his head, "We stole nothing." then pointed at Charlie. "They stole it."

"I agree…and so does *A*." Charlie ran his hand over his chin. "You made the switch right in front of MP's?"

Jaime smiled, then pointed to Ben. "And he led the mission."

Charlie shook his head. "Was it headed to the amusement park?"

"Yeah, but it took off on the way."

Charlie rested his hands on his stomach and chuckled as he eyed Jaime. "I really would read this book."

"There's more. We've seen a second invisible ship floating overhead, since the dusting."

"You saw a second?"

"Yeah. When we're…" Kye held up his plastic bag. "…we can see anything that is…"

"But now some idiots won't leave us alone." Faith scowled at him, "My mom is scared to death."

"You know she doesn't know anything." Ben's breathing increased as he motioned to Kye. "And there's footprints in their yard, we think are not from any of us. And somebody may have been in our house."

"Seriously?"

Jaime stared at him. "We didn't do anything wrong, and you need to convince some old friends to leave us alone."

"Especially our mom."

Charlie sighed and nodded. "I agree."

"Can you get them to leave us alone?"

"Life isn't that simple or easy." Charlie inhaled. "Now it's time to share with you." He leaned forward as his voice lowered. "The toy replacement went to a special lab."

"Area fifty-one."

Charlie's head shifted back as he eyed Faith. "How do you know that?"

"We were sitting in A's office listening to most of your conversations."

"And the control room." Ben shrugged. "Sorry for stealing your cookies."

Charlie slapped his thigh and laughed. "Wait till I tell A it was you."

"So what's happening, on your side."

Charlie eyed Steve and sighed. "We got intel they isolated a small sample of gel, and a general wants more." He frowned. "And no one is above or immune to the tactics he'll use."

Becca motioned to the group. "Are they in danger?"

"We don't know, but they're starting to re-engage, and if they have gel, they may not be visible when they visit. " He refocused on the friends. "If you can see other objects ...when you're... we can see if they're around or not." He rubbed his forehead "But remember, they'll be able to see also, so with great care, check regularly."

Kye nodded at Ben. "We can do that."

"Good."

Faith sat up. "Do we need to go somewhere and listen for you?"

"No, but it'd be nice if *A* and I had the ability." He studied their faces. "Please think about it?"

Ben raised his hand. "I'm done thinking about it."

Jaime held her closed hand, thumbs up, "Yes." then turned it down. "No."

Charlie smiled at the unanimous result. "Show me how?"

Mitch's alarm beeped, and Amber stirred. "What time is it?"

"Earlier than normal." He wrapped his arm around her and kissed her after pressing the alarm. "Go back to sleep."

He exited the house in the dark and drove to the obscure office building in silence, rehearsing what approach he should take, then realized the reason for his impending polygraph failure, and smiled. He parked and fixed his hat before removing his briefcase from the back seat, then followed his previous path to the third-floor suite. He pressed the beige button and stood at attention.

"May I help you?"

"Captain Cooper." He reached for the handle before the buzzer sounded, and sat in the same metal chair, unable to fully eliminate his smile.

The *veiled-threat* gentleman from the day before, appeared after a short wait, and Mitch's smile grew. "Hi."

The gentleman squinted before inhaling. "Follow me."

"Gladly."

They walked past the room he occupied the day before, and two unrecognized gentlemen stood as they entered a different room. "Welcome, Captain."

"Thank you." Mitch extended his hand. "And you are?"

The man glanced at his hand without accepting it. "The person administering your polygraph today."

"Would you like me to call you poly, or do you prefer something else?"

The lead gentleman stepped forward and motioned to the chair. "I do not appreciate your attitude, soldier."

"Why not?" He turned toward the familiar face wearing an exact replica of yesterday's black jumpsuit. "This is a joke and we both know it. I read every transcript produced for this set of incidents and that intelligence information makes this little game, an obvious joke. And I do not appreciate you threatening my rank. I earned my rank, and no anonymous a-hole is going to jokingly threaten its removal, without extensive comment."

"Gentlemen." The third jump-suited attendant extended his open hand. "We're on the same side."

Mitch smiled as he faced the man. "You have yet to show any indication, that statement is fact."

"So are you saying you won't help our quest to accomplish our goal?"

"Psychology one-o-one?" Mitch's eyes narrowed as his grin twisted. "Seriously?"

The last gentleman pressed his fingers through his thinning hair. "All indication shows your lack of willingness to perform your tasks to the level expected of a person in your authority, and we *will* share that with military council, if necessary."

"My effort shows the opposite, and your opinion is based on what facts you subjectively give credence." Mitch shook his head. "And that's twice you've vacillated on what sides you think we're on. I will lay my life down for people I believe are on my side. I fight the enemy, like a soldier."

"We're on the same side, Captain. Are you willing to help us uncover whether or not the civilians had an active role in your mission's failure?"

"What do you think some high school kids could possibly do, to stop a fifty man military mission that went off without a hitch?"

"That's what we're here to uncover."

"And how do you think this exercise can add to the extensive reports the mission generated?"

"We're about to find out." The lead gentleman pointed to the chair next to the polygraph machine. "Sit."

"No, Sir."

"Please sit, Captain."

He turned toward the second operative. "Gladly."

A gentleman lifted Mitch's hand and began connecting electrodes. "We're going to ask base questions first, please answer truthfully."

His eyes moved from his wrapped fingers to the man's eyes. "Before we begin, please tell me what offense the kids committed, if they did interfere? What is the crime and punishment for interference?"

He watched the three men ignore his questions. "Gentlemen, this session is over unless those preliminary questions get answered."

"You will take this test today, Captain…whether you like it or not."

"And I will name the seven dwarfs as my answers, unless you answer my questions." He glanced at each individual. "They're not unreasonable and they're not difficult questions, are they?"

"Why are you being insubordinate?"

"Sneezy …Grumpy?"

"What is your full name?"

"Doc …Bashful."

The lead interrogator pounded the desktop. "Are you kidding?"

He stared into the man's eyes. "Dopey …Sleepy."

The gentleman glared at him, then stood and pointed. "Get him out of my sight, NOW!"

"Are you sure you don't want to see if I can name all seven?" Mitch's smirk morphed into a grin. "Dopey, Sneezy, Grumpy, Doc, Bashful..."

An associate quickly unhooked him as the lead gentleman pulled the door open and exited.

"...Grumpy... wait, I already said Grumpy." He extended each wrapped finger, "Sneezy, Doc, Bashful..." then sighed as the other two men left the room.

He disconnected the armband and continued speaking as he walked toward the exit. "Sleepy, Dopey, Bashful, Grumpy, Doc, Sneezy. Aw man, what's the last one?" He started over as he opened the glass door, "Dopey, Sneezy." then shook his head as the door latched behind him.

Mitch drove in silence, then eyed the Field Op's building differently as it came into sight. He rubbed his eye after opening the gray metal door, then exhaled as he opened the Control Room door.

Charlie smiled after spinning in his cubicle seat. "How'd it go?"

"Disaster."

"Took her whole ass off?"

Mitch squinted. "What?"

"Dis...assed...her?"

Mitch's grin grew as he shook his head. "That's bad."

Charlie pointed to his grin. "Then don't laugh."

Mitch tossed his hat at the table behind them, then plopped into the chair in the next cubicle as the hat hit the floor. "The other disaster."

"So you failed a test." He offered a half-smirk. "If we were good at tests, we wouldn't be in the military."

"I never took it."

"They decided not to give it to you?"

Mitch shook his head. "I was all hooked up, and decided to ask two questions before we began, and they ignored me…and I pretty much lost it."

Charlie grinned as he sat up. "I need details."

"I told them if they didn't answer my questions, my answers were going to be the seven dwarfs."

"Oh, that must have went over well."

Mitch leaned forward. "They wouldn't even tell me their names!"

Charlie glanced at the phone. "The colonel's call goes immediately on speaker."

"I had enough. I don't care what the kids' role was." Mitch sighed. "It wasn't a crime."

"Want to hear what their role was?"

Mitch looked around. "Seriously?"

Charlie stood, then motioned to the coffee machine. "Fill your mug and let's sit out back."

"Let me forward the phone to my cell first."

"Perfect. The cell speaker is undetectable." Charlie led Mitch out the back door, then sat across from him, and Mitch rubbed his hand on the worn wood tabletop. "If I'm still here tomorrow, remind me to get two airmen out here to refinish these."

"You ain't going nowhere."

"Don't bet on it."

Charlie sipped his coffee. "On to better news. I met with them last night."

Mitch folded his hands on the table. "And?"

"We did have it, until the airport."

Mitch squinted. "How?"

"Wait till you see." Charlie stood. "Leave your coffee."

Mitch followed him into bay three, and Charlie extended his hand as he turned. He stepped five feet away, held up a finger as he reached in his pocket, then displayed a small plastic bag. He opened it, turned it inside out, motioned to open an invisible second one, then dipped the corner of the first, inside…and disappeared.

"Damn!" Mitch stepped back before reaching forward. "Are you still there?"

"Yep." Charlie suddenly reappeared twenty feet away. "Ain't that amazing?"

His eyes widened. "Damn."

Charlie waved him toward the inside bay door. "I have a story to share."

~*~

Faith turned the hallway corner and stood behind the loveseat. "Where's Ben?"

Taylor lowered the TV volume. "Where else?" She pointed in the direction of the Fergusons' house.

"Mind if I go to Jaime's?"

"Will you invite her here?" She shuddered. "I'm still not over what happened."

"Sure." Faith swiped her phone open and pressed keys. "Will you share what happened with Jaime and me?"

Taylor frowned after shaking her head. "I don't want to. I don't want you to worry or be scared." She shivered again. "It was very intimidating."

"I'm sorry you had to go through that." She sat on the sofa and patted her mother's hand, then eyed her phone as it beeped. "She's coming over, and we'll be right upstairs."

Faith opened the front door and smiled as Jaime approached. "Thanks. My mom wants me close. She's still not over what happened."

Jaime nodded. "I don't blame her. It must have been crazy scary." She paused before following Faith upstairs. "Hi, Mrs. McCloud."

"Hi, dear."

Jaime shut the bedroom door as Faith turned on music. "Can you believe school starts in a week?" She fluffed a pillow, then propped it against the dresser.

"I know, and I know I should be sad about summer ending, but I'm not. I'm actually looking forward to seeing everyone."

"What are you wearing?"

Faith sneered at the song, then reached for her phone. "I haven't thought about it yet, but I'll text you when I figure it out."

Jaime sat up as her phone indicated an incoming text. "It's Ben. He wants to know what time we're practicing tomorrow."

Faith shook her head. "You know, he bounces off the walls waiting for the time you've set. Between that, sit-ups, and push-ups, it's all he does. Oh …and video games. He read somewhere it helps when you want to be a pilot."

"I read that somewhere too." She caught herself smiling. "He's so cute, and he's going to be an unbelievable catch in a few years."

"You know he has a crush on you."

Jaime smiled. "Of course I know. How could I not know?" Her chin lowered and smirk grew. "You know Kye has a crush on you."

"Yeah and I think it's cute. I love that he knows how to make me laugh, but don't tell him."

"I'm pretty sure he figured it out. He works hard enough at it."

"You know we can't tell either of them we know."

Jaime sighed. "Not yet anyway."

"You do mean, after he graduates college or turns forty or something, don't you?"

Her smirk turned apologetic. "Well…"

Faith stared. "No way."

"I might be secretly pissed if I'm not his first kiss."

"My little brother?" Faith sat up. "Seriously?"

Jaime sighed as her eyes widened. "I think I am."

"I'm not sure I know how to process that."

She ran her fingers through her long blonde hair. "You have time. He's still way too young."

~*~

Mitch's office phone rang, and he inhaled as he lifted the receiver. "Captain Cooper."

"Mitch …what's going on?"

"Sir?" He quickly opened his phone and texted Charlie. *GET IN HERE*

"I'm going to ask one more time. …What's going on?"

He inhaled and lowered his head. "To be honest, Colonel, a few different things." He quickly listened for Charlie's footsteps. "But of all the things, the childish bully tactic doesn't digest well. They really can't tell me their names?"

"It doesn't matter what their names are, Captain. You take orders from anyone I tell you to. I sent you there. That means you do as they say while you're there."

"Yes, sir." He held his finger to his lips, then waved Charlie into a seat as he appeared. "But why are they using intimidation tactics?"

"Intimidation?"

"They threatened my rank. I like to think I earned that, Colonel, and I don't appreciate them threatening me with it." His breathing quickened, then his eyes widened as he glanced at Charlie during the silent pause. "They have the ability to bust me?"

"If you cooperate, it isn't an issue."

"Colonel …did I not execute your orders flawlessly? Didn't I initiate and implement the entire acquisition and transport process perfectly?"

"Mitch, I'm catching hell from above for our failure, just like you, and your interactions with the investigation team aren't winning either of us any points."

"And I'm not allowed to disapprove of their tactics?"

"You definitely don't want to leave on the terms currently being discussed."

Mitch inhaled. "One day I did good enough to earn a promotion, and two months later I'm threatened with dismissal ...over the same actions?"

"New insight has come to light."

"Why was this how they addressed it?"

"Don't try to figure out how the military works, Mitch. Just be a soldier and do as you're told."

"But my career? Instead of offering the respect commissioned officers deserve; they threaten my career?"

"They threatened mine, Mitch."

"With impunity?"

"I don't make the rules." The colonel paused then spoke softer. "Are you going to cooperate when you meet with them, next?"

"Do I need to ask for legal representation?"

"You'd be ending your career."

"Wow, Colonel. I initiated and executed above and beyond." His eyes narrowed. "Don't you agree?"

They heard the colonel's breathing.

"What part of the mission did I fail?"

"Just one, Mitch, and it's the same one they're holding against me." The colonel exhaled audibly. "The result."

"Have they interviewed you? ...Threatened you?"

"I'm not as uncooperative as you." The colonel paused. "Indications are, something went down that prevented the mission's desired result, and the investigators are doing nothing more than uncovering the source of the failure. I don't believe you're that source. If you agree, then what's your problem helping them identify the culprit?"

"Colonel ...teenagers? Are they going to intimidate and possibly incriminate teenagers?" He stared at the phone. "And they expect me to sell out four kids?"

"Mitch, the adolescents have already been found guilty. You read the transcripts."

An extended silence followed.

"Will you please meet with them, with a different attitude?"

Charlie stood and stepped toward Mitch's desk, emphatically nodding yes as he displayed a note.

Mitch's eyes widened as he stared at his friend, and adjusted his demeanor. "Yes, Colonel. And I apologize for not understanding where everything stood."

"Mitch."

"Sir?"

"Please keep this conversation between the three of us."

"Sir?"

"Have a great day, gentlemen."

The phone clicked and Mitch placed his elbows on his desk and rubbed his eyes. "That was different."

Charlie's brows rose. "It actually went well."

"How do you figure?"

"He gave us more information than he intended, and it means he doesn't hold your failure against you. He confirmed we can't trust him on our team, and he'll sell anyone out if it comes down to him or the other person, and his side has already concluded the guilt of the four kids." Charlie nodded. "He gave away a lot to keep you on the team. He doesn't want to lose you."

"I'm not sure it isn't too late, for what this experience has exposed."

"Good. Then you'll operate without split allegiance."

Mitch's eyes narrowed. "You have no alliance issues, do you."

Charlie exhaled slowly. "I risked my life volunteering for advanced levels of military service, hoping to prove people like me are as trustworthy, loyal, and normal as anyone in the world; then learned, certain entities I was hoping to persuade, weren't interested in what I so desperately wanted to convey. When I realized they were only using me for their agenda, I decided to adopt the same regard for them, as they have for me." He grinned.

Mitch pressed his fingers through his short hair. "And this was my dividing act."

"And you'll keep that fact to yourself by being a model soldier. Apologize to the interrogation team when you go for your polygraph; act contrite …and tell them what they want to hear."

Mitch raised an eyebrow. "And why on earth would I do that?"

"So you can keep your current position and help us protect those families. You can't protect them if you're suddenly stationed in South Korea, or retired."

Mitch shut his eyes as he rubbed his temples. "But I'm not helping them if I bury them."

"You heard the colonel. They've already been tried and convicted. You telling them you're not on their side, serves no one. Want to make a difference? You know the rules. Play the game."

"So you think these aholes are giving themselves an excuse to abuse these families?"

Charlie's head tilted. "You and I know they don't need an excuse, and they want their stealth capability."

Mitch's eyes narrowed. "And the people in hell want ice-water."

Chapter Three

Fifth Wheel

Kye sat up and lifted his phone off the coffee table as it vibrated.

I'm home from the dentist

He tossed the TV remote onto the loveseat, then typed. *Wanna play vid games over here?*

Sure. R we looking out back first or did you already?

No. Just chillin waitin for you

Ok ...On my way

Ben knocked and opened the door minutes later. "It's me."

"Hey." Kye led him directly upstairs and shut his bedroom door.

Ben removed the plastic bag from his pocket. "Do you think we should do this every day?"

"It's probably a good idea for a while at least." Kye opened his plastic bag.

Ben waited for him, then dipped his covered finger in the gel and disappeared. "You don't think we're gonna spot anyone, do you?"

"We're about to find out." Kye disappeared, then moved to his bedroom window.

Ben held the curtain in front of his face and peeked out the corner of the window, then immediately dropped to the floor. "I can't believe it!" He knelt then inhaled before taking a confirming glance. "I was dreading this."

"Tell me about it. Everyone's going to freak when we tell them." Kye continued staring from behind the curtain's edge.

"I'm not worried about who we can tell. I'm worried about who we can't tell."

Kye spun against the wall. "Our parents?"

"…Hell yeah… My mom would freak if she knew there was an invisible soldier in our alley." Ben turned from the window and slid down the wall. "How long do you think he's been out there?"

Kye frowned. "The footprints."

"Do you think he's the one who came in our house? Do you think he watches us leave, then comes in and does whatever he wants?" Ben clutched his phone. "We have to tell everyone."

Kye reached for Ben's arm as he swiped his phone open. "Not till we see them. It'll freak our sisters out if we text this, and if they're with anyone, it may give too much away."

"Agreed." Ben swiped his second phone. "What about texting Becca and telling her to tell Steve and Charlie?" He held the phone. "We're really not going to text our sisters?"

"Not yet. Let's think about this first." Kye knelt below the window and peeked around the curtain. "Look at this."

Ben inched the curtain open before raising his head.

"Look at this little old lady walking toward him."

Ben covered his mouth as he stared. "Oh man, could she be any older?"

"Or bent over any further?"

Ben softly chuckled. "Why do little old ladies wear scarves and sweaters, even when it's summer?"

Kye shook his head. "And where do they buy those wrinkled stocking socks they all wear." He snickered. "Look at her ankles."

"She must be a zillion years old."

"And she has no idea what's in front of her."

Ben smiled. "Thank god. She'd probably shit herself."

"That's probably alright. She's probably wearing a diaper."

Ben chuckled. "Now that's funny."

"Damn!" Kye released the curtain and dropped to the floor, then immediately knelt and watched. "What the hell just happened?!"

Ben held the curtain below his eyes and stared. "She dropped him!"

"Damn! Did you see how?"

"She raised her cane when she got close, and he just dropped like she shot him!"

"Did she? How did she even know he was there?" Kye held his stomach, ready to vomit. "Is he dead?"

Ben rubbed his eye. "Oh god …we're dead if he's dead. Who the hell is ever gonna believe we didn't do it!?"

"Man, this is messed up!" Kye inched closer to the window. "Look at her! That hunchback little old lady just dropped an invisible, undetectable fully armed soldier! …In an instant!" Kye ran his hand over his hair. "Alright. Don't panic. We didn't do anything wrong."

"I gotta text Aunt Kitt." He motioned to the window. "Take a picture of her! Is she still there?"

Kye's phone clicked. "Got it, I think."

"Your mom's downstairs and knows we're up here." He heard a car and reached for the curtain, then both watched a pick-up truck stop next to the old woman and her and the driver lift the unconscious soldier into the truck bed before driving away.

"Are they gone? Is that it?" Ben scratched his head, then rubbed his neck. "Should we go down and see if there's blood splattered on the construction garage or something?"

Kye spun and slid down the wall. "He was invisible. We won't be able to see it."

"Yeah we will. Whatever separates from you when you're invisible, becomes visible. Remember your puke?"

Kye chuckled. "Oh yeah."

"Damn. If there's blood, we have to wash it off."

"On the white siding and garage door?" Kye nodded before frowning. "Yeah we do."

Ben removed the gel bag from his pocket. "Come on. Let's go see the damage."

"Man, I don't want to see what we're gonna see." He rose slowly, holding his stomach. "I may throw up."

Ben tucked the gel bag into his pocket after reappearing. "What's your father say about doing what needs to be done and collapsing later?"

Kye shook his head as he reappeared. "Wonderful. Now you're quoting my father?"

They hurried downstairs and Ben paused as they entered the family room, heading toward the back door. "Hi, Mrs. Ferguson."

"Hi, Ben. Hi, sweetheart."

"Hi, Mom." Kye slid the glass door open, then stepped out behind Ben, before hurrying to the alley. "She didn't hear a thing?"

Ben shrugged. "Neither did I. Did you?"

Kye passed through the gate as he stared at the patchwork alley surface. "No." He studied the ground before each step. "Do you see anything?"

Ben examined his path as he walked to the garage. "Nothing."

"Nobody's gonna believe this." Kye shook his head as he examined the large garage door.

"It's why we took a pic."

Kye slid his fingers down the siding. "But we didn't get her in the act."

"Who would've ever guessed that's what she was about to do? She could barely walk." Ben's phone beeped and he opened the text. *Theres an invisible soldier in your back alley?*

"It's Aunt Kitt." He showed Kye the message, then quickly typed. *Not any more*

He left?

Ben scratched his head before typing. *...sort of ...but you aint gonna believe how*

Did you do something?

Not at all. We just hope someone believes us

What happened?

He typed as he held the phone so Kye could read. *Some little old lady just knocked him out cold or killed him or something, w out even doing anything Then a pick-up came and they loaded him in the back n drove off*

Are you serious?

Kye opened his phone and typed, before glancing at Ben. "I'm finding out where our sisters are."

Yeah we re out back looking for blood ..nothing! Ben hit send, then glanced at Kye. "Okay."

"Man, this is freaky." Kye shook his head as he typed. *Where R U and Faith? R U together?*

His phone beeped a minute later. *Yeah we re at the mall with Muhammad Alice Skyler TJ ...why?*

Kye glanced at Ben. "They're at the mall. Should I tell them to come home?"

Ben continued searching. "Why? What are they gonna do?"

Nothing ..we were just wondering where you are Kye frowned after hitting send. "Man, that doesn't sound good."

Ben refocused. "What?"

"I just told them, we were just wondering where they are."

Ben chuckled as he shook his head. "That's not good."

~*~

Mitch sighed after canceling his alarm, then headed to the bathroom. He dressed quietly after showering, kissed Amber as she lay asleep, then shut the bedroom door behind him. He caught himself sighing as he left the house, and shook his head. This ordeal was getting tiresome, and the orders he'd follow today were further from his inner beliefs than his career had ever taken him. He chortled at how he had changed over the years. How innocent he viewed his profession when he chose it, and how different it currently appeared.

The drive seemed quicker than he remembered or hoped, and he pressed the buzzer after following the path to the glass entry door, then waited patiently in the metal vestibule chair, until the gentleman appeared and waved him to follow.

He sat after entering the room then allowed another gentleman to attach the polygraph machine while he answered general questions. The man nodded to the lead officer after establishing baseline, and another gentleman opened a file.

"Have you read all Fallwater incident related transcripts, numbered one through twenty-eight?"

"Yes."

"Do you conclude, the four teenagers were actively involved with thwarting your mission?"

He hesitated, then exhaled. "Yes."

"Were you aware of their involvement, during your mission?"

"I never felt they did anything more than watch us execute our mission."

"Yes or no, Captain. Were you aware of their involvement during your mission?"

"Yes, under the terms just described." Mitch's eyes widened as he studied the lead operative. "Honest. We really didn't think they could interfere or prevent our efforts. Four teenagers? We're the Air Force."

The lead operative nodded at his associate without acknowledging Mitch's explanation, and the gentleman refocused on his open folder. "Do you believe their ability to thwart your mission was aided by their stealth abilities?"

"I see no indication they have stealth abilities."

"Please answer yes or no, Captain."

Mitch shook his head. "No."

"During your review of the transcripts, did your opinion of their intent change?"

Mitch felt his smile appear. "Yes. Clever little bastards, aren't they?"

"Do you still think this is a joke, Captain?"

Mitch sighed as he eyed the lead gentleman. "No, sir, but I am impressed with their accomplishment, if they did thwart our efforts. A good soldier admires the talents of his enemies, even as he fights them, don't you agree?"

The gentleman inhaled, then exited the room.

Mitch smiled as the door shut. "Am I done?"

"Roughly twenty more questions."

He continued answering until the polygraph administrator removed the electrodes, and he eyed the two remaining men as he rubbed his hands together. "And you don't want to hear whether I can recite the seven dwarfs?"

He caught the administrator's smile before he exited, then fixed his hat and followed the route to his car. He eyed the building as he exited the lot, then released a long deep breath as he lost sight of it, driving away.

He pulled into the Field Op's parking lot two hours later, then finally smiled as he opened the Control Room door and spotted Charlie. "Hey friend."

Charlie spun in his chair. "Welcome back. Are you having coffee with me or heading to your office?"

He lifted his briefcase. "Let me go drop my stuff off and grab my mug."

"Mind if I bring the pot and join you there?"

Mitch smiled. "Not at all."

He unlocked his office and froze as he leaned his briefcase against the desk, then studied the phone sitting in the middle of his desktop, under the camouflage bow. "Is this from you?"

Charlie froze as he followed Mitch's eyes to the device. "No. No it's not."

"Seriously?" Mitch pulled his hand away as he reached for it.

Charlie inhaled as he continued staring. "Seriously. I've only been in the Control Room since I got here."

"Are our friends here?" He grinned. "Guys?"

They waited, then eyed each other. "Anyone? Is anyone here?"

Charlie's eyes narrowed. "This doesn't make sense. We discussed communication protocol."

Mitch shrugged before lifting the phone and removing the bow. "Kids wouldn't have added this." He tossed it in the trash before swiping the device open. "It has text messages."

"This can't be good." Charlie stared at Mitch's hand.

"You don't think it's anything dangerous, do you?"

Charlie met Mitch's stare. "I'm not referring to the device."

"What the hell could it say?" He touched the screen and studied the display. "Ready for message one?"

Charlie inhaled without answering, and Mitch read aloud.

"A new era has arrived. It came during daylight but only four angels witnessed the event. These angels have been measured and their grades are exemplary. They exude character beyond expectation. ALL have been and will be measured against them."

Mitch glanced at Charlie as he began copying the message. "This is interesting."

Charlie rubbed his eyes but sat silently as his breathing deepened.

Mitch inhaled before scrolling to the next message.

"I am the teacher. I teach coexistence ...tolerance ...acceptance ...at whatever severity necessary to deliver the lesson. I will now teach those who have forgotten or never learned.

Lesson 1: The Golden Rule - The four angels will live in the environment they have extended to others."

Mitch finished writing, then scrolled and continued reading.

"The four angels discover and understand like young angels. I am neither."

...

"Share the messages but keep the device if you wish the ability to communicate."

A new message appeared as he copied the last.

Thank you for reading. Copy and share. These are final warning; peace should be declared and coexistence honored. If enemies announce peace, you will not notice me. The opposite is equally true.

Mitch shut the text window and opened the phone contacts. Only one appeared, entered as the single letter *T*. He inhaled and smiled at Charlie. "I'd swear this was you if I wasn't staring at you."

"Mwah?" Charlie grinned. "I see no resemblance whatsoever."

Mitch shook his head. "I'm sure you don't."

The phone indicated another text and he read it aloud. *"Tell the enemy I also have the next thing they'll seek."*

Charlie stared at the device. "It looks like our old side made enemies of people not opposing them."

He re-read the copied notes. "Yeah...and that's never good."

"I hate cryptic messages."

"You're not alone." Mitch tapped the notepad with the back of his pen. "What do we do with this?"

Another text appeared as the phone beeped. *Tell the angels it's safe to talk again. Neighborhood surveillance has been dismantled. Any attempt to reassemble will not be tolerated*

Mitch slid his hands over his hair. "We told Alex... You don't think..."

"Delay action until we process the messages." Charlie stood and reached for his mug. "I'm taking a long lunch if I can set up a meeting. Our friends need to know about the new addition to our team."

"You don't think they know about this entity?"

Charlie glanced at the phone. "I don't know for sure, but I'm guessing not."

"Why?"

He watched Mitch finish writing. "Many reasons ...from who the kids are, to how this was received. These also indicate a different level of engagement."

Mitch placed the paper in the copy machine. "How do we say we received these?"

"They were written on paper that lit on fire without warning, and burned in a flash after we copied them. It's called flash paper." Charlie smirked. "Ever hear of it?"

Mitch raised his mug. "No."

"You've lived a clean life, haven't you."

Mitch inhaled. "You have secrets, don't you."

"Everyone has secrets." Charlie sipped his coffee. "Even angels keep secrets."

~*~

"What do you mean there was an invisible soldier out back?"

Ben grimaced. "Not so loud."

"There's nobody home." Faith's eyes widened as she stood in his face. "Why the hell didn't you share this earlier?"

"I was waiting for you to wake up'"

She raised her hand to her mouth. "Is he there now?"

Ben's face contorted as he rubbed his eye. "This is where the story gets strange."

She eyed him before walking toward the stairs. "Yeah ...*this* is where the story gets strange."

His voice softened. "Okay ...stranger."

"Did you tell Jaime or any of the adults?"

He followed her down the stairs. "We texted *P* and told her he was there, then gone."

"Well if he's gone, maybe it's over."

"Not the way he left, it ain't over."

She glanced at him as she entered the kitchen. "Well, how did he leave?"

"We need to get together so we can tell you." He pressed a phone button, then raised it to his ear as he entered the kitchen behind her. "Did you tell her?" He listened. "Over here or there?"

He ended the call. "They're coming."

She opened the fridge and removed a yogurt. "It's too early for this."

"Trust me. It's not."

They sat in silence until the doorbell rang and Ben darted from the room, then led Jaime and Kye to the kitchen table. Faith stared at Kye as he sat next to Ben. "What's going on?"

He glanced at Ben before leaning forward. "We were playing video games and remembered we were supposed to look out back for anyone invis ...and there was." His eyes widened.

"Yeah yeah. He already told me that part." Her breathing deepened. "Then something strange happened?"

"Very." Kye glanced at Jaime as his voice lowered. "We saw this little old lady walking toward him..."

"She was ancient and bent over."

Faith reached across the table and patted Ben's hand before staring at Kye.

"…and when she got close, she pointed her cane at him and he dropped like she shot him!"

"She killed him?" Jaime covered her mouth. "Is he still there?"

Ben's second phone beeped. "It's *P*. She wants to know if the four of us are free and can take a ride."

Faith eyed Ben's phone. "What time?"

Kye motioned for Faith's attention. "Wait. I'm not done."

Jaime tapped his hand. "Is the guy still there or not?"

"No." He refocused on his sister. "A pick-up came and the driver and old lady slid him into the back and drove away."

Faith sat back. "Then what are we worried about?"

"The government blaming and arresting us."

Kye nodded at Ben. "Then maybe we should accept *P*'s invitation and get the hell out of here?"

"Okay."

"I say we shower and leave asap."

Kye smiled at Faith. "Individually?"

She snickered and Jaime hit her arm before sneering at him. "Do you ever stop?"

He spread his open hands as he stood. "What… Just thinking of ways to save time."

~*~

The phone rang as Mitch studied the messages, and he pressed a button. "Captain Cooper."

"Mitch, you and I have to report to the airbase immediately. We have a meeting with the general, about Fallwater."

"I was just about to call you, Colonel."

"You know about the missing Fallwater soldier?"

Mitch audibly gasped. "That's what the message meant."

"What message?"

"Sir, we received multiple communications from a previously unknown entity." Mitch slid his keyboard away and moved his notepad closer. "One of the messages said, tell them I have what they'll search for next."

"How do you know the entity is previously unknown?"

"To be honest, Colonel, it's an assumption based on the messages."

"How many messages are there?"

"Seven, Colonel."

"And how were these messages received?"

"The phone was sitting in the middle of my desk, with a bow on it when I returned from my polygraph appointment."

"Bring the phone to the meeting."

He glanced at the file cabinet. "I was told, if I do, the entity goes stealth."

"Do you see any other way of convincing the general, the teenagers aren't to blame for the missing soldier?"

"Why are people assuming these kids are soldiers?" Mitch audibly inhaled. "Nothing could be further from the truth, Colonel, and I have all indication, we're about to start a war we can't win, if we continue believing that lie."

"That's not for us to decide, Captain."

"I respectfully disagree, Colonel, and I've been designated the communication liaison between us and this entity, with explicit instruction; give up the communication line, and it goes dead. May I share them now?"

"Sure."

He read the rewritten notes, then inhaled when he finished. "Are they significant enough to want to keep communication open, Colonel?"

"Yeah."

"I have the messages written on a notepad and I'll come to the meeting with twenty copies."

"Damn, Mitch. I really do understand your argument. I always see your argument and your awareness is always impressive …but these are decisions for people far above us. First and foremost, we're soldiers, and soldiers obey orders without question."

"With all due respect Colonel, you and I both know that's a poor counter-argument."

"Do you think it'd be wise to not have the device if it's requested?"

Mitch rubbed his forehead as he stared at the messages. "No, Colonel."

"How long before you're here, Captain?"

"Roughly an hour and a half, sir. I'm leaving now."

"Come to my office first. We'll go to the meeting together. And I'll take the lead regarding the messages and the device."

"Yes, sir."

Mitch knocked on the Colonel's open door, after acknowledging the desk sergeant. "Hi, Colonel."

"Good morning."

He followed the colonel through the headquarters' corridor and past the general's assistant as the yelling behind the door grew louder. The colonel approached the door and hesitated.

"… teenagers brought to me immediately! And if my soldier isn't returned unharmed, immediately, I'm charging them with every felony I can think of, including kidnapping and possibly attempted murder!"

The lieutenant looked up. "The general's waiting for you, Colonel."

"…This is all a joke to them? They won't see freedom until they're too old to remember it! The joke ends today!"

Colonel Sorelo glanced at him, then inhaled as he stared at the general's door. "I'm aware." He straightened before opening it, then changed his demeanor as he nodded. "Good afternoon, General."

The general glanced at him without acknowledgment, then refocused on the group. "What can we charge these four punks with?"

The woman shuffled through the papers in her hand. "Nothing at the moment, sir, but we can declare them persons of interest and use that identification as a reason to bring them in and hold them for questioning."

Mitch smiled as he reached for an empty conference room chair. "Hi, Cowboy. Share any good rumors lately?"

The general straightened. "That is Captain Harris, Captain."

"I noticed." Mitch eyed Cowboy. "…Who's first, beats who's right."

The general's voice rose. "Are you done, Captain?"

Mitch's voice softened. "That no longer seems to be in my control, General."

The general's eyes narrowed. "It never was, Captain." He motioned to the conference table. "Sit."

Mitch extended his hand to the only person he didn't recognize. "I'm Captain Cooper."

The captain shook his hand after a quick smile. "Captain Mia Madison. We talked once before."

"Intelligence?"

She nodded.

The general pointed to each in turn. "Captains, Harris, Madison, Cooper. Colonel Sorelo." His chest expanded. "Are we done the pleasantries?" He began pacing between the table and desk. "We lost two invaluable things today, and I am so thoroughly angry, I'm considering declaring war on the people responsible." He balled his fists as he placed them on the table. "Do you understand?"

He scanned the group. "One of my soldiers is missing in action, and he was on guard in a small town, in our own freaking country!"

"General, new information has come to light, regarding this situation."

He stared at the colonel. "What new information?"

Mitch opened his briefcase and handed everyone photocopies of his notes.

Colonel Sorelo raised his copy. "We've been contacted by a previously unknown entity."

The general reached for a copy, then sat as he read. "What is this?"

"Communications from a new participant."

"How were these messages received?"

The colonel glanced at Mitch. "Phone text, General."

"Who received them?"

Mitch lowered his copy. "They were already on a phone, placed so it would be found, at the Field Ops building."

Mia pointed to her laptop. "Sir, we just confirmed, only two of the original subjects were in the vicinity of the event."

"Does video surveillance confirm their interaction?"

"Sir, video and audio surveillance went down prior to the event. We have nothing."

"Are you kidding me, Captain?"

Her shoulders drooped. "No, sir."

His volume increased as he stared at her. "Is someone working on that, Captain?"

"Yes, sir."

Mitch raised his photocopy and pointed to the last message. "Our new participant suggests not."

"I really don't give a damn what some anonymous idiot suggests."

"The entity shows abilities beyond ours, General, and they may have abilities beyond the ones we've identified. May I suggest a less invasive alternate solution?"

"And what would that be, Captain?"

"The entity said it has our soldier, and he'll be returned when we declare peace and end the conflict."

"And what are our terms of surrender, Captain?"

"There is no surrender, General. Just peace."

"And my second prize?"

"We can present a request."

"I don't ask for things, Captain. I command an army. I take what I decide to take." He stood, then pounded his fist on the table. "Re-establish our surveillance, and bring me those four punks." He stared as they all hesitated. "Now!"

They rose and immediately headed for the door.

"Halt!" He eyed the colonel. "Where is this new communication device?"

Colonel Sorelo reached in his pocket, and it immediately indicated a new incoming message as he held it out.

Captain Madison hesitantly reached for the phone. "May I, General?"

The general barely nodded, and she opened the phone, then read. "Debellatio"

"What?"

"Debellatio, General."

"What the hell does that mean?"

Mitch inhaled. "It's military jargon for *the end*, General."

"Hooray. The idiot knows a military term." His eyes widened. "Go!"

Mitch dialed his phone after leaving the airbase.

"Dixon here."

"It's me."

"Is this my boss, or my ex-boss?"

"I'm still your damn boss." Mitch shook his head as he caught himself smiling.

"Good, cause I got shit to share."

Mitch merged onto the highway. "So do I."

"Want to wait till we're in the office tomorrow? It's been a long day."

"It can't. Can you send a message telling the kids, they're about to be taken into custody?"

"Are you serious?"

"Very." Mitch glanced over his shoulder before switching lanes.

"Did the general declare war?"

He sighed as he moved into the far left lane and sped up. "Did you really think he wouldn't?"

Charlie's voice turned solemn. "Okay. Priorities. What do we tell the kids and their families to do?"

"Did they have anything to do with the soldier's disappearance?"

"Nothing. They're as twisted as anybody about the ordeal. They were shocked the soldier was there, but far more frightened by how he left."

Mitch glanced at his phone. "They know more about it than we do?"

"Benny and Kyle watched it happen."

He lowered the phone as he passed a slower car. "Who did it?"

"Some little old hunchback lady in a shawl and wrinkled anklet stockings."

Mitch chuckled. "That story ain't gonna fly. They better make up something better."

"They're dead serious. I'll fill in the details." Charlie exhaled into the phone. "What do we tell the kids? Do we tell them to hide?"

"The general won't stop looking for them until they're caught."

"I can't tell them to just surrender."

"That's their decision. They can hide, fight, or go peaceably and get the interrogation over with." Mitch lowered the phone as traffic increased. "I suggest they go and try to wrap this up before school starts."

"That suggestion ain't gonna fly well with anybody; especially the parents."

"I know." Mitch increased the volume. "Tell them to hide what needs to be hidden and not bring anything they don't want confiscated, except their phones. They might lose them, but they need the ability to contact everyone."

"Do you know a good lawyer?"

"This is going to take more than a lawyer." Mitch sped past a group of slowing cars. "We'll talk back in the office."

"What's your ETA?"

Mitch glanced at the upcoming overhead sign. "An hour …maybe."

"See you here."

"Wait till I tell you who's an active-duty captain again."

"Huh?"

He smiled as he eyed his phone. "Talk to you in a bit …partner."

"No! Are you kidding!?"

~*~

Becca's second phone beeped and she glanced at it. "If we're all together, this can only be from one person." She removed it from the driver's door pouch and handed it to Jaime.

She eyed Becca and inhaled as she swiped the phone face, then twisted in the passenger seat before reading the message aloud. *Military coming for 4 kids. Their choice: flee, fight, surrender.*

"What do you mean?" Faith grabbed the back of Becca's driver seat. "Aunt Kitt …all those choices suck!"

"I agree." She glanced in the rear-view mirror. "Okay, let me think. First, you have to decide what you want to do but whatever it is, we'll handle it together and go with you if that's your choice."

Ben scratched his eyebrow as he leaned forward. "What if they don't let you?"

77

"Then we'll follow them, but be sure of one thing; we're not leaving you."

Kye shook his head. "There's no way our parents are letting this happen."

Faith slouched in her seat. "Mom's gonna have a heart attack when she finds out."

"Okay, before I drive you home, you have to decide what you're doing."

Ben tapped his sister's arm. "What if we do something about it?"

"Like what?" Her brows rose as she studied him.

He smiled. "What if we got all our friends to block our front door, and tell them we all helped save the ship?"

Kye grinned. "Yeah!"

Jaime leaned against the headrest and covered her eyes with her forearm. "How many times?"

"What do you mean?"

Ben sat up. "What if we called the news too?"

"And all they'll do is wait until the hype dies down before coming for us?" Jaime sighed. "You know they'll keep hounding us until we finally go."

Ben gently gripped the back of her seat. "So you're saying, we should just go and get it over with?"

She pressed her fingers through her hair. "Any other choice doesn't change the inevitable. It just prolongs it."

Ben shook his head. "Mom and dad ain't gonna listen to that argument."

"Neither are our parents."

Kye eyed his sister. "Then we have to convince them ...or not tell them yet."

Faith grabbed the corners of both front seats. "I don't want to get interrogated by these aholes."

Kye smirked. "What can they actually do to us? They're not going to kill us. I doubt they're even allowed to touch us let alone torture us."

Becca eyed Kye through the rearview mirror. "You're not scared of going with them?"

"A little. You'd have to be crazy not to be, but we'll survive."

Faith's eyes widened as she stared at him. "Wonderful. I feel much better now."

"Maybe our secret protector will help us. She's got to be the baddest zillion-year-old on the planet!" Ben made a karate motion.

Faith glared at him. "I don't think she's a match for a whole army."

"A whole army isn't after us. Just a few idiots"

She frowned. "Yeah …a few colonels and generals."

Jaime straightened in her seat. "I swear, if I can't play soccer this year because of these idiots, I may do some things with our gel, that I'm not going to be proud of."

Becca reached for her hand. "Don't stoop to their level."

She glanced at Becca. "Do you mean, don't be as childish as the adults?"

"I'm gonna hope *T* helps us, and we don't have to worry about it."

Kye leaned forward and eyed Ben. "If anybody can help us, she can; the way she dropped that soldier?"

"Yeah, but do you think she will?" Faith reached for Kye's hand. "We don't even know how to get in touch with her. What if she doesn't know about this?"

"She knew about the soldier."

Jaime sighed. "She could live behind the alley, but then she won't see the military come for us if they come down our street."

"Do you think she saw the ship?" Ben energized. "Do you think she knows what happened because she watched the whole thing?"

Faith tapped Jaime's shoulder. "We know the people behind us. No old ladies live there."

"What if the outfit is a disguise?" Kye smacked his thigh as he grinned.

"Guys, am I taking you home or not?"

"Man, it was a good one if it was. …fooled me!" Ben held his fist toward Kye.

"Can we call our parents first, just so they know?"

Kye fist-bumped him. "Fooled that soldier too. He didn't know what hit him."

Jaime eyed Faith. "Why worry them. They'll panic and come home, but they can't do anything."

She frowned. "My father's gonna punch the first person who tries to touch me."

"Maybe we should just play this out. It may be time to trust our side?"

Faith glanced at her brother. "The only people I trust are the ones who already proved they can be trusted."

"*T* kinda already has."

She glanced at Kye, then sighed. "Saving that ship is proving to be more trouble than I ever imagined."

Ben rubbed her forearm. "Would you do anything different?"

She shook her head and frowned. "Not a thing."

~*~

Mitch reached for his briefcase in the back seat, before opening the car door, then hurried to the side entrance as the thundershower teemed around him. The door slammed shut from the wind and moments later, Charlie opened the Control Room door. "Looks like the gods disapprove."

Mitch wiped the rain off his hair and shoulders. "Then they're not going to get any happier anytime soon. My office in ten?"

"Will do."

Charlie walked in and froze as he began sitting, then pointed to the bow-topped gift in the middle of the desktop. "What's that?"

"I haven't touched it, but I'm assuming."

"Another phone from our mysterious friend?" Charlie's eyes narrowed.

"It appears."

He refocused on Mitch. "What happened to the last one?"

"I gave it to the colonel and he gave it to the general."

"You didn't like the flash-paper idea?"

"I didn't think they would believe me and I didn't want to get caught in a lie."

"Fair enough. Are we unwrapping the new one, together?"

Mitch shared an uneasy smirk before removing the bow, then swiped it open and read the single text entry. *Do not share this possession with anyone.* He eyed Charlie. "I can't seem to please anybody today."

"Some days are like that, my friend." Charlie offered a faint smile. "But this may work out."

"How?"

"The Teacher now has access to us and the general, if she so chooses." He scanned the office walls. "And all indication is; she hears more than anyone's acknowledging."

"Good. I hope I'm talking to more than you, right now." Mitch followed Charlie's eyes around the room. "I have nothing to hide."

"Then let's share."

Mitch rested his forearms on the desktop. "The general got word his spy was abducted. When I told him we were contacted by a new entity and shared the messages, including responsibility for the abduction, he blew me off completely and demanded we bring the kids in for questioning."

"Does he think they were involved in the soldier's capture?"

Mitch glanced around the room, then leaned forward and lowered his voice. "He's a four-year-old throwing a temper tantrum and doesn't seem too concerned with facts, no matter how plainly they're laid out."

"Wonderful. Someone bruised his ego, and he's looking for retribution?"

"It sure looks like it."

"My turn." Charlie reached for his coffee mug, then smiled. "This new entity …the teacher… is a hunchback little old lady. And Ben and Kye watched her walk to the invisible soldier, raise her walking cane, and drop him in an instant. Then a pick-up came, and they loaded the invisible body in the back, and drove off."

"Did they give you a description of the woman?"

"Not much of one. A scarf covered her hair and blocked her face. Her shawl covered her arms, hands, and most of her house dress. The rest of her legs were covered by wrinkled stocking socks." Charlie rubbed his forehead. "She uses a metal walker with multiple rubber-tipped feet, but it seems to be more than a walker."

"But she had no problem lifting a fully outfitted limp soldier into a truck?" Mitch's head tilted and eyes narrowed. "Does the outfit sound a little too perfect?"

Charlie nodded. "They couldn't tell how tall she is, what her skin color is …nothing."

"Is anyone questioning how she knew the soldier was there?"

He chuckled. "Not yet, but I'm sure someone eventually will. The kids have no idea how she dropped him, either. She extended the cane and he hit the ground."

"Wonderful." Mitch smiled. "But to you and me, she's definitely a hunchback little old lady."

Charlie sipped his coffee. "Of course she is."

~*~

Faith took Becca's hand as they entered the family room, then motioned to the other three. "Do you mind if the four of us go upstairs? We want to discuss some things."

Jaime held Becca's other hand and offered an apologetic stare. "We want to decide what we're doing, alone."

"So you haven't decided?"

"Not yet." Jaime inhaled softly. "But I think we all want this over with."

"I understand." She watched them head toward the stairs. "Don't forget to hide everything."

Faith raised the music volume as Ben shut her bedroom door, and Kye pointed to the speakers. "*T* said the surveillance is cut."

"Oh yeah." She lowered the volume, then sat on the floor.

Jaime eyed everyone as they formed a circle. "Are we fighting, hiding, or surrendering?"

"We can't fight them."

Faith smiled at Kye. "And I'm tired of hiding."

"Maybe we can end this if we just go."

Jaime reached for Ben's hand, then glanced at each friend. "We're going with them without a fight?"

They nodded.

"Okay …what's our interrogation story? Do we tell them we did it and it needed to be done because they're intelligent beings? …Do we deny it?"

"What if we tell them we just watched the whole thing but didn't help?"

Ben nodded at Kye. "What if we tell them we hid it and didn't do anything after they discovered it in our yard, then we hid because we didn't want to be in trouble."

"Any other options?" Jaime glanced at each friend.

"Yeah. What if we tell them we saved it but when they mention the gel, we act clueless?"

Faith shook her head at Kye. "We can't. They know about the gel and we can't give any clue we used it."

Ben sat up. "Are we voting which one of those options we're going with?"

Jaime extended her hand, thumb down toward the middle of their circle, then turned it thumb up. "Which was first?"

"I vote for the one where we hid it till they found it, then we hid."

Faith nodded at Kye before refocusing on Jaime. "I think so too."

Ben nodded. "It's the one I want to pick."

"But then who do we say rescued it?"

"We don't have to say anybody, but we can tell them, maybe it was the teacher."

"Yeah! They don't know it ain't her. Let's blame her!"

"Guys, I don't think we're supposed to know her name. She shared that with Mitch and Charlie …not us."

Ben frowned at Jaime. "Oh yeah. We'll just call her the old lady."

"We can't say we know her at all. We would have had to be invisible to see what she did to the soldier."

"Then we can't even know they're coming for us. Charlie told us that too."

Faith sighed. "This is getting way too complicated."

"We can just say we don't know who did it, and they can do the math."

Kye shook his head at Ben. "I don't think they can do math, but maybe they own a calculator."

"Okay, is that our story? We hid it until they found it, then we hid because we were scared?" Jaime watched them nod.

"How come this feels so ominous?"

Kye grinned as he shoved Ben's shoulder. "Ominous?"

"Yeah. Ain't that the right word?" He glanced at both sisters.

Jaime nodded at him, before squinting at her bother. "Why are you such an idiot?"

"Somebody has to be," He pointed as he grinned. "...cause you three are way too serious."

Faith scanned the room. "Okay. Is everything hidden?"

Ben hopped as he stood. "All taken care of."

"Then let's go keep Aunt Becca company till they come for us." Jaime opened the bedroom door.

"And we all have to act shocked when they do."

"What's that noise?" Jaime opened the front door as they filed downstairs.

"I don't believe it." Faith raised her hand to her mouth as she peered over Jaime's shoulder and watched the utility truck extend its boom.

"*T* ain't gonna be happy."

Kye patted Ben's shoulder before continuing toward the family room. "I'm okay with that."

The knock on the door came twenty minutes later, and Becca whispered. "Are you sure you don't want to call your parents?"

"It would be a fight we won't win, and I'm not getting my father arrested."

"But I'm gonna do some acting on your behalf." Becca motioned to the front door as she stood. "Don't get upset when I make a scene."

Ben rubbed his hands together. "Good idea Aunt Kitt! Pour it on!"

She smirked as she watched Ben and Kye head to the door, then reached for Faith's hand. "I promise I'll come back to tell your parents, right after I find out where they're taking you."

Faith kissed her cheek. "Don't worry, Aunt Kitt. We're *The Invizibles*!"

They heard Ben's voice at the door. "You're who?"

"Are your parents home?"

"Hi, Cowboy. Nice costume. I'll go see if we have any candy." Kye peered down, then pointed as he grinned. "Where's your boots? You having the shit stain removed?"

"Kyle!" Becca gently nudged his shoulder and he stepped aside. "Can I help you?"

"Yes, ma'am. I'm Captain Mia Madison from military intelligence." She presented her identification as she stepped forward. "And we'd like your children to come with us."

Becca eyed the plastic card, then her eyes narrowed as she spotted Cowboy. "You again? Aren't we done with your petty bullshit yet?" She turned to the woman. "And no you can't have my children. Come back and try to take them from their parents, when they get home."

"Ma'am, these four are coming with us."

She turned toward the gentleman. "Not without someone's balls getting a lot closer to their neck."

An MP stepped back and placed his hand on his pistol holster.

She pointed at him. "Draw it, asshole, and give me a reason to bury my toe in your ass."

"Calm down Aunt Kitt. It's alright. We'll go with them."

"The hell you will!"

"Hey look!" Kye stepped onto the porch and pointed at the hints of smoke coming from the utility truck's cabin.

Faith stepped next to him and waved to the man in the extended boom. "Hey mister! There's smoke coming from inside your truck!"

Jaime stepped beside the MP and waved. "Get down!"

Ben hopped off the porch, and Faith moved next to him. "Hurry! Get down!"

Kye shook his head as he stood near Cowboy. "I love *T*"

Cowboy's head spun. "What?"

Kye grinned. "I'm thirsty and could go a nice ice tea …couldn't you?"

Ben glanced at Kye, then smiled at Cowboy. "Can we stop for a *T* on the way?"

Jaime placed her hands on their shoulders and smiled as she watched the smoke begin billowing from the truck windows. "Can we?"

Kye waved at Cowboy. "C'mon. Let's go get a tea."

Ben pointed to the man lowering the utility truck lift, as flames began flickering from the open truck windows. "Do you think we should invite him?"

Faith giggled as the man in the lift stumbled to the ground and hurried away. "He may have just had a *T*"

"Maybe he wants another."

Faith grinned as she glanced from Cowboy to Jaime. "I wouldn't think anyone would want more than one *T*."

They watched the flames flicker as it mixed with thick gray smoke. "One way or another, he needs a ride home."

Ben faced the female captain. "Are we going his way?"

Kye's hand jolted up. "Shotgun!"

Ben bolted toward the military vehicles. "Race you for it!"

Kye pointed to his friend as he pouted at Cowboy. "Tell him *I* called it!."

Chapter Four
Interrogatory Response

The general locked the door after exiting his office. "Forward my phone line, Lieutenant. Send all communications to the Tancil numbers, and send all non-essential communications to Colonel Immar. Tell him I might be gone a few days."

"Yes, sir."

He shut the car radio off and tried to enjoy the temporary peace of a quiet drive, but his thoughts continued racing. He remembered the peaceful and serene feeling the location offered when he first arrived; how sparse the traffic was when he assumed command of the base. The area had gone through significant changes over the last few years, and none of them to his liking.

He parked in the almost empty lot an hour later and stared at the obscure office building while walking to the door. Except for their temporary set-up, it appeared unoccupied. An agent came to attention as he turned the last third-floor hallway corner, and saluted as he held the door. "Welcome, General."

The general eyed his pristine black jumpsuit and spit-shined boots without reply, then walked along the inside hallway to the last door.

"General!" The gentleman behind the desk immediately stood as his four associates came to attention.

"At ease." He eyed them. "Are we ready to do this?"

"Yes, sir." One operative raised a tentative finger. "What level of intensity are we using, General?"

His chest expanded as he inhaled. "I want what I want."

"Does that include physical?"

The general stared at the interrogator. "Do you need that level to get answers from four kids?"

The agent lowered his gaze. "No, sir."

"No physical contact." The hint of a smile broke on his face as he faced the lead interrogator. "But push the Ferguson boy to his limits. He seems to have an attitude that needs adjusting."

Captain Madison appeared at the door as the gentlemen filed out. "General."

He raised a finger, then refocused. "What is it, Captain?"

She stood in the doorway. "May I come in?"

He motioned to the chairs facing the desk.

"Something or someone seems to be preventing us from re-establishing Fallwater surveillance."

He clicked his computer mouse before raising his stare. "How?"

"We're not sure how the surveillance went down, but the installation truck just caught fire while our operative reconnected our equipment. It's a total loss."

"Why would you assume an unnatural cause?"

She glanced at the clipboard in her hand. "We also lost the three assigned domestic drones."

"When?"

"This morning, sir."

"How?"

Captain Madison sat upright. "Exploded, sir. The three broke communication, concurrently."

"Aren't they almost undetectable from the ground?"

"Yes, sir. Pin-dot profile."

"Find out if we have any photo source whatsoever for the area, then visit the Ferguson boy's interrogation. I want an in-depth analysis of that conversation."

"Yes, sir."

The two agents hesitated as she entered the interrogation room, but Kye energized. "Hi, Captain!"

The lead interrogator's eyes narrowed before leaning on the table. "You act like you're not bright enough to know what kind of trouble you're in. Do you have any idea?"

He continued his grin as he refocused. "I'm bright enough to know I'm not in trouble …unless you're just a piece of shit."

"Not in trouble? We can charge you with kidnapping, which would take half your life away in an instant, and would be the equivalent of J-walking compared to the domestic terrorism charge we could prosecute you on."

The interrogator sighed as Kye stared. "We have multiple affidavits indicating you were actively involved in preventing your country from executing a military operation."

Kye shook his head. "No you don't."

He smiled. "We do and could charge you, and ruin the rest of your life. If one of you shares, or even slips, the other three are getting prosecuted. But you can be the one we don't press charges against."

He leaned back and rested his hand on the table. "Now there's an incentive to talk."

The agent stepped closer. "Did you have anything to do with stopping your country from capturing an alien entity?"

"No."

"Were you able to talk to them? Are they friendly?"

Kye squinted. "Are you kidding?"

"We know what you and your three friends did and it's okay if you just admit it. I'll make sure you don't get in trouble. Just say it so we can move on and learn more about them."

"Sorry to disappoint you, but we didn't."

"That's a lie. You did, didn't you."

He shook his head. "No."

"Try again!"

"Sure. …No."

"You did and we know it." The agent moved closer and stood over him. "So try again."

He inhaled and pressed his fingertips to his temple as he concentrated, then opened his eyes and smiled. "Sorry …still no."

The man sat on the table's edge. "No?"

Kye grinned. "What part of *no* don't you understand?"

He leaned intimidatingly close. "I don't appreciate your attitude."

"I don't have an attitude when I'm not taken into custody and interrogated." Kye placed his elbow on the table before resting his chin on his palm. "I'm a pretty happy-go-lucky kid at home."

"You'd *be* home if you didn't decide to play terrorist. Instead, you're going to spend the next few weeks with us and you and I are going to spend hours together, until you're not sure of your name. You can end this quickly, or you can see how long it takes me to break you. Just give in now. I promise it's a better alternative than going through what we put people like you through."

"Yeah …people like me. Everything about me says, terrorist."

"You're the definition, when you work against your own country's military to help an alien entity escape our control."

"We hid it until you captured it from our friend's yard, and you weren't even involved when we found it."

"But you didn't stop being involved like you should have, did you."

"Wrong. We're not stupid. We hid it before you showed up and had nothing to do with you or it from the time you took it away."

"We both know that's a lie."

"So what? You captured it. Take your toy and go home."

"We don't have our prize. We have the toy replacement you stupidly put in its place."

Kye sat up and slapped the tabletop. "You lost... ...our spaceship?!"

"You stole our spaceship!"

Kye pursed his lips as he paused. "It'd be nice if I had a part in saving highly intelligent living beings, from a bunch of immature aholes, but we really didn't do anything except protect it until you captured it."

The interrogator shook his head. "We have strong reason to believe you four exchanged it for the toy we now have, and you have access to alien technology, which is how you performed your little terrorist mission."

Kye's mouth opened as he stared at the interrogator.

"Yeah ...we're calling it a terrorist mission and will ruin your lives because of it." The interrogator leaned forward. "And we're going to disassemble your houses, looking for the little alien gift you used ...unless you tell us where it is."

Kye's eyes narrowed. "What the hell are you talking about?"

"You know damn well what I'm talking about, and you can give us what we want, or we can do this the hard way. I'm not going to spend much more time playing this game before I tell my constituents to proceed with your prosecution and our extraction plan. We're literally going to rip your houses apart and if you think we're building them again, you're a bigger fool than you pretend."

"You seem to like making enemies." Kye leaned back and crossed his extended legs. "Why is that, Corporal? Why do people like you travel around the world, killing people, and then wonder why you have so many enemies? And now you're starting a war with kids who are citizens of your own country ...in your own country? Can't you see how that makes you scum, besides being an ahole?"

The interrogator leaned forward and pounded the table with his fist. "Who do you think you're talking to!?"

"Really? You really need me to draw you a picture?" Kye leaned forward, then shook his head. "Do you really want me to say it out loud?"

"I dare you."

"A moron." Kye tilted his head as he smiled. "You asked."

"Well, wise guy, right now you're being charged with kidnapping, arson, and four terrorists acts against the military. Your ass ain't gonna see freedom ever again."

"Is the arson, the utility truck barbeque?"

The agent smiled.

"And how many other acts did I commit, while in your custody, genius?"

"You're a little punk, aren't you."

"No. I'm what you hoped to be when you grew up, but instead, you sold your beliefs for a career and some security and you hate me because I make you realize your life is a joke."

"I'm going to bury you."

Kye grinned. "You realize you probably shouldn't say things like that out loud, don't you?"

"And why not?"

"Because it goes against the golden rule …or haven't you learned that higher life lesson?" Kye adjusted in his chair. "You really are a moron."

"We'll see who has the last laugh."

"Yeah we will, Corporal." He raised a hand as he pretended to fight an apologetic smirk. "My bad …General?"

An operative knocked and the second agent quickly turned back after reaching for the door handle. "May I?"

He nodded, then refocused as it opened.

"Sirs! There's a fire at the base."

Captain Madison stood. "Where?"

"The general's office, ma'am."

Kye raised both hands, laughing, "I swear it wasn't me!" then softened his smile. "You people seem to have pissed off a significant someone. See why mommy always told you, be nice to strangers?"

Captain Madison hurried to the far office. "Have you received the latest intelligence information, General?"

"I have, Captain. Send Captain Harris in."

The captain immediately spun and disappeared.

"You wanted to see me, General?" Cowboy hesitated before entering.

"Shut the door and have a seat, Captain." He motioned toward the chair facing the desk.

"Yes, sir."

The general placed his forearms on the desk and leaned forward. "I thought you said you were positive these kids were the source of our difficulties."

"They are, General. I know it."

"Well, we've lost one surveillance truck, three drones, and now my office, all while they've been in custody. Please explain."

"Maybe family members?"

"You're guessing now, Captain? A week ago, you were adamant."

"They're involved, General. I'll stake my career on it."

"That's already been done for you, Captain."

The general refocused on his computer screen before breaking the next silence. "Staff meeting. Here. Now." He pointed to the door. "Get everyone in here, now."

The general leaned back as the room filled. "Is this everyone?"

The lead agent nodded as he eyed each associate. "Yes, sir."

"Shut the door."

The general pointed to an interrogator as the door closed. "Report."

The gentleman came to attention. "Subject Faith McCloud insists the four concealed the ship when first discovered, then hid after we discovered it in their yard, afraid they would be reprimanded for hiding it. She says it recloaked itself during their contact, and they placed it where we found it, hoping it would depart without assistance, once it had shown life. She swears they disengaged when we engaged."

"Your measure of her sincerity and truthfulness?"

"I cannot measure. My first inclination when I read the transcripts was; they're active participants, but her sincerity is convincing, and the latest developments support her story."

"Just because we seem to have uncovered a new vigilante, doesn't exclude or excuse them from their involvement, Captain."

The general nodded at the next interrogator and he straightened in his chair. "Subject two is Jaime Ferguson. Her story matches, General."

The general frowned. "Is it too close a match? Is the story collaborated?"

"The story is short and simple General, but consistent."

"Compare transcripts when they're assembled. I want to know how exact their stories are." He eyed the group. "Subject three?"

The interrogator came to attention. "Benjamin McCloud, sir. Same story. The ship disappeared on its own as they had it hidden on a shelf, and they put it in the yard, hoping it would depart. Then we came along."

"Subject four?"

The operative straightened. "Kyle Ferguson. Same story, General, but he quoted one of the new vigilante's messages."

"How so?"

"He mentioned the Golden Rule."

"Really."

An agent raised his eyes. "What's the Golden Rule?"

Captain Madison inhaled. "Do unto others as you would have them do unto you."

The general eyed her. "Why would they both mention it? What's it from?"

The lead agent pointed to his computer screen. "Sir …may I read?"

The general stared at him.

"The quote is attributed to Christ and found in the Gospel of Matthew. The Sermon on the Mount; considered Christ's longest and most enlightening lesson to his followers." The man inhaled as he read the screen. "One of his names is, Rabbi …which translates to *Teacher*."

"So this vigilante thinks he's god? No problem. I'll show him who's god."

"I think you're misinterpreting the message, sir."

"I'll tell you the message, Captain." He stood as his volume increased. "I don't have my prize, and shit is going to get ugly until that fact changes!"

"One or more adults could be involved, sir." Cowboy straightened. "The kids interacted with adults during the period in question."

The general's brow rose as he stared. "Are you telling me two fifty-year-olds thwarted our military mission?"

"It's as feasible as four high school kids, sir."

The general's eyes narrowed as he stared at the interrogator. "The relatives."

Captain Madison's breathing deepened. "The aunt and uncle haven't missed a day of work since their ill-timed mini-vacation."

"But they were both off for the week in question?"

"Yes, General."

"And the kidnapping incident?"

"Both were accounted for and in the company of others, General."

"Parents?"

"Proximity and company make them non-starters, General."

"Beyond question? Are you sure?"

Captain Madison nodded. "More than any other part of this investigation."

"The drones. Have we recovered any debris?"

"None, sir. It's as if they disintegrated, and the wind disbursed the dust."

"And my office? How extensive is the damage."

"Very, General. With the office door shut, there were no signs of fire until the flames engulfed the room."

"Is anyone hurt?"

"Your assistant is being treated for flash burns he received opening your office door. No other injuries have been reported."

"If we lose another thing, I'm going to declare war and dismantle a specific section of that town." He inhaled, then rubbed his forehead before scanning the room. "So what are your recommendations?"

"We've identified, but haven't captured our combatant, and the four are non-combatants, General."

The general eyed the agent, then pointed in sequence to the remaining interrogators.

"Non-participants."

"Not accomplices."

"Non-factors."

He placed both balled fists on the table as he leaned forward. "I disagree, ladies and gentlemen. I think they were involved. Heavily involved. And I order you to stop coddling them."

"Sir?"

He stared at Captain Madison, then met each soldier's eyes. "Do not let them sleep tonight, do you understand?"

"Sir, we can't really detain them unless we start formal processing."

"You'll do as I order, Captain."

She lowered her gaze. "Yes, sir."

~*~

"Our children are where?!"

Becca sighed as Taylor began panicking. "In a little town called Tancil, about an hour from here."

Owen pointed to the still smoldering utility truck outside. "Did our kids do that?"

Becca shook her head. "No. They were standing with the military when it caught fire."

Taylor pointed in the truck's direction. "Does it have anything to do with what's going on?"

Becca offered a conciliatory frown. "Yeah."

"Good. Serves the bastards right."

Cal shook his balled fists. "And I'm gonna light some more bastards on fire."

Steve smiled as he extended his open hand. "Relax. Word has it, someone's already taken up that mission."

Amanda reached for Becca's hand. "So you do know more than you're saying?"

Cal inhaled as he gestured toward Steve. "Come clean, my friend. They're my kids."

"Shit. When you use that angle, I have to give in." Steve raised a finger. "But understand, it's our love for them that stopped us from sharing."

"How do you figure?"

Becca eyed her sister. "When they questioned you, you were adamant about their innocence. In a few minutes, you'll have to lie, claiming the same innocence."

Steve eyed Becca, before motioning to the walls. "You're going to tell them here?"

"The teacher said it's fine." She pointed to the front window. "The fried utility truck proves her word is good."

He raised his open hands. "You're right."

Owen looked at each in turn. "What?"

"Your kids have a friend…"

Steve held his hand toward Becca. "Should we start from the beginning?"

"Cut to the chase. Are our kids alright?"

Becca smiled at Taylor. "Your kids are more alright than you could possibly hope."

"I don't understand."

"The chase." Becca smiled. "Faith is adorable. So feminine. Beautiful heart. She was scared to death for what they planned, but she was amazing."

"Ben is the bravest young man I ever met." Steve eyed Cal. "He has more guts, and more drive than you and I combined."

"Jaime is brilliant, analytical …a thinker but not an over-thinker. And Kye pushes them through any overwhelming circumstance, with a comedic stoicism worthy of a seasoned warrior."

Steve nodded in agreement. "Their loyalty is unbreakable, and they all show a tolerance and acceptance of others that would make most leaders blush."

Amanda's eyes narrowed. "What the hell did they do?"

"They took on the country's military, and kicked their ass."

Becca shook her head at Steve, then refocused on the two mothers. "They rescued an alien spaceship, with lives onboard …after the military captured it."

"How?"

Becca glanced away from Owen as Steve's hand motion caught her attention. "We helped."

She smiled and reached for his hand. "We did …didn't we."

"Guys …how?" Taylor moved to the edge of her seat.

"Can you love them enough to trust them?"

Taylor voiced indignance. "Are you saying I'm not allowed to know?"

Becca's brows rose as she inhaled, then Cal extended his hand. "Don't tell us anything they wouldn't want us to know."

Steve sighed. "Thank you."

"Are you kidding?" She refocused on Becca. "I want to know."

Steve shook his head. "It's like unringing a bell."

She spun in his direction. "What?"

"Can you unring a bell?"

Her eyes narrowed as she offered an admonishing stare.

"Please don't ask to hear something you can't unhear."

She pursed her lips and stared at Becca. "You suck."

"I love you and I adore your children."

Her voice softened as her eyes became glassy, and she placed her fists on her thighs. "You both really suck."

Becca held out her arms as she walked to her, then hugged her. "You're amazing parents. Your kids are proof."

Owen stood. "So, what are we doing? Are we rescuing them?"

"They're probably safer right now, then they've been in a few weeks."

"Are you saying, do nothing?" Amanda's eyes darted between Becca and Steve.

He grinned. "Oh, something is being done, don't worry about that."

Becca met his glance, then refocused on everyone. "What we're saying is, don't get arrested trying to fight battles you can't win."

"But our kids can?"

"Our side is potentially more powerful than anyone is crediting at the moment. Trust the process."

Taylor rubbed her face with both hands. "Why do we ask you two anything? You both manage to never answer anything."

Steve exhaled. "And yet you still know more than we wish you did."

Becca raised her hand. "Wait. Do any of you realize what we *did* tell you?"

Taylor sighed. "And what's that?"

"Your kids rescued and saved intelligent alien life by taking on the military …and kicked their ass in the process!"

"And that calls for a celebration!" Steve pointed to the kitchen. "Cal's beer for everyone!"

Cal raised his hands and laughed. "Ah, what the hell."

Taylor whispered to her sister as they stood. "Are you protecting my babies?"

Becca grasped her hand as they walked to the kitchen. "With my life."

~*~

"Is it necessary for me to visit the base tonight? Will everything still be burnt to a crisp, tomorrow?"

"Yes, General."

He yawned. "It's been a long day, Will. I'll stop in tomorrow morning."

"No problem, General. Get a good night's sleep."

He hung up as he eyed the last glimpses of sunlight piercing the whisper-thin clouds above his house, then pressed the garage door opener and noticed the lack of house lights as he removed his briefcase.

The inside garage door creaked as he opened it. "Dianna?"

He searched his phone for messages, then turned on the kitchen lights and exhaled in exasperation as he patted the empty kitchen counter. "Dianna?!" A simple message is all he asked for. How hard was it to leave a quick note? He shook his head knowing if he did this, he'd catch hell.

He dropped his briefcase in the foyer, then began removing his tie as he climbed the stairs. "Dianna!"

He turned from the closet as he unbuttoned his shirt and the yellow sticky-note on their leather headboard caught his attention. He quickly glanced around the room before approaching, then froze. This wasn't how they communicated. Notes were always left on the kitchen counter.

The doorbell rang as he studied the hand-drawn smiley face, and he stuffed it in his pocket before hurrying toward the stairs. "Coming!"

He watched the uniformed officer step back as he opened the door. "What can I do for you?"

"Sir, are you General Aidan Dimitri?"

"Yes. Has something happened?"

The second officer stepped closer. "Do you have identification, sir?"

He held his collar between his finger and thumb, displaying the silver star. "This is my identification. Do you know what this means?"

The officer stepped back as his partner read from a clipboard. "Are you the husband of Dianna and father of Allison?"

"Yes." His eyes narrowed. "Get to the point."

"Your daughter's daycare has your two grandchildren and is requesting you to pick them up immediately. Do you have any idea where your wife, daughter, and son-in-law are?"

"No. Have you been to their house?"

"Officers have knocked repeatedly, but we haven't forced entry, and all efforts to contact them have failed." The officer motioned to the inside. "May we quickly walk through your house?"

He straightened. "You've got to be kidding."

"The quick walk-through will not only help us spot any obvious foul play, but also remove you as a person of interest."

"I'm an active Air Force general!"

"We're aware sir, but we'll be back in an hour with a court order, and your grandchildren will stay where they are. Or we can expedite our process with your permission."

He inhaled, then stepped back.

The two officers quickly searched the house, then met the general at the front vestibule. "Thank you for your cooperation, General. We see no sign of anything unusual." The officer glanced at his clipboard. "Have you seen anything out of the ordinary, sir?"

He inhaled, then inconspicuously placed his hand in his pocket and grasped the sticky-note. "No officer, I haven't."

"Do you have the daycare's address and phone number?"

He slid his hand over his hair. "Yes."

"Please call them immediately."

~*~

The harrowed woman held the crying child toward him, as he opened the daycare door. "The hundred dollar overtime fee is due tomorrow with their arrival, or admittance will be denied."

"Where's our mom?!"

He glanced at his grandson, "Not here." then faced the daycare worker. "Will you help me?"

"I already did, and it cost me my evening plans." She handed him their nylon bags and held the door. "Have a great night."

Ian tugged his pant leg as they walked to the car. "Why isn't mommy or daddy picking us up?"

He balanced the bags and the crying baby before unlocking the car. "They're helping grandma."

"Give me my sister! She don't like you! You make her cry."

He patted the crying baby as he opened the back door. "You can hold her and take care of her when we get home."

"She needs mommy! Is mommy and daddy there?"

He laid her in the back seat and buckled her in. "No. You're coming to my house."

"We don't want to go to your house! We want to go home!"

He waved Ian inside. "You can't right now."

"We can't go to your house." Ian pointed to the back seat. "You don't have seats for us!" He folded his arms and frowned. "We have to stay here with Miss Rayna!"

"You can't."

"We have to! It's the law!"

He inhaled. "I know, but I need you to be my little soldier right now."

"I'm not your little soldier!" Ian stomped his foot. "You don't love us and I don't want to be anything you want!"

"You have no choice tonight."

"I want to go with anyone but you." Ian began crying. "You're mean!"

He sighed, then motioned to the back seat. "Get in."

Ian squeezed his arms tighter across his chest. "No! You can't drive us or you're a *crinimal*!"

He rubbed his eye. "I know."

Ian pointed at his face. "You said only crinimals break the law."

He patted the crying baby then smelled the odor coming from her diaper. "I know."

He cleaned and changed the baby before making dinner and putting both children to bed, then turned a living room reading lamp on and enjoyed a moment of relaxation. He read emails and sent a few texts before retiring early, then jolted awake from the sudden sound of the blasting sound system after what seemed like moments of sleep.

Instant Karma's gonna get you. Gonna knock you on the head.

He jumped out of bed as the words to the *John Lennon* song resounded throughout the house.

You better get yourself together. Pretty soon you're gonna be dead.

He ran halfway down the stairs before remembering the two children, then ran up and grabbed both crying babies as the music blared.

Instant Karma's gonna get you. Gonna look you in the face. Better get yourself together. Join the human race.

He ran from the house and crossed the front walkway before lowering Ian onto the hood of his car, then answered his ringing phone as he held his crying granddaughter. "What."

"It's Captain Madison, sir. Two messages were just received on the confiscated phone."

He watched the music's resonance, rattle the front bay windows. "Whose phone?"

"The phone Colonel Sorelo gave us."

"What's it say, Captain."

"Innocent angels aren't home or asleep because someone chose poorly."

His breathing intensified. "And the next, captain?"

"It is… Review Sherman's war philosophy. There will be a test. …And the text is signed …Karma."

His eyes narrowed as the curtains danced from the pounding bass notes. "Our on-base daycare is open twenty-four seven, correct?"

"Yes, sir."

"Send someone from the facility to pick up my two grandchildren. I have to go to Tancil."

"Sir?"

"My wife, daughter, and son-in-law are missing, and I have my two grandchildren." He adjusted the baby in his arms and buried his finger in his other ear as the music blared. "Send someone to my house, with a toddler and baby car seat …immediately!"

"Yes, sir! I'll find someone immediately, sir."

Ian's heels bounced against the car fender, in rhythm with the pounding beat. "I like this song."

He grabbed Ian around his waist and carried them across the street as the sound reverberated, then sat the baby on the sidewalk and motioned to Ian after two police cars screeched to a stop in front of the house. "Stay with your sister."

He recognized the approaching officer as the second officer headed toward the house. "Hello again."

"Hello, sir. Are they your grandchildren?"

He nodded.

"Let me get them blankets." The officer hurried to his vehicle, then presented the blankets as he approached. "Any word from your family?"

"No."

"I take it you're not the cause of the music?"

He inhaled. "No."

"We've called for a swat team. There may be someone inside." The officer tightened his bulletproof vest straps.

"I searched the house after putting them to bed. I don't think you'll find anyone." He ran his hand over his hair. "But I don't like the song's lyrics."

"Is there concern, General?"

"It's top-secret, officer, and I can't explain."

"Fair enough sir, but one way or the other, we'll make sure your house is safe." The officer squinted as he pressed his palm to his ear. "And we'll see about shutting the music off."

He pointed to the house. "The electric panel is in that corner of the basement."

A SWAT team filed out after the black SUV screeched to a halt, and five fully armed men sprinted to the front door.

Ian pulled on his pant leg. "Can you babysit Kaylee? I wanna watch."

"Only if you stay next to me."

Ian turned after an extended mesmerizing stare, then shared a toothless squint as he pointed. "Why does your house have loud music? Did you lose the remote control?"

He rubbed his temple without acknowledgement.

Ian took one giant step forward. "Can we move closer?"

"No."

"Why?"

"It's dangerous."

Ian's voice lowered. "I know why people don't like you."

He glanced without responding, and Ian looked away. "…You're mean."

A lieutenant approached, then saluted as the moon lit the night sky. "Lieutenant June, facilities daycare, General."

He half-saluted, then motioned to the two babies wrapped in police blankets asleep on the lawn. "Do you have two car seats?"

"Yes, General." She removed a marker from her shoulder bag. "Please mark the bottom of their feet with their sir name and a contact phone number." She eyed the baby before removing a clipboard from her bag. "Then please repeat the information on this form."

He inhaled slowly. "Seriously?"

"No exceptions, General." She eyed the children. "They hold higher priority and rank than your direct orders, sir. Your information will be in your handwriting, and photo identification will be demanded upon retrieval."

She glanced at the well-lit house. "I'm sorry for your difficulties, sir."

He mumbled as he began unwrapping the baby. "You won't be the only one."

The lead officer approached, as the daycare vehicle turned out of sight. "Your house is safe, but has no power until you re-engage the main breaker." He pointed to the bottom of his clipboard and extended a pen. "I hope your day gets better."

"It will." He pressed phone keys and listened as he watched the officers depart.

"Sir."

"Interrogation team meeting, back office, in forty-five minutes. And those kids better be awake and exhausted when I arrive."

"Yes, sir."

He walked into the office fifty minutes later. "Is everyone here?"

"All but one, present and accounted for, sir."

"Who's missing?"

"Captain Harris."

"Why?"

"We don't know, sir. He told us he was on his way when we called this morning, but as of ten minutes ago, no one's been able to reach him."

"Keep trying. No one requests recommission, then goes AWOL."

The special phone indicated an incoming message, and Captain Madison swiped it open, then read the message aloud.

"Peace or war. The four angels ... or no one ... will eat breakfast at home."

She stared at the general. "Sir?"

He pointed to the device as he rubbed his eye with his palm. "Then no one will eat breakfast at home."

The boom shook the building and the general looked out the window in time to see his car flip in the air and land on its roof. The team hurried to the window, then as they watched flames engulf the general's car, six additional cars exploded in succession.

"You're right, General. No one is going home for breakfast."

The general inhaled as he eyed the agent. "Get out of my office."

Mia stood behind him and watched the cars burn. "Sir, can we reconsider sending the children home?"

"No."

"Sir, will you at least reassess your hardline approach …at least until we evaluate our adversary?"

He pointed to the captain. "Put a plain-clothes platoon together and confiscate the two Fallwater houses. Arrest occupants on suspicion of terrorist activity."

"Sir. Please reconsider. We seem to pay for every act of aggression."

He eyed Captain Madison. "Then let's get what we're paying for, Captain. Find the dog vomit responsible, and then make it disappear."

They filed from the office and one agent whispered as the door shut behind them. "That's our problem, General. It has already disappeared."

~*~

Mitch heard the beep in his desk drawer and inched it open, then lifted the lit phone before swiping the screen.

Good morning Captain

He immediately pressed the office speaker and direct dial. "Get in here."

Moments later, Charlie hurried through the doorway. "What."

Mitch displayed the strange cell phone in his hand. "We seem to have an invitation to talk."

Charlie lowered into a guest chair. "Really."

Mitch shared as he pressed keys. "Hello."

The phone beeped. *Call me Karma*

He typed. *"Hello, Karma. I'm here with Charlie."*

The reply appeared before he finished typing. *Hello Charlie*

Charlie glanced at the walls. "Hello, Karma. Is there anything we can do for you?"

The text appeared as Mitch typed.

Yes

Charlie raised his hands to his head and his eyes widened as the phone beeped after the short break.

Inform the parents:

1   Stay calm and remain inside

2   Our children are being watched by their guardian

"Our children?"

Specifically the 4 angels but whose children are not OUR children?

Charlie's eyes narrowed as he stared at Mitch. "Stay calm and remain inside? What's happening?"

The phone lit. *An unsuccessful raid*

"Right now?"

Shortly. Tell them to go upstairs and peek out the windows without being seen. They are your eyes.

"The children saw your interaction with the alley soldier." Mitch scanned the room. "How did you spot him? Are you as you appear?"

He scratched his nose as the silence indicated non-response.

Charlie keyed a text, then tapped his second phone. "Message sent."

Your daily lives at the facility are not monitored. I only listen when we talk. You show no need for supervision. I exterminated your building. You had other bugs, but only a recent infestation

Mitch eyed the ceiling. "Is the soldier alive?"

I do not kill. It is one of our most sacred don'ts. That man did nothing wrong just like my angels did nothing wrong. 4 are detained like my 4 angels are detained ...and will be freed accordingly.

"Can we help free them?"

No. The lesson must be learned. My latest message to the leader: Study Sherman. All or none go home

Charlie's head tilted. "Without death?"

Death isn't necessary. Loss is. Lessons are learned through failure and loss. Death is the end of loss and the end of lessons

Mitch inhaled after placing his forearms on the desktop. "Can our side have access to the invisibility gel?"

We can't give dangerous toys to children.

"I know, but asking means I did everything I could to get access to it. That's my duty as a commissioned officer."

I'm aware

Charlie's stare lowered. "Is there anything else you'd like us to do?"

Share: war is not a means to an end. It is the end. My last message is my first: Peace or war

Mitch stared at Charlie during the extended silence, then rubbed his face with both hands before sitting back. "What do you make of that?"

Charlie inhaled. "One line scares me more than the rest."

"What line?"

He frowned. "Study Sherman."

"Why?"

"Sherman loathed war. No man ever hated it more."

Mitch's eyes narrowed. "We should all hate war."

"We should, but talk is weak when action is contrary, and his hatred manifested into action, directly correlated in magnitude to the atrocity. Did you ever study him?"

"Yeah. He was a war hero who later became a war villain when everyone changed perspectives on his actions."

"Do you remember why?"

Mitch chortled. "Why was he a hero or why was he then declared a villain?"

"The dynamic from one point to the other."

"Please share your thought."

Charlie lowered his coffee mug. "His insight into war is intriguing, and I'm fascinated by the different perspectives time produced." He stared at the strange phone resting on the desktop. "He loathed war."

"Then why would he become a soldier?"

"For the reason many of us do. Governments make it sound glamorous. Our side is going to right the world. Then you experience battle and find out it's an atrocity …unarguably the most vulgar human act. Then you study it through history and realize, the atrocity has no lasting result. No one ever learns anything, or the next war would be unnecessary."

Mitch frowned as he reached for his coffee.

"So why did people initially love him?" Charlie's brows rose.

"He put an end to a horrendous atrocity."

"And why did people come to hate him?"

Mitch raised fingers to his chin as his eyes narrowed. "They didn't like how he put an end to a horrendous atrocity."

"And to this day, people dislike how sides end wars, more than the idea they must end."

Mitch motioned with a nod. "How do you feel about the severity implemented to end certain wars?"

"I don't measure that, since I can't live that moment, but for that specific conflict, I have more of a problem with the initial post-war peace …on both sides." Charlie's voice turned solemn. "It taught an unacknowledged lesson. Nothing we fought for ended. Nothing was resolved. Definitions and descriptions change. Philosophies and mindsets don't …which proves war useless."

Mitch motioned to the strange phone. "This entity is trying hard, not to fight."

"And her retaliations are immediate, but can be viewed as attempts to end the conflict, without escalation."

Mitch nodded. "She isn't initiating."

"But that doesn't mean she can't …or won't."

He continued staring. "Her warnings most likely mean she can."

Chapter Five
Secret Spectacle

Owen pressed his fingers through his hair. "Okay ...how are we doing this?"

"Is anyone else as terrified as me?" Taylor moved the front window curtain and stared down the street.

Cal glanced at Owen and Amanda. "Should I get a gun?"

"No!" Amanda placed her open hand over her heart. "Please no. You're not threatening them with it and you can't shoot anyone without devastating both our families for years to come."

Taylor eyed him. "Becca said it'll be unsuccessful."

"How do we know? How does she know?" He extended his arms as he scanned the room. "They already have our kids, and these are our homes."

Owen eyed the front window before refocusing on Cal. "Let's trust others right now ...at least for now."

"I can't and won't lose everything I love without a fight."

"If you take out that gun, you will."

Owen glanced at Amanda, then rested his hand on Cal's shoulder. "Neither can I, friend, but we aren't winning this battle with a single handgun, and we were told we'll be alright."

Cal rubbed his forehead. "And if it isn't?"

"Then you and I will consider our options, together."

Cal snorted. "Like our kids?"

Owen laughed. "Exactly like our kids. Together."

Amanda waved him to the door. "Come on. We have to hurry if they're on their way."

"Calls connected?" Cal raised his phone.

Owen grabbed Amanda's hand. "Dial us now. We'll connect as we run."

They hurried across lawns as both answered their phones, then ran upstairs to their bedroom after locking themselves in. Owen knelt by the side window as Amanda sat between the front bedroom curtains and raised her phone. "Are you upstairs?"

Taylor whispered. "Yeah. You?"

"We're both upstairs and safe" She inhaled, trying to calm. "...for now."

"Do you see anything?"

"Not yet." Amanda scanned the street. "I hate this."

"Me too."

"Holy shit!" Amanda knelt and peered out the window. "An enormous tractor-trailer just came into view! If a bunch of soldiers jump out of that thing, I'm going to have a heart attack!"

"Shh!"

She eyed Owen as he raised his finger to his lips, then lowered the phone and glared at him. "Well I am."

She moved the curtain and knelt at the windowsill, then whispered into the phone as she peered down the street. "Something's going on."

The giant vehicle stopped five houses down as a rusty white sedan coming in the opposite direction, stopped after trying to fit between the truck and a parked car. Two heavyset workers wearing coveralls nonchalantly stepped from the truck's cab and left both doors open as the two black SUVs following behind, honked at the massive carrier.

They heard hydraulics as they lost sight of the tractor-trailer driver. "What are they doing?"

Owen glanced at Amanda. "Making a delivery?"

116

The lead SUV driver exited his vehicle and pointed to the truck, then suddenly fell to the ground as everyone in the two SUVs slumped in their seats. The second SUV's back passenger door opened and a helmeted occupant hung face down under it, suspended only by a seatbelt.

"Oh my god!" Amanda covered her mouth. "Can you believe this?"

"What's happening?"

She raised the phone. "I think it's the two SUVs!"

The truck driver drug the unconscious lead driver to the first SUV's passenger door, as his partner lifted the slumping passenger in the second and shut the door. They removed the second driver and placed him in the back seat before the co-worker took his place and inched the vehicle forward.

"It's the SUVs..." Amanda pointed and Owen raised his fists in celebration as they heard hydraulics whine in the distance.

Owen snickered as he raised his phone and stared out the window. "This is unbelievable."

Taylor's voice caught Amanda's attention. "What's going on? We can't really see!"

Amanda raised her phone after moving the curtain. "The truck ...it's stopping them!"

Owen glanced at his phone. "Cal! Can you see the tractor-trailer?"

"Just barely. What's happening?"

Owen pointed. "Two SUVs full of what look like sleeping soldiers are being loaded into it. Hot damn, this is fantastic!"

"What?"

"There are two SUVs behind the tractor-trailer, and they have people in them. I think they're the raid. And they never even made it here!"

Amanda turned and sat against the wall as Owen peered out the side window. "That's it? That's really it?"

She held her phone closer as she knelt again. "Two burly guys are driving the SUVs into the back of that gigantic truck. Taylor, a tractor-trailer is going to pass your house in a little bit! Wave to it! It'll be driving our raid away!"

Cal's voice made Owen lift his phone. "Would it be wrong to go out front and wave as it passes?"

"You're only joking, right?"

They heard his deep cackle. "Half joking?"

Amanda eyed her phone. "Taylor, please convince him to stay out of sight. We don't need to let anyone know we saw anything."

"Agreed."

Amanda heard Taylor's voice. "Stay put!"

Cal laughed into Owen's phone. "Did you just get me hollered at?"

Owen snickered. "Why are you blaming me? You just got you hollered at!"

The oversized tractor-trailer's back doors clanked shut, then both large men climbed into the cabin as the white car reversed into a driveway. The truck ground into gear, then the air-brakes released and it began moving.

Amanda jumped with excitement as the truck approached. "I feel like we're watching a parade!"

Owen whispered into his phone. "One military raid, coming to you."

Taylor's excited voice echoed from Amanda's hand. "I see it! I see it now! I'm dialing Becca!"

"No!" Amanda stared at her phone. "No! Please don't! It's bad enough we're on the phone with each other!"

"Oh, Jesus. You're right." They heard Taylor sigh as her voice turned solemn. "We'd make lousy bad guys."

Amanda raised her phone. "Yeah we would. Cause we ain't!"

~*~

"Sir. We lost communication with the search and seizure crew."

The general's eyes widened as he faced the open doorway. "What do you mean, we lost communication?"

Captain Madison continued standing in the doorway. "Last communication placed them at the corner of Tangent and Third Avenue, and all subsequent communication attempts have failed."

"How long ago was that?"

"Roughly fifteen minutes."

"Is someone…"

"We have an investigation team en route, sir. … Oh!" The confiscated phone vibrated as it beeped in her pocket, and she removed it before studying the device. "It's a media message, sir."

"Good. Maybe the coward will show their face while gloating over what they've done."

She held the phone so he could watch, then opened the message, and a musician's face appeared as a Talking Heads song began.

Watch out, you might get what you're after. Cool babies, strange but not a stranger. I am an ordinary guy. Burning down the house.

"End that."

"Sir, there may be something after."

He pointed. "Get it out of here!"

She hurried through the doorway as the song continued…

All wet, hey, you might need a raincoat. Shakedown, dreams walking in broad daylight. Three hundred sixty five degrees. Burning down the house.

She knocked on the open doorframe moments later. "Sir, we just got word your house is engulfed in flames."

He stared out the window. "I know what the song meant, Captain."

"Will you declare peace, General?"

"Why? What else could this bastard do to me?"

"Say *peace* and we won't find out."

"I have a couple of choice words for this puke. None of them include the word *peace*."

She stood motionless, and he glanced at her. "What?!"

"Can we release the four adolescents?"

"Get out of my sight."

A knock on his door broke the extended seclusion. "Leave me alone."

The door opened and Captain Madison stepped in, flanked by two MPs. She raised a paper and began reading. "Sir, you are hereby relieved of this assignment. Please gather any personal belongings and accompany these two soldiers to the awaiting vehicle. You are also hereby requested to meet with the general's council at Ryan Air Base, eighteen hundred hours today." She inhaled. "Signed, Generals Mahir and Avory, Division Command."

Her voice softened. "It is suggested you stay on base tonight, since you no longer have accommodations or transportation, but a driver is instructed to take you to your residence after your meeting, if you desire."

She exhaled. "I'm sorry for your loss, sir."

His chest expanded with a reactionary breath, but he remained silent as he finished packing his laptop, then walked past her without glancing at her or the accompanying MPs.

She waited until the three exited the office suite before opening the first interrogation door. "Gather everyone, including the four adolescents. Meeting in the back office. Now."

"Yes, Captain."

She gestured Jaime, Faith, Ben, and Kye to sit after they entered, and she grasped her wrist behind her back and inhaled as the remaining personnel finished filing in. "Ladies and gentlemen, I am Captain Mia Madison and I've been given authority over the remainder of this incident, by order of Generals Mahir and Avory, Division Command …and I declare peace."

"Hooray!" Jaime smiled. "Sorry."

"Please don't apologize. Peace should always be celebrated." She smiled before lifting the confiscated phone high enough to visibly text.

"And declared." Ben's eyes widened as his three friends faced him, and he extended his hands apologetically. "Don't you think?"

She nodded and smiled at him, then read her text. "We declare peace. Our four guests are going home as soon as transportation arrives." She pressed the send button, then focused on an agent. "Has transportation been requested?"

"Yes, Captain."

"Has someone called their families?"

An agent raised his hand. "I'll do it immediately, Captain."

"What were the explosions we heard?"

She smiled. "Your side, demanding we declare peace and release you." She motioned to the windows. "Take a look."

Ben's eyes widened as he stood. "We have a side?"

Kye raised his fist after moving the blind. "Yes!"

Faith covered her mouth. "Was anyone hurt?"

"No."

"Thank god."

The captain eyed Jaime. "That's your first concern?"

Faith grasped Jaime's hand. "Yeah. How could it not be?"

Ben turned from the window. "We don't want anybody getting hurt."

"…Anybody." Kye grinned. "But I do like your cars like that."

She chuckled. "The teacher says you're four angels."

"Our teachers?" Faith's voice rose as she pointed to her chest.

"We're four average kids who just want to be left alone."

The captain eyed Kye, "I know, and I apologize on behalf of our military." then refocused on Faith. "Don't you know about the teacher?"

"Which teacher?"

"One of our teachers is protecting us?" Ben peered between the window blinds.

"We need to have a meeting. Lieutenant, please remain. All others are dismissed. Shut the door."

"What teacher is it? Are they in trouble?"

Kye pointed to the window. "I doubt a teacher blew up your cars."

"Please sit." She opened a briefcase and removed a handful of papers. "I have legal documents indemnifying you and all family members involved. Signing them comes with financial retribution. Placing the retribution in your bank accounts will be the legally binding action indemnifying our organization. The four of you will also receive full scholarships to any state college or university, but does not include private schools."

Jaime pointed at Ben. "No one signs unless he gets full guaranteed commitment papers and recommendation letters for admittance into the Air Force Academy."

Kye nodded emphatically. "Yeah! Before we sign anything, or we're not signing."

Ben eyed Jaime as tears welled. "You would do that for me?" He quickly wiped his eyes.

Jaime smiled, then pointed to the papers on the table as she eyed the unnamed associate. "Go get it done, or this ain't happening."

He hesitated until the captain nodded, then immediately left the room.

Mia smiled at them after he left, "You're impressive young adults." then turned to Ben. "You want to join the Air Force?"

"I want to fly something! ...Anything!"

"We'd be proud to have you."

"I'm taking a lot of science and math courses, and I made the freshman soccer team …and I'm joining ROTC as soon as school starts!"

"Then you'll qualify."

"Oh wow!"

Jaime smiled at the captain. "And in a few years, if that isn't honored …we keep our money, and share this entire fiasco with everyone." She inhaled. "And it's well documented."

"Understood and agreed." The captain extended her hand and Jaime shook it.

Ben stood and reached for Jaime's hand, then pulled her close and hugged her. "I can't believe you just did that for me."

Kye stood with his arms out. "I did it too. Don't I get a hug and a kiss?"

Ben reached for him and he jokingly shoved his shoulder. "Get away from me, you weirdo."

Faith smiled as she stood. "I'll give you a hug."

He raised a finger. "I believe the offer was a hug and a kiss?" He pretended he didn't know how to hug her, then covered his mouth and feigned a bashful smile as Faith kissed his cheek.

Jaime shielded her eyes in playful disgust. "Oh, brother."

"Aw shucks. Ya shouldn't have."

Her head tilted. "Are you done being an idiot?"

Faith giggled. "It's like asking him to stop breathing."

They signed the papers, and Ben eyed the captain as they were approved and collected. "Is our ride almost here?"

Mia glanced at her watch. "Within fifteen minutes."

"Well …how about we say goodbye here …you know …so it's not awkward …and don't be a stranger." Kye pointed to the window. "We're just gonna go hang by the fried cars." He smiled. "Sorry. Is one yours? I didn't mean to be insensitive."

Jaime grabbed his shirt. "We'll be outside."

The captain raised her hand. "There's one more thing. We'll be investigating two incidents that happened since your internment. You're not the target, but your immediate vicinity is. Don't be alarmed if you spot unusual activity."

"And then will you go away?" Kye extended an open hand. "It's not like we don't enjoy your company. No, wait. It is like we don't enjoy your company. Are you done after that?"

"We're done with you as of your deposit but there are other issues in your area we must address."

Faith grabbed Kye's hand as she studied the captain. "But you promise to go away as soon as you can?"

She nodded. "Yes."

Kye inhaled as he exited the building. "It's not restaurant grease, but fried car isn't terrible."

"You're disgusting."

He rubbed his stomach. "I'm hungry."

"So am I." Ben eyed the burnt cars. "Do you think our teacher bullshit was convincing?"

"I think we were flawless." Faith twirled with her arms out. "You're all better actors than I thought."

Jaime laughed. "Practice makes perfect."

"One; bring the toy. Two; the cardboard box. Three..." Kye grinned.

Jaime's eyes widened. "Shut up. If it wasn't for the teacher, our asses would be heading anywhere but home."

"Remind me to give her an apple."

Ben extended his fist toward Kye. "...A day, for the rest of her life."

He fist-bumped him. "I wonder if she still has teeth to eat one."

Faith smacked Kye's shoulder. "Be nice to her!"

"Just wondering."

A driver stepped from a vehicle after stopping between the building and burnt cars. "Fallwater?"

"Yes, please."

They rode in uneasy silence, and Kye broke the prolonged discomfort after exiting, "See ya!" then waved at the departing car as their parents ran from both houses.

"Babies! Our babies!"

Ben spun as Taylor approached. "Jesus, mom. We know we're your babies, but do you have to scream it in the middle of the street?"

"Shut up and hug your mother."

He returned Cal's smile before hugging her, then switched with Faith. "Hi, dad. It's good to be home."

"Good to see you, son."

He waited for Jaime to finish hugging Amanda. "You'll never guess what she did for me today."

Faith jumped. "We have college scholarships!"

Kye removed a folded paper from his pocket. "And checks to deposit."

Jaime smiled. "Rather nice checks."

"Wanna go inside and hear?"

Owen eyed Faith. "Together?"

"Always." Ben smiled after glancing at Kye and Jaime.

"Can we make it a pizza party?" Kye grinned. "I'm starving."

Owen caressed the back of his head. "Yeah, sport. Let's get some pizza and have a small welcome home party."

"Our house?" Amanda eyed the McClouds.

Ben interrupted Taylor. "Okay."

"We have to call Aunt Becca and Uncle Steve."

Taylor reached for Faith's hand. "Sure, sweetheart."

Jaime pointed to Faith's phone. "Call them before they have dinner."

Amanda smiled at the McClouds. "I'll order the pizza."

Ben ran ahead as they left their house, and knocked on the Fergusons' open door. "It's only me."

Owen yelled from the family room. "Come on in."

He hopped as he reached the end of the hall. "I love when we have parties together."

Amanda caressed the back of his neck on her way into the kitchen. "You're so cute."

Cal followed the others inside, carrying the pizza, and laid the boxes on the kitchen counter. "You owe me twenty."

They ate and laughed until Taylor waved a hand. "Who's starting?"

Ben lowered his pizza slice after eyeing the others. "We'll take turns."

Cal stood with his plate as Kye finished explaining their confinement. "Well, that worked out alright?"

Faith smiled. "A little bit better than alright, though I'm not sure I'd volunteer to do any of this over again."

Jaime lowered her half-eaten pizza. "We didn't volunteer. We had no choice."

"So who is this teacher?" Amanda's eyes narrowed as she fed Chichi a small piece of crust.

"We have no idea, mom."

"But she saved our lives." Kye rested his plate on his folded legs after sitting on the floor. "I think we're in deep trouble if she doesn't show up."

Ben glanced out the sliding glass door at the houses across the alley. "And we can't even thank her."

"Thank every old lady you see."

"Do you really think she's an old lady?" Jaime bit her pizza.

Ben nodded. "She sure looked like an old lady to me."

"From the neighborhood?"

Kye shrugged. "Where else would she be from?"

Taylor wiped her mouth with her napkin. "I just want things back to normal."

"So do we, mom."

"I'll never be happier to go to soccer practice tomorrow. I hope I'm still on the team."

"We'll talk to your coach, and the principal if we have to."

"This is why we missed all those baseball games this year."

Owen smiled at Kye. "We'll talk to him too."

"So you didn't go to Florida and visit Aunt Aerial?"

Faith's head tilted. "Sorry."

Cal smiled at her. "Nothing to be sorry about. You had business to take care of."

"But it's over now." Amanda sat forward and reached for Jaime's hand. "And everything can get back to normal."

"So we're cashing our checks?"

"Depositing." Owen pointed to each in turn. "Depositing your checks."

"But we owe Aunt Kitt and Uncle Steve about…"

Jaime eyed Faith. "Three or four hundred dollars?"

Ben straightened. "Yeah. We should pay for our other phones, and dinner that night driving home."

Amanda's voice rose. "Phones?"

Jaime motioned toward him. "Don't forget the toy."

"And the delivery." Faith sipped her soda. "It was overnighted."

"We have to pay them back." Kye stood as he finished his slice. "Can we take a hundred from each of our deposits and give it to them?"

"Please?" Faith joined her hands as if praying.

Taylor exhaled audibly. "Are you ever going to tell us what you really did?"

"Probably not." Ben kissed her cheek before following Kye to the pizza on the kitchen table.

She shook her head after attempting to smack his arm as he walked away. "Wonderful."

~*~

"Good afternoon, General. They're waiting for you, sir."

Aidan ignored the desk sergeant and opened the conference room door.

"Welcome. Please have a seat." General Mahir motioned to the empty chair with paper stacks lined within reach.

"It's good to see you." General Avory extended his hand across the table.

"Can the bullshit and cut to the chase."

"If you insist." General Mahir folded her hands on the tabletop. "You've had a distinguished career Aidan, and the Air Force is honored to have had your extended loyal service."

"This is it?" He eyed his two contemporaries after glancing at the two unintroduced strangers sitting silently across the table. "This is my unceremonious departure?"

"You openly ordered a combat mission on United States civilians, then botched the mission. Do you understand it's to your great advantage to retire effective immediately?"

"The base fire and soldier kidnapping have brought your activities to the attention of those best left unnotified."

His eyes shifted from Avory to Mahir. "That mission was for the posterity of all we believe."

"Aidan, you can't possibly mean that."

"We're on the precipice of acquiring the greatest warfare technology we could ever imagine. How can you not support maximum effort, at all costs?"

"Let me reiterate. You ordered and continually sanctioned an ongoing combat mission against United States civilians within the United States borders. You could get court-martialed and sent to prison." General Mahir folded her hands on the table. "You have a choice. Sign, or contest our decision and request representation for your court-martial. What do you prefer?"

"Have you read the transcripts?"

Avory leaned forward. "We've read enough"

"That's a bullshit answer for a subordinate, not an equal. Especially someone who's reached our rank." He pointed at the window. "There's something out there that proves what I'm after is worth breaking a few rules for, and you know it."

"A few rules?" Avory inhaled. "You crossed the line, and have subsequently brought our entre command across the line with you, and it's unacceptable, Aidan. Time to retire."

He pressed his fingers through his hair. "Damn you."

"What's your answer, General?"

"You know damn right well what my answer is."

"Say it."

"I'll retire. I'll retire! There! Are you happy?"

"Effective...?"

"Immediately." He pointed toward a window. "But you see what just happened. There's something out there that singlehandedly just kicked our ass, twice. How could you not want that power ...that ability?"

General Avory reached into his briefcase and presented paperwork. "You'll receive full retirement, and I suggest any and all information leading to today's events be kept everyone's secret, understood?"

"Yeah yeah yeah." He shook his head in disgust.

"We'll wait while you read and sign."

His eyes rose from the document. "I don't have to read it, do I?"

"No. It's military policy not to dishonor those who've served at such a high level."

"Thank you." He leafed through the document, signing where indicated, then slid the papers across the table.

The generals examined each page, signing where necessary, then Avory handed it to an associate. "Six copies plus original."

"Yes, sir."

"It's been a pleasure serving with you, Aidan."

"Yeah. I'm noticing what you think of our time together."

"In time, you'll have a different perspective. We're sure you'll eventually realize this action is for your own good."

"I risked my life and sacrificed myself for the good of our nation. I hope you both don't come to realize, not helping me find the cause, was your biggest mistake."

"Let's hope better for all involved, Aidan."

The associate re-entered the room and handed the general seven copies.

"Thank you, Lieutenant." General Mahir reviewed a copy then slid it across the table. "Understand, any further action on your part starts a military inquiry."

Avory frowned after turning from his peer. "And suspends your retirement privileges, until the matter is resolved."

General Mahir folded her hands on the table. "But do yourself a favor, Aidan. Take a well-deserved vacation."

"Do I still have my car and driver?"

General Avory nodded as he closed his briefcase. "And a room on-base for as long as you need."

He slid the document into his briefcase as the group left the conference room, then wrote his address on a separate paper before leaving.

He opened the car door after exiting the building, then extended the note toward the driver. "Take me here."

"Yes sir." The driver accepted the paper, then entered the address into his GPS.

They drove in silence until they turned onto his street, and Aidan spotted his wife's car as the driver approached his smoldering house. "Stop here."

"Should I wait for you, sir?"

He exited the car with his briefcase. "Yes, Sergeant. But park a hundred yards down the street, and don't leave unless it's by my direct order."

"Yes, sir."

He tapped the car roof. "Move."

"Yes, sir."

Dianna spotted him as the car pulled away, and thrust a pointed finger at him as she crossed their front lawn. "You bastard."

He stepped onto the sidewalk. "It's good to see you too."

"Seriously? Sarcasm?" She pointed to the house. "You cost me every possession, memory, and keepsake I have." Her voice turned bitter. "You're not even close to the man I thought you were."

"I'm exactly the man you thought I was."

"…In your dreams."

"Why are you blaming me for this?"

She waved a handful of loose-leaf papers. "I know exactly what you did."

"You don't know what happened."

"You captured and interrogated four American teenagers?" Her brows furrowed. "Who are you?"

"I really don't feel like discussing this tonight."

"Oh don't you?" She mock saluted. "Well excuse me, General Asshole." She peered around him. "And where are our grandchildren?"

"At the base daycare."

"Mom! Are you alright?!" Allison appeared as she ran around the corner of the building. "I heard your voice."

Dianna turned as she pointed behind her. "Look who decided to show up."

"Hi, Allie."

"Damn, Dad. Is it true?"

"What?"

She pointed to the papers in her mother's hand.

"I doubt what you think you know, is the truth."

"You're not a liar too now, are you?"

"Why do you think you have access to the truth?" He motioned to Dianna's hand. "My enemy gave you their explanation and you believe it wholeheartedly?"

"All you had to do was say *peace*?"

Dianna pointed to Allison. "Answer her. All you had to do is say *peace*?"

"Do you think this is that simple? ...Life is that simple?"

"We were released as soon as the *peace* text was received ...so what do you think?"

He inhaled without answering.

"What could four kids have done that would make you declare war on them?"

"They stole something extremely valuable."

"Your enemy says they had nothing to do with what you lost."

"Again ...you believe my enemy?"

Dianna raised both open hands waist high and inhaled calmly. "You still haven't answered the main question."

"I'm not going to answer any question regarding this incident."

"You seem to lean on your title whenever it's convenient, and I'm sick and tired of it."

"There are things you can't know."

She pointed to the smoldering wreckage. "Can I know why my house is destroyed? Can I know that?!"

His voice lowered. "I'm afraid you can't."

"Then you lost one more thing. Can you guess what it is?" She exhaled in disgust. "You'll be hearing from my lawyer."

He raised his voice as they began walking away. "Where were you? Do you know where you were taken and held captive?"

She stopped and turned. "We were treated nicely, actually. The only problem with our stay was, we were told we couldn't leave until you released the four teenagers, and declared peace."

"And we were told you never did, Dad. You had to be relieved of duty, so someone else could say it?"

He silently eyed his daughter.

"Where are my children?"

"At base daycare. You'll need picture identification."

"We don't need you to get them?"

He shook his head.

Dianna hesitated as Allison walked to their car. "Have a great life, Aidan. Rebuild my house, then understand you're not welcome in it. Go live your military life and stay the hell out of mine."

Ben ran down the stairs and jumped as he saw Taylor in the kitchen. "Hi, Mom!"

She smiled. "You're in a good mood this morning."

"Yeah! School starts in a few days and the only thing I have to worry about today is soccer!" He reached for a cereal box. "I think I'm playing soccer all day, until you come home."

"That sounds great."

"Then can we all borrow your car after dinner, to go to the mall?"

"I don't see why not." She finished fixing her coffee, then kissed him. "See you tonight."

"Okay, Mom. Have a great day."

"Thanks. You too."

He heard the garage door shut, then texted Jaime. *Want to head over the fields early and warm up together?*

His phone beeped. *Sure. When?*

Im ready now so whenever

Out front in forty?

Sure

He instinctively hopped when he saw her, and she registered her responding heart ping. "Hi, Benjamin."

He lifted the soccer ball at his feet as she approached. "Hi, Jaime."

She smiled as he fell in step. "It's fun playing soccer together, isn't it?"

"I really like it."

She glanced at him. "I like hanging out with you too."

"I really like hanging out with you. I'm glad we're friends."

"I like the idea I'm friends with a future Air Force pilot." She bumped into him softly as they walked onto the asphalt pathway leading to the school fields.

"I can't believe you did that for me. I'll never forget it."

"I loved doing that for you."

He glanced at her after toeing his ball as it dropped. "I hope I can pay you back someday."

"Oh, I'm thinking you probably will." She dropped her ball as they stepped onto the field. "Want to stretch together?"

His eyes widened. "I always want to do whatever you want to do."

"I hope that's still the case when you get older and more popular."

"It'll always be true." He inhaled as he eyed her. "Always."

She smiled as she registered his deeper meaning, but hid her accompanying exhale. "Help me stretch my hamstrings."

Jaime led the ball-handling and opposite-foot drills as other players arrived, then spotted Ben's coach as he walked toward the field. "Let's go talk to him."

Jaime controlled her smile as Ben kept pace jogging to him.

"Hi, coach Jefferson."

"Hi, Ben. What can I do for you?"

"I wanted to apologize and explain why we weren't here for a few days."

He handed Ben the ball net. "I got a call from the principal yesterday explaining everything, and both of you are fine."

"Principal Jessica called you about us?"

Coach smiled. "She told me an Air Force Captain called her."

Ben hopped. "Who? Captain Cooper or Captain Madison?"

"She didn't say, but she said the Air Force needed you for a few days, and we shouldn't punish you for your absence." He motioned to the different fields. "Go get with your teams."

"Thanks, Coach!" Ben sprinted away, dragging the ball net behind, and Jaime chuckled before heading toward a different field.

Ben waited for Jaime after practice, then fell in step with her as she headed toward the path. "Want to go to the mall after dinner?"

"Sure, if we can borrow a car."

"I already asked my mom and she said yes."

She fought her smile as she glanced at him. "Are you trying to squeeze two months of normal into our last four days off?"

"No. I'm completely okay with what happened." His eyes widened. "Are you?"

"It was a pretty crazy summer."

"But we saved lives and got paid for it …and got scholarships."

She smiled. "I love how you always focus on the positive."

He inhaled as their eyes met. "Because that's what we should focus on."

Ben paused as they reached his house, then motioned back toward the school fields. "Did anyone ask you what happened?"

"Yeah."

"What are you telling everyone?"

"That none of it's true."

His eyes softly widened. "Is this going to make us popular this year?"

"For a little while, but I'm sure it'll fade in time."

He grinned, then whispered, "We saved lives."

She patted his shoulder and smiled before walking away. "We did, didn't we."

~*~

Aidan ignored the ringing phone as he hung his uniform pants in the dank unfamiliar closet, then reached for the matching shirt before eyeing the device on the small nightstand. The phone immediately rang again after the first sequence ended, and he offered a hard exhale but made no move toward it.

He sat on the bed and removed his shoes as the phone began its third sequence, and he slammed his open hand on it before picking it up. "What!?"

Laughter came from the speaker. "General Dimitri. This is Commander Lacey from FARO. Mind if I interrupt for a few minutes?"

He exhaled audibly, then breathed deep. "Not at all, Commander. I apologize for the greeting. It's been a trying few days."

"I've heard."

He scanned the dimly lit room. "News travels fast."

"Satellite and fiber-optic fast."

He placed his hand over his eyes as he shut them. "What can I do for you, Commander?"

"I'm wondering if you'd have interest consulting here, on project *I* as in indigo, seven four zero one eight three, otherwise informally known as our *Toy Gel* project."

"I'm sorry?"

"From what I understand, the Air Force may be ending its Fallwater investigation and subsequent material procurement efforts ...but we don't answer to the Air Force."

He stood and began pacing. "Please continue."

"If you feel you still have services to offer regarding that previous goal, we'd like you to consider being a distinguished member of our investigation and procurement team, here in our beautiful desert facility."

"Paid consultant?"

"Well compensated, even for a general, and supplemental to your retirement earnings."

"I'm very interested. Highly interested."

"Then I'll assume your forgiveness for my intrusive phone pursuit, this evening?"

"Thank you for your aggression, Commander."

"I'm sure you have civilian logistics to address. Once completed, call this number and we'll arrange your formal acceptance and create travel plans."

"I should be in contact within a week."

"We'll discuss further logistics at that time, but we apologize, there's no place for your spouse here, though we can arrange furlough every ninety days or so."

"That won't be necessary, Commander."

"Don."

"And please call me Aidan. That won't be necessary, Don." He eyed his temporary lodgings. "I no longer have civilian ties."

"Then you can devote your energies toward our goal, while you build new ties here."

"You'll hear from me within the week."

"I look forward to it, Aidan."

~*~

Faith grabbed Jaime's arm. "Oh! Let's go in there!"

"I thought we were sticking to the stores we can all shop in."

Faith snickered. "You can come with us."

Jaime rubbed Ben's arm. "Relax, will you? We won't be long."

Faith raised an eyebrow at Kye. "Do you want us to come alone, the next mall trip?"

"We don't mind you going in any stores you want." Ben discreetly nudged Kye's arm.

Faith grabbed Jaime's hand before glancing at Kye. "Why can't you be more like him?"

"Do you mean it?" Ben's voice rose as they hurried away, then Kye yelled louder, "You're kidding, right?"

They glanced back before disappearing into the store.

"I hate when they do that." Kye gestured behind him as he faced Ben.

"I don't hate anything Jaime does."

He leaned against the glass and metal guard rail surrounding the second-floor walkway. "Well start, will ya?"

"Yeah, like you hate anything Faith does."

"That's different. She ain't my sister."

Ben smiled as he shook his head, "That makes no sense." then motioned to a couple pushing a baby stroller as they looked for friends and people watched. "Wouldn't it be funny if the four of us go to the mall together for the rest of our lives?"

"Damn, dude. Seriously?"

"Yeah." He leaned close. "…like you and Faith and me and Jaime."

Kye's chin lowered as he stared. "And us out here with the baby strollers when they go into stores and take way longer than …anything?"

Ben grinned. "Yeah."

Kye shook his head. "You're torturing me."

Ben leaned a shoulder into him as he turned toward the railing. "Don't give me that shit. You know you'd like it as much as me."

"And if you ever share that, I'm beating you with whatever's in reach."

Jaime and Faith reappeared, laughing and holding hands. "Are you two ready?"

"Yeah. We've been ready."

"We know." They glanced at each other and giggled.

Kye smirked. "You're both so funny."

"We think so." Faith slid her arm inside Jaime's before leading them along the walkway, and they wondered in and out of every clothing and shoe store.

Faith inhaled the sweet scent of the cookie stand at the food court entrance. "Anybody else hungry?"

"I could eat."

"There's news." Jaime grinned after glancing at Faith. "Are you two buying?"

"You got your own money."

Faith slipped her hand inside Kye's arm. "Yeah, but it's not a date unless you buy us something."

Ben's eyes widened. "This is a date?"

Kye shook her loose. "And what do we get out of it?"

Faith slid her hand down Kye's arm, then held his hand. "Maybe another date?"

He frowned as Jamie giggled. "Very funny."

Jaime's head tilted. "It was pretty funny, actually."

"Oh yeah …things are back to normal." Ben sighed.

Jaime playfully eyed him. "How so?"

"You two are back to torturing and abusing us."

She stared into his eyes. "Kind of, but someday we might not."

"But not today?"

Faith poked Kye's arm, "Nope …not today." and they giggled as they strolled through the food court.

Jaime sat facing Ben as Faith placed her tray on the table, then smacked Kye's hand as he reached for a french fry. "Mine."

Ben held his soft pretzel toward her and she broke off a piece. "Thank you, Ben."

She motioned to her fries and smiled at him, then faced Faith. "I want those tan sandals with the ankle strap."

"They did look good. Were they comfortable?"

Kye leaned forward. "Can we talk about anything else? …Something more serious?"

"Like baseball?" Faith frowned at him.

Jaime stared at her fingertips. "I seriously want to get my nails done for school."

Kye placed his hands on his head. "Yeah …that's serious."

Jaime smiled. "It could be."

"How do you figure?" Kye sneered as Ben offered her another piece of soft pretzel.

"Oh!" Faith hopped in her seat. "What if …instead of our plastic gel bags, we paint our nails so we can touch the gel to them, and disappear?!"

"The plastic lunch bags are a little lame, but I'm not painting my nails." Ben motioned to Kye. "But you can."

"No thanks."

Jaime nudged Faith's shoulder. "Yeah! Then we could cover the gel with a clear coat."

Kye leaned forward. "We ain't painting our nails."

"Don't be babies. Besides, you can use a masculine color."

Faith giggled at Jaime before eyeing their brothers. "Yeah."

Ben inhaled. "I have no problem with any guy painting his nails, but some guys don't want to."

Faith lifted a fry. "Favio wears nail polish."

"And if anyone gave him shit for it, I'd defend him. Everyone's allowed to wear nail polish." Kye leaned toward Ben. "We choose not to."

Faith sneered at him. "What about clear?"

Ben's brows rose as he eyed her. "No."

Jaime reached for Ben's hand. "One?"

"None."

"No ...one nail. Clear?"

Ben sipped his drink. "Why are we discussing this?"

Faith pointed. "He said he wanted to discuss something serious."

Jaime examined her fingers again. "Turquoise or teal with one gold, is serious."

"How about turquoise with gold tips?"

"Or a turquoise gold swirl!" Her eyes widened as she grabbed Faith's hand. "Wanna go tomorrow?"

Ben frowned. "Yep ...everything's back to normal."

~*~

Mitch walked into the Control Room and laid his open laptop on the workstation. "The latest Fallwater intelligence report is in. Did you see it?"

"No." Charlie tabbed to his email program. "Did you open it?"

"Yeah." Mitch smiled as he reached for the coffee pot. "Some crazy shit's been happening."

"Crazy good or crazy bad?"

He filled his mug as he gestured with his chin. "Open it. You have clearance."

Charlie frowned and Mitch laughed. "Just read the damn thing."

Charlie fought his smirk as he opened the document.

He spun the closest chair and plopped down. "Did you get to the part where cars exploded, or the general's house burnt down?"

Charlie glanced at him as he scrolled. "You have no intention of letting me read this, do you."

He adjusted his laptop and paged down to the pictures. "You're taking too long."

"No …you just like gossiping."

"I'll shut up." Mitch sipped his coffee.

"The general's house burnt down?" Charlie glanced at the screen. "Cars exploded?"

He grinned. "Isn't that what the report says?"

Charlie fought his smile. "I just opened the damn thing."

Mitch pointed. "The kids and their families are exonerated."

"The families?"

"Everybody."

"Are you mentioned?"

Mitch sat back and smiled. "Not directly, but their declaration means we're back in the right."

Charlie scrolled down. "Slightly inaccurate, but hooray for us."

"Meanwhile …our side's getting their ass kicked. Did you get to the part about the botched raid?"

"Botched raid?"

"A dozen soldiers are missing."

"How?"

"There's no mention, but they're gone without a trace."

"Damn. Karma can do shit."

Mitch smiled. "Oh yeah. Read more."

"She really lit the general's house on fire?" Charlie rubbed his temples as he examined the screen.

"Study Sherman." Mitch sighed. "Precedent had been set. But the cars exploding must have been more spectacular."

"Where?"

"The interrogation building."

Charlie looked up. "The one you went to?"

"Yep."

He slapped the edge of his workstation and laughed. "She blew up military intelligence cars, in front of them?"

"And the general's." Mitch pointed to the screen. "There's pictures."

He clicked on the accompanying photos. "Anybody hurt?"

"Not a single soul."

"The raid …was it headed to the kids' two houses?"

Mitch nodded. "Two SUVs full of agents."

"Any details?"

"Last communication contact specified location as supposedly on their street."

"We're getting our asses kicked…again." Charlie shook his head as he studied the pictures.

"I really didn't think we'd lose round two."

"You ain't the only one, but it ain't over." Charlie leaned closer to the screen after clicking on the next picture. "Is that the general's office?"

"I forgot to mention that. Right on base. But there's more to that particular incident." Mitch fought his smile. "It's no longer the general's office."

Charlie laughed as he pointed to the picture. "I guess not."

"No. He resigned his commission and retired." Mitch spread his joined fingertips as he raised his hand. "Poof. Gone."

Charlie laughed. "She made a general disappear?"

"There's a lot of that going around, lately."

"This is unbelievable." Charlie pushed his chair away from the desk. "I need to tell them."

"No you don't." Mitch pointed to the screen. "Keep reading."

He scrolled down. "Ha! We surrendered and we're paying them to shut up?"

"If we're smart."

He chuckled. "And scholarships?"

Mitch grinned. "Ben has an Air Force Academy invitation, with admission recommendation letters from Mahir and Avory."

"Hell yeah. We want him on our side before he destroys us." Charlie eyed the ceiling after slapping his thigh, "Thank you, teacher." then his head shifted. "The other soldier!"

"Safe and sound. Found, wrapped in a blanket."

"What?"

"Wearing nothing but a blanket and a note."

Charlie rubbed his forehead. "Don't tell me it was from his teacher."

"Aw, c'mon. That's funny shit!"

Charlie turned away from his workstation. "She took everything?"

Mitch sipped his coffee. "Everything."

"Damn. I see another theme."

"You're not the only one."

Charlie continued reading. "So the kids are home, safe and sound?"

"A little worse for wear, but yeah."

"So much for not telling them we exist. Do you think the other side will leave them alone?"

Mitch smirked. "The other side?"

"Did I mistakenly say the other side?" Charlie chuckled. "Of course, I meant our side."

"Only time will tell." Mitch shook his head, then raised a finger as his smile grew. "Oh. Cowboy is missing."

"Wow." Charlie's eyes narrowed. "I wonder how long she's been watching."

"I'm wondering the same thing."

Charlie's computer programs beeped in succession and he tabbed to a surveillance program. "You've got to be kidding."

Chapter Six
Subterranean Ecosphere

Commander Lacey reached for the incoming fax after raising his phone volume, then smiled as he examined the signature. "I have the signed contract in my hand, Aidan. Welcome to our team."

"I'm looking forward to the new start, and appreciate the opportunity."

He scanned the document, then attached it to an email. "My pleasure. And you're going to be pleasantly surprised by the accommodations."

"I'm sure it's impressive, but I plan on burying myself in the work."

"You're more than welcome, but we have some nice leisure venues, so bring civilian sweats, bathing trunks, and anything that would make you feel at home. We also have a small strip of stores, and a commissary onsite if your palate isn't too discerning."

"I'm not a man of particular tastes."

"No career soldier is, are they?" The commander placed a stack of papers in the fax machine, then dialed. "You'll be receiving reading material in a moment. Enjoy it while traveling, and don't be concerned by your lack of proper greeting, upon arrival. I've decided, a subdued welcome will be prudent, considering the nature of your focus."

"I prefer that, actually."

"Excellent, Aidan. Your vehicle should arrive momentarily."

"It's already here, Commander."

"The vehicle and driver are at your beckon. Use them for any last-minute procurement on your way to your departure point."

"I appreciate the offer, but my preparation has been thorough."

"Then we'll welcome you before the next sunrise. Have a safe trip."

Aidan tucked the faxed documents into his briefcase, grabbed his suitcase, and exited the building. The driver immediately opened the back passenger door. "Welcome, sir. Momodu at your service, sir."

"Good morning, Momodu. Please take me to my departure destination."

"Gladly, sir."

The TVs intermittently lining the airport terminal displayed different news channels, but only a local channel shared audio. The weather-person stepped away from the national map. "Now back to the Sunrise Morning Show."

The camera view scanned the studio before stopping on a smiling brunette as she folded her hands on the news desk. "All local schools are back in session tomorrow, so take extra precaution on your morning commute."

He identified the departure gate as he walked past the TV, and sat as far from the check-in podium as possible, then focused on the faxed documents. Three soldiers broke his concentration as they sat in the next aisle, and he straightened, about to take offense at the lack of proper greeting, before realizing he wore no identifying insignia. He inhaled as he straightened his unadorned collar, and refocused on the document in his hands. Every current unwelcoming experience could be attributed to the incident it detailed, and his breathing intensified as he resolved to rectify the accrued displeasure.

The sun had set by the time he entered the last connecting flight's boarding gate, and he smiled after observing the designated area. No gate number appeared. No destination displayed. No departure time posted. The flight attendants bore no airline affiliation and checked no boarding passes as the ten additional passengers passed the gate-side podium.

He discreetly sighed in pleasure, for the precision and preparation that went into such an ongoing clandestine operation. This flight functioned in secrecy, under the watchful eye of everyone, yet only those needing to know, knew its purpose.

He glanced at the news channel on a terminal TV before entering the boarding walkway, and smiled. The news never shared this flight's existence. This flight flew its passengers off the existence grid.

The landing gear deploying, broke the comfort of the uneventful flight, and he peered out the window. The brilliantly bright moon lit the expansive night sky, and offered a unique birds-eye view of the local terrain as the secret flight approached its destination.

A soft voice came over the intercom. "Cabin, prepare for landing."

A flight attendant walked the aisle. "Please stow away any previously removed items, buckle in, and return your seats to their upright position."

Distinct hydraulic whines accompanied the wing reconfiguration, and the resulting wind resistance rocked the cabin as they made their approach.

"This is Captain Julian Kelsey, ladies and gentlemen; on behalf of the entire flight crew, I'd like to thank you for traveling with us. Welcome to this wonderfully unique destination. We hope you have a successful stay, and we look forward to being part of your departure plans."

The chill in the air caught Aidan's attention as he exited the plane, and a smiling attendant motioned to the waiting bus after he stepped onto the tarmac. "Welcome, sir. Your luggage will be delivered directly to your living quarters."

The dark and silent ride offered no precursor to the contrasting sights and sounds accompanying their building entry. Inside, the bright light and surrounding commotion gave the appearance of mid-day activity at any active military base. A sharply dressed woman smiled at him as he stepped from the bus. "Aidan Dimitri?"

"Yes."

"Welcome to Homeland Facilities' Forward Analysis and Reconstruction Operation, otherwise known as FARO. I'm Assistant Commander Alysiah Izzy Jared and we're honored to have such a distinguished new associate." She extended her hand.

"Thank you, Commander Jared."

"Please call me Izzy."

"It would be my pleasure. Call me Aidan."

"Gladly, Aidan. The commander sends his regrets he couldn't personally welcome you, and hopes you understand."

He smiled. "Unlike the recently departed, I trust the unexplained actions of new and old friends alike."

"Wonderful." She gestured to an electric cart parked along the side of the expansive entryway. "You'll enjoy your stay with us. Only the invited experience our amenities."

He admired his surroundings as he sat in the cart. "I already feel fortunate to be included, and to be honest, I haven't felt all that fortunate lately."

"May I offer an impromptu briefing, while escorting you to your residence?"

He smiled. "I'd be honored."

She looked behind the vehicle before heading down the expansive corridor. "We'll have an informal meeting tomorrow at eleven, in the assigned laboratory conference room, then let you familiarize yourself with the facility's amenities. Normal business will begin the following day."

"I'm leaning toward burying myself in this project, without concern for the niceties."

"All personnel are self-sufficient and the complex is extensive enough, your familiarization is mandatory." She turned the cart into one of the massive open elevators, then pressed a series of numbers. "This site is twelve stories deep and has two five-lane tunnel egresses leading into and under a bordering mountain. The outer shell was constructed over a geological depression, and before the hidden remainder, so no one who hasn't been informed, has knowledge of the expansiveness of our secret world. There are roughly seven thousand personnel here at any given time and the inclusion prerequisites are rather daunting. But if necessary, the facility could accommodate up to twenty thousand."

He smiled as the elevator opened. "Impressive."

"Each floor is far more expansive than the surface footprint. The designers believed, an open feel would be more conducive to advanced and innovative thinking. It also helps with claustrophobia."

Aidan peered down the spacious corridor. "What floor is this?"

"This is level six. The levels can be likened to a cruise ship. The top levels are mainly admissions and social activities. Certain guests only have access to the top three levels, and those levels are operationally self-sufficient. The bottom two levels are mechanical and logistical functionality."

"Very impressive."

She turned at a corridor intersection. "You can only access certain levels with your six-digit personal code, found in your welcome folder. An easy way to memorize it is to picture it as two, three-digit numbers. It's your key to places you'll need access."

"Understood."

"Laboratories are on levels two, three, and eight through ten, depending on its degree of privacy. Your project is on level nine." She glanced at him and smiled as she drove.

"Interesting."

"Other levels are housing, additional entertainment, more private entertainment and dining, procurement, and warehousing. We not only function autonomously, but we can also sustain and even defend ourselves autonomously."

He inhaled as his brows rose. "Really."

"Would you like to be included in our deterrent force, while here?"

"I'd like that very much."

"Consider it done." She drove into an expansive corridor and stopped at a residence resembling a fairly typical townhouse in any civilian community. "Why would anyone think such an advanced and extensive facility wouldn't have the capability?"

"I never thought about it."

"We rely on outsiders not thinking about our existence. It's why there's as little activity as possible on the surface, and that activity is kept to the privacy of night." She handed him the door key as they approached. "We track unfriendly satellites and note when the moon waxes and wanes."

He opened the door and stepped into a plush and expansive living area. "This is impressive."

"It's different than the hotel facility located on the second level. This housing accommodates more distinguished, long-term guests."

"I hope my next civilian residence is this nice."

"We're happy you're pleased." She extended her arm toward the kitchen. "We took the liberty of stocking your refrigerator with a few essentials, and your bedroom suite is ready to accommodate you."

She smiled as he nodded approvingly, then opened a cabinet face in the hallway and exposed a bank of switches and controls. "There are a few peculiarities not found in a typical, above-ground residence, I'd like to share."

She explained the amenity's idiosyncrasies, then led him to the front door. "Considering your travel today, I don't expect you to remember much of what I've shared, but don't be concerned. Further explanation is available through multiple means, and you'll get used to everything in a shorter time than you realize. We hope you'll make yourself at home."

"I appreciate the amazing hospitality, but I'm not concerned with anything as much as my primary task."

She smiled. "Then we'll say goodnight and address other concerns tomorrow at eleven. Codes, directions, and estimated travel times are in the packet on the living room coffee table. Have a great night."

"Before you leave, I'd like to request one thing."

Her brows rose as she released the door handle.

"May I have access to all notes, correspondences ...everything connected to this project?"

"It's on your new laptop, sitting on your laboratory office desk."

"Everything?"

"Look around, Aidan." She smiled. "...Everything."

He inhaled as he extended his hand. "Thank you."

The abbreviated night passed quickly, but he woke with an invigorated sense of purpose; equating the feeling to a projected allegiance he hadn't perceived since his last foreign tour. There were no political undertones, misguiding missions here. This facility's goal was singular in purpose, persistence, and performance, and he noted how those disciplines were noticeably lacking, his last few years in the military.

He removed the residence's floor plan and a site map from the welcome package as he sipped his coffee, then studied the directions leading to the ninth level laboratory. The bright morning sunlight shining behind the dinette curtains suddenly caught his eye, and he inhaled before smiling. No morning sun existed here ...only the detail invested in this impressive facility. He walked to the sheer floor to ceiling curtains and opened them enough to admire the perfectly etched visually impenetrable glass.

He shut his eyes and leaned his head back as he enjoyed the accompanying warmth the light emitted, then inhaled as he shook his head. No amenity had been overlooked or omitted.

He opened the door leading to a small garage, after studying the orientation packet, and chortled as he noticed the electric cart's number matched the address. No detail had been missed. He pressed the garage door opener after unplugging the vehicle, then followed the site map toward the closest elevator bank.

Pressing the elevator button, prompted a soft feminine voice. "Please enter your six-digit access code and floor number."

He did as instructed, and the automated voice responded, "Thank you." as the doors closed.

The site map offered precise directions along the unmarked corridors, and he parked in the designated area, then keyed his code into the laboratory's double entry door.

"Good morning."

He stopped and backtracked after passing a doorway. "Hello."

"I'm Abraham Yaseer. Abe for short." He extended his hand. "I'm the team coordinator and liaison."

"Aidan Dimitri."

Abe smiled as they shook. "Our new member. It's good to meet you."

"Same here."

"I didn't expect you, but decided on an early start, just in case." He motioned to the expansive laboratory. "May I give you a quick tour?"

"Tour later, new friend. Right now, I'd like access to all pertinent information."

"Then let me show you your office." He extended his hand as he approached the third door. "Your computer is docked and charged. Your unlock name is your six-digit ID and the password is the last four of your social security number. Lock it whenever you're not using it. Everything is recorded, as is your phone for as long as you're inside the facility."

He smiled. "How is that different from outside?"

Abe chuckled. "We all extend our societal fallacies, don't we?"

He sighed as he unlocked the computer. "I'm growing more tired of the bullshit, each and every day."

"On that note, I'll leave you to your studies." Abe turned and pointed along the partition, after stepping to the door. "There's always coffee in the kitchen alcove, or your beverage of choice if you share the preference with me."

"Thanks, Abe."

Commotion broke his hours-long concentration, and he glanced at his door as the smiling figure appeared. "Aidan."

He quickly assessed the uniform adornment, and stood at attention. "Commander."

"Leave the formalities on the surface, Aidan." He extended his hand. "We're all equal under the sod…or sand in this case." He chuckled as he patted Aidan's opposite shoulder. "The only difference is, someone has to conduct the symphony."

"Is it close to eleven?"

"About two minutes of." Don glanced at his watch, then refocused. "How long have you been down here?"

Aidan slid his hands over his hair. "Since around seven."

"So you haven't toured the facility?"

"Not yet." He pointed to his laptop. "More important things."

"A good host would frown at that reply, but not a good commander. We're going to enjoy our time together." He stepped aside and gestured toward the expansive lab. "Come. Let me introduce you to your esteemed colleagues."

He lifted his laptop, then followed the commander past the electronic equipment, and through the glass conference doors at the opposite end of the suite.

"Good morning, Don."

"Good morning Doshmere, Jocilyn, Nong." He stepped aside. "This is Aidan."

"Welcome, Aidan."

He nodded as he shook each extended hand. "Doshmere ... Jocilyn. ... Nong."

Commander Lacey removed his laptop, then placed his briefcase beside his chair. "Please share introductory thoughts with Aidan, lady and gentlemen."

Jocilyn eyed the commander. "From the beginning?"

Aidan raised an open hand. "I've read all intelligence reports and am familiar with all the overt interaction between the military and our civilian counterparts."

Nong gestured to Aidan's laptop. "And your computer documents will share almost everything else…"

Jocilyn nodded. "…But there will be an underlying perspective not fully evaluated in that material, which we'll expose."

"And teach you how to expose." Doshmere joined his hands as he leaned forward.

"Such as?" Aidan's brows rose as he eyed the three unfamiliar faces.

The associates glanced at each other, then shared in turn.

"The photographic differences between the captured ship and the item delivered to this location."

"The replacement item's man-made cavity used to eliminate all trace of the object delivered here."

"The material found in its cavity eliminating all traces, and how these findings indicate a far greater application potential."

Don rested his hand on the table. "We appreciate you spending the last five hours re-familiarizing yourself with the events, but we're going to share specific pathways which will allow you to dissect and evaluate this ordeal, far more extensively."

"And once we share all perspectives of all events, we believe your military expertise will help us apply our findings."

He faced Jocilyn. "To what end, may I ask?"

"The procurement of more of this." Doshmere raised a small vial.

Nong smiled as Aidan tilted his head. "The vial isn't empty."

Jocilyn pointed to his hand. "But what's inside is undetectable."

"What we would like you to do is what we've been doing for some time." Doshmere moved his laptop aside. "Study and record alone for a period, then we'll come together and study as a group, pointing out individual observations and insights which will add to and feed our collective insight."

Don raised a finger. "But first, we'd like you to share your knowledge of the incidents, from your perspective. Please gather all your current knowledge of the Fallwater incidents and construct as thorough a report as possible. We're interested in viewing the events from every angle possible, and your individual viewpoint will feed our collective insight."

"I'd be happy to share."

Jocilyn smiled. "Reasons why certain actions were taken, are more important than the actions taken."

Doshmere nodded in agreement. "They give insight into unaware perceptions and resulting motivation."

Nong motioned to his associates. "We're already familiar with the actions. We're interested in the cause-effect dynamics. They help us understand and predict future adversarial actions."

Don interrupted the momentary silence. "Shall we convene weekly for the foreseeable future?"

Jocilyn smiled. "As you wish, Commander."

He glanced at his watch, then stood as he refocused on Aidan. "You have much to share, study, and learn. Meanwhile, your associates will acclimate you to our process." He smiled as he straightened the front of his uniform. "Have a great week, lady and gentlemen."

Chapter Seven
Fortified Allegiances

Kye met Ben and Faith at the sidewalk, and adjusted his backpack before turning toward the school. "I'm not ready for this."

Ben grinned. "I can't wait!"

"You're as strange as ever, little brother."

He hopped as he fell in step. "You love me."

"Stop." Jaime pointed a finger as she joined them. "Both of you …fight nice."

He continued grinning as he headed toward the school. "This is gonna be the best year ever."

Jaime wrapped her arm around Faith's shoulders and smirked as they followed behind. "It has to be. It's our last year together."

He hopped as he turned. "Who has sixth lunch?"

Faith smiled at him. "We all do!"

He thrust a fist skyward. "Yes!"

"No we don't." Kye bumped his shoulder. "She's messing with you."

Ben's eyes widened, and Jaime scolded her. "Stop doing that to him."

Kye motioned to Faith as he eyed her. "Or what? You both won't let her be your baby's godmother?"

Jaime smacked Kye's head. "Haha."

Ben spun and walked backward. "Nobody has sixth lunch?"

Jaime pointed to Kye. "We both have fourth."

"And I ain't eating with you."

Faith frowned. "Fifth."

Ben sped the last five steps then held the door, and Kye snickered as he passed. "For a second, I thought the old Ben was back."

He sneered. "Very funny."

The morning went quickly as Ben greeted old friends and answered questions about the rumors, then spotted Jaime in the hallway after third period.

She smiled. "What class do you have next?"

"Science, but I have to go see the principal." He frowned after displaying his note. "How's it even possible to already be in trouble?"

"Relax. You're not the only one." She raised a yellow paper. "And it doesn't mean we did anything wrong."

"You think?"

"Yo!"

Ben smiled, then pointed to the paper in Kye's hand as he approached. "You too?"

"What?" He waved his note. "You two too?"

Ben laughed. "Tutu?"

Kye playfully shoved him as he passed. "Idiot."

He raised his arms as he followed. "Come on …that's funny."

Kye whispered as he fell in step with Jaime. "You think Faith too?"

"We'll see in a minute." They turned the hallway corner as Faith opened the gym door in the distance.

"That answers that question."

"Did you get one?" Ben waved his paper.

She displayed hers. "All four of us? What do you think this is about?"

"We don't know, but when is getting called down to the principal's office ever good?" Kye held the door, and Ben scowled as he passed. "You just want to be last."

Kye smiled as the door shut behind him. "I ain't as dumb as you look."

"Good morning everyone."

Faith peered into the adjoining doorway. "Good morning Ms. Jessica."

She pointed to the table in her office. "Come in and sit."

Faith slid a chair out. "We're not in trouble, are we?"

She shook her head and smiled. "No, not at all."

"Then I have a suggestion for the yellow slips."

"What's that, Benjamin?"

He pointed to the corner. "A little box on it that you can check when we're not in trouble?"

She chuckled. "I'll take the idea into consideration."

"...Cause it really is awful not knowing."

"I apologize."

"You don't have to apologize." He shrugged. "...Just saying."

"What are we here for then?"

She inhaled as she eyed Jaime. "To know if the rumors are true. There's a buzz around the entire school about you four." She lifted her coffee as her smile grew. "And we're wondering if we should be nominating you for some kind of community award or something."

"None of that stuff is true."

"Really, Kye?" Jessica smirked. "Captain Cooper was lying?"

"To be honest, he doesn't know what happened, either."

Jessica folded her hands after facing Ben. "So you're admitting you four are involved in something?"

Kye grinned. "No ...but you'll have to give the whole school an award if you think we're lying. Do you know how many people helped us not do what we didn't do?"

Jaime sat straight as she shook her head at her brother. "What did the captain tell you?"

159

"That the Air Force needed your assistance for something very important."

Faith reached for Jaime's hand. "We didn't do anything special."

Kye leaned forward. "And the entire school helped us do nothing. Not that we can't do nothing by ourselves. I'd like to believe my grades prove that I'm very good at doing nothing."

Faith covered her grin.

"You have a very good sense of humor, Kyle."

He covered his chest with his open hand and bowed in his seat. "Thank you. Thank you very much. I'm here till June. Enjoy your salads."

Jaime raised her hand to her forehead as Faith snickered. "Seriously. We didn't do anything special."

"And about twenty other students really did help, and another twenty were ready to."

Kye pointed at Ben. "Help us do nothing."

"I'm so confused." Jessica reached for her coffee mug before refocusing on the group. "The captain didn't give specifics either. Are you telling me this thing you didn't do, was that special?"

Faith extended her hand. "Okay. What we did, was something anyone would do."

Ben straightened in his seat. "And seriously, about twenty of our school friends helped."

"So about twenty students do know what you did?"

Kye smirked apologetically. "Kind of, but not really."

Jaime glanced at him before refocusing on the principal. "And the rumors need to die, or the wrong people might hear and start things again."

"Oh."

Faith nodded. "…Things that need to be forgotten."

Jessica eyed them. "And we can't celebrate what you did?"

Jaime shook her head. "We really can't."

Faith placed her hand on Jaime's. "We really can't."

"Can I at least know what you did?"

"Do you know what we'd have to do to you if we tell you?"

Jaime smacked his shoulder. "Kyle!"

He extended his arms as Faith snickered. "Aw, c'mon. That's funny!"

Jessica chuckled as she stood. "Alright, you missed enough class."

"So we can just let the rumors die?"

Jessica's brows rose. "It may take a while. The entire school is buzzing."

Jaime tucked her hair behind her ear as she stood. "And something will happen in a week that'll be the new buzz."

"I don't know. I hear this was pretty special." She motioned them toward the door.

"Teenagers exaggerate."

She shook her head as Ben stood. "Well, whatever it was ...congratulations."

"Thanks, Ms. Jessica." Faith stepped behind Jaime.

Kye turned and pointed to her eyes as he reached the door. "You know nothing."

She grabbed his finger. "You didn't tell me anything."

"Oh yeah." He grinned.

She shook her head. "Have a nice day, everyone."

"Thank you, Ms. Jessica."

"You too Ms. Jessica."

~*~

"Good night Aidan."

"Are you staying late again?"

"Good night Abe."

He stopped typing as he acknowledged Doshmere's disembodied voice. "Yeah, Dosh. I need to finish this." He raised his head at the soft knock on his office door.

"Are you sure you don't want to join us for dinner?"

"Next time, Jocilyn. I promise."

Her head tilted. "That's what you said last time."

He offered a faint smile.

"Alright then. See you tomorrow."

He continued typing. "Have a good night."

The knock forty minutes later, startled him, and his eyes widened as he focused on the figure in his doorway.

"May I come in?"

"Of course, Commander."

"You've been burning the candle quite extensively lately."

"Just trying to catch up to my colleagues."

"Your colleagues have doctorates in multiple sciences." He shook his head as he fought a wry smile. "They're a wonderful commodity, but we don't need any more of them."

"But they're helping me see patterns and strings of events."

Don nodded as his smile intensified. "You meet my expectation for a seasoned warrior."

He pointed to the computer screen. "My written submission is far from coherent."

"There's no deadline."

"I'm concerned the time gap will cause missed opportunities."

"I see a different picture." Don continued smiling. "Let's have dinner and share some nice Scotch."

"I'm more of a beer man."

"I know a bar where both are abundant."

Aidan rubbed his eyes. "Sure. Why not."

"A driver will pick you up in roughly half an hour, and we'll meet at the bar." Don gestured toward the laptop. "Shut it down."

Aidan snickered as he moved the computer mouse. "I haven't received a direct oral command in quite a while."

Don chuckled. "It's what I do."

He closed the laptop as he stood. "So where is this watering hole?"

"Plug, seven nine two four six one into your vehicle and it'll show you, but tonight we have drivers. Plug in your *six* at the security gate, then again at the door."

Aidan raised his stare after keying the code into his phone. "Gate and door?"

"You'll understand when you get there, but in case you haven't figured it out; we track everyone and everything down here. It's how I know you need a break."

Aidan followed him to their vehicles. "Your visit wasn't a happy accident?"

Don offered a wry smile. "Nothing I do is a happy accident."

Aidan joined the driver at his residence, then marveled at the expansive complex as the sergeant negotiated unfamiliar corridors on previously unvisited levels. He used his code on the gate and noticed the cart blink as it passed through the steel barrier.

The unusually lit tunnel that followed, offered no indication of what lie beyond, but the corridor suddenly transformed into a café-lined city street at nightfall. The driver continued along the narrow roadway and stopped at a beautiful English drinking pub, with a dark ornamental wood façade and stained glass windows.

"Your destination, sir."

He exited the cart. "Thank you, friend."

He reached for the ornate twisted metal handle on the oversized door and grinned at the authenticity and attention to detail as he entered.

Don turned from the bar and raised his scotch as he approached. "Welcome, neighbor."

"I feel like I crossed the ocean."

"For all intents and purposes, you have."

Aidan eyed the intricate bar-face and Don chuckled. "On this side of the pond, we stand at the bar."

The server placed a coaster on the dark wood surface. "What can I get you?"

Aidan smiled. "What do you have on draught?"

The server reached under the bar-top and produced a list. "All our beers are made on-premises. You may sample one or all, or order by the *flight*, which are four different selections, served in four-ounce glasses. Single selections are served by the pint."

He pointed to the list. "I'll try a flight. The session IPA, Helles lager, brown ale, and Belgian wheat."

Don grinned. "You know beer like I know scotch."

He inhaled the venue's earthy musk. "I've been studying for quite a few years."

Don rested his arm on the bar's edge. "I'm sure we both can say that about a number of things."

Aidan nodded as the server placed his flight, then lifted the first. "To differences."

"That complement one another." Don clinked glasses then touched his to the bar-top before sipping.

Aidan returned the small glass to its holder, then examined the room, with its wood and etched glass partitions dividing different size cubbyholes. "I'd swear this was Liverpool or Manchester if I didn't know better."

Don laughed. "We'll eat and drink in Nuremberg or Tuscany, next."

His eyes widened. "Does the facility make its own wine?"

"No. It's too easy to buy confirmed quality, but we do have nice selections, delineated by type and country." Don glanced at him after lowering his drink. "I told you to investigate the facility."

"There's a job to do first."

"I disagree. I prefer it hold its priority as intermittent perks periodically rejuvenate the heart, mind, and soul."

~*~

Mitch lifted the phone receiver and pressed the direct line. "Get in here and bring a notepad."

Charlie laughed. "Aye, aye, matey"

He knocked on the doorframe moments later, holding his notepad like a butler tray. "You rang?"

Mitch nodded as he smiled. "Lurch, my good man."

Charlie pointed and laughed. "Whatcha need?"

"I want to talk to Karma again before everything becomes too distant a memory." Mitch removed the phone from a lower desk drawer. "Feel like?"

"Yeah, but why didn't you tell me over the phone? I got a whole page full of questions."

"Where?"

Charlie pointed in the direction of the Control Room. "In my desk."

"Well don't just sit there. Go get them."

"Ugh!" Charlie stood and turned toward the door.

"And stop your bitchin."

He smirked. "Anything else you need while I'm down there?"

Mitch spun in his chair and leaned back. "Yeah. Pee for me, will ya? I gotta go real bad."

"You know …you coulda came down, did your thing, then popped your head into the Control Room afterward."

Mitch followed him into the hall. "Are you telling me you don't like my management style?"

"You pain in my…"

Mitch pointed as he opened the bathroom door. "Captain pain in the ass, to you."

Charlie chuckled as he opened the Control room door. "Nope. You got one more promotion coming before your title works."

Charlie laid his notepad on the edge of the desk as Mitch re-entered the office. "How are we starting this?"

Mitch shrugged. "How about we tell her we want to talk."

"Pretty pathetic opening line."

"I'm not trying to date her." He lifted the phone sitting on his desk, then keyed a text. *Hello*

"Good thing."

Mitch shook his head as a text reply appeared. *Hello*

Mitch glanced at the ceiling. "Hi, Karma. It's Mitch and I'm here with Charlie. Can you hear me? May we talk?"

You may talk. I prefer to reply by text. Use the text to voice app

"Fair enough." Mitch pressed the buttons and played the message as he scanned the room.

Can I help you? Is everything alright?

Mitch frowned as he stared at the phone. "I can't promise *alright*, but things are quiet."

What would you like to discuss?

Charlie pointed to his notes and Mitch read the first question. "We're wondering if you'd share how and when you became involved, and your current involvement or communication status with the visitors?"

To what end?

Charlie raised a finger. "We're two fairly intelligent people who believe, the more intelligent minds in communication, the stronger the group."

A sound philosophy. Are you committed to the angels?

Mitch frowned. "My commitment to them almost cost me my career."

Charlie glanced around the room. "If you've been monitoring, you have proof."

Past proof is not future proof. I want your word.

Charlie nodded. "You have ongoing proof, and my word."

"Mine also. Would you share?"

I will share what I wish

The electronic voice interpreter broke the following short silence.

I also heard the original squawk and thud in the Fergusons' back yard, and their pet can bark the dead back to life. I watched them encounter the strange object, then almost immediately discover the unearthly characteristics of the accompanying gift.

"The invisibility gel?"

The older boy accidentally stepped in it and they panicked for a bit.

"Where did you see this from?"

Charlie frowned at the lack of response, then examined the phone. "When did you do more than view?"

The angels cleaned the site and hid the guests, just before a suited man entered their yard. I knew his interaction wouldn't end with the short encounter so I took the liberty of cleaning up after the four. In the process I also secured gel.

"Have you been experimenting with it?"

The result of my concern for the four was unintentional and can be summed up as nothing more than carelessness. The experimentation has also been unintentional.

"Please explain."

I came in contact with the gel as I did a more thorough cleaning. I stopped trying to wash it off weeks ago. I cannot turn visible. I don't know how the angels do it.

"They don't touch the gel. They touch a plastic bag to it, then release the bag when they want to turn visible."

Excellent. It's imperative they not touch it if they wish to have a normal life.

Mitch's eyes narrowed. "Did the aliens release the gel on purpose?"

No. The encounter was accidental.

Charlie continued writing. "How do you know? Can you speak to them?"

They don't speak or hear.

"But you communicate?"

Communication is an ongoing learning process, and difficult. They share telepathically and receive both telepathically and empathically. Their thoughts are highly complicated and imparted at a higher complexity and speed than we can comprehend. I've expressed their need to slow and singularize their communications, but it often takes multiple exchanges to grasp their information.

"What have you learned?"

There were living sentient beings on the ship the angels saved. They delighted in the angels efforts, but their greatest delight was the angels' welcoming reaction to alien life. They're pleased the four look so different yet seem inseparable.

"Have you learned anything else about these beings?"

They're members of a community of worlds with interstellar travel ability and they're patiently waiting for our world to reach an existence level which would allow them to welcome us to the next level of community. They're anxious to get to know us and share knowledge and their first encounter, though accidental, has fed their excitement.

"But the first encounter wasn't positive. The actual authority tried to capture and kill them."

All they want to discuss is the angels, their welcome, and their heroism.

"They don't understand we're not ready?"

It is difficult to receive information and more difficult to impart information. From what I've gathered, they don't understand or are unwilling to fully accept.

"Can they comprehend they're in danger if they make full contact?" Mitch rubbed the back of his neck. "…Our leadership is on the side wanting to harm them?"

They aren't worried about being harmed. They realize the dangers of first contact. Those who die during first contact, become great heroes in their community. The sacrifice helps the newcomers realize they aren't dangerous. The new world is also named in honor of those lost befriending a planet.

"This communication ability …Are there other qualities of the gel the four don't know?"

It seems to have amplified a previous skillset.

"Please share?"

The ability to persuade influence suggest

"Did you use these abilities to terminate a military mission without confrontation?"

I had an ability before I touched the gel, that has been intensified. My efforts to communicate with the beings have positively and negatively increased those communication skills. The sun also strengthens the gel's effects.

"Telepathically?"

It is far more complicated than a simple answer explains. Communication efforts have taught that accompanying aspect.

"I don't understand." Mitch eyed the phone after writing. "Will you be more specific?"

I'm hesitant. I don't want the angels becoming curious and losing their potential for normal lives.

Charlie referenced his questions list. "Do you have accomplices?"

It isn't necessary to concern yourself with how I operate. Focus instead on my results.

"Do you know the whereabouts of the twelve raiding soldiers or the one called Cowboy?"

Yes. The twelve are returning to base as we speak, without their equipment. The other soldier is enjoying a few relaxing days with a new friend.

"He's been missing a while."

He's being trained for a new mission and has a sufficient alibi.

"May I ask what his new mission is?"

My new ally.

"But those he reunites with will tell him what's happened."

He'll be prepared.

"May I ask why you went to such quick extremes with the general?"

They stared at the phone as its voice synthesizer continued interpreting Karma's replies. *What's the objective and end game of a chess match?*

Charlie slid his hand over his chin. "Capture the King."

Does anything else end the game against the loser's will?

Mitch inhaled. "No."

War is a chess game as chess is a war game and the game needed to end quickly. Young adults are in danger of irreparable harm. He threatened and frightened families who are not criminals or his enemy.

"But his house?"

Was anyone harmed?

Mitch sighed. "No."

No one injured, yet the loss will linger for years. And as the loss is contemplated, so will the decisions leading to the loss.

Mitch scanned the ceiling after jotting a note. "Lessons."

Charlie's gaze lowered. "But not all evaluate to that level."

An expedited end result with no lives lost or permanent damage done. How many generals can make that claim? Can you assert, the other side's first concern is the same?

Charlie stared at Mitch after lowering his pen.

Any other questions?

Mitch rubbed his face with both hands. "No, Karma. Thank you for sharing."

People don't acknowledge the great difference between solicited and unsolicited acts, and my solicited actions carry the intensity needed for others to learn their unsolicited actions have quick and complete consequences.

"Understood."

Goodbye

The phone displayed an icon, and Mitch stared at it as Charlie's eyes rose from his notes. "Anything you want to discuss?"

Mitch slid his fingers through his hair as he refocused on his notepad. "I don't know what to make of all this, but I don't want to make her an enemy."

"I think it means she's human, isn't sharing more than necessary, and possibly has a borderline personality disorder."

Mitch glanced at his notepad. "Or is just jaded by age. You know you can only fight immature bullshit for so long before raising your hands in disgust."

Charlie reached for his coffee mug. "That's fine if you stop playing after realizing it. Some decide to upend the game table, after quitting."

"But it sounds like she had stopped playing, and was only cleaning up after the new players."

"Okay, you convinced me." Charlie tapped the notepad with the back of his pen. "I'm now less sure of her motives, than I was a minute ago."

"Think about it. She hasn't initiated or escalated a thing." He raised his coffee. "She's only offering consequences to their …our actions."

Charlie nodded. "You're right …so far."

Mitch studied the notes. "She has powers."

He exhaled. "Abilities. Let's use the word, *abilities*."

"Any word you want is fine with me. She can do shit, others can't."

"And we have to warn the kids not to touch the gel." Charlie scanned his notes, then raised his eyes and smiled. "Our old thorn is now an ally?"

"I was hoping you wouldn't bring that up."

"Why?"

Mitch inhaled. "Because it means our double-role just got harder."

"Maybe …but we were never on the other side."

Mitch slid the notepad in a folder, then tucked it in his file drawer. "How come I feel like I need a shower?"

Charlie frowned as he lifted his coffee and stepped to the door. "Because we're elbow-deep in some really murky water."

~*~

Faith stood at the open stadium gate as Ben reached the edge of the soccer field, heading toward the locker room. "I can't believe I just watched you play high school soccer."

"It's only freshman, but did I do alright? I'm not embarrassing myself, am I?" He acknowledged Kye before refocusing on his sister.

She chuckled. "You're actually pretty good!"

He grinned. "Really?"

She slid her fingers over his jersey sleeve. "Don't get me wrong. You have a long way to go, but you run twice as much as everyone else on the field. How do you do it?"

"I like running."

Kye stepped beside Faith. "We know."

Ben's focus changed as a school bus pulled into the parking lot. "That may be Jaime."

"I doubt it. She won't be back for a while. Besides, varsity games are longer."

"They are not. Are they?"

"Yeah." Kye squinted. "Do you know anything about soccer?"

"I like playing it."

Faith fought her smirk. "You like that Jaime plays it."

"McCloud! Get in here and get changed."

He stepped toward the locker room door. "Do homework together after dinner?"

Kye nodded. "Sure."

Ben's bedroom door opened without warning and startled both brothers as Jaime led Faith in and sat on the edge of his bed. "So I hear you were pretty good today."

Ben rolled onto his side before moving his laptop from the middle of the floor. "But we lost."

"Your job isn't to worry about the final score. Your job is to get better at your specific job on the field. Let the coach worry about wins and losses."

He grinned. "How'd you do today?"

"We won."

"Did you score."

"Yeah."

"I hope I score someday." His eyes widened as he stared at her. "Is it fun to score?"

She smiled. "It doesn't suck."

Faith frowned at the exchange. "Are we going back to my room?"

"You can do homework in here with us if you want." Ben sat up and moved his notebook.

"Sure."

Faith's brows rose. "Are you kidding?"

Jaime grinned. "For a bit. I have things to ask."

"What?"

Kye's eyes darted between the sisters as he sat up. "Yeah …what?"

She ignored him as she turned and smiled at Ben. "There's a rumor going around school that Jacquelyn Marannda and her friend Tiana are fighting over which one is going to ask you to the Sadie Hawkins dance. Want me to tell them which one you want to go with?"

Faith sneered at Kye. "And the other one gets you."

Ben's eyes dropped as he shook his head. "I don't want to go with either."

"But Jacquelyn is gorgeous." Kye turned to his sister as he rubbed his hands together. "I got a fifty-fifty chance of getting asked by Jacquelyn?"

"Only so she can hang with cute little Benny here." Faith laughed as she pinched his cheek. "Why? Is there someone else you hope asks you?"

Kye smacked his arm. "C'mon. Pick Tiana. It'll be fun."

"Can't we just say someone else asked us and the four of us go together?"

"Uh…no."

"Stop picking on him." Jaime smacked Faith's arm, then refocused. "It's only a dance, Ben. It doesn't betroth you."

"Betroth? What the hell does *betroth* mean?"

She frowned at her brother. "Going to marry …idiot."

Faith giggled. "Or the idiot you're going to marry." She bounced her finger in a two-inch arc. "The noun works on either end of the sentence."

Kye smirked as Jaime softened her voice and smiled at Ben. "You can't start dating the person you're going to marry until you're older. The relationship won't make it."

He stared into her eyes. "It could with me."

"I know." She patted his shoulder. "But there are circumstances that make delaying it, better."

His eyes widened. "Are you going to ask someone?"

"Yeah."

"Who?"

"Whichever one of our friends doesn't get asked."

"What if I don't get asked?"

Jaime smiled. "Rumor has it, that isn't possible."

"Him?" Kye waved dismissively.

Jaime smiled. "I told you he's gonna get more girls than you."

He raised his nose and pointed at his chest. "The other one's asking me."

Faith grinned. "Yeah. The loser gets his hand-me-down."

"Well if Jacquelyn is his hand-me-down, I'm a happy camper."

Ben finished typing. "Should I stop doing sit-ups and push-ups?"

Jaime inhaled as she refocused. "Not if you want the girl of your dreams."

He continued staring at her. "Okay."

Kye turned Ben's laptop so he could view the screen. "Are you doing homework?"

"I thought that's what we were doing."

Kye gestured to their sisters. "Do you see anyone else doing homework?"

He pushed his book aside.

"You know who we ain't seen in a while?" Faith swiped her phone open. "Becca and Steve."

"We should visit." Ben smiled. "Wanna go visit?"

Kye grinned. "They are pretty great."

"We don't have to stay long, but we really should. They saved our asses."

Ben eyed Jaime. "But what would we talk about?"

Faith raised each finger in turn. "Our interrogation, cars exploding, our scholarships...getting a general fired. They couldn't make the coming-home party, remember?"

"Wait a minute." Kye raised an open hand. "I'm not getting this close to a date with Jacquelyn and letting it drop."

Jaime ignored him. "I could hang with them for a night. They really are fun."

Ben whispered, "You can have her. I like Tiana." He lifted his laptop before facing Jaime. "So could I. They're funny, the way they torture each other."

Kye smiled. "Thanks buddy, but you're crazy."

"Call and see if we can come over Friday or Saturday night." Jaime motioned to Faith's phone, then shook her head at Kye. "And you ain't getting her. You're her reason to hang with him."

Kye smirked. "Yeah, right."

Chapter Eight
Involuntary Disclosure

Karma walked down the basement steps and unlocked the partition door, then knocked before entering. "Hello, Captain."

Cowboy pressed the bed remote and the headboard rose. "Hi, Rachel. I've been waiting for you."

"You know what time our daily appointment is." She placed her folder and notepad on the side table.

"I do, but I like when you come early and chat."

"You're such a flirt."

He smiled. "I like talking to you"

"I like talking to you too." She tapped his arm. "Lean forward. Let me check your wound."

He winced as she began peeling the tape.

"Is this still sensitive?"

"Not as much as it was."

She carefully removed the bandage. "It must have been a large bullet. You're lucky to be alive, Captain."

"Thank you for helping me."

"Thank god our operatives were able to rescue you and bring you here. You could have bled to death." She slid a cabinet drawer open, then removed gauze and hospital tape. "Has the doctor been in to see you today?"

"No." He inhaled as she touched his shoulder. "Tell him I don't need him anymore. I don't like him."

"I know. You like nurses." She shook her head.

"What can I say. I'm a red-blooded male."

She removed an antiseptic wipe and swabbed his shoulder. "Be careful, Captain Harris. You don't want me falling in love with you, do you?"

"As long as you realize my mission means I may never see you again."

She gently rubbed ointment around the wound. "Are you sure you want to continue your mission?"

"Yeah. They don't suspect a thing, do they? You haven't heard anything, have you?"

"No we haven't. You've been brilliant." She began replacing his bandages. "I can't believe you're going back in."

"I have to. I have their complete confidence."

"But to continue infiltrating their inner sanctum? I can't comprehend how you can risk your life every day."

"I do it for you and everyone who believes in our way of life."

"Handsome, intelligent. You'd make a movie spy jealous."

He winced as she pressed the edges of the new bandage and she paused. "Are you alright?"

"I'm fine. Better than fine during your visits."

She sighed audibly. "I'm going to have a hard time forgetting you, Captain."

"I hope I'll be a good memory."

"The best, I'm afraid." She sighed again. "Shall we get started?"

"Let's"

She adjusted her chair. "I suggest we use hypnosis again. Don't you agree?"

"Of course I do."

Her brows rose as she eyed him. "Do you feel it helps?"

"It's amazing." He smiled. "The story is so real."

"And I must re-emphasize, if they find out otherwise, they'll torture you."

"I know." He patted the bed. "Do you want to sit up here so you can face me better?"

She feigned exasperation. "Oh, you're definitely feeling better, aren't you."

He grinned. "I was only thinking about my cover story."

"I'm sure." She opened the folder. "Do you want to go through the entire program, the next few days? You'll be leaving as soon as the wound heals."

"With you? And it extends our time together?" He smiled. "Of course."

She shook her head. "Do you ever stop flirting Captain Harris?"

"Not with pretty girls like you."

He winced trying to get comfortable and she stood. "Let me fix your pillows." She fluffed them, then touched his shoulder, guiding him. "I'm going to miss you, Cowboy."

He exhaled after leaning back. "Are you ever going to tell me your real name?"

Karma sighed. "You know operatives can't do that. We're well outside protective territory and have to take every precaution."

"I know, but I want to know your name."

"You know the spy game, Captain. Our precautions increased, once you told me they identified and procured our advantage. But it would be nice to look you up when our tours-of-duty are over and I hear you're home safe and sound." She smiled. "Are you ready to get started?"

"I'm ready." He inhaled, then tried to calm. "Make me impenetrable."

"Okay. First, I want you to tell me what you're going to tell them. And remember, I'm going to interrupt you and ask questions, and we're going over any spot you stammer."

"I know the rules, and I appreciate your insistence on perfection."

"It's the only way to keep you alive." She nodded with admiration. "Let's begin. What happened to you?"

"I got a call from Major Mattie, and was heading to an early meeting when I was abducted between my apartment and the car."

"Does that seem real to you?"

Cowboy sighed, then stared at Karma. "It really does."

"Can you see the abductors and how you struggled against them?"

"Definitely. There were two …well disguised. I don't know how I was knocked out. I don't have any head contusions."

"Excellent. They may ask you to take a lie detector test, and you must feel it."

"I understand." He inhaled. "But I actually do."

"Excellent. Let's continue. What happened next?"

"I don't know. I was unconscious for a period."

"When did you wake up?"

"I don't know how long I was out, but when I woke, I was in a cage in the woods …under a tree. The thickest tree in the area and its canopy blocked most of the sky."

"What could you see around you? Did you have time to study your surroundings?"

"Yeah. I felt like I was there for days, but I don't remember nights."

"Did you try counting days? Can you try now?"

"I didn't think to count, but I think it was maybe five to seven days."

"Did anything stand out during the time?"

He shook his head. "Not really. It was just a cage in the woods."

"How big?"

"I'd say roughly ten by twelve. Leaves covered the bottom bars, almost to the point where the ground felt comfortable …like the cage had sunk into the dirt."

"And you don't know how you got there?"

"No. I woke up in it."

She wrote a quick note. "Did you examine the bars?"

"Yeah. It's the first thing I did. They were welded. Everything was welded together. There was rust, but not a lot …surface rust on some of the bars. A lot of leaves inside."

"Animals?"

"Occasional squirrel …birds." He shook his head. "Wow, it's so real."

"It needs to be." Karma smiled softly, then inhaled. "Ready?"

He nodded.

"Did you see anyone?"

"No."

She studied his eyes. "You were ever told who captured you?"

His eyes narrowed. "No."

"Do you have any idea who they are?"

"None."

"You were there, days?"

He inhaled and nodded. "Yeah."

"Is it believable to you?"

"Scary believable."

"Excellent. I'm going to jump around with the questioning."

"Good." He adjusted his pillow.

She inhaled. "Tell me about what you could see from the cage?"

"Trees. Thin to medium size. Very typical for this area. What I would call woods or a wooded park, but nothing but trees in every direction. I couldn't see past them."

"Sounds? Smells?"

"Nothing but woods …forest."

She read from a notebook. "Cars? Traffic?"

"No …none. It was peaceful, actually."

"How were you fed?"

"I was told to put a bag over my head and pull the strings, tightening it around my neck. Then put my hands through the cage and they were tied. When they were untied, I lifted the bag and food was there."

"Did you look for people when you lifted the bag?"

"I was told if I looked behind me, there'd be no more food."

"How were you told? Who told you it was time to wear the hood?"

"A voice in the distance." He sat up. "A male voice."

"Any distinguishing accent or feature?"

"No."

"Same voice every day?"

"I think so, but it was indistinguishable and from a distance."

"What did you eat?"

"Fruits and vegetables mostly." His eyes narrowed. "Bread. Hard-boiled eggs."

"And you never saw anyone, your entire confinement?"

"No."

"What do you think they wanted?"

"They told me they wouldn't harm me, but I was a hostage, in exchange for a hostage if needed."

"So how did you escape?"

"I didn't. They let me go."

"Understand, we're going to let you go in a few days, so that answer isn't a lie. When you give it, picture the truth. We're releasing you." She paused. "Can you picture the truth when you answer that question?"

He nodded. "I can."

Karma smiled before patting her notepad. "You did excellent, Captain!"

"Thanks, Rachel."

"Is everything believable? Did all these things actually happen to you, or are you just reciting memorized answers?"

He inhaled as his eyes narrowed. "This all happened." He faced her. "This all really happened."

"That's excellent." She slipped the notepad in the folder. "Okay. Shut your eyes and relax. Let me have control."

"You know you can do anything you want with me."

"Then I choose to save your life." She placed the folder on the hospital cart.

He inhaled deeply. "I'm counting on it."

"Shut your eyes and relax. You're going to sleep on the count of three, and when you wake, you're going to be blindfolded and wearing a deprivation hood." She paused. "One, two, three."

The commander removed a document from his briefcase, then placed it on the laboratory conference room table before tapping it and eyeing Aidan. "Is this the final draft?"

"It is." Aidan's breathing increased. "I decided to be completely forthright, even if the information places me in a compromising light."

Doshmere opened his laptop. "Our latest findings vindicate your actions."

"And your insight negates any uncomplimentary light."

"Thank you, Jocilyn, though my soon-to-be ex-wife disagrees."

Nong placed a notebook next to his computer. "And the latest confirmations justify your determination."

"Thanks." He glanced at his associates. "Has anyone finished reading the report?"

"I've gone through it once, but I haven't studied it yet."

Dosh nodded after eyeing Nong. "Same here."

Aidan opened a separate notes document. "Should we reschedule?"

"No." Don gestured toward Aidan's computer. "This particular weekly meeting isn't perfectly timed but it's slotted in my schedule, so if you're comfortable, let's discuss this in the detail you can present and we'll continue the discussion as needed."

"Is the document open?" Aidan registered everyone's affirmation, then scrolled to his red highlights. "The first thing I'd like to do is finalize confirmation of the active participants, through video proof. Please refer to addendum one, page thirty-eight."

They refocused after completing the request.

"We have accusatory audio conversations, but I'm going to present visual proof. There's no questioning visual confirmation."

"You discovered visual proof?"

"It isn't beyond all doubt, Commander, but it's highly suspect, considering the time and place aspects."

The commander pointed to the smartboard on the conference room wall. "Let's display this on the large screen." He eyed Aidan. "Have you been shown how?"

"He has." Doshmere eyed him. "Let me know if you need help."

Aidan clicked on the attachment after activating the integration, and the wall unit beeped. "The first embedded video is security cameras from the fast-food restaurant next to field operations building two-eleven, which housed the prime exhibit before being shipped to this facility. Note the surveillance time and date. It's within an hour of the confirmed transport of exhibit prime." He forwarded to the twenty-minute mark and hit play.

Don leaned back as the video showed two cars entering the picture. "Let's refer to it as *the ship*. No one's going to overhear us."

"Understood." He refocused on the screen. "Those two cars are owned by the aunt and uncle, and they're about to be joined by three of the four prime suspects as they exit their vehicles."

He adjusted the video. "So where were the kids, that they suddenly come running from the restaurant?"

Don moved his laptop and leaned forward. "Isn't that also on surveillance video?"

"This discussion will branch in a few different directions, Commander, but first I'd like to establish the suspects' presence at this time and place. This fact helped us confirm our main assumption, and as soon as their presence verified our belief they were involved, we began studying with a different mindset."

"May we?"

Aidan nodded at Nong.

"That was the next thing we searched for, Commander; them entering the restaurant. We were looking to establish their direction into the building."

"We discovered something far more interesting." Jocilyn finished typing and lowered her laptop screen. "There is no surveillance video of them entering the restaurant."

Doshmere nodded before eyeing the commander. "This started as a quest to prove the adolescents actively participated in our mission, then suddenly turned into proof they possess something otherworldly."

"And gave us reason to pursue a greater goal." Nong pointed to the smartboard. "We think, if we succeeded in capturing and transporting the ship, we might have failed to emphasize the more practical and purposeful prize."

Don placed his elbows on the table and joined his hands. "Both would've been nice."

"Yes, but the one within grasp is much more practical and attainable, and we now have a much better idea where to look, to find it."

"We're getting ahead of ourselves." Aidan smiled at Jocilyn before facing the commander. "We're about to expand the potential sources of our desired prize."

Don rested his hands on the table. "I'm listening."

"Watch instead." Aidan motioned to the screen, then clicked his computer mouse after maneuvering over a different link.

Another surveillance video began, and Aidan pointed to the bottom of the screen. "Do you recognize the cars?"

"Where is this?"

"The cargo ship parking lot across the street from the airport hangar housing the crated ship."

"Timeline?"

Aidan paused the video, then walked to the screen and lifted a special red marker. "The beginning of a seven-hour window, starting roughly a half-hour after the ship arrived at the hangar."

"You're kidding." Don glanced at each associate. "Who's idea was it to secure surveillance videos?"

"Just an old military habit."

Nong pointed. "…That changed our entire game plan, Aidan."

"Please continue the video." Aidan stepped to the screen and drew two red circles as Doshmere clicked the computer mouse. "These are the aunt and uncle's vehicles. Focus on the SUV."

Don glanced at his computer screen before refocusing. "What am I looking for?"

"The strange dance it exhibits, without a human in sight." He nodded at Doshmere, "Pause it." then erased the drawn circles before sitting and continuing the video.

Don pointed to the screen and broke the extended silence. "What's the significance of repeatedly driving slowly backward?"

"This is only a guess, Commander, but we believe the four kids are there with the aunt and uncle and they're practicing their rescue mission."

"When you say *there*, you mean physically present but invisible?"

Jocilyn looked up from her notepad. "Doors open and shut without assistance. So does the back hatch at the end. It's the only logical explanation. It's their vehicles and no one's in sight."

Dosh tapped his laptop screen. "Occam's Razor, Commander."

"Brilliant, but how would they know our plans?"

"Deductive reasoning leads us to believe they infiltrated our command locations." Aidan inhaled. "What would you do if you had adversaries to defeat, and stealth ability?"

"Infiltrate my enemy's command centers." Don eyed Abe as he sat silently taking notes. "I want more information on the seven adversaries."

"We have no clue who the last adversary is, Commander, and we're not sure if number seven participated in any event prior to their known introduction."

"Understood, Nong." He refocused on Abe. "Seven, Lieutenant. Available individual information. I want a new and in-depth study perspective, for future cross-reference."

"Yes, sir."

Aidan refocused the group as he stood. "We believe their ability is the prize; not the ship. Rumor has it, you already have one of those."

The commander grinned. "Rumor has it."

Aidan smiled, then pointed to the screen. "There's more. This parking lot activity stops when the C-130 arrives for landing. All time references have been confirmed."

"I can't believe seven civilians thwarted an entire military mission."

"Civilians armed with the one advantage above all others …the ability to operate stealth."

"And this third video's timeframe is roughly five and a half hours after the last, and fifty minutes after the C-130 departs." Aidan started the video, then walked to the screen and pointed. "Watch the aunt's back hatchback open and close with no one in sight, then a while later, the car doors open and close without assistance, then the aunt appears in the driver seat before driving away."

"You think they're all there?"

"One better, Commander. We think they're all there, and they just loaded the ship into the back."

Don pointed to the screen. "What's going on with the uncle's truck?"

"He appears hours later in the driver seat, before driving away."

"What's your assumption regarding the delay in his departure?"

"We assume he was making sure the others were safe and undiscovered."

"So …what's our course of action?"

Aidan gestured to the document resting beside Don's computer. "The report is new, Commander. Let us analyze it in greater detail, but know we have full intentions of preparing a response."

Don eyed the group, then placed his hand on the table. "Excellent impromptu presentation, team."

"Thank you, Commander."

"Please also give kudos to the facility's video department in your travels." Jocilyn closed her laptop. "They've been amazing."

"They produced this for you?"

Aidan nodded. "And spent hours searching for and identifying what I requested they find."

"Excellent. I like confirmation, our team is exceptional."

"Their work for this project was exemplary."

Don stood after returning his laptop to his briefcase. "I look forward to further insight as we continue our scheduled meetings."

"Yes, Commander."

~*~

"Hi honey, I'm home" Steve waved like the lead in a sixties sitcom as he entered.

Becca looked up from the coffee table, in playful disgust. "What? Am I supposed to stop everything I'm doing and come running to you, because you're home?"

His brows rose. "Yes. You should be greeting me with a smile and a kiss as I smell the aroma of your fine cooking. ...And why are you wearing shoes?"

"Ass." She finished wiping the table.

He chuckled. "It's great to see you too."

She pointed to the front closet. "Vacuum the floor for me after you get changed."

"Why? And why are you cleaning tables? Is the Queen coming again?"

She smiled as she moved to another table. "Better. The kids are visiting tonight."

"Faith and Ben?" He leaned over the loveseat and motioned for a kiss.

"And their better halves." She kissed him then continued wiping the table.

He laughed as he headed toward their bedroom. "Now *that's* funny."

He walked into the living room after changing. "Where are you?"

"In the kitchen."

"You're not making dinner, are you?"

"It's Friday night. I wouldn't make dinner for the Queen."

"So when ...how did this happen?"

She stacked a washed container on the drainboard. "Faith called me and asked if they can come visit."

"Why didn't you tell me?"

"In case they backed out. They're kids. And I know you'd be crushed if you knew and they didn't come."

"You're right. But they are?"

She turned from the sink. "I confirmed before you walked in."

"They're the most impressive kids I ever met."

She shook her head as she finished washing a plastic container lid. "I wish you had a tolerance for adults, like you do kids."

"I can't. Most kids already know things some adults never learn." He headed toward the front closet.

She heard the vacuum a minute later and smiled knowing, he'd do almost anything for the kids, with far less bitching than he would otherwise.

He vacuumed the hall near the powder-room and spotted her inside. "Damn. You're going all out."

She smiled. "I miss them and I'm looking forward to this. That was a crazy, exciting thing we did together."

"It was nerve-wracking but it was fun."

"The most exciting thing I ever did in my life." She wiped the sink top. "And we made an even deeper connection …it's just too great."

He smirked. "Are you going to cry?"

"No, you ass." She threw the wet paper towel at him.

He laughed as he picked it up. "What are we feeding them?"

"I figured we'd order take-out when they get here."

"Let's have it here when they get here. They're kids. They'll be hungry when they walk in." He scanned the room, then raised a finger. "Dessert."

"I bought a cake and ice cream on the way home …and soda."

"Beautiful. What time are they supposed to get here?"

"In an hour."

"I got time to go get a square pizza. Need anything else while I'm out?"

"I don't think so." She looked around. "I'll order everything else."

He kissed her. "Perfect."

He opened the inside garage door as he balanced the pizza boxes. "Hi honey, I'm back."

She shook her head and smiled.

"Is the rest of the food on the way?"

"Yes." She reached for the large plate on the counter, as he placed the boxes next to her. "Don't you dare put this on a serving plate."

"Why not?"

"Because pizza needs to be taken out of the cardboard box." The doorbell rang. "Is that the kids or the food?"

"How the hell would I know?" She chuckled as she followed him to the door. "God, you're like a little kid."

"Only mentally and emotionally …but don't tell them."

"I don't think I have to."

He opened the door. "Peoples!"

"Hey Uncle Steve …Hi Aunt Kitt!"

"Hi, Steve." Kye smirked as he extended his hand. "I'm still not used to calling you that."

Steve rubbed Kye's shoulder after releasing his hand. "Do you love me?"

"Hell yeah."

"Then get used to it."

Faith led them into the living room after they kissed and hugged. "We have so much to tell you!"

"Yeah. We couldn't think of what we would talk about, then we thought of a whole bunch."

"Ben! You're not supposed to tell them that!"

His brows rose as he eyed his sister. "Why not?"

"Relax. All of you. Everyone feels that way at your age. He didn't say anything we didn't already know."

"Thanks, Aunt Kitt."

She slid her hand down the back of his hair as she passed, heading into the kitchen. "Who wants a drink? We got soda …ice tea."

"I'll have a beer."

She eyed Kye and laughed. "Not for about six years."

"Then can I have a beer?"

The doorbell rang. "Food!" Steve grabbed his wallet and disappeared, then returned with an arm-full or boxes and bags.

"Cool. I'm hungry." Kye opened bags as Steve placed them on the counter.

Ben eyed the boxes. "Did you get a square pizza?"

"Ha! Yes!" He pointed.

Faith opened the box and inhaled the aroma. "I swear, I'm gonna think of you for the rest of my life, every time I see square pizza."

They gathered in the living room after fixing plates and drinks, and Steve lifted the remote after placing his plate on the coffee table. "Basketball?"

"Can you put on that soft music so we can just talk?"

He smiled at Faith. "Absolutely."

Becca fixed a sofa pillow on her lap, then balanced her dish. "So what's new?"

Jaime brightened. "We all got scholarships!"

"That's wonderful! From where?"

Ben shrugged. "The military or the government. We don't know which."

"They're kind of the same thing …but how?" Becca bit her sandwich.

"You know about us getting captured."

"I was there …remember?"

Kye grinned. "Oh yeah."

Faith reached for her drink. "We weren't captured."

"Oh yeah!" Ben pointed at Becca. "You threatened to kick that guy's ass if he drew his weapon." He refocused on Faith "We weren't arrested."

Jaime shook her head. "We went voluntarily."

"Guys …what happened after you went with them?"

"Cars blew up!" Kye's arms shot up. "You should have seen the parking lot!"

Faith reached for a french fry. "Oh! We have money for you."

"What do you mean you have money for us. Wait. Cars blew up?"

"Hell yeah!" Kye sat up. "Karma likes blowing shit up. It looked really cool. You guys know about Karma, right?"

"Yeah, we know about Karma."

"Well, she saved our lives."

Becca eyed Kye as she reached for her drink. "How do you figure?"

"We figure we're going to prison unless she shows up and starts blowing stuff up, but she told a general he had to declare peace, or she'd keep blowing stuff up, and when he didn't, they relieved him of duty."

Jaime nodded. "And then they declared peace and apologized and gave us scholarships."

"And really nice checks." Faith smiled before biting her sandwich.

Ben pointed. "And Jaime got me committed to the Air Force Academy."

"Admitted, genius."

He sneered at Faith. "It's a commitment letter."

Becca motioned with her pizza crust. "Can you two cut each other some slack?"

Steve grinned as he sat back. "You guys are too great."

"Can we give you the money now?" They reached into their pockets, and Jaime collected it. "We want to pay you back for some of the things you bought us."

"You don't owe us anything."

"No. You don't understand." Ben sat up. "We got checks from the government."

"Nice checks." Faith nodded.

"And this is like nothing." Kye grinned as he reached for the french fries.

Jaime laid the money on the coffee table. "Plus we asked permission, so our parents know we're doing this."

Ben's voice softened. "So we don't feel so guilty for costing you so much."

"Who feels guilty for what the whole ordeal cost?" Steve watched all four raise hands. "You guys are the frigging best!"

"So are you."

"The money's already spent. Don't worry about it."

Faith smiled at Becca, then motioned to her plate. "Then it can pay for dinner."

"We were already ordering take-out."

"Yeah. Three large sandwiches, three pizzas and how many orders of fries?" Faith pointed to the containers circling the coffee table.

"We were hungry." Steve stood before reaching for Faith's empty plate. "Are you done, precious, or do you want to keep your plate?"

Kye popped up. "I'm not done."

"We have news for you too." Becca watched them face her. "Charlie sent a few messages recently. He and Mitch talked to Karma, and she wants you to know, you have to be very careful with the gel."

"Why?"

"She accidentally touched it, and she can't wash it off."

Ben's eyes widened. "She can't turn visible?"

Becca frowned. "She hasn't figured out how yet."

"That's sad."

"And scary."

Steve nodded at Jaime. "Exactly."

Faith sighed. "Is she alright?"

"There has to be a way. The ship had it, then released it and was visible."

"And the blanket. Remember?"

Jaime tilted her head at Kye. "Is your sneaker still invisible?"

"No idea." Kye bit his pizza.

"Are they still in the yard?" Jaime's eyes widened. "You never brought them in?"

"It ain't like I could wear them."

"Check when we get home."

"Oh …Karma's got Cowboy." Becca sipped her drink.

"Do you think she'll blow him up?" Kye walked to the kitchen, carrying his empty plate.

"That's disgusting."

"What does she want with him?" Jaime sat back with her drink.

"She said he's going to be her new accomplice."

Ben paused as he lifted a fry. "How's she doing that?"

Becca shook her head. "They didn't say."

"But this is all over. We deposited the checks." Faith sighed. "Wasn't this all supposed to be over after we cashed the checks?"

Steve patted the back of her hand. "We see no reason not to believe or hope so, but we can't be sure until time proves it."

Becca broke the uncomfortable silence. "So what's going on in school?"

Laughs filled the next few hours, followed by cake and ice cream, then hugs goodnight.

Jaime buckled her seatbelt before waving as Faith pulled away. "That was fun!"

"That was great!" Ben continued waving out the back window.

Kye playfully smacked his arm. "Knock it off. They can't see you."

"I love them."

"So do I, and that was fun, but I'm tired." Jaime slouched in her seat.

He bounced in his. "I'm wired."

They yelled in unison. "We know!"

Jaime spun in her seat as they giggled, then wrapped her arm around the headrest. "Find your sneakers when we get home."

"What for?"

"To see if one's still invisible." Jaime sneered. "Don't be an idiot."

Ben playfully shoved his shoulder. "Yeah, Kye …don't be an idiot."

Chapter Nine
Capture Strategy

Mitch's ringing office phone startled him and he hesitated before pressing the speaker button. "Captain Cooper."

"Open your afternoon, Mitch. I'm visiting today with a few others."

"Hi, Colonel. Any specific time?"

"After twelve."

"Is there anything I should prepare?"

"No. We just want you present."

"Sure, Colonel. Just me, or should I tell Charlie to take an early lunch?"

"Make sure Charlie's there."

"Will do."

"Different idea …set up the conference room and have lunch delivered."

Mitch lifted a pen then adjusted his notepad. "How many people, sir?"

"Four are visiting."

"Lunch for six, here by noon."

"Excellent, Captain. See you then."

The call disconnected and he immediately hit the direct line button. "Dixon."

"Noon conference room lunch meeting."

"With who?"

"The colonel and three others."

"D-Fac?"

"Hell no. Decent food. And the delivery person is calling the Control Room phone number when they show up."

"Sounds like a blast, but I have a hair appointment."

Mitch smiled as he reached for the phone button. "Cancel it."

"But it's for a color and style. You don't want my roots to start showing, do you?"

He pressed the button ending the call.

Charlie knocked on Mitch's office doorframe, hours later. "I heard the colonel's car doors."

"Who's he with? Any idea?"

"By the sound of the doors shutting, I'd say it's a female and two males."

Mitch fought his smile as he unplugged his computer. "Why do I ask?"

Charlie raised his arms. "You know there are no windows. What did you want me to tell you?"

Mitch shook his head as he followed Charlie into the corridor. "You got your computer, notepad, pen?"

"Yes, sir."

"Cellphone silent?"

"Yes, sir."

"Such a good... Hi, Colonel." Mitch extended his hand as he approached.

"Good to see you again, Colonel."

"Mitch ...Charlie." He inhaled. "Food smells good."

Charlie grinned as they shook hands. "I ordered it with my own two hands."

The colonel smiled as he turned into the conference room. "...Always the comedian."

Mitch extended his hand as he held the glass door. "Good to see you again, Captain Madison."

She smiled politely as they shook. "Captain Cooper."

He eyed the next gentleman as he reached for his hand. "Captain Mitch Cooper."

The stone-face gentlemen accepted his extended hand. "Captain Griz Griziani. We met in Tancil."

Mitch nodded as his smile disappeared, then focused on the last gentleman. "Captain Mitch Cooper."

"Lieutenant Jeremiah Jeffreys"

The colonel placed his hands on the conference table after everyone set up notepads and opened laptops. "Gentlemen, this meeting is about the future, and our place in it. Do we decide to make a name for ourselves by successfully carrying out our new mission, or do we fail and become less than an afterthought moving forward?" He straightened after eyeing each associate. "Military intelligence has had no luck identifying our new Fallwater adversary and our higher-ups have requested, we help find this person-of-interest. She is not only responsible for quite an impressive amount of domestic damage, but at this moment, holds an impressively high terrorist ranking for military damage done inside our borders. She has taken the fight to us, and seems to have gotten away with it." He inhaled. "And that just isn't acceptable."

Captain Madison acknowledged his nod before facing the others. "Does everyone understand who we're referring to?"

Mitch inhaled. "The teacher? What's her name?"

Charlie flipped the page on his notepad and searched previous notes. "Karma."

"Yes. She's been labeled a domestic terrorist, and currently holds one of our military officers hostage, and we believe she's in close proximity to the original four persons-of-interest."

"Intelligence reports thirteen hostages. Is that no longer accurate?"

"Twelve have been released."

Charlie glanced at the three new acquaintances. "When? Where were they?"

"They're still being processed."

Mitch's eyes narrowed. "We understand the original four have been exonerated, along with all family members?"

The stone-faced captain inhaled noticeably. "We wouldn't go that far, Captain."

Charlie slid his hand over his hair as he sat back. "What do you mean?"

"The intelligence discovery process didn't end with our agreement to discontinue pursuit of the six. It just went stealth, and we've since discovered irrefutable evidence the original perpetrators actively participated in our mission."

Mitch continued writing. "But we're not pursuing them again?"

Captain Madison shook her head. "No. We intend to honor our signed agreement if their participation has terminated."

Jeremiah raised his pen. "But any new activity on their part voids any existing agreement."

Mitch refocused on Mia. "What is our agenda today, Captain?"

She placed her pen on her notepad. "Our interest at the moment is solely this new terrorist, and we're here to devise a plan to lure this individual from hiding, capture her, and bring her to military justice."

"But you have new proof the original six were actively involved in thwarting our mission?"

"Substantive proof."

Charlie inhaled. "Was this Karma person involved from the beginning?"

Mia began typing. "We have no verification to date."

"Lady and Gentlemen, this is not a meeting to rehash past incidents. We're here to move forward." Colonel Sorelo gestured to Charlie and Mitch as he eyed the visitors. "And our team wishes to assist you in developing and executing any newly adopted plan."

Charlie nodded. "Absolutely, Colonel."

He smiled at Charlie before studying Mitch.

"Absolutely, Colonel."

"Excellent." The colonel placed his hands on the desk as he rose. "Let's have lunch, then turn this meeting into a think-tank."

Charlie's voice brightened as he stood. "Excellent idea."

The colonel interrupted the casual silence as everyone ate. "Anyone object to a working lunch?"

Mitch lifted his drink. "Not at all, sir."

"Good." He glanced at the others. "Any idea how to flush her out?"

Griz's voice deepened. "We know what worked once."

Mitch's brows rose as he eyed the group. "The soldier has no recollection what happened?"

"He remembers this little old lady with a cane."

Charlie lowered his fork. "And nothing else?"

"Nothing." Mia released her pen and began typing as she stared at her computer screen. "He has no recollection where he was or how he arrived where we found him."

Griz concentrated on his notes. "How many people do we think we can hide in the alley, with vision access?"

Jeffries tapped his notepad. "We only need one operative with sight access. The rest can work off his eyes, and we can do that at great distance."

The colonel pushed his plate aside. "Have we decided to lure her out in the same manner we previously used?"

"We know she monitors the alley."

Mia eyed the group. "Any suggestions on another option?"

"Have we searched the neighborhood? ...Looked for her by description? ...Community records? Monitored the surrounding streets looking for anyone fitting her description?"

"Of course, mister Dixon."

"Door to door?"

"No. But we've searched census and school personnel records since she calls herself a teacher."

"We're military intelligence, gentlemen. Our methods are extensive." Griz pushed his plate away. "We also believe, remaining stealth is the more prudent option at the moment. Non-typical community activity might cause an awareness better left undisturbed."

"So we lure her out with an invisible soldier." Mitch inhaled. "Then what? She seems to have abilities we haven't countered well."

Captain Griziani lowered his pen. "We can silently put her to sleep from a distance."

"Without harming her." Mia leaned forward. "We want her alive and well in our custody."

The captain broke his stoic stare. "The little dart leaves nothing more than a welt."

Lieutenant Jeffries continued writing. "Advanced scouting." He eyed Griz. "How many days?"

"I suggest two-tiered. Tier one, two weeks. Let's run through two week-long cycles, looking for patterns and measuring human and vehicle activity. Then we'll secure in place for roughly twelve hours before we set the bait."

"Are we attempting electronic surveillance set-up?"

"Yes, but with stealth placement. The adversary has destroyed all known surveillance, to date."

Mitch's voice softened. "She also told us not to place more."

The captain stopped writing. "Yeah …the enemy gives orders."

Mitch tapped his notepad. "How many days between last soldier placement and capture?"

"Two."

Mia raised her drink. "The previous example holds no merit, Captain."

"Who provides the soldier and how do we make him invisible?"

Charlie glanced at Mitch, then eyed the group. "Does our side have the ability?"

The captain's eyes narrowed. "Intelligence will provide the soldier."

"What would you like from us?" Mitch raised his pen and adjusted his notepad.

"Initial logistics, general layout, basic intel."

Mitch looked up after writing the reply. "What do you need first?"

"A secure local base."

"How close?"

"The closer, the better."

Mitch nodded at Mia. "Gladly, Captain."

"We'll work start date off procurement of that initial resource."

"Is our involvement, pre-capture only?"

Charlie smiled at the silence his unacknowledged question produced, as the colonel slapped his hands together. "Anyone not on-board with this plan?" The colonel sat back after eyeing the group. "Okay. Everything set?" He watched the team finish their last notes, then stood. "Thank you for your hospitality, Captain."

Mitch rose. "Our pleasure, Colonel."

"Be in touch, lady and gentlemen, and keep me informed."

"Yes, sir."

Mitch waved Charlie into his office, after walking the group to the exit, then looked up from his notes as Charlie entered. "Is it me or do we not have anything important to do for this joint assignment?"

Charlie extended his open hand, then brought his index finger to his lips. "That's normal when military intel is involved, but why are you complaining?" He motioned between them, then pointed toward the back of the building. "I could go a coffee. You?"

"I could always go a coffee." Mitch stood after lifting his mug, then reached for the special phone in his lower desk drawer, and slipped it in his pocket.

Charlie turned after exiting the office. "So what are you thinking regarding their temporary base?"

"An abandoned business along one of the bigger streets."

Charlie led them into the Control room, then raised the coffee pot as Mitch extended his mug. "Are they looking to house vehicles or just personnel?"

"Good question. I'll ask." Charlie filled his mug then followed Mitch toward the back door. "I'll need neighborhood plot plans and layouts."

"No problem."

Mitch waited for the exit door to latch shut, then sat and sighed. "Have we been set up?"

He smiled. "If it looks like a duck and quacks like a duck…"

Mitch gripped his mug with both hands and stared at its contents. "Wonderful."

"Now, we have to figure out if the colonel thinks we're as stupid as we look, or if he's as stupid as we look."

"Hey!"

Charlie grinned. "I'm sorry, but you look way too serious."

Mitch's eyes narrowed. "You really think the colonel is setting us up?"

"I'm as unsure as you but we obviously don't know, so we need to assume."

"What would be another scenario?"

"He's trying to get his team back in good graces? His team looked really bad after evaluation of the initial confrontation, and it made him look bad." Charlie glanced at the back door, then leaned forward. "That's all he's worried about. We've already established, he's out for himself. Our new question is, how far is he willing to go, to get back in good graces."

"Do you think he set us up voluntarily, or is he being pressured by Intel?"

"Let me share something about military intelligence."

"Besides the fact, there's no such thing?" Mitch grinned.

Charlie smiled before rubbing his face. "They have allegiance to almost no one but each other …and that's questionable."

"Do they train that into them or look for borderline personalities to recruit?"

Charlie inhaled. "That's a good subject for another time, but a wrong path for this discussion."

"I'm listening."

"Right now we have to decide if and who we tell." Charlie pointed to the building. "We have to figure, the only people aware of this mission are the six at that lunch meeting. If anyone gets warned, it comes back to us, and only us."

"Do you think they rewired this place?"

"I still can't believe they haven't put cameras around it, but we should assume it's wired."

"Damn."

"So we enjoy the back yard once in a while, and inside we act normal."

Mitch rubbed his upper arms. "But it's getting brisk out here."

Charlie pointed past the parking lot. "Then we'll visit next door."

"Do we let everything play out without warning any of the players?"

Charlie smiled. "I don't think it's necessary to go to that extreme, but we don't have to share just yet."

"If a decision isn't necessary, then it's necessary to not make a decision." Mitch grinned.

Charlie chuckled. "He got his ass blown away in Newbury, so he was one made decision short."

"Who?"

"Falkland." Charlie sipped his coffee. "…The guy you just quoted?"

~*~

Jaime walked up behind Ben between classes and whispered in his ear. "Wait for me after soccer practice, so we can walk home together. I have something to give you, but don't say a word to anyone. Understand?"

His back straightened and he nodded without facing her.

"Our secret?"

Her sweet warm breath made his breathing deepen. "Okay."

She slid her fingers down the back of his curly brown hair. "Then it's a date."

She walked by him without further acknowledgment, but turned after walking a distance, and pointed at him. "Secret."

His eyes widened but he offered no reply, and she smiled before turning and walking away.

He showered and changed faster than he ever had after practice, then stood by the gym doors, waiting anxiously. He stammered, greeting her when she appeared, and she smiled. "How are you?"

He took a calming breath. "Good."

She chuckled. "Are you alright?"

"Sure." He nervously fixed his damp hair before straightening his shirt.

"That was the most unconvincing *sure* I ever heard."

He inhaled audibly.

"You're too funny." She nudged him toward the exit doors, then broke the next silence. "How was soccer?"

"Good."

She fought her smile. "How's school?"

"Good."

She led him across the parking lot. "You really like school, don't you."

He nodded. "Yeah."

"What's your favorite subject?"

"Science." He hesitated. "What's yours?"

"Soccer." She motioned toward the back alley.

He chuckled. "You're really good at it."

She broke the next awkward silence. "You think I'm special, don't you."

He breathed deep. "You are."

She glanced at him. "Do you think I'm pretty?"

He looked down after turning onto the back alley. "I think you're the prettiest girl I ever saw."

"That's the sweetest lie you ever said."

He met her eyes. "I'm not lying."

"Yeah you are, but I really like it." She glanced at him. "Do I make you nervous?"

"No. But I'm a little nervous about the secret thing you're giving me."

"You can't figure it out?"

"No."

Her brows rose. "No idea?"

"No."

She smiled as she shook her head. "God, you're so frigging cute."

He hesitated at his back gate. "Is that good or bad?"

"How could being cute be bad?"

He shrugged. "I don't know."

"Well it isn't." She gestured toward the construction garage. "You have to come with me."

He glanced at the back of his house before following her. "Did I do something wrong?"

"You haven't done anything wrong since I met you."

"Are you mad at me for anything?"

"Not at all."

He fell in step with her. "Then what?"

"I told you I want to give you something." Her eyes narrowed. "Why are you breathing so hard?"

"I'm not."

"Yeah you are."

"It's from soccer."

She smirked. "Okay. If you say so."

"And you promise I didn't do anything wrong?"

"No Benjamin, you didn't do anything wrong."

"Then what is it?"

"I'll show you in a minute." She unlocked the side garage door, then re-hid the key.

"From the construction garage?"

She held the door open, then shut it behind them. "*In* the construction garage."

"And it's a secret Faith and Kye don't know about?"

"Yes, Benjamin, and they can never know. Understand?"

His eyes widened after adjusting to the light. "Okay, I guess."

"And you can't figure out what it is?"

"How could I?"

"Do you know what tomorrow is?"

His eyes narrowed in thought. "Friday?"

"The dance?" Her head tilted.

"What about it? You're not going with Jayden anymore?"

"It's not about me going with Jayden. It's about you going with Tiana."

"What about her?"

She stepped in front of him. "I'm afraid she's going to give you something I want to give you."

"Girls give guys something at the dance?"

She gently pushed him against the wall. "Not always. But I have a feeling she's going to, and I want to first."

She watched him stand stiffly against the wall. "Okay. Shut your eyes."

He inhaled and complied.

"Now just do what I say." She moved closer and whispered. "Put your arms around my waist."

He slid his hands along her hips, and she moved closer as she slipped hers around his neck. "Now part your lips just slightly." She smiled as she pressed her cheek against his. "Now do you know what I'm going to give you?"

She felt him stiffen as her lips gently pressed against his, then softly part as her tongue touched. "Is this okay?"

He leaned toward her and she opened her mouth, then silently elated at his eager innocence. Her tongue felt his soft tongue, and she tilted her head enough to seal her open mouth against his.

She felt him inhale and wrapped her arms tighter around his neck, and he held her as if she would break with any force. The kiss ended after an extended moment, and she fought her grin as his breathing raced. "Was that alright?"

"Wow."

He leaned closer, and she opened her mouth on his a second time, then slid her cheek against his after their kiss ended. "There."

He stood, frozen. "Wow."

Her voice softened. "Was it everything you hoped?"

"It was the best thing …ever."

"You never kissed a girl before?"

His breathing continued intensifying. "Not counting my mom, sister, and aunts?"

"Am I your first kiss?" She giggled. "You can open your eyes now."

He continued holding her. "I don't want to."

"Why?" Her voice softened. "You don't want to look at me?"

"I don't want the moment to ever change."

She gently teased the back of his hair with her finger. "So was I your first?"

His brows rose as he opened his eyes. "My first and second."

"Oh …right."

His eyes widened. "Can you be my first five kisses?"

"Are you sure you don't want other girls in the first five?"

He smiled. "You could be my only ones ever, if you want."

She giggled. "We'll go with first five for now."

"Okay!"

"Shh!" Her arms surrounded his head as their lips met, and he sighed as their tongues softly pressed together.

She broke the extended kiss. "Can I ask you a question?"

He answered with more breath than voice. "Yeah."

"Did you want to kiss me before anyone else?"

"Can I share a secret?"

She smiled.

"I want you to be the only one I kiss, for my entire life."

"Other girls aren't going to let that happen, but remember what I told you about dating too soon?"

"Yeah, but you don't have to worry about that with me."

"We're not dating until you graduate."

"Then we're dating?"

She kissed him tenderly. "Yes, Benjamin. Then we'll date."

"For real?"

"Yes."

His brows rose. "Will you be my date, graduation night?"

She fought her smile as she shook her head. "We'll work out the details later, okay?"

"Two more kisses."

"One more. I just kissed you."

He sighed, then brightened. "Can we kiss again before we date if we're ever anywhere alone?"

She slid her fingers through his dark curly hair. "Yes, but we can't get caught."

"Okay." He smiled. "One more for five?"

She shook her head and smiled. "That's four more than I planned, but okay …one more for five."

~*~

Faith wrapped her shawl over the back of a folding chair, and Jaime placed her soda in front of the next seat, then scanned the gym for friends. "Angelina, Myasia, Emine!" She waved, then pointed at the closest round table. "Put your stuff here so we get both tables."

Myasia shuffled in her high heels and extended her arms as she reached Jaime. "I love your dress!"

"Thanks! I love yours!"

"Welcome to the twenty-sixth annual Fallwater high school Sadie Hawkins dance, ladies and gentlemen. Tables are first come, first reserved. The cafeteria is also set up, and refreshments are available. I hope you have a great night!"

Faith hugged Emine after the announcement. "You look beautiful!" Where's your date?

"The one my parents think I'm with, or my real one?"

Jaime placed her hand on Faith's shoulder. "Em, where's Muhammad?"

"Waiting for his date."

Jaime hugged her. "Aren't you his date?"

"Shh! I'm really here with Erik." She pointed. "Don't tell anyone or my parents will kill me."

"Then who's Muhammad here with?"

Emine adjusted her beautiful silk hijab. "Samantha. But you can't tell their parents either."

Faiza squinted. "Not Lucy's little sister."

"No. She's here with Nina …but nobody's supposed to know that either."

TJ slapped his thigh. "I love this group and this school."

Jaime nudged Faith as she spotted Kye at the entrance. "Look at the grin on his face."

Faith smiled. "Better yet. Look at Jacquelyn. She's gorgeous."

Jaime leaned closer as music filled the decorated gym. "You're not jealous, are you?"

Faith nudged her. "I could have him if I want, but he ain't ready yet."

Jaime snickered. "Tell me about it. Oh my god …look at Ben. He looks like a young European soccer star in that suit with the turtleneck."

"That's my father's look."

She nodded. "Oh yeah. It works."

"He asked me a million questions about you and your date, last night."

Jaime smiled. "Really."

"What are you two doing?"

Jaime hugged Isabela. "Watching our little brothers walk in with their dates."

"Tiana looks happy."

Isabela smiled. "I don't blame her."

"Anyone sitting here?"

"You." Faith smiled as Brianna draped her shawl over the back of a chair.

"Here." Jayden handed Jaime a soda as TJ stepped next to Faith.

"Anyone see Muhammad yet?"

"Not yet." Jaime smiled as she sang her next greeting. "Hi, Ben."

"Hi." He hesitated, then gave her an extended hug as Tiana's eyes widened. "Where's everybody sitting?"

Tiana reached for his hand and gave him a tug. "We're over there with Seara and Kendra."

Jaime smiled after spotting their joined hands. "Bye guys. Have fun."

"Don't be strangers." Faith snickered before turning to the group. "Muhammad! Happy birthday!" She hugged him as greetings came from everyone. "Happy birthday!"

He grinned and pointed. "If you start singing, I'm leaving!"

Hugs ended and everyone claimed seats, then Faith grabbed TJ's hand as another song began. "C'mon everyone! This is a *dance*!" She drug him to the dance floor as Jayden extended his arm to Jaime.

She yelled to Faith. "I'm not dancing next to you!"

Cheyenne whispered as they walked to her. "None of us should dance next to her unless you want to be invisible."

"Not to mention how gorgeous her legs look in heels and that clingy red dress." Muhammad placed his hands on Jaime and Angelina's shoulders, then leaned closer. "Or the rest of her."

Angelina playfully smacked his head. "Then why are you mentioning it!?"

He rubbed his head as Samantha gripped his other hand and drug him along. The friends danced in every combination and visited every table as the night progressed. Jaime watched their brothers throughout the night and decided to visit when she spotted Ben and Tiana sit after dancing. She rested her hands on the back of their chairs. "Are you guys having fun?"

Tiana's eyes narrowed. "Yeah."

"Do you want to come over and meet Ben's other friends?"

Kye plopped in a seat, out of breath as Jacquelyn sat between him and Tiana. "We're going to the caf for a snack."

Jaime raised her hands. "Okay. Stop by later if you feel like."

She walked away, then leaned close to Faith before sitting. "I invited our brothers over, and Kye completely blew me off."

Faith laughed. "Don't take it personally. They're having fun."

"I'm not complaining."

Faith grabbed her hand and drug her toward the dance floor. "Yes you are."

"I just wanted one dance with Ben, but Tiana keeps looking at me like, *go away* ...every time I'm close."

Faith raised her arms as they started dancing. "Leave him alone. He's hers tonight."

Chapter Ten
Arcane Imperatives

The commander entered the conference room and laid his briefcase on the table. "Good morning everyone. Are we making progress?"

Doshmere smiled as he adjusted his seat. "We're making excellent progress."

Jocilyn glanced over her laptop. "We're actually becoming experts on the Fallwater incidents."

"Including the adversaries." Nong adjusted his computer screen.

"Did you work up character profiles?"

Aidan nodded. "Extensive character profiles."

"Karma?"

He inhaled. "Incomplete, but we've gathered what we know. She's been the toughest to grasp, due to the nature of the contacts we've experienced, but completing it is high on our agenda."

"Excellent. So tell me who the other six are."

"Gladly, Commander. Mind if I take the Fergusons?" Dosh glanced at his associates, then tapped his touchpad before concentrating on his computer screen. "Jaime Savannah Ferguson; seventeen, first child, older sibling of blue-collar parents. Excellent athlete, but shows a unique psychological kinesthetic perspective. She's not afraid to score. I mention this because psychologists insist, many athletes freeze when winning opportunities present themselves, and this shows a hesitation and uncertainty she doesn't possess. This is a mental toughness which shows, she would be the most levelheaded, and most likely to think clearly in times of crisis. Her kinesthetic abilities are also impressive. She stands out among her peers, even when her physical attributes aren't dominating. Intellectual quotient; she is slightly above average, but she doesn't study. Her ability to retain enough intellectual content to do better than average seems to come naturally, but shows less than average motivation for all things not soccer. But I re-emphasize; her mental toughness with regards to physical circumstances, should not be discounted."

He inhaled as he tapped the touchpad repeatedly. "Kyle Ronald Kye Ferguson; fifteen, youngest child, oldest son, younger sibling; a jokester. Physically above average size. An athlete, but not on the level of his sister. Fairly motivated scholastically, though he doesn't seem to do more than demanded. School profiles mention he's calm emotionally, bordering on stoic. His reactions to our encounters show a high realism perspective. Not easily rattled. Socially, he's not extroverted or introverted, but has a measuring personality. The psychological term is called, slow to warm, but once accepted into his social circle, shows an extremely high loyalty quotient. He isn't a person who will even consider selling out another, let alone a friend. He has no selling point, to date. This was extensively tested." He tapped the touchpad and folded his hands.

Jocilyn sat up as she turned her focus from Dosh to her computer. "Faith Galilea McCloud, eighteen; first child of white-collar parents; older sibling. Gifted kinesthetically, though in dance, not sports. Extremely feminine perspectives, non-confrontational, highly loyal. Strong emotional personality, but not fully developed. Socially accepting ...believed the weakest of the four, regarding crisis management. Intellectually above average; above-average work ethic and motivation. High creativity quotient. She would be most likely to think her way out of a situation, but only after initial panic." She eyed Nong. "Want to take Ben?"

"Sure." He maneuvered his computer mouse, then studied his screen. "Benjamin Khalil, Ben McCloud, fourteen, youngest child oldest male child, younger sibling. Ben is a slight enigma. A strong loyalty quotient, but an almost unrealistic positivity. Scholastically highly motivated overachiever. Goal setter with persistence and just enough obsessive compulsiveness to attain desired goals. Generous and welcoming socially. Slightly compulsive emotionally. Good insight for his age. More daring than common sense would dictate. School records show a well above average percentile in natural leadership qualities. He also wants to join the Air Force and be a pilot."

Don sat up. "Fighter pilot, or pilot?"

"Records indicate, pilot."

"Adolescents that age never use one word without the other."

"No sir, they don't."

"Impressive." Don pointed to Dosh. "Aggression level of the four."

"One to ten, I'd say Jaime is a four, Kyle, a seven or eight."

Don nodded, then motioned to Jocilyn.

"Faith …a two if not lower."

Nong inhaled. "Benjamin is tough to measure, though if put on the spot, I'd have to say, five. He's equally disinclined and non-hesitant to initiate, depending on his perception of the inevitability of the proposed situation."

"Fight or flight impulse?" Don pointed to Dosh.

"Jaime …six or seven toward fight. Natural competitor unafraid of competition. Kye, a clear eight toward fight. Young testosterone."

Jocilyn straightened. "Faith, a nine toward flight."

"Ben..." Nong shook his head. "I'd say dead even between the two. He will if he has to, but could just as easily walk away."

"Leader qualities."

"Yes, sir."

Don eyed Aidan. "Do you have the adults?"

Aidan nodded. "I do."

The commander sat back and folded his arms.

"Steven Raphael, Steve DiMarcantonio; forty-eight. Husband of twenty-six years, to Rebecca Franklin DiMarcantonio, uncle through marriage, to Faith and Ben McCloud. Diverse background. Son of blue-collar parents. Ex-Army; honorable discharge. Used the GI bill for his education and entrance into the computer industry. Prior, he was a commercial carpenter."

Aidan maneuvered his computer mouse. "Personality profile; blue-collar mentality, typical work ethic, though not measurably successful. Realist by perspective. Well stated admiration for younger generations. Socially, he prefers the company of younger people, to peers, though he and his wife have no children. Typical family man, from what we can tell through family social media. Not a social media user, so his profile is limited"

"The wife?"

"Rebecca Anastacia Franklin, Becca, Kitty, DiMarcantonio, forty-seven. Second oldest of six sisters. Sister to Taylor Franklin McCloud. Blood aunt of Faith and Ben McCloud. Ex-Army, honorable discharge. Above-average maturity, mentally, intellectually, emotionally, and socially. Successful career in real-estate sales, which has honed her social maturity. Bread-winner of her household and she earns her money through successful relationships and transactions. Physically, she's forty-seven. Her strength though might be her weakness. We assume, her maturity allows her to be aware of her limitations. A strong family sense. She is very close to her sisters, and they show signs of acting with one mindset. A trait her niece and nephew seem to have adopted from the sisters."

"Why do you think the kids sought their help instead of parents?"

"Psychologically, adolescents are more inclined to seek counsel with adults who are less likely to judge or demand. We can only assume, but their family dynamic indicates a high probability toward that reasoning."

"Group dynamic perspective?"

"With regard to the four adolescents …cohesive. Single-minded." Dosh pushed his computer away. "Conversations indicate, they torture each other emotionally, like typical adolescents but their ability to work together, and group loyalty is extremely impressive. Our attempt to brake them proved completely futile."

Aidan clicked his computer mouse. "We have audio indicating Ben is the leader, though his natural tendency is to delegate leadership whenever prudent."

Don chuckled. "Future Air Force General?"

Aidan's breathing quickened. "He reminds me too much, of a young Aidan Dimitri."

"Then we look forward to having him on our team in the not-so-distant future." The commander motioned to Abe. "But in the meantime, share these profiles and use our psychology department to find ways to break them if needed." He leaned forward as his smile vanished. "Adversary seven?"

Aidan nodded toward Dosh, and he maneuvered his computer mouse. "Karma, the Teacher. We have no additional identifying information. We are assuming she is female, based on our only eyewitness account. Age …the eyewitness account has her as elderly, though we're not sure that isn't a ruse. Personality …intellectually, she is arrogantly self-assured. Articulate, which more than likely shows intelligence if not just advanced education. Little to no self-regard. Her moral-reasoning quotient is far more dominant. Emotionally, she is restrained but shows high loyalty traits. She is quick to defend though she shows no sign of preemptive actions, to date. Social perspective …incomplete. Physical strengths and weaknesses …incomplete. Overall weaknesses and subsequent vulnerability …incomplete. But we are continually analyzing her actions so we may formulate ways to combat her."

Don finished typing, then scanned the group. "Is there anything else we need to discuss? Any preliminary thoughts on plans for future engagement?"

Aidan nodded softly as he stared. "There's no other reason to be here."

"Anything to share along those lines?"

"Yes. We'd like authority to remotely plot movement on the aunt and uncle."

"For what purpose?"

"There's a significant probability they house a portion of the material we're pursuing."

"Are you thinking of a stealth search?"

"Yes, Commander."

"Observation duration?"

"Minimum two weeks. Preferably three."

"I'll send authorization, and share access with the appropriate personnel." He scanned the group. "Anything else?"

"No, Commander." … "No, sir."

He placed his hand on the tabletop, "Good session today, team. See you next week." then refocused on Aidan. "I'd like a further discussion."

"Gladly. Here?"

"Your office." The commander faced the others. "Thank you for your exemplary work."

Aidan followed Don to his office, then turned after shutting the door. "Is everything alright?"

"Absolutely."

He motioned to the large leather chair. "Please use my desk."

Don placed his laptop on the table between the guest chairs. "I'd like a more casual discussion."

"Your preference is my pleasure." Aidan sat in the second guest chair. "What can I do for you?"

The commander smiled. "I just want to counsel with a peer, regarding the multiple facets of this project's future."

"Such as?"

"I'm being asked to surrender the remainder of what little invisibility substance we have, and I'm disinclined."

"Whose request?"

"Air Force Intelligence."

"Their intentions?"

"Their purpose wasn't divulged, but I'd venture a guess and say, potentially, stealth soldiers in the pursuit of the entity which caused many of your final difficulties."

"How much matter do we possess?"

"A small drop from the original object, of which we previously surrendered half at their request, in the hope they would secure additional material."

"The alley soldier."

"Correct."

"Did he produce anything before his capture?"

"A miniscule amount on the toe of an invisible sneaker."

"Was your original supply returned once they secured more?"

"Karma supposedly confiscated the original quantity, when she captured the soldier."

"Do you think that's truthful?"

Don smirked. "Would you be?"

Aidan fought his reaction. "Do you think that's why Karma stripped him?"

"I don't believe it would've been her primary reason, though it produced the result. But I'm inclined to believe our colleagues have additional material."

"So am I, but a soldier always expects the worst." Aidan breathed deep. "Do you plan on turning any over if we secure more?"

"I'm weighing my response, which is why I requested your consultation."

"Have you planned a proposed course of action for the quantity you've kept?"

Don removed two pads and pens from his briefcase and handed one set to Aidan. "Write your top three ideas regarding what we should do if we find more, and I'll do the same."

Aidan's eyes widened as he accepted the pad and pen, then quickly wrote.

Don paused after finishing. "Done?"

Aidan nodded before extending his pad, and Don smiled as he read Aidan's reply. "I said three."

Aidan inhaled. "There's only one."

Don chuckled as he displayed the same answer on his pad. "Correct. And I want control of the entity we create."

"Are we creating one or multiple soldiers?"

Don rubbed his chin as he contemplated his answer. "One is easier to keep secret, and manipulate."

"Where are we recruiting this soldier?"

"He'll be a member of our special forces." Don pointed to the pad in Aidan's hand. "Write a memo to those organizations, requesting applicants, and I'll authorize. Our prestige will offer us a voluntary supply pool."

"I think we should also recruit a military associate, mentor, partner. The second part of a team."

"Expound on the thought."

"A second set of eyes and ears. A non-participating mission accomplice, companion, sounding board, advisor, training partner, potential rescuer."

"Non-stealth?"

Aidan nodded. "Non-stealth except his communication capabilities. It also gives us better tracking proficiency on both soldiers."

"You've thought about this."

"I have."

Don lifted his coffee mug after adjusting in his chair. "Would you take charge of this new project?"

Aidan inhaled. "I'd like nothing more."

"Then it's done. Write a concept proposal. I'm interested in making this soldier and his partner, highly technological and cutting-edge advanced." He tucked the pads into his briefcase. "In the meantime, we only have a few droplets, and I don't want this to be a contention between us and intel, but we feel they'll use the remainder for military purposes, without using it to procure more material, and our intention is to procure more substance, so there's longevity in its military application."

Aidan stood and adjusted his chair. "Have you made that argument?"

Don shook his head as he closed his briefcase. "Not yet. I wanted to counsel with you first, considering your inclination toward their mindset."

"We're in possession?"

Don smiled.

Aidan placed his laptop in its desktop docking station. "Debate settled."

~*~

Sweat droplets beaded on Karma's forehead as she sat on the floor in the dark. She wrapped the blanket tighter around her shoulders, then pressed her fingers gently to her temples, trying to concentrate past the throbbing ache. "Yes, it's okay, but you're still going too fast."

Her head twisted and she winced as multiple parallel thought-streams entered her consciousness. "Slower ...please ...slower."

She rubbed her pounding temples as one concept dominated the incoming barrage. "Yes I know you're trying and you're improving, but it's still too strong ...too complicated." She visualized the perception of aging, trying to convey the process without word association, then frowned at her inability. "It's just going to take time."

She rubbed her burning eyes and lowered her chin in frustration. "I'm sorry we're so primitive."

Karma flinched, and her breathing intensified. "No …it's okay. Yes, it hurt, but you're forgiven. You're always forgiven." She pictured the joy of their desired connection and friendship. "I'm as willing and excited to communicate with you, as you are with us."

"No." Her eyes squeezed shut as she tried to decipher the incoming messages. "Please continue to learn through and with me. You're teaching me how to communicate in wonderful new ways."

She reached for a tissue and wiped her forehead. "I know you don't want to hurt me …us …but someone has to help you learn."

"…But saying the words helps me envision the thought."

"Yes …this thing I call sound, is how we communicate. It's simpler and slower than your communication. …Slowly shared single thoughts. Vibrations physically traveling between us."

"Yes! A lot like the vibration of the universe. No, we don't feel them …we hear …our instruments hear as they record it. But things make sound to us …noise. No, we don't hear you fly." She pictured the tree and the ship next to it. "We heard you crash. It's how we knew you came."

"No. Our sound is very local." She pictured a small area …her immediate surroundings. "The others used special instruments …machines…devices…tools to identify your vibration signature."

"Waves. Yes! Waves! We call them sound waves." She tensed and gasped as increasing concepts bombarded her. "No. We don't feel them or use them. We hear many directly, but we hear many more with our instruments …our machines."

"No!" She looked up. "Please don't reveal elsewhere! No! There are fewer beings here who'd accept you, than you understand."

"Other visitors? Here?" She gasped at the pressure pulse accompanying the increase in concepts. "Before? We have not made contact before."

"We have? When?!"

"Primitive man." She shuddered as sweat beads trickled down her neck. "That's prehistory ...before our history. We have no records ...no memory."

Cave drawings and pyramids around the world suddenly came into vision. "Yes, but so many ignore encounters so long ago."

"Like me? ...I'm sure, but not now." She concentrated and covered her face as she tried to communicate without words. *No, I'm not typical. Most aren't ready for your next contact. We've not advanced in many ways. In many, we've regressed.*

Karma smiled. *No. I'm not special. I just want to enjoy and share our mutual existence ...to learn from each other. But most don't.*

Yes, the angels are like me. Many younger people are more willing to accept you. "Yes ...by their actions."

A short time alive. Less time. She pictured a newborn. *Closer to birth than death.*

But our young don't make our rules or decide matters of this magnitude.

...Will not accept. ...I don't know why. ...Scared. Afraid of being destroyed. She shivered as the perspiration from the intensity, dampened her shirt. *No. Ancient paradigms influencing current beliefs.*

...The end of primitive paradigms. Many fear advancing to that awareness. Many wish to continue believing we're alone.

No. Not good news for many. Great news for some like me ...like the angels. But not most.

...Alters ...Adjusts their spiritual theories. Old comfortable inaccurate concepts.

Images flashed into consciousness. *No. Leaders don't. They prefer status quo ...things as is.* She shook her head and sighed. *No. Our wise men don't rule us. ...Our society is more hierarchical.*

We don't communicate directly with our leaders. Our communication is different. We cannot share thoughts over great distances without using machines.

Yes. It is pleasure...hope.

Images inundated her and she winced. *No. Pain is okay.* She pressed her palms into her temples. *...You're teaching me. This is necessary. This is good ...desired.*

"Wait. Stop. ...I need rest." She placed her hand on her chest, and breathed deep, trying to relieve the anxiety, then wiped the perspiration from her face.

She gasped as the visitors shared their displeasure while reading her fleeting thought. *Yes, I understand it's forbidden on your planet, but I promise to use only when necessary. They were coming to harm the angels. I promise not to use what I've learned except to prevent harm or death.*

I understand those actions are grave on your world. They are here, too.

No. We have not reached that existence level. Many purposefully harm others.

He is not harmed... She inhaled as the vivid image of Cowboy's abduction flashed in her mind. *...But he'll help prevent harm.* She pictured a barrier blocking aggression. *I swear I'll only use the skill to prevent harm.*

Her head twisted as her eyes teared. *I know, but the ability is part of learning to communicate with you. Would you be happy if the angels were harmed?*

She concentrated as thought streams overwhelmed her, and she pressed her hands against her head. *I haven't injured him, but his inclination was to harm the angels. All I've done is give him the opposite reasoning.*

Yes, that's a secondary effect ...for the same reason.

I do understand, but please let my actions show...

I know. She held her temples as beads of perspiration outlined her face and dampened her hair. *We also have circumstances beyond our control, but I can use the abilities to nullify conflicts between the angels and those who wish them harm. I showed you and I'll continue showing you.*

She held her breath as multiple communications overwhelmed her. *I understand your respect for life. I have that too, but many of us lack that reasoning.*

Yes. Please discuss it. But I haven't injured anyone and there are many here who would harm you and the angels, without concern. She moved her damp hair off her neck. *We have not advanced beyond that maturity. Our actions confirm.* She pictured conflicts around the globe. *We aren't ready.*

She sighed. "Different. So different. Less advanced in many ways. ...Less mature than you think."

No. I'm sorry. I'll release him, but he is no longer the threat he once was. Her sweat-soaked hair made her shiver, and she wrapped the blanket tighter before lowering to the floor with her eyes squeezed shut. *Please stop now. It's too much*

~*~

Cowboy struggled trying to keep warm as he huddled in the roadside ditch and studied the passing cars. He stayed hidden until a pick-up drove close enough to identify a single male driver, then held the wrapped blanket securely before standing. "Stop! Please! Stop!"

The driver swerved as he stepped to the edge of the secluded road, then stopped twenty yards beyond as he waved his arm. "Thank you! Thank you!"

The man opened his door then quickly extended a hand after exiting. "Stay where you are or I'll drive off!"

"Buddy! I'm not dangerous. I'm a kidnapping victim. I have a number you can call to prove it."

"I'll call nine-one-one for you." He reached in the truck.

"No! No police! Please! You'll get others hurt."

"What? You're not alone?"

"I'm alone. Just please don't call nine eleven."

"Look …All I want is to see if I could help but I can't afford to get involved in some kind of high federal crime."

Cowboy stood, shivering. "Well do you at least have something I could wear?"

"I may have an old shirt tucked behind the seat." He lowered his head, then raised it as he stared frantically and pointed. "But stay where you are!"

He shivered. "Okay, but I'm getting down the embankment. It's breezy up here."

The man placed his hand on his head. "Ah, damn! Just get in!" He revealed a tire iron as his stare followed Cowboy to the passenger door. "But I swear if you make one stupid move, I'll be the worst thing that's happened to you today …and it don't look like you're having a good one to begin with."

He hurried to the passenger door. "Mister …the only thing I'm going to do is hold this blanket tight, and shiver."

"I'll crank up the heat." He motioned to the passenger door. "And buckle up. You're going to be hard enough to explain if anything happens to us."

Cowboy noticed the mile marker. "What road is this?"

"Midland Bypass."

"What township?"

"New Sharon. I'm heading to Redmont. Where you going?"

"To find a phone." Cowboy held the blanket tight.

"Public phone?" The man chuckled. "How long you been out in these woods?"

Cowboy eyed the desolate road. "I have no idea."

"Are you sure I can't drop you off at a police station?"

"Positive."

The stranger glanced at him. "It's up to you."

"Could I use your phone and make a call? Just one call. Please?"

"You have my time, gas, and heat. You can't use my phone. I want no connection whatsoever, with whatever this is."

"No one's going to bother you. The police would, but I'm not calling them. I'm actually trying to reach the Air Force base. I'm a soldier."

The man glanced at his blanket before refocusing on the road. "I don't want to know."

"Then just drop me off near a town, and thanks for letting me get warm."

The stranger leaned forward and eyed the sky, "Why?" then inhaled. "One call. And you gotta tell everyone, my phone number was just some guy who stopped when you hailed him, and let you make a call."

He released the blanket and exposed his hand. "I promise you won't hear a word from anyone I know."

"Damn." The man reached into the door pocket and offered his phone.

He accepted it and dialed. "Captain, it's Captain Harris. I was just released. I'm on Midland Bypass, driving with a hailed stranger, passing mile marker twenty-nine point one in New Sharon, heading to Redmont. They took my clothes, and this phone is the stranger's."

He inhaled as he listened.

"Please. As soon as you can …and bring me clothes. All I have is a blanket."

"No idea where I'll be. I've never been around here."

The driver motioned to him. "You can stay in the truck till they pick you up."

"I'm in an old black pick-up."

"Tell him you'll be in front of a place called *Rhema's*." He reached for the phone. "Let me talk to him."

"The guy wants to talk to you." Cowboy extended the phone.

"Ask for Rhema's when you get to town. Everybody knows it. Is this guy really a captain in the military?" He listened. "I had nothing to do with his situation, understand? I'm just doing a kind deed." He handed the phone back.

"He really didn't. I waved him down from the side of the road, at mile marker twenty-nine point four." He listened. "Okay. See you there." Cowboy ended the call and returned the phone. "Thanks. If you watch, you'll see the people who come for me are in uniform. If you trust me and just relax, I'll buy you lunch while you wait"

Two military police walked into the restaurant as the stranger sat at the counter. "Is there a military captain here?"

"Damn." The man squinted as he pointed at the large storefront window. "He's in the black pick-up out there."

One MP turned as the other rushed through the door.

"He's really a captain?"

"United States Air Force."

"What's he doing naked in the woods?" The man raised both hands as he faced the counter. "Sorry. I don't wanna know."

The stranger dropped his fork when the MP appeared at his side, minutes later, "Relax, friend. You won't hear from us again." then dropped a twenty-dollar bill on the counter before eyeing the server. "The meal's on us. The change is his."

Cowboy placed his hand on the dashboard and chuckled as the man spun on his counter stool and watched the MP exit, and he tipped his cap as the military vehicle departed. "I'll pay you back when we get back to the base."

"I appreciate it, sir."

"We're going to the base, Captain, but you're not to talk to anyone before you're admitted into the infirmary. You've been scheduled for an extensive examination and debriefing."

"Will it be warm, with a decent meal, a stiff drink, and nap after?"

"I'm not sure, sir."

"…Sounds like a blast."

~*~

Ben cut across the neighbor's dew-covered lawn, running to Kye as he walked behind Jaime and Faith. "Guys, you know what today is?" He adjusted his backpack straps as he caught up.

"Thursday."

Faith crumpled her protein bar wrapper. "I got a math test."

Kye pointed to Ben's pocket. "You know… your phone tells you when you open it."

"Haha. You're all so funny. Guys, it's four months since we became famous, somewhere."

"Somewhere else." Kye wrapped his arm around Ben's shoulder. "Call me when we become famous here."

"Is it just me or does, famous somewhere else, feel exactly like tired, overworked, and overwhelmed, here. Anybody else already tired of school?"

"I'm more interested in how long it's been since we heard from the other side."

Kye tapped Faith, "Not long enough." then placed his hand on Jaime's shoulder. "Does tired of classes count?"

"I like my classes."

Faith zipped her jacket as she glanced back. "Oh, little brother. You're still as weird as ever."

"I wonder if anything is still happening. Has Steve or Becca heard from anyone?" Jaime gently bumped Faith as they walked across the parking lot.

"You mean *C*, *A*, or *T*?"

"I love it! Cat." Ben pulled on the locked school entrance door. "We should call them or something."

Jaime eyed him as she leaned against the building. "That's the last thing we should do."

"Why?"

"Because we want them to forget we exist." Faith's head tilted. "And leave us alone?"

"Oh. We should go to Field Op's and visit! Get invisible, camp out the night, and reappear in Mitch's office."

"Yeah, that's exactly what I just said." Faith sneered at her brother as she moved against the gym's outer brick wall. "Has anybody looked out back for anything strange lately?"

"I haven't touched that stuff since watching *T* drop that guy." Kye shuddered. "That scared the shit out of me. I really expected to find blood everywhere."

"We really should check once in a while."

Faith eyed her brother as she placed her backpack at her feet. "I'd just as soon not know."

"That's probably not a good reason not to look." Jaime hopped, trying to keep warm.

Faith checked her phone. "I can't wait till we don't discuss this anymore."

"You know who I miss?"

Faith turned away from Ben. "So much for not discussing it."

Kye tapped his arm. "Charlie."

"No."

"Make-up lady?"

"No …Karma. We never thanked her or found out if she figured out how to turn viz… and she saved our lives. I wanna know if she's alright."

"There's only three ways of doing that." Jaime offered Faith a contrite smirk, then raised fingers. "We ask *A* and *C* to ask her, we go to the interrogation building and steal the phone she texts to, or we go to Field Op's and try to learn how *A* and *C* contact her."

Ben pulled his hoodie strings tighter. "I wanna talk to her."

Jaime glanced at him. "I wouldn't mind, now that you mention it."

"It'd be nice, even to just say thank you."

Kye pointed to Faith's phone. "Text Becca and ask."

"Why can't we all just leave this alone?"

Jaime nudged her. "It's just to make sure she's alright."

She frowned. "Okay. I'll text, but not till lunch. We don't need to wake her."

"Should you call her instead. We don't know if they're still reading our texts."

She pointed to Ben's pocket. "Then text her on your secret phone, but not till lunch."

~*~

Mitch entered the Control Room and filled his mug. "Let's go next door for a coffee."

"I was going to ask if you wanted one." Charlie reached for his mug then held it out.

Mitch filled it. "Really."

He followed Mitch out the back door and sat at the picnic table. "What's new?"

"I secured the facility Intel requested, and they can occupy it legally, starting Monday."

"Intel identified and requested it?"

Mitch nodded. "Yeah. It's a foreclosure property on the next street."

"And why did they ask us to do it?"

"Is this a test? Because I know you already know."

Charlie grinned as he raised his coffee. "Was that the last part of our participation?"

"Yeah."

He wrapped both hands around the mug as he placed it on the table. "Where?"

"An unoccupied property on Segment Street, with an additional garage facing the alley." Mitch removed a folded survey map from his notepad and pointed to the lot. "Five houses in from Third Avenue."

"Nice work."

"I don't like it."

"I know." Charlie sipped his coffee. "Me either."

"Do we say anything?"

"Not yet. Do you know if the scouts are set up?"

"No, and I don't want to know." Mitch placed his mug on his notepad as the wind picked up. "Intel hasn't shared a word more, and I know better than to ask."

"Don't even ask if we can help. The further removed we are, the better. And if the colonel volunteers information, cut him off. There's only one reason they'd share now."

"Agreed." Mitch rubbed his face. "But I want to affect the outcome."

"I know. So do I. But if we're caught affecting the outcome, we probably go away for the rest of our lives, and military prison isn't a good career move."

Mitch twisted his head as he rubbed his neck. "So, do you have any idea how we can?"

"Not yet."

Mitch broke the momentary silence. "And why did you want to go next door?"

"Pool Lady called. The angels want to contact their teacher."

"Why?"

Charlie lowered his coffee. "Wait. We'll know when the mission starts. The bait will be in the alley."

"We'll only know the bait is set if someone tells us, and I don't want to ask anyone to look."

He sat back and stared. "I don't either."

Mitch raised his mug. "So why'd you mention it?"

"I'm trying to work it out in my mind."

"And?"

Charlie's brows furrowed. "I'm working on it."

Mitch lifted his pen and adjusted the notepad. "In the meantime …the angels?"

"…Want to thank their teacher."

"That's it?"

"With these four?" Charlie smirked. "I doubt it."

"You don't think they know anything, do you?"

"The only way they'd know is through us…" Charlie studied the rear door. "And those little bastards better not be still haunting this place."

Mitch chuckled. "They wouldn't be the only ones, but that's about the only question we can ask them. Everything else shares too much information."

"We can put out cookies and see if they disappear." He snickered. "Those ghosts love cookies."

"That's some funny shit. The brats sat right in the rooms with us?"

Charlie saluted with his mug. "Either a whole lot of guts or amazing stupidity."

"They already proved they ain't stupid." Mitch rubbed his upper arms as a cool wind picked up.

"True. But they're young and inexperienced, so we're not telling them anything."

"Inexperience." Mitch frowned. "Young intelligence's greatest secret enemy."

Chapter Eleven

Draft Deviation

The single streetlight illuminating the alley entrance suddenly went dark, and the darkness lingered as the scout secured his predetermined location. He quickly nestled between the untrimmed bushes and outer shed wall, then hand planted the leafy fake weeds around the ones attached to his disguise. He finished scattering debris, then settled in the shallow trench dug the day before while disguised as a building surveyor setting the property's boundary markers. He tossed more dirt and leaves on his back and legs, then signaled his team leader and the streetlight began powering up.

He lay quietly for days, recording all movement as his team infiltrated the property's house and back garage, then crawled inside the rising garage door during the night, as a second scout crept unnoticeably to the side of the building, and established his position.

Days later, a utility van parked at the curb and a middle-aged couple exited as a rental truck backed into the property's driveway. A loaded pick-up arrived minutes later, and the four began unloading the vehicles. The SUV drove into the alley after the occupants finished, and parked in the back garage, then a person wearing jeans and a baseball cap exited the garage and entered the house through the rear door. The TV flickered through the newspaper covered windows, and the new occupants displayed normal daily activity as they secretly set up unseen monitors and motion cameras at side and back windows.

Major Madison lifted the phone receiver and waited for the connection. "Griz, are you busy?"

"No, Major."

"Grab Jeffries for a quick meeting. Stake-out reports are in."

She glanced over her laptop as they appeared at her open door. "Have a seat gentlemen."

Both walked to the front of her desk, saluted, then extended their hands. "Congratulations, Major."

"Thank you, gentlemen." Mia returned the salute, then gathered her laptop and file folders before joining them at her office table. "Have you both read the Fallwater scouting report?"

Lieutenant Jeffries nodded as Captain Griziani slid his chair back. "Yes, ma'am."

"Is it analyzed and annotated? Are we ready to go?"

"Yes." Lieutenant Jeffries patted the file folder he had placed on the table. "Just awaiting orders."

"Do you agree, Captain?"

"I believe so, Major." The captain opened the file, passed duplicate annotations, then turned the page and skimmed over his notes. "Initial scouting proceeded without incident, and our operatives have been embedded and monitoring as our systems plot all neighborhood logistics tendencies."

"How many days' data?"

The lieutenant ran his finger down his notes. "Nineteen."

"Is that sufficient?"

"We believe so." The captain studied his notes. "We have a field command and three separate egress viewpoints. We occupy the foreclosed property. Two soldiers are posing as a couple, and reside in the house, while a team has set up access to the alley through a back door. Two sniper units in two piles of road stones with multiple sightlines have been established. One egress post at the far end of the alley, where it meets the high school property. One post is situated at the edge of the school property, with additional visual along Segment Street. An operative occupies an electric relay junction barrel at the top of a utility pole at the intersection of Third Avenue and the alley, and a sixth sniper is positioned at the property's back window. We're also using the back garage as a station for additional soldiers and the transport vehicle."

"Do you recommend we begin phase three?"

"Yes." The captain glanced at Lieutenant Jeffries as he nodded.

"How many men will be positioned outside?"

"Ten, counting the five egress personnel. Three additional on the north and two on the south, along the alley. Another three are in the garage, and four more occupy the residence."

"We're set for overkill, Major."

"No, Captain. We're preparing for a very quick and uneventful removal of a single unknown entity who has displayed unusual abilities." She studied both men. "This is not a war battle. This is an extraction."

"Understood, Major."

Lieutenant Jeffries looked up from his laptop. "And we're not notifying the police?"

"Do you think they'll let us take away a citizen, without extensive explanation? If they discover that citizen is stealth, do you think their requested information decreases?" She finished writing in the margin, then placed the document in her file. "Give the orders. Phase three starts tonight at oh-two-hundred hours." They stood and gathered their belongings as she stood. "Notify me when our team is ready, and we'll release the bait."

She turned as they reached the door. "And gentlemen ...we're approaching this encounter with a different mindset. We're in search of a single entity, and I want an uneventful, covert engagement. Non-confrontational."

"Understood."

239

"Put her to sleep and get her out of there. Nothing more is acceptable."

"Understood, Major."

Captain Griziani grabbed Lieutenant Jeffries' arm as they left the major's sightline, then motioned him into his office and shut the door. "We're not informing our task force of her last …suggestion. Our soldiers are professionals and we have a job to do."

"You know it was an order."

"I don't believe it was an order, Lieutenant."

Jeffries inhaled and stared forward as the captain faced him. "We don't get to decide the level of confrontation they'll encounter, so why put the extra burden on our operatives? If we make someone hesitate, we may cost them their life." Griz smiled and patted his arm. "Let our operatives do their job as they're trained."

"They're not trained for domestic conflict against civilians."

"They know what country they're in. And a terrorist is a terrorist."

"This is team leader. We are *go* for phase three. Crow's nest, report."

"This is crow's nest. We are secure and ready for release."

"Sightline?"

"Visual east to eight hundred yards."

"Copy. Rock pile one?"

"Last operative installed at plus fifty minutes. Secure and ready."

"Sightline?"

"Visual to seven hundred yards, west. Two hundred yards, south."

"Rocks-two?"

"Both occupants secure, plus fifty minutes."

"Sightline?"

"Visual to seven hundred yards, west. Three hundred yards north."

"Copy. Mark time …now. Remaining scout deployment is *go* minus three hours. Full *go* command is minus seven hours. Hourly confirmation is required. A missed report is automatic abort."

"Roger."

Monitors registered the normal increase in pedestrian and car movement during the expected morning hours, and the team watched the activity decrease as the surveillance model projected.

"Last report."

"Crow …go."

"Rocks-one …go."

"Rocks-two …go."

"Command …requesting authorization."

Captain Griziani hurried from his office and knocked on Major Madison's open door. "All is *go* at minus one hour, Major. Do we have final approval?"

She sent a text then shared the reply. "We are *go*."

He displayed his phone and pressed the send button. It beeped moments later and he nodded. "We're live minus one hour."

"Report any and all deviations from normal."

"Yes, ma'am."

A police cruiser and SUV sped silently into the alley from Third Avenue, then activated their oscillating colored lights, and the crow's nest scout pulled the soundproof blanket over his head. "We have potential abort! Repeat …potential abort!"

His earpiece crackled. "Explain."

"Local police just entered the alley from Third Avenue."

"Hold in place."

The first vehicle screeched to an angled stop a few houses past the command location, as the trailing SUV idled by the alley entrance.

"This is rocks one, Command. Local police have just entered the alley at the high school end."

Identical vehicles crept along the alley's far end, and a trailing cruiser blocked the entrance.

"Stand by."

Tires screeching, resonated between the buildings, and oscillating colored lights reflected off walls, as more police surrounded the fronts of homes on both bordering streets.

"Rocks one requesting orders, command."

The lead officer exited the cruiser with his weapon drawn, and took immediate cover behind the vehicle's open driver door. "Come out with your hands up!"

"Abort in position."

"I said, come out with your hands up!"

Spotlights began scanning back yards and the second cruiser crawled forward as more blue and red lights reflected off sheds, fences, and houses.

"They're too close, Command. Soldier in danger!"

A cruiser's bullhorn blasted. "Surrender, now!"

"Who's in his sightline?"

"Field op seven, command."

"Single reveal only! Field op seven …reveal. Everyone else, remain in position."

A single soldier moved to his knees with his hands up. "Please don't shoot!"

The officer pressed his shoulder communicator. "We have suspect one. Configure for apprehension."

"This is rocks one …was bait released?"

"No. Bait is not exposed."

The officer stared down his gun barrel at the kneeling figure. "Anyone else! You have a two-minute reprieve. After that ...any movement receives immediate gunfire!"

"What do we do, Command?"

"How well are you hidden?"

The lead patrolman pointed to the house as assisting officers ran toward him. "Start searching here."

The crow's nest scout pressed his eyepiece against the barrel opening. "We can't get trampled and they're not satisfied!"

"Scouts and inside personnel, stay! Everyone else ...reveal! Hands up. Surrender! I'm coming out!"

Soldiers began kneeling with hands raised, as officers exited vehicles and took immediate cover.

"Don't shoot. We're unarmed!"

The lead officer pressed his shoulder com. "Assist! ...Alley between Segment and Tangent! House six, Tangent! Multiple suspects."

His com sounded. "All available units. Officer assist. Alley between Segment and Tangent, Third Avenue and the high school."

The lead officer pressed his com button as he continued aiming at the kneeling soldier. "What do we have?"

"Multiple suspects along the entire alley!"

The command lieutenant turned from the closed-circuit monitor and handed his communicator to an associate, "You're communication lead until the residence is compromised." then slid the back sliding glass door open, and immediately raised his hands. "Officer! We surrender! You will not receive gunfire!"

"Assist! Multiple assist! We need back-up immediately!" The second officer raised a bullhorn from his open trunk. "Come out with your hands raised!"

"Officer! I'm in charge and I've ordered everyone to surrender!"

The lead officer scrambled around the side of his cruiser with his gun pointed toward the voice as multiple sirens blared in the distance. "Show yourself!"

"The garage is between us! I'm standing in the yard with my hands fully raised!"

"Face away from the alley and walk backward!"

Officers rushed between the houses with guns drawn, as soldiers started appearing in the alley with their hands raised.

"Stop!" The officer pointed to an associate, then at the first revealed soldier. "You have him!"

The command lieutenant raised his hands and walked backward past the garage as an officer yelled in the distance at the escorted soldiers, "Down on the ground! Arms and legs spread! Hands open! Face flat on the ground facing right!"

Tires screeched and sirens blared, as assisting officers ran into the alley.

"On the ground, face down!" The lead officer waved his gun at the soldier as he appeared from behind the garage. "You're the leader?"

"Yes, sir."

The officer walked behind him then glanced at the patrolmen in the distance, frisking the soldiers lying in the alley as others pointed guns. "Are you a drug cartel? Drug dealers?"

"No, sir. We are not."

The officer pointed to his associate. "He came from that house! Surround it with SWAT."

"That's not necessary, sir. We're military and we surrender."

The officer pressed his com button, "SWAT back-up!" then squinted as he faced the prone man. "What?"

"We're military and we can prove it."

"Whose military?"

The lieutenant's voice softened. "United Stated military hunting a domestic terrorist."

"Bullshit. I never heard of the military hunting terrorists domestically. Besides, they would have contacted us."

"We couldn't, and we'll explain after we prove who we are."

"You can do that at the station. Right now ...you're under arrest."

"But I have identification in my back pocket."

"And I've never seen a fake ID in my life." The officer placed a cuff on the lieutenant's wrist, then twisted the soldier's arms behind his back and cuffed the second.

~*~

The school alarm blared, and everyone in the class moaned. The teacher smiled as she turned from the smart-board. "Aww... Are you guys enjoying the lesson?"

"Excuse the interruption. Fallwater high school is now in lockdown. Lockdown in place until further notice. Lock all classroom doors, cover windows, and remain out of sight. This is not a drill."

"Oh, stop your moaning." Ms. Lopez pointed to the windows. "Get the shades. Everyone else, huddle in the corner." She hurried to the door and peeked down the hall for straggling students before locking it and covering the window.

Faith's phone beeped with an emergency alert, and she read the screen. "It's not in the school, guys, but the police activity is right down the street." She read further and frowned. "My street."

"Too much has been happening on your street lately."

"Tell me about it." She smirked at Francesca before texting Jaime and their brothers. *Trouble on our street ...again*

"Shh! Whisper." Ms. Lopez eyed the students, huddled out of sight, then smiled at Faith. "What did happen on your street over the summer?"

Segment too. Tangent Segment and the alley

Faith shrugged after glancing at the reply. "A utility truck caught fire."

"Anything else?" Natalia moved a desk and sat closer. "There's no truth to the rumors about something visiting you?"

Do you think they caught ...anybody?

Her eyes darted from Natalia to Ms. Lopez as she hid her inhale. "Visiting?"

Ashley smiled at her. "Visitors as in aliens?"

It could be something diffrent. Its the police

"Someone got that from a burning utility truck?" She shook her head as she eyed her classmates.

Ms. Lopez's voice softened. "And it isn't true you helped them escape?"

Yeah it culd b something diff ...but what r the odds?

Faith glanced at the text, then chuckled as she lowered her phone. "That's what the rumor is now?"

Should we tell P?

Francesca sat up. "My mom heard, you and your brother rescued somebody who was in danger. Were they kidnapped or something?"

Not yet. No need to scare her

"There was no kidnapping." She shook her head as she leaned on a desk seat. "Seriously, how do these rumors get started?"

Was anybody caught?

"Just rumors?" Ms. Lopez smiled. "...if you say so."

Natalia frowned. "A really big rumor. It not only spread through the whole town, but my cousin in Medwin asked if I know you."

Only 1 person to worry about

Faith smiled as she pointed a finger to her heart. "Well, I didn't start it."

...Only 1 person worth catching

Faith eyed the speaker above the whiteboard as Mrs. Krull shared an announcement. "The school is still in lockdown, but normal classroom activity can resume. However …No one is allowed to leave the building or go near a door. There is police activity in the area."

We need to find out

Faith quickly typed as she rose from between the desks. *Meet after school*

"Alright, everybody. Get in your seats and phones away. Let's get back to work."

"Aww."

Ms. Lopez chuckled. "Fifteen minutes ago, you were all complaining we had to stop the lesson."

Christian sat in his desk with his legs stretched forward. "That doesn't mean we liked the lesson. It just means we like complaining."

She stared at him, fighting her smile. "How are there not more comedians in the world, when every one of my classes has more than one?"

~*~

The sniper huddled inside the sound-proof blanket and waited for the call to connect. "Captain. Captain Griziani. It's the Fallwater crow's nest scout. We have a situation."

"Explain."

"The Fallwater police showed up. The mission is aborted and they're arresting everyone but the five embedded scouts."

"Do you have communication with the other four?"

"Yes, sir …so far."

"Remain inactive in place until further orders. Keep a watch for the direction anyone appears. Photograph anyone who comes out to gloat."

"A caged prison bus just showed up. They're arresting the entire team."

"We'll send a rescue team, but we're an hour away."

"There's no way for me to tell them, sir."

"We'll make some calls then be on our way."

The desk sergeant sat back and smiled as the military officers approached. "Welcome. May I see picture identification?"

Both presented their military photo IDs and the sergeant scrutinized the information before returning the cards. "Thank you, Major Madison …Captain Griziani. Chief Craven is expecting you. First door on your right." He gestured toward the table at the side of his desk. "Help yourself to coffee before you go in."

"Thank you, Sergeant."

The chief greeted them at his office door after they fixed their drinks. "Welcome." He stepped aside as they entered. "Make yourselves comfortable."

"Thank you, Chief Craven."

He moved around his desk. "I'm Joe."

The major smiled. "Mia, and this is Griz."

He sat and folded his hands on the desk. "I'm sorry we're not meeting on different terms."

"I'm sure you'll see this as just a misunderstanding, after we explain."

"Then you'll have changed my initial perspective, Major. Please share why you were conducting a military mission in my town, without notifying its police force."

"Gladly."

He smiled. "Will the information include your unauthorized apprehension of four adolescent residents, or is that a topic for another conversation we're going to enjoy today?"

Mia tilted her head and squinted in confusion. "I'm sorry?"

"This isn't a small town, Major …but it isn't a big one either. People know people who know people, and your actions are fleeting enough to end before we get notified, but we do receive notice."

Captain Griziani straightened in his chair. "We all have jobs to do, Chief, and one of the reasons our large organization runs so efficiently, is our ability to honor and respect command, without question, so we may not be able to provide you with the explanations you request."

"I have a small organization, Captain, and one of the reasons I don't need a large one is, our primary honor and respect go to the people we serve. Forgive me if I'm mistaken, but I thought that was part of your organization's policy also."

"There are individual concerns and there is the greater good."

"And who decides this difference, Captain?"

"Our level of leadership doesn't ask that question, Chief."

"Well for my town…" He gestured to the walls. "Welcome to the decision maker's office. Now convince me why I should change my perspective."

Mia sat forward. "We have a terrorist, we believe resides in your town, and we'd like to apprehend her, without fanfare."

"International terrorist?"

She shook her head. "Domestic terrorist."

"One of Fallwater's residents?"

"We're sure."

His eyes narrowed. "A single entity?"

"We're fairly certain."

"Not the four teenagers?"

She chuckled. "No. Not the latest incidents, but we're still processing other event participation."

He reached for a pen and notepad. "Do you know this resident's name?"

"We don't."

He inhaled. "And what acts of terrorism have they committed?"

"We're not privy to say."

"Do you need me to swear to secrecy?"

"We would need you to get security clearance."

"Who do you think is the first line of domestic protection, Captain? The military?" He set the pen on the notepad, then rested his folded hands on his desk and leaned forward. "When you go away ...and you will. My group will be left to manage any confrontation initiated by anyone not willing to live peaceably." He paused as he eyed them. "What level of terrorist do I have living in my town?"

Griz glanced at Mia, then sat forward. "They've destroyed military vehicles and attacked a military base."

"In this country?"

"Yes."

The chief lifted his pen. "Please be more specific."

"We'd rather not."

"In this state?"

The captain glanced at Mia. "Yes ...in this state."

"How long ago?"

"Recently."

"Any reason why I've not seen or heard any reports of these events?"

"It's in our best interest if these incidents remain beyond public knowledge."

The chief rubbed his forehead. "I'm going to step from my office and get a cup of coffee, and when I come back, we're either going to have a much more open and mutually beneficial information exchange, or I'm going to expose this entire story, because ...it seems to me ...you people are two bullshitters, and you'd like nothing better than to keep your bullshit story as buried as you've kept your actions."

Mia's eyes narrowed. "And why do you think we're not being forthright?"

"I hinted it earlier, but I'll spell it out for you since you missed my initial effort. One of my officers has a daughter who goes to high school with the previously mentioned adolescents. And I do my homework like I'm sure you do yours. Now, how about you be as forthright as you're claiming, or I'm going to make local headlines, exposing a military operation, in a place most citizens might find …disturbing."

"We'll win that battle, Mister Craven, and all you'll have done is make the wrong enemies."

"My residents are the only people I worry about making enemies of, Captain, and I work very hard making sure they know I protect and serve them. I even expect to sacrifice myself for them. It's not only my sworn duty …it's my purpose." He stood. "Excuse me while I get my coffee."

Mia displayed her phone as the chief re-entered the room. "Our general would like to know when you're releasing my team?"

"When you've proven they're not domestic terrorists and have broken no laws."

Griz leaned forward and placed his closed fist on the edge of the desk. "We're the United States Air Force."

"And we're the Fallwater Police." He sat back and folded his arms.

Mia chuckled and shook her head. "Alright, Chief. You win. You really want to know what we're doing?"

"I'll compromise. I don't need details, but I'd like the argument, your actions are legitimate."

"Fair enough, but please understand some of the information is currently classified, and you'll be hurting me by sharing."

"I'm the only person who has to know, and I'll honor your concern."

"We discovered..." She smirked. "…through a planet monitoring system, we identified and procured an interesting item which was then taken from us while on its way to an examination facility. From a nationalistic standpoint, the fact it was taken from a major branch of the U.S. military against our will, in our own country, is highly concerning. How it was taken, is scary concerning. What we're trying to do …with as little fanfare as possible, is gain access to the material and method used against us."

"And you don't know who executed this act?"

"We're still working on many aspects of these events, and I cannot compromise our efforts with speculation regarding involvement."

Chief Craven stared at Mia, "Understood. Thank you for sharing." then slid his hand over his hair. "Was the vehicle and base attacks, truthful?"

"Yes, but there may be more to the story than we're sharing."

"Fair enough." His gaze narrowed. "Are you more concerned with the method and material, than you are the …terrorist?"

"I'd have to say yes, until the person uses their abilities against us again."

"How concerned should I be that they'll use their abilities against the civilian population?"

Mia exhaled after contemplation. "Currently, we believe your concern should be minimal."

"Thank you for your honesty."

"Would you mind sharing something in return?"

He raised a finger, then pressed two buttons on his office phone.

"Sergeant's desk."

"Release the military." He ended the call, then looked up. "Please ask."

"How were you tipped off about our presence?"

"A motion sensor doorbell."

"A what?"

He turned to the captain. "A woman called, rambling on about her back doorbell sending her phone, video clips of peculiar movement in the alley, and someone dressed in black, digging near the trash cans in her yard."

"Back doorbell?"

He tapped his phone and displayed a short video. "No. Inexpensive anti-burglar motion sensor with video relay, but it's also a doorbell when mounted by front doors."

"Technology." Mia shook her head as she rose from her seat and extended her hand. "Thank you for pushing our dialog past the awkward beginning."

He stood and accepted her hand. "Thanks for rethinking your approach."

"You deserve the explanation, Chief. Does our release involve any further action on our part?"

"Not if you're done in Fallwater." His brow rose. "Are you?"

"We have no current additional plans, but most likely, we're not. What was taken and how it was taken, are a grave concern."

He stepped toward his office door. "Is it too much to ask you to keep me informed?"

"No. It's a very fair request."

"Your wish that I keep your situation private, is also a fair request." He extended his hand as they approached the exit. "Thank you for serving our country."

"It's reassuring when I discover, I'm serving people like you."

He smiled. "Even when we disagree?"

She hesitated before walking through the building's vestibule and entrance doors as Griz held them open. "That's exactly what makes this place, and the people in it, worth serving. I put my life on the line, for our ability to peacefully disagree and coexist."

Mia tapped the captain's arm as they walked from the building. "Seventy minutes to the office?"

He swiped his phone and displayed the paused stopwatch. "Seventy-four."

"Are the car and crew still in the alley garage, and snipers still in place?"

"I believe so, but I'll confirm."

"Confirm, then release in ninety minutes, with twenty-minute temp hold intervals if there's still a police presence."

"With pleasure, Major."

"No activity until the target is down, then I want an extraction so fast, police on the next street aren't in time to intervene."

"Yes, Ma'am."

She walked to the loaded military bus as Griz turned toward the SUV. The bus door opened and she immediately yelled, "At ease." before stepping inside.

She entered and faced the team. "Nice try ladies and gentlemen. You did nothing wrong. There is new technology available, that we didn't account for, and we'll need to update our systems accordingly."

A soldier's hand rose.

The major's eyes met his camouflaged face. "Yes?"

"What did we miss, Ma'am?"

"A motion-activated doorbell sensor, connected to the owner's phone."

Another hand raised. "Was the bait released, Ma'am?"

She looked at her watch. "Contingent countdown has been re-initiated." She turned to the driver. "Take our team home."

"Yes, ma'am."

She watched the bus drive away before entering the SUV, then sat quietly until they exited the lot. "Six, Tangent?"

"That's what he said."

"The actual address?"

"Two forty-three Tangent. The report should be on your desk by the time we get back."

"Request the doorbell company's records."

"Already in process."

~ * ~

Ben raised his hood after stepping from the school building and into the cool steady drizzle, then ran to catch up to Kye, Jamie, and Faith. "Did you call *P* yet?"

Faith continued walking. "I'm not getting my phone wet."

"Wait. I'll call on my other phone."

Kye glanced at Ben's calf. "It's for emergencies."

"This may be an emergency." Ben removed the hidden phone from his sock. "Besides, they can't trace this one."

Jaime slipped her arm inside his as they walked. "Our leader is right."

Faith waved a finger. "He isn't our leader anymore. That mission is over."

"Well, I vote for him to be the permanent leader of the invisibles."

"It's spelled with a Z. You know that, don't you?"

"You've been agreeing with everything he says lately." Kye pointed to her arm in Ben's. "And what's with that?! Are you two secretly dating or something?"

"No. We just became better friends since we play soccer together."

"And she's my hero."

"You're pathetic." Faith moved her pointed finger to Jaime. "And you better knock it off."

"What do you mean, he's pathetic …and so what if I like him?"

Kye leaned back and stared at the drizzling sky. "I will laugh my ass off!"

"Then I'm going to start liking him." Faith slid her arm under Kye's.

"Wait! I'm her punishment?"

"You're everyone's punishment." Jaime sneered at him.

He sneered back. "And you're a riot."

Ben's voice softened. "Can I make a suggestion, not as the leader?"

"No."

Jaime tapped Faith's calf with her foot. "Stop messing with him or I'm dating him when he gets older."

Faith turned. "And you won't date him …ever… if I stop picking on him?"

"I can't make that promise." She wrapped her other arm around Ben's and glanced at him with a smile.

Kye pointed. "I knew it! I know he likes you, but you like him too?!"

Faith stared at her brother as she spun Kye around. "You told him you like her?"

Ben straightened. "He told me he's liked you since fourth grade, and he thinks you're gorgeous now!"

She smiled at Kye. "You think I'm gorgeous?"

Kye placed his free hand on his head. "Bro! That was a secret!"

"You said I liked her first. I told you, I go down, we both go down."

"Yeah, but damn!"

"Guess what, brainiacs. We already knew."

Kye wiggled his hips as he taunted. "But we didn't know about your secret love for him!"

Jaime fought her smirk and glanced at Faith. "This is all your fault."

Her eyes widened. "I'm the only one who didn't do anything."

Ben wiped the rain off the edge of his hoodie. "You said I couldn't be the leader."

"Well, now I'm positive you can't."

"Why?"

"Because I said."

Kye glanced at her. "So …what …are you the leader?"

"I'd be a better leader than him."

Kye laughed. "Doubtful."

Ben nodded. "She could be, as long as we're on the ground and it's daytime." He turned to her and grinned. "Who leads if there's a ladder or it's dark out?"

"Or bugs." Kye mock-shivered. "Don't forget…they give her the heebie-jeebies."

"Ugh!"

Jaime turned Ben toward his garage door. "Are we going in and calling Becca?"

"Of course."

She felt her hair as she glanced at Faith. "I have to use your hairdryer."

"After me. I'm mad at you."

The sisters walked into Ben's room after drying their hair, and Kye looked up from his open computer as he sat on the floor. "Do you both like red begonias? We're planning a double wedding. It'll be cheaper."

Ben leaned back on an elbow. "Oh my god! Your name would be Faith Ferguson!"

"Shut up, twerp."

"Faith Ferguson." Jaime chuckled as she shook her head.

Ben moved his computer and sat up. "Okay …I'm not the leader, but I'm calling *P* on the other phone." He removed it from his sock. "Agreed?"

"Whatever you say …leader."

Faith stared at Jaime. "I'll quit this damn team."

Kye nudged him and whispered. "Just text her, in case she's working."

Jaime sneered at her. "No you're not. You're a lifetime blood member, and there's nothing you can do about it."

Ben began typing.

"Then I'm asking the superhero board for more money."

"Why? They make all superheroes, gazillionaires with high-rise penthouses."

Ben shook his head at Kye as he continued keying the message. "Not accurate. You only get a high-rise penthouse if your dad was already a world-famous scientist."

Jaime pointed to him. "You get one if you're the son of the king of a different planet."

Ben raised his phone, "The text is sent." then shook his head. "Only on that planet. But if you're just an ex-soldier, you're living in a one-bedroom apartment, on a soldier's pension."

"Or on welfare if you're a foreign superhero with no regular job."

Ben tapped Kye's calf as they laid on the carpet. "She could teach martial arts on the side."

Faith frowned. "Wonderful. We're going to be broke, and hope for side jobs?"

"Or you could be a lawyer."

Faith raised a finger. "A broke lawyer."

Jaime sighed. "A cute broke lawyer."

Kye stopped typing. "That's because he helps clients who don't have any money. He's a *good guy superhero*."

Jaime nudged her. "Not that broke. He was in two TV series."

"Cancelled TV series."

Kye tapped his keypad. "The best canceled TV series ever."

"The superheroes who make movies must do decent."

"Only if they pretend to be other characters in other movies." Ben's secret phone lit and he read the message. "Guys. She's going to text *A* and *C*."

"What did you tell her?"

"That something happened in our back alley today while we were at school, and we're worried about *T*." He nudged Kye with his foot. "Want to get *Izzy* and take a look?"

"Are you inventing a different language, a word at a time?"

He grinned at Jaime. "Necessity is the uncle of invention."

Faith leaned off the bed and smacked his shoulder. "Mother, idiot."

"The uncle's mother?" Kye grinned at her. "That would make necessity the great aunt of invention."

"And what's spelled with a *Z*?"

"The invizibles ...our name?" Ben smiled at Jaime as he opened his computer. "Instead of an *S* ...it has a *Z* in the middle."

"Since when?"

"Since before we did our first mission." Kye frowned at her. "You really need to pay attention."

"And who decided that?"

"The old leadership." Ben smiled at Faith. "Wanna see the symbol?" He searched his phone, for the picture they drew.

"We have a symbol?" Jaime's eyes widened.

"Of course we have a symbol." Kye grinned. "Even Superman would look stupid without a symbol on his pajamas."

"I had Superman color pajamas when I was little." Ben passed her the phone after opening the picture.

Kye pointed. "But no *S*, and that's another reason why we have a *Z*. The *S* is already taken."

Faith leaned against Jaime and stared at the symbol. "What's the rest of the stuff?"

"It's one of the symbols from under the ship." Ben studied the pic. "Don't you remember?"

"I never looked. I was too busy worrying about hiding the thing."

Kye moved next to him. "Well, there it is ...one of the symbols, anyway."

"I don't remember it either." Jaime frowned. "I still can't believe we never took pictures."

"Tell me about it." Ben stood and removed his gel bag from his pocket. "Are we looking out back?"

"Are the four of you up there?"

Ben opened the door. "Yeah, Mom!"

"Who's eating here?"

"Can they both stay?"

"If they get permission."

Faith's voice softened as she glanced at Jaime. "Do you want to eat here?"

"Yeah, but do you want us to?"

Faith's gaze widened. "Why wouldn't I?"

"You said you were mad at me."

"I'm over that. Are you?"

Jaime extended her arms. "You know I am."

Kye leaned back on both elbows as he rested on the carpet, and shook his head. "Girls are strange."

Jaime turned her head as they hugged. "Yet both of you love us."

~ * ~

"Rocks-one. Report."

"All clear, team leader."

"Crow?"

"Sightline clear."

"Rocks-two."

"Silent and all clear."

"We're a go, people. Live in three minutes."

An SUV turned into the alley and stopped by the confiscated garage, and the operative stepped from the vehicle wearing a high school jacket, jeans, and a baseball cap. He opened the back hatch and removed a nylon sports bag without shutting the back passenger door as a young woman waited in the driver seat. The man shut the back hatch and passenger door, then tapped the side of the SUV. "Thanks for the ride."

She waved and drove off.

"Alley teams report. Do you have visual of the bait?"

"Rocks-one. Affirmative."

"Rocks-two. Negative."

"Crow's Nest. Unobstructed."

The fifth half-hour update broke the major's concentration, and she read the message. *Still live. No engagement.*

She refocused on her computer as the secret phone in her possession lit, and she inhaled before opening the message.

Hi. Visiting again?

Mia tabbed to a computer program and typed an instant message. *TRACE MY TEXT CONNECTION. START TRIANGULATION IN ALLEY BETWEEN SEGMENT AND TANGENT IN FALLWATER*

She pressed reply on the secret phone. *Thank you for sharing your proximity.*

We both know where you think I am or you wouldn't be here

Mia smiled as she typed. *It's only a matter of time before we find you*

And you've given me a reason to leave but I don't trust you to leave the angels alone.

She read the text, then continued concentrating on her computer. Minutes later, the phone beeped with another message.

What will it take to end your interest in Fallwater?

Mia lifted the phone and pressed keys. *Your capture*

Your failure to reply 1 sentence earlier says differently.

She finished analyzing her laptop screen before pressing phone keys. *It's just a matter of time*

...before you continue a war you can't win?

She stared at the reply, then typed. *Every war starts with both sides believing they'll win*

The phone lit its response. *But I've already displayed abilities you can't stop or defend*

Mia concentrated as she typed. *And we have abilities we haven't displayed*

Can't you see how it is best if we don't share additional abilities?

You destroyed some things you need to answer for

If that was how war worked ..it would never end

She exhaled. *It's the way terrorism works*

We both know the word is nothing more than a convenient pretext. I abused buildings and cars. Your side abused living intelligent beings. I react. You initiate. Do you care to measure the differences?

Soldiers don't measure

...and 2 sides fighting is war and we declared peace. Do I assume your breach of terms has already answered the question of our re-engagement?

Her computer displayed an instant message pop-up. *Five or six more texts, Major.*

She rested both forearms on the desktop and pressed keys. *...so where do we go from here?*

...why don't you finish your four active wars, and come and visit when they're done

Your unique talents would help us finish our current conflicts. Please share your skills

Then what would you do with all your soldiers

A rather cynical perspective I'd be glad to prove inaccurate. Share your abilities and help us end a few.

You already have that power but I can't give you the intelligence to use it

Mia smiled as she typed. *And you have the power to end our presence in Fallwater*

Your pretense makes that a lie. We both know you're not after people.

Our motives aren't secret but we're leaving the four teenagers' houses alone ...would you like us to reconsider that option?

Common sense would say they're also aware... and your prize is not there.

Mia placed the phone down and typed on her keyboard, *Do we have definitive coordinates?* then pressed phone keys. *But we're eventually going to need confirmation*

...and invite consequences

The price of war

Then why don't you try peace?

Her message program lit. *A few more, Major.*

Mia's breathing increased as she typed. *We are very interested in peace, and you have a tool we would like to incorporate to promote peace*

The phone lit in her hand. *I've been a tolerant teacher, but your pursuit triggers my belief- you will need lessons repeated.*

Mia stared at the phone as she keyed the reply. *Is this conversation finished?*

Are you finished triangulating?

She tabbed to the instant message program, then pressed phone keys. *Yes*

Then we're done

She lowered the phone and typed an instant message. *Do you have it?*

The pop-up appeared instantly. *Yes*

Address?

Not an address, Major. A utility pole on Third Avenue, facing the alley.

How accurate?

Two to three meters

263

She placed both elbows on the desktop before lowering her head into her hands.

What action do we take, Major?

She typed, *None* then tabbed to a different message. *How long can the snipers stay in place?*

The rock piles can remain indefinitely, Major.

How is service set up?

School district maintenance vehicle and special groundskeepers

Bring crow's nest down. Let's pretend we're done, and service the rocks locations indefinitely until further notice

~ * ~

Aidan entered his six-digit code and opened the glass door, then walked between the mass of computers and electronic equipment surrounding the center of the tech lab. "Hello, ladies and gentlemen."

"Hello again, General. How are you this fine morning?"

Aidan glanced at his watch. "Is it morning outside? It's been a while since I saw a sunrise."

A technician glanced at him while typing. "It's just an inside joke, General."

Another tech turned from his computer. "We like to scramble the computer clocks and make up our own time since we're nine stories down."

"Then we have an office pool for most accurate."

The team leader spun in his seat and smiled. "What can we do for you, sir?"

"The Toy-Gel team is thinking, if the four untraceables had phones and were communicating while undetectable, then communication is possible when stealth, and if a signal can be received when stealth, then it may be possible for our soldier to send an otherwise untraceable sensor signal so we can track him."

"Interesting thought." The technician looked up after jotting the note. "It's good to hear your plans are proceeding. Have you identified the soldiers?"

"The finalists are going through psychological evaluation, but we've named them. The stealth operative will be called Narmer, and the support operative will be Sobekkare, or Sobe` for short."

A technician turned from her workstation. "You're digging up the long-dead."

Aidan smiled. "You know the names?"

"Of course, General? We know who we work for."

The tech leader shrugged. "After all …the new greatest house *is* nicknamed after the old greatest house, spelling notwithstanding."

Another technician chuckled. "…is there a greater ancient or current house?"

Aidan grinned. "I'm impressed."

"If you weren't, we wouldn't be in the current version."

"So what would you like us to do for you?"

"I want you to build subcutaneous sensors for our two pharaohs, with a continuous untraceable signal to individual designated off-grid computers. And I want Sobe` to have an additional ankle sensor that will signal him where Narmer is …direction and distance."

"Subcutaneous?"

"Not Sobe`'s. Make it inconspicuous, but both global signals will have to be implants. There's no other way to guarantee our unbroken connection, especially in a worst-case scenario."

"Program orientation?"

"Magnifying map-based. Continual unbreakable signal. Off-line, worldwide military global positioning."

Multiple techs began typing.

"We can hide the signal in plain sight. You're talking about a glorified telephone connection."

"With a call block on every other phone in the world."

Aidan followed the conversation as it crossed the room.

"Send and receive."

"Default, muted. But with emergency communication ability."

"Silent ability."

"Morse code."

"An oldie but goodie."

"Will the pharaohs be aware of their tracking devices?"

Aidan scanned the circle of technicians. "Both will only know Sobe`'s ability to track Narmer."

A technician chuckled as she typed. "Like every woman wishes she could."

"Don't tell the second pharaoh he's named after a woman."

"A pretty damn impressive one for our time and place, let alone hers."

"There are no signs they were less advanced socially, then we are right now."

The lead tech walked to a clutter-covered whiteboard. "Authorization code, General?"

"Indigo seven four zero one eight three."

He uncapped a marker and wrote the number under a list of existing numbers. "And our timeframe?"

"Undetermined. Can you project a rough lead time?"

"I'll contact engineering to make sure their timeline is concurrent, and if it is, it's doable within a three week period. We can add what material we'll need to the next requisition list, so overall, you're looking at a four or five week window."

Aidan rose from the metal folding chair. "Then we're well within projected operating parameters."

The tech capped his marker. "Consider your request scheduled. You're on our current tasks list in the order received, unless you share an approved, adjusted timeline."

"Thank you, ladies and gentlemen."

"You're welcome General, but understand, this is not our forte. This is very doable, and we only specialize in the impossible."

Chapter Twelve
Mortal Demigods

Ben knocked on Faith's bedroom door, and she opened it a few inches. "Hello interior decorator. Sorry. I don't need anything decorated."

"At least I have some school spirit."

"Hallway decorating?"

"It was just outside Mr. Linwold's room and it was for extra credit." He shrugged. "Besides, it was fun."

She closed the door slightly. "What do you want?"

"It's been a whole day since we heard back from Aunt Kitt and I'm worried about Karma."

"And I just want a day off from my new job."

"Can the four of us talk about it?"

She leaned against the doorjamb. "Didn't we talk enough yesterday?"

"Yeah, but we didn't solve anything."

"Oh, let them in."

She huffed. "Is Kye here?"

"Yeah. He's in my room."

Jaime called from behind the door. "They can come in."

Faith frowned as she swung the door open. "Go get Kye."

They returned with their backpacks and Ben sat on the floor as Jaime spun on the bed and faced him. "Don't look so bummed."

"Aunt Kitt should have texted by now. I hate when people don't text back."

"Maybe she's waiting for *A* to text her."

"What if *T* is captured?"

Kye grinned. "I know a team of superheroes that'll rescue her."

Faith covered her face with her hands. "Oh god, I don't want to have to rescue anything else this year."

Jaime's voice softened. "We may have to rescue things for the rest of our lives."

"We need to be able to contact Karma directly." Ben lifted his secret phone, then dropped it as it beeped in his hands.

Kye chuckled. "That was classic!"

Faith leaned over the edge of the bed. "Is it Aunt Kitt?"

He opened the text. "Yeah. She said she hasn't been able to reach them."

Jaime frowned. "So we have no way of finding out and no way of contacting Karma?"

Kye tossed a stuffed frog in the air. "This is BS."

Ben raised a fist and used his deepest cartoon voice. "This sounds like a job for the Invizibles!"

Faith watched her toy repeatedly rise and drop. "You're just dying to use the gel, aren't you."

Ben raised his eyebrows and shook his head. "No. I'm dying to work as a team again."

"So you can be the leader?"

"So we can get along and not be mad at each other. Nothing we did bothered us when we were on our mission. We all had the same weirdness, but instead of making fun of each other or being frustrated …we got along and accepted each other." He frowned. "I don't care who the leader is. I just want to have what we had before."

"Aww …that's so beautiful. Someone get me a tissue." Kye shoved him.

He raised his arm. "I vote for Faith to be the leader."

Jaime sneered. "Nah."

Faith gasped, then grabbed her pillow and started hitting her. "You're supposed to be my best friend!"

"I am! I am!" Jaime giggled as she defended herself. "But did you hear the speech he just gave? He's the leader."

Faith hugged her pillow and frowned.

Ben watched her. "She can be the leader."

Kye swung his arm toward him. "No she can't."

She stuck her tongue out at Kye before facing her brother. "So what does the leader suggest we do?"

He glanced at Jaime and Kye. "What's everybody think?"

"Some leader." She shoved Jaime with her foot.

He leaned against the dresser. "Should we go to the Air Force base and try to find out what the military is doing?"

"That's a long ride, considering we don't have the slightest idea where to go or what to look for once we're inside." Jaime sat up. "And we don't even know if they were part of the police thing yesterday."

Kye tossed the frog on the bed. "Should we stop at Field Op's and talk to *A* and *C*?"

"We should camp out there again! It'll bring back great memories."

Faith's eyes narrowed as she stared at her brother. "You think our time there is great memories?"

He glanced at Jaime and Kye. "Well …yeah. Don't all of you?"

"God, you're strange."

Jaime nudged her. "And why he's the leader, and you can't be."

Faith smacked Jaime's arm. "How we gonna get there?"

"You drive."

"We can't borrow mom's car, overnight."

"Let's call a new-age cab."

"You mean where you get in a stranger's car and he hopefully drives you where you want?" Faith shivered.

"Our next leader, ladies and gentlemen." Kye held his arm out.

Faith hugged her stuffed unicorn. "You better all stop abusing me."

Kye grinned. "But you always hurt the one you love and we're just showing you how much we love you."

"Cab driver could be a superhero side job." Ben smiled.

Kye gasped and covered his mouth. "Our cab driver may be a superhero?"

Jaime hugged a pillow and rocked on the bed. "Guys …what are we doing?"

"Why don't one of us get invisible and check out back. See if any idiots are back there again, or better yet …maybe Karma will appear and let us know she's alright, or talk to us or something." Ben glanced at each in turn. "Anybody think that's a good place to start?"

Faith sneered. "It's as good as any."

Ben eyed Jaime and Kye. "Agreed?"

"Sure …after we make sure there's not an invisible soldier out there."

"Volunteers?"

Faith glared at Ben. "Please don't."

"But…"

Kye closed his computer. "I'll do it this time."

Jaime shook her head. "I think it should be me."

"Why?"

"Because if Karma comes out, I don't want you handling our introduction."

"Are you kidding? I'm getting on my knees and worshipping her."

Faith sat up. "And that's the reason I vote for Jaime."

"You're just jealous Karma's a god and you're a mere mortal."

"Yeah …that's my concern." Faith raised a finger. "And for the record, I'm not driving a cab."

Kye stood as he slid his computer into his backpack. "Okay, we'll let you have first pick of what side job you want." He looked around. "Where are we doing this?"

"Are we doing this now? Mom's downstairs."

Jaime gestured toward the door as she stood. "Then let's go over our house and do it from there."

Faith slid to the edge of her bed and slipped into her shoes. "Are the rest of us watching from upstairs?"

"The tree and back garage stops us from keeping an eye on her." Ben zipped his backpack. "Someone has to be in the back yard."

"And whoever is upstairs has to be invisible, so we can see her, and anyone else invisible." Kye swung his backpack over his shoulder as he stood.

Jaime led them from the room. "And everyone on the phone, agreed?"

"Sure."

They exited the house from the sliding glass door, and walked along the alley. Kye spun slowly and scanned the pathway as they strolled between the houses. "Everything looks normal to me."

"Let's make sure no one's lying in the alley, invisible."

"If they spotted her and did something, they probably took her away."

Faith turned to the others. "Then we really don't have to get invisible, do we?"

"Not really since we can look for an invisible soldier from the window."

"And we'll check the alley for anything else incase that isn't what it was." Ben turned to Kye. "Wanna ride bikes and scout the area?"

"Sure. Meet you around front."

Ben spun and sprinted toward his back gate as Kye jogged to their sliding glass door.

Jaime stopped at her back fence gate and faced Faith. "Feel like strolling the alley with me?"

"Nah. There's nothing here and it gives me the creeps, lately. Besides, I have a five-hundred word essay due tomorrow, and I need to write the last four-hundred and fifty."

Jaime chuckled. "Okay. Good luck with that. See you tomorrow."

Captain Griziani knocked on the major's open office door. "We have a deviation at the Fallwater stakeout."

Mia turned from her monitor after clicking the computer mouse. "Captain, Lieutenant …come in."

Lieutenant Jeffries pointed to her computer. "It's on our network, under Foxtrot, Alpha, Lima, one three seven one."

"What's going on?"

"Rocks-one sniper base has the four original targets walking alone in the alley …and we were wondering…"

She laid her hand on the desktop and grinned. "Here we are, fishing with artificial bait, and real bate comes along, ready to be hooked."

"That's what we were thinking, Major."

"Are we ready to strike and run?"

"The striker is waiting for permission."

"Understand, whoever we take is a minor and gets treated like an esteemed guest, for their duration here."

"Understood."

"Do you have a plan?"

"Yes." Griziani leaned against the office table. "We leave their phone and shoe at the site, then wait to see if a target finds and identifies the items. If they don't, we notify with an anonymous call. Once they're informed, we wait for their communications to reach our prize. She found them before. There's no reason she won't find them again."

"Let me send a message, then we'll turn the game on while we wait for permission." She typed an instant message, then accessed the secured communications channel and raised the volume.

"Targets Bravo and Delta turned north toward their dwellings. …They're no longer visible. Target Alpha is on foot, at point zero plus four, west. Range two hundred and eighty yards, moving east, and closing. Target Charlie at point zero plus five, west. Range three hundred and ten yards and holding."

"Copy, rocks-one. Mobile one?"

"Mobile one is loaded and covered. Awaiting permission."

"Copy."

Mia studied the computer monitor. "What's he mean, Lieutenant?"

"Point zero is the lot where our prize was found. He's counting plus or minus residences from that point. Zero plus five is residence two. Closing means target Alpha is walking toward him. Holding means target Charlie is stationary. Sniper position is east, so all sight demarcations will be west." He pointed to the monitor. "Mobile one is our SUV. Covered means it's in the closed garage."

Mia glanced from the screen. "Do you know the names of the target letters?"

"Alpha and Bravo are Faith and Ben McCloud. Charlie is Jaime Ferguson. Delta is the brother Kyle"

"Authorization communication has been acknowledged. Awaiting permission."

"Rocks-one. Copy, team leader. All is clear, awaiting authorization."

"On my mark, we will work at T minus eleven seconds. Dart release at T minus eight. Mobile one will uncover, then enter the alley eastbound at T minus five."

"Copy, team leader."

"Do not harm the bait. She is not our target. Repeat. She is *not* our target. Her phone and right shoe get left behind. Place them visible but away from harm."

"Copy, team leader."

"Target pinpoint?"

"Upper right thigh"

"Feed us running audio, rocks-one."

"Roger. Target Alpha approaching point zero, west. Range one hundred fifty yards and closing. Target Charlie's position unchanged. ...Target Alpha at point zero, heading north toward residence. Four seconds till sightline lost. ...Target Charlie, now last visible target. North edge of alley, retreating west on foot, from point zero plus five. Range three-hundred and twenty yards."

Major Madison's IM beeped and she tabbed to the program. "We have authorization. Repeat, we have authorization."

Lieutenant Jeffries typed on his laptop as the captain raised his phone to his ear. "We are *go*, team leader. Repeat, we are live."

"Target is texting. Distance, three-hundred and thirty yards."

"Authorization received. We're are *go* minus eleven seconds, mark now."

"Mobile one uncovering."

"Rocks-one. Sightline unobstructed. ...Dart released."

"Dart extraction and antidote first. Check for head contusion and possible bleeding."

"Mobile one exiting."

"...Target hit. Side collapse."

"Mobile one has visual. Two seconds to load."

"Move! Move!" Doors opened as the SUV came to a halt and three jump-suited operatives quickly exited. The first removed the dart and checked for head trauma as the second administered the antidote, while the third agent slipped Jaime's sandal off and laid it near her phone.

The second agent circled the vehicle and entered the back seat as the others slid the limp body next to her. Doors closed seconds later, and the SUV proceeded to the Second Avenue alley exit.

"We have a clean extraction, command. ETA one hour and twenty minutes."

Ben stopped pedaling as his vibrating phone caught his attention, and he read Jaime's text. *Why is the alley so dingy? I don't like it back here*

He typed as he rode with no hands. *Because it isnt as pretty as the street*

He stopped with his bike between his legs and keyed a second message. *We'll come around and keep you company*

He circled toward Kye, "Jaime's searching the alley by herself." then stood on his bike pedals and raced ahead.

"Man, you two are getting way too friendly." Kye stood on his pedals and sped up.

He looked back. "This ain't about that."

"Dude …everything is about that."

"Guys and girls can be friends too."

Kye waited until Ben reappeared after turning the corner. "That's about the dumbest thing you ever said. Friends with my sister? Have you met her?"

Ben pulled his bike handles and launched a few inches as he rode over the sidewalk apron, then coasted as he eyed the alley. He stopped and stood with the bike between his legs, then swiped the phone face and typed. *Where are you?*

He stared at the phone and waited for her response, then lowered it. "Jaime!"

Kye rode forward. "Jaime!"

"Jaime!" Ben sped past him and raced along the alley. "This ain't funny!"

Kye caught up and watched him text. "What the hell is happening?"

"I don't know, but this is bullshit."

Kye pointed. "Jesus, is that her sandal?"

Ben glanced twice before circling on his bike and racing to the shoe, then jumped off and it scraped to a stop. "Her phone!"

"You've got to be kidding."

Ben inhaled, then spun in a circle as he scanned the area. "Somebody's kidding but it ain't funny."

"Do you think she's in one of these houses?" Kye stepped off his bike and hopped over the adjoining fence. "Check around. Make sure she's not laying anywhere."

"Jaime!" Ben hopped the next fence and sprinted to the corner of the house as he searched frantically. "Jaime!"

Kye opened a shed, then turned after searching. "We need Faith."

"We need the cops."

Kye sighed. "We need Karma."

Ben lifted his pant leg. "Time to call everybody." He dialed, then held the phone to his ear as he continued searching. "Aunt Kitt! Help! We think Jaime's been kidnapped!"

He listened. "Only you so far. We want to know if the military took her. ...I don't know, but please keep trying and call us when he answers."

Major Madison's computer speakers interrupted her office silence. "Rocks-one reporting at extraction plus fifteen minutes. Target Charlie's phone and sandal discovered by targets Bravo and Delta. They are now north of the alley, searching yard zero plus seven. Sightline sporadic."

"Roger, rocks-one. Continue interval updates. Mobile one report."

"En route to home base. *T* minus one hour. Target dart removed and antidote administered. Bait is unconscious and resting comfortably. No head contusions. No bleeding."

"Your arrival is already cleared, and our subject goes straight to the infirmary."

"Roger, team leader."

Mia leaned back and exhaled. "Time to discuss what we're doing with the bait, and how we catch any fish it attracts."

"How do we catch her? We haven't found a detection process. She could be standing in this room, for all we know."

She eyed the lieutenant. "I have an idea how to expose her. Did we house the remaining diatomaceous earth from the Fallwater event, on base?"

"I believe so, Major."

"Find out, and then tell base command we need a *C*-one-thirty *T-O-A-L* training exercise, during the next twenty-four hours."

"Sure, Major. What are you thinking?"

"We deploy the same method we used to discover the Fallwater ship." She turned from her computer and nodded softly. "But we use a more thorough and overwhelming delivery system."

"Are we working out the specifics?"

A knock on her doorframe diverted their attention, and she smiled. "Captain Harris."

"Hello, Major."

"Welcome back." She stood and extended her hand.

Griz stood. "Good to see you, Cowboy."

"Thanks. It's good to be back." He shook Lieutenant Jeffries' extended hand. "I understand you're discussing my last field-agent assignment. Mind if I resume participation?"

"It'd be our pleasure, Captain." She pressed two phone buttons. "Cancel all calls until further notice, but notify me by *IM*, after each call."

"Yes, ma'am."

Jeffries stared at his computer. "Base command would like to discuss your request for *C*-one-thirty takeoff and landing drills."

Mia tabbed to an open computer program and began typing. Her computer blinked moments later and she read the reply. "We have permission to run a full base emergency exercise over the next twenty-four hours, including *T-O-A-L* training with four C-one-thirties on rotation. Base command is notifying all personnel." She opened a file, then adjusted a notepad. "Do we have Hercules in-flight dispersal systems, on base?"

"Always, Major."

"Griz, have engineering fit each participating Hercules with a particulate dispersal system, then load each plane with twenty yards of diatomaceous earth, and I want continuous contact with each flight crew. Flight paths will be coordinated over the base's main roads, and if ordered, those roads and surrounding areas are to be dusted."

"Understood Major. I'll set up a quick pilot briefing."

"Lieutenant, coordinate with munitions through base command. Sniper training will commence immediately. Focus on all command buildings along the main streets. Same ammunition as utilized in our Fallwater event, today. Anything suddenly appearing after being stealth, gets put to sleep."

"Understood, Major."

She placed her elbows on the table and rested her chin on her closed fists. "You know what we're looking for, and expecting. Any sign of rustling, or any unnatural noise gets reported. Our fish is stealth, and we're going to have to be on our *A* game to hook her."

"Or she does what she did in Tancil."

"What are we hunting, Major?"

"A teacher." She smiled at Cowboy. "Help Griz and Jeffries coordinate, until you're re-acclimated." She closed her file folder and placed her pen on it. "I expect full operations mode within twenty minutes."

"What do we do with the bait, Major?"

She rubbed her hands together. "I'll take care of her. ...Dismissed."

"Nothing!" Ben hopped the next fence and continued his frantic search. "There's no sign of her!"

Kye rubbed his face as he walked to the fence separating their neighbor's yard and the alley. "Does her phone say anything?"

Faith shook her head. "Ben received the last message."

"Nothing open or saved in drafts?"

"No."

He watched Ben, two yards away. "She ain't back here."

"I'm not giving up until I check every yard." Ben darted around every nook, frantically searching.

"I know you want to find her, but we gotta work smart, instead of hard."

"No! I gotta find her or I'm gonna..." He fell to his knees and slumped over, and Kye jumped the two fences, then lifted him and hugged him. "I get it. I want to find her as bad as you."

He wiped his eyes. "I know. But what are we gonna do?"

"Exactly what we did the last time." Kye placed his hand on Ben's shoulder and stared into his eyes. "Whatever it takes."

They walked to Faith after climbing the fence, and she displayed her phone as Jaime's sandal dangled from her finger. "Becca is still trying to reach *C*."

"*G* has *A*'s number!"

"Shh!"

"He does! I forgot all about that." Faith swiped her phone open.

Kye placed his hand over it and whispered. "Not here. I don't trust that ears aren't listening."

Faith's eyes darted around the area. "Where then?"

Ben's voice softened. "Are we telling our parents yet?"

"No."

Ben pointed. "Your construction garage."

They ran inside and locked the door, before Faith dialed.

"Hello?"

"Uncle Steve!" She listened. "Not good. I'm putting you on speaker."

"What's going on?"

"We need help. Jaime is nowhere around and we think she's been kidnapped."

"How sure are you?"

"She was in our back alley, texting Ben, and when he and Kye came around on their bikes, all they found was her sandal and phone."

"That ain't good."

"Something happened in the alley earlier today. Our school was on lock-down and our phone alerts said it was police activity."

"Do you think it's our old friends?"

"Can you call Mitch and ask, please? Aunt Becca hasn't been able to reach Charlie."

"Sure. Did you tell your parents yet?"

"No."

"I think you should tell them. This is serious."

"I don't want to tell them. They're gonna freak!"

Kye faced the phone in Faith's hand. "I know. We can buy a little time by telling them we're over each other's houses."

"No. With kidnapping, the quicker we act, the better. Call the police. In the meantime, I'll try to get ahold of Mitch, Becca, and Charlie. Act now! No delay. Call and meet them, and explain everything."

Ben's brows rose. "Everything?"

"No. Absolutely not. Just everything about the kidnapping."

He stared at the phone and nodded. "Okay we will."

"Becca and I are coming over, and I'll call you back as soon as I can."

"Thank you for helping us."

"Don't ever doubt my help. That is always a given. Call the cops and I'll call you right back."

Faith ended the call, then eyed Kye. "Do you want me to call or are you?"

"It sounds more terrible coming from a girl."

"It's terrible either way."

Kye glanced at Ben and frowned, then eyed Faith. "You do it?"

She pressed three buttons and the speaker.

"Nine one one dispatch."

"We have a kidnapping in the alley between Tangent and Segment Streets in Fallwater."

"How long has the person been missing?"

"About an hour."

"The reporting time for a missing person is twenty-four hours."

"Look …she was in the alley with me, then I left her and ten minutes later, her brother finds her phone and one of her sandals laying in the alley, and she's gone. Can you please send someone?"

"Resident address?"

"Two fifty-one Tangent. Jaime Ferguson is missing. I'm Faith McCloud here with her brother Kyle Ferguson and my brother Ben. Please hurry! We're in the alley."

They stared at Faith's phone as the dispatcher relayed the message. "We have a possible kidnapping. Two-hundred block alley between Tangent and Segment. Victim's name, Jaime Ferguson, two five one Tangent."

"Roger, dispatch."

"They're on their way, Ms. McCloud."

"Thank you."

The desk sergeant knocked before opening the office door. "Chief, we just got a dispatch call from a Faith McCloud, reporting a Jaime Ferguson kidnapping in the alley between Tangent and Segment."

He placed his elbows on his desk and rubbed his face. "That's all the major players directly related to the bullshit earlier today."

"What?"

"I want every available car there. Surround that alley and search everything."

"Are we calling the FBI?"

"I have a call to make first." He found the major's business card and dialed the number.

"Major Madison's office."

"Is she available? This is Fallwater Police Chief Joseph Craven."

"She is not in her office at the moment. May I leave a message?"

"Yes. This is an urgent call from Fallwater Police Chief Joseph Craven. Emphasize, urgent. She is now a person of extreme interest in a kidnapping and has twenty minutes to call me or I come with a crowd, looking for her."

"I don't know if she'll be back by then."

"And I'm sure you have the ability to share my message with her, wherever she is. I'm trying to be civil and give her the benefit of her title. In twenty minutes, I request an executable warrant for her arrest." He disconnected the call, then walked to the sergeant's desk. "I'm heading to the Segment, Tangent alley."

Faith led Kye and Ben to the back gate as the police cruiser's siren welped, and they met the officer as he exited his car. "Hi. Are you Faith McCloud?"

"Yes, sir. And this is my brother Ben, and Kye Ferguson. His sister is missing."

"What makes you think so?"

Sirens blared from all directions, and oscillating lights reflected off every exposed surface as police cruisers entered and surrounded the alley.

She raised Jaime's sandal and phone. "We found these in the alley, where we left her minutes earlier, and we can't find her."

"Can you show me exactly where?"

The screen door shutting caught Kye's attention as his mom appeared. "What's going on!?"

"I got her." Kye patted Ben's arm before darting toward her.

Ben watched him, then glanced at her concerned face and hesitated before following Faith and the officer.

"We were hanging together, then decided to split because I have an English essay to write." They heard Mrs. Ferguson shriek in pain and both wiped their eyes. Faith breathed deep, trying to compose herself. "And she told me she was going to take a walk before heading in." She stopped where Ben had originally pointed. "We found her sandal and phone about here."

"I found them. I was texting her, riding my bike with Kye out front, and told her we were coming around to keep her company." He pointed toward Third Avenue. "And by the time we rode around, she was gone. We found her stuff and started searching, and we yelled her name a bunch of times."

"Did you see any cars leave the alley?"

"No, sir."

"You entered the alley from Third Avenue?"

Ben pointed to the far entrance. "Yes, sir."

The officer smiled. "You can call me Derek."

"Thanks, Officer Derek."

A police cruiser crept to a stop and a silver-haired officer exited before walking toward them. "Hi."

"Hello, Chief."

"Is their claim legitimate?"

"Very."

Ben straightened. "Hi, sir."

He extended his hand. "I'm Chief Craven, and you are?"

"I'm Benjamin McCloud and this is my sister Faith."

He smiled reservedly. "It's nice to meet you both. I've heard wonderful things about you and your friends."

"How would you know us?"

"Do you know Bre Cassidy from school?"

"Yeah."

"Her father is one of my officers, and your adventures aren't as secret as you think."

Faith frowned. "Don't believe everything you hear, but believe one of us is missing and we really need your help."

"Do you trust me?"

"You're the police Chief. If we can't trust you, we're in trouble."

He patted Ben's shoulder. "I promise to earn that compliment, and we have to get to work …so I want you both to go home, but you're allowed to watch from your windows."

Faith hesitated. "Do you know about us and the military?"

"I do."

"Were they part of the raid that locked down our school today?"

"Yes. They said they were hunting a terrorist. Do you know about a terrorist?"

Ben shook his head as he stepped closer. "She ain't a terrorist. She saved our lives."

He eyed Ben. "So there's no terrorist?"

"No. Is that what they told you?"

"Did she do anything that would give them a reason to call her that?"

Ben frowned. "She blew up their cars, rescuing us, but she asked them to release us before she did it, and they refused."

Faith grabbed his arm and pulled him away. "Okay …let the man get to work"

"Thanks for the help, Ben. We're going to make some noise and do some shouting. Don't be alarmed."

He tapped Faith's arm as they turned toward their houses. "Are we going home or to Kye's?"

Faith grabbed his shirt sleeve, as she opened Jaime's back gate, and Ben glanced back as they heard a bullhorn.

"This is Chief Craven. Seal and secure this alley. No one in or out until we turn over every rock, and arrest everything that breaths." He opened his phone and redialed the major.

"Major Madison's office."

"It's police Chief Craven. Put me through."

"Yes, sir." He heard the beep.

"Hello, Chief."

"Major …however you answer this next question …it's going to disappoint me. Do you have our Fallwater kidnapping victim?"

"Yes we do, but she's just visiting for a few hours, and being treated like a dignitary."

"I need to hear how accommodating her host is, and how voluntary her visit is, from her please."

"She's being given a tour of the facility at the moment, but I'll have her call you as soon as possible."

He turned from the activity at the alley entrance. "Give me a rough time estimate."

"An hour and a half …maybe two?"

"That's absolutely unacceptable, Major. She needs to be on her way home within the next ten minutes."

"I'm sorry, but that isn't possible, Chief. We're in the middle of a base-wide emergency readiness exercise, and lockdown is part of the initial phase. Access on and off base is not permitted for the first hour."

He stood in the middle of the alley and rubbed his forehead. "Major, I don't know what authority you think you have…"

"Chief! We found something!"

He raised a hand toward the voice as he began walking. "…but I'd suggest giving that kid just about anything she wants to verify your lies, because your ass is mine if any of six people don't swear by what you've just told me. Meanwhile, have your military attorneys work on stopping me from arresting you on felony kidnapping charges."

Chief Craven drew his gun as the officer stood behind the stone pile, pointing hers. "One move and you visit God today!"

"We surrender. Don't shoot!"

Chief Craven heard the hidden voices as he ran closer. "What do we have?"

"Bodies in this stone pile."

"Are you part of the morning raid?"

"Yes, sir. Don't shoot?"

"Why didn't you surrender this morning?"

"Orders, sir."

"Are you armed?"

"Yes, sir, but the rifle is disassembled and inoperable."

"Are there men in the other rock pile?"

"Yes, sir. Don't shoot."

"Do you know if there are any other hidden bodies in or near this alley?"

"There are none, sir."

"Dig yourself out …now!" Chief Craven holstered his gun. "One stupid move and you get to receive the purple heart, but we can't promise it won't be posthumously." He pointed to the pile as he turned to the officer. "Charge them with domestic terrorism and kidnapping. I'm going to go tell the family, we've located Jaime." He walked to his cruiser and raised the bullhorn from the trunk. "Officers, our victim has been found safe and sound, and we know the perpetrators. Focus on finding any hidden bodies for the remainder of the search." He pressed his shoulder communicator.

"Sergeant, leave four officers in the alley to finish the search, and have the rest resume normal duties."

He walked through the back gate and knocked on the Fergusons' sliding glass door and Ben slid it open. "Hi, Chief Craven."

He nodded at everyone in the room, then removed his hat. "May I come in?"

"Please." Owen stepped forward with his hand extended. "I'm Jaime's father, Owen." He gestured around the room. "Jaime's mother Amanda, brother Kyle, Charlie, Steve, Becca, Cal, Taylor, Ben, and Faith."

"Hi everyone. I'm Chief Craven. We've located your daughter and she's fine. She is at the Air Force base with a Major Madison."

"Why would they take her?"

"I'm not sure, but I will be investigating, since I was told they're looking for someone completely different."

Amanda placed her hand over her heart. "Who?"

"Someone Ben told me helped you?"

"Karma?"

Chief Craven turned to Kye. "That's the name of the person they're looking for? Do you know her?"

"Well, not really." Faith glanced at Kye, then faced the officer. "That's what they told us she called herself when they talked to her."

"They, the military?"

"Yes, sir, but we never talked to her."

"But she's the one who helped you by blowing up cars?"

"Well, we don't really know for sure. It's just what the military lady told us."

Ben stepped forward. "Are they bringing Jaime back?"

"Yes, but there's a delay due to a base-wide emergency readiness exercise. But they insist she's fine and in good hands. I'll keep in touch with them, and inform you when she's on her way home."

Amanda stepped forward. "Thank you for finding her for us, and all your work."

"You're very welcome." Chief Craven smiled before exiting the sliding glass door.

Mia glanced twice at her office doorway as motion caught her eye. "Welcome. It's good to see you again."

"That shit ain't funny." Jaime limped into the office, holding her thigh. "You shot me?"

Mia's head tilted. "In our defense, only with a dart, but I'm sorry."

"Sorry for shooting me on purpose? …And why?"

Her gaze narrowed. "Don't worry. We're not interested in you."

Jaime limped around the office table. "I know who you're after. One of us isn't as dumb as the other."

"That's a little harsh, don't you think?"

"I don't know. I remember a promise, this wouldn't happen again, yet here I am." She winced as she rested against the edge of the table. "You could have made friends with some interesting people. Instead, you choose to make enemies?"

"We want your little secret, more than we want your friendship."

"And we told you we don't have it."

Mia shook her head. "We know better, and we're getting tired of asking for it."

"Better suggestion; if I were you, I'd put a really nice sum in my bank account, so I don't sell your prize to someone a little more worthy."

"You admit you have what we want?"

Jaime's brows rose. "No. We actually don't."

"Then why should we pay you?"

"For starters, so you don't go to jail for kidnapping."

Mia placed her folded hands on the desktop. "I'm not worried about that, but I don't believe you no longer have the prize, and I will tear your houses apart to confirm your ...honesty."

"Be careful making threats. Your predecessor lost that battle in the not so distant past."

"Scare tactics on an active duty military officer? Really?"

Jaime stopped her reply and smiled. "A million dollars in my bank account, before I talk to the FBI, or your headaches become personal."

"Now blackmail?"

Jaime's eyes narrowed. "Don't play holier than thou with me. You have a kidnapping felony pending ...of a minor no less, and society frowns on that. All I'm doing is trying to settle on the way to court. A philosophy a great teacher once encouraged. But understand his words ...on the way to court."

"Don't get so bent out of shape. You'll be home by bedtime."

Jaime folded her arms across her chest. "It's not me I'm concerned about."

"Who are you concerned about."

"Let's talk in court, shall we?"

Mia shook her head. "You won't win in court. We learn our lessons better than you think. Lesson one; get permission. Then I was told to inform you, we're a branch of the government, and we'll bury you so deep in legal fees, you'll end up broke and homeless. Oh, I forgot to mention. Rumor has it, your aunt and uncle's cars were recorded at the fast-food restaurant near one of our facilities, about the same time our shipment departed that facility, and then they're on surveillance video in a cargo ship parking lot, while our mutual prize was being readied for transport across the street. We seem to be equally unholy." Mia walked to the front of her desk and leaned against it. "So let's revisit the negotiations. Instead of giving you a million dollars to leave you alone, give us what we want or we readdress our main contention with you."

"Do you have a lighter, pencil, and a piece of paper?"

"For what?"

"You'll see."

Explosions suddenly diverted their attention, and they ran to the windows.

Mia smiled as she watched. "Looks like your teacher is back."

Jaime glanced at her after separating the window blinds. "I thought she was your teacher. She taught you more than she taught us." She watched the mangled cars burn. "It's a shame the lessons don't stick."

"It doesn't matter. She was what we hoped you would bring, and neither of you disappointed."

Jaime faced the window as they heard a second set of explosions. "You can't catch what you can't see."

"No we can't, but if you remember, we found a solution for the first invisible object." She raised the window blind. "Let's watch."

The roaring vibration rattled the building's windows as the massive *C*-one-thirty strafed so close, Jaime stepped back in fright, then she rushed to the window as a plume of white powder fell in its wake, making the outside look suddenly like winter. A body appeared out of nowhere as the fine white dust reached the surface, and Jaime shrieked as the distinct pop of a rifle sounded just before the figure collapsed to the ground.

"No!" Jaime placed both hands on the window as she stared at the prone figure being surrounded from all directions.

"Do yourself a favor and realize we're the military, with resources beyond your wildest imagination, and contrary to popular belief, intellectual might to match our physical prowess."

Jaime pressed both hands against her head after losing sight of the soldiers carrying the limp body, and turned as Mia lifted the phone receiver. "Call your parents and tell them you're on your way home."

She dialed the phone as Mia raised her cell and pressed keys. "Hello, Chief. Jaime is leaving as soon as she finishes her call with her parents."

"Mom!" She listened. "Yeah. I'm on my way. Tell them they captured the Teacher!"

Mia smiled as Jaime hung up. "Be careful of the action you take, regarding that bit of information. Any strange happenings connected to our mutual acquaintance will invite a less than welcoming revisit." She waved her hand toward the open office door. "Are you ready to leave?"

Jaime winced and grabbed her thigh as she turned, then followed Mia from her office, down the elevator, and through the front door to a waiting sedan.

Mia gestured to the dust-covered sidewalk before opening the back passenger door. "Be careful getting this dust on your shoes. It leaves footprints where surveillance videos focus."

She smiled at the major as she sat. "We already figured that out."

~ * ~

"I'm so glad you stopped sharing. It's so hard not to volunteer information to friendly authority, isn't it?"

Kye stood behind the loveseat and pressed his fingers through his hair as he eyed Charlie. "I hate that I can't control it."

"Work on it." Owen rested his hand on Kye's shoulder. "Know it's one of your weaknesses, and work on sharing only the bare minimum, unless they're your closest allies."

"Not sharing will serve you well. Mark my words." Charlie chuckled. "Never volunteer either."

Faith's brows rose as she looked up. "Hear that, Ben?"

"Guys…" He sneered at her as he paced in front of the sliding glass door. "What are we doing!?"

Taylor raised a finger. "We're doing nothing, young man."

His eyes darted around the room and finally focused on Steve. "But someone is, right?"

Steve fought his grin but kept silent as Ben's phone lit with a message. He glanced at Becca, then sat quietly.

Taylor waved a finger. "I'm telling you all. You got away with whatever you did the first time, without getting in trouble. The next time, I will ground all four of you until you're all twenty-one…mine or not."

Faith's brows rose as she glanced at Amanda. "Can she do that?"

Owen raised an open hand. "I ain't stopping her."

She continued waving a finger. "You all eat and sleep at my house enough that I can, and will."

"I'm calling you Mom T."

Ben frowned at Kye before eyeing his mother. "What if we promise to be real careful?"

"Ladies and gentlemen, stop." Steve peered out the sliding glass door as a police cruiser's lights flashed through the alley. "We're not doing anything …especially tonight, so let's just relax and be happy Jaime is safe."

Becca shrugged. "And Karma may be able to handle herself."

"One person against the Air Force?" Cal scratched his head as everyone stared. "Did I say that out loud?"

"Do you know where they'll keep her?" Ben sat on the carpet and faced Charlie. "Is there a jail there?"

Taylor pointed to Charlie. "Don't go there."

Cal reached for her hand. "Aren't they allowed to ask?"

"No. It just gives them ideas."

"They're just ideas. Besides …it helps them with their problem-solving skills."

Taylor faced Becca. "But that leads to actions, with these four."

"That's a good thing, sweetheart."

"And the discussion helps them cope with the injustice." Amanda reached for Taylor's hand. "Don't force the injustice to remain bottled up in our children. It's what creates anger and hopelessness."

Taylor's eyes welled. "Don't you understand, I wouldn't be able to handle something happening to them?"

Amanda's eyes turned glassy as her voice softened. "Am I not their mother too?"

Taylor wiped her eyes. "Our baby was kidnapped today."

"All the more reason why they need to at least be able to discuss this."

Taylor pointed to Faith, Ben, and Kye as her eyes reddened. "I will die if something happens to any of you. Do you understand?"

Faith shared a faint frown as she sighed. "Yeah, Mom. We really do."

"So then you agree you won't do anything?"

"We promise, Mom T." Kye rose and hugged her.

She patted his back as her chin rested on his shoulder. "You're such a liar."

Ben stood and started pacing again. "So is there a jail they would take her to?"

"There's a jail on base, but there's also an interrogation process."

"Wonderful."

"I have to go to the Commissary on base. I'll look around …visit some old friends while I'm there."

"What's a commissary?"

"A gigantic military discount store."

Ben hopped as the front door opened, then ran toward it. "Jaime?!"

"Hi."

He hugged her tight, then stared with wide eyes after releasing her. "Are you alright?"

She smiled as everyone appeared in the hall. "I'm fine. My thigh is a little sore, but otherwise…"

Amanda pushed through the small crowd and embraced her, then held her by the shoulders. "What happened to your thigh?"

"It's where they shot me."

Amanda gasped, then raised her hand to her mouth. "They shot you!?"

"Only with a dart, but damn, it hurt when I woke up."

"Jesus, child." Owen held her.

"I'll be alright. I've had worse injuries." She squeezed Faith tight.

Kye whispered in her ear as he hugged her, "Glad you're safe."

"I'm safe, but our friend isn't." She hugged everyone else as they drifted toward the family room, and she glanced at Charlie and Becca after they sat. "Did you make any plans yet?"

She followed everyone's eyes to Taylor. "What?"

"We don't want you doing anything."

"Tell me about it." She gestured toward her brother and friends. "We don't want to do anything either, but something keeps taking away our choice."

Taylor reached for her hand. "Sorry honey, but I forbid you to do anything."

"But if it wasn't for her, we'd be in jail, and in more trouble than you think." She looked around. "Guys …we have no choice."

Becca raised her hands. "Nothing has to be done in haste. Let Charlie go to the base and do a little advance scouting." She eyed their new friend. "Agreed?"

Charlie nodded. "And the four of you shouldn't be the ones who do anything, anyway. You have too much to lose."

Ben's phone lit again and he inhaled trying to calm, then discreetly forwarded Becca's message.

Kye waited until Taylor looked away before glancing at his phone, then forwarded the message. "You're right. We can't do anything. They're the military. We can't fight them anymore." He stood and drew Taylor's attention, as Faith's phone lit.

"Let me and a few other military friends handle this." Charlie stood, blocking Jaime from Taylor's view. "You've all been wonderful, but Taylor's right. You've done enough. You got lucky once. Time to disengage."

Jaime buried her phone in her back pocket, then stood and rubbed her thigh. "He's right. It isn't worth the risk."

"Poor Karma." Ben raised his hand to his hair. "What do you think they'll do to her?"

"No idea." Charlie inhaled as he eyed the group. "But short of stupidity, we still have cards to play."

Jaime smiled. "Is it time we share our adventures with the world?"

Becca sat forward. "It's an option, but I think you should share your abduction with the police, as soon as possible."

"I think everyone should think of all our options and share them with each other."

Steve chuckled at Ben. "I like the way you think, Boo."

Jaime sat up. "It's why he's the leader."

"Leader to what?!" Taylor sat forward. "What's he the leader of?"

"Nothing." Cal raised a hand toward her. "Relax."

"I'm telling you. Don't even…"

"We really won't, Mom, but we can at least think of ideas for others."

"Okay, It's been a long day, everybody." Owen stood and yawned. "Time to call it a night."

~ * ~

"Well done." Steve started the truck, then glanced at Becca as she buckled in.

"Did I pull it off?"

He clicked his seatbelt. "Taylor never suspected a thing."

"It wasn't easy typing with one thumb, and not looking."

He chuckled. "You're brilliant, I swear."

She waved out the passenger window as they pulled away. "I'm not just a pretty face?"

He grinned. "You haven't ever been just a pretty face."

"Are you saying I'm ugly?"

He laughed as he patted the steering wheel. "But only you could twist that statement all the way around to that."

She removed a second phone from her purse, and sent a quick message. Moments later, it lit in response. "We're meeting Charlie at the Iron Creek Diner."

"Sounds good. I could go some…"

She raised her hand and playfully cut him off. "Brown gravy cheese fries."

His grin widened. "We've been together a long time."

She patted his forearm. "I love you long-time."

He snickered as he reached for her hand, and they drove to the restaurant in peaceful silence. Charlie appeared as they entered, and she turned to the hostess. "Booth for three."

"Yes, ma'am. Follow me."

The hostess laid three menus on the table. "Anything to drink?"

"Coffee."

"Same."

"Three." Steve leaned forward as the young lady walked away. "Thanks for being part of that tonight."

"No problem." Charlie frowned. "Sorry I never saw your earlier messages. I just thought this bullshit was over and had put it in my desk, never thinking…"

Becca leaned back as the waitress placed her coffee. "It's okay. Who would've expected this?"

"I knew the pursuit of Karma wasn't over, but I really thought the kid's involvement, was." Charlie sipped his coffee, then eyed Becca. "So what did you text the kids to appease them?"

Steve turned to her. "Yeah. What could stop Ben in mid-motion, and make him sit calmly?"

She smiled at Charlie as she patted Steve's shoulder. "First, I want credit for deciphering your little hand signal." She motioned with her two thumbs. "As if anybody but me could interpret that as a signal."

Steve lowered his coffee. "Fine. You're the best secret agent here. What'd you tell him?"

"Just a few words. It was all I could type without looking." She sighed. "I told him, agree and trust me. He forwarded it on his own."

Charlie chuckled. "Wow. Fantastic."

"They love us, and know we love them."

"I'm noticing."

The server smiled after approaching. "Are you ready to order?"

Charlie slid his cup closer. "I'm good with just coffee."

"We're going to get something we used to order when we were dating. You're more than welcome to try them." Steve eyed the server. "A double order of french fries covered with melted cheese and brown gravy …and three plates."

Becca watched the server walk away, then leaned forward. "So …we have the kids' trust. How do we earn it?"

"First tell them, absolutely no traceable communication between them or any of us, regarding this business. We can bet their communications are being monitored. Yours most likely are too. Mitch and I aren't sure ours aren't."

"We have throw-away phones."

"We figured. Keep them active, with no association trail. And I promise I'll keep mine on me until further notice."

"What do we do about Karma?"

"I really can't tell you anything until I visit the base and see what's happening, but I'll go sometime tomorrow and give you thoughts by tomorrow night, but to be honest with you, we all might not like the reality I share."

Becca scanned the room before leaning forward. "You know they're going to do something, even if we say there's nothing they can do."

"Yeah ...and I'm not thrilled about that. If they get caught trespassing, they may get in more trouble than any of us ever bargained for."

"Here you go." The server laid the plate between them. "Can I get you anything else?"

"More coffee."

"Ah, memories decades old." Steve lifted a gravy-covered fry. "Help yourself."

Charlie smiled as he stabbed a fry with his fork. "How long have you two been together?"

Becca's eyes widened. "A lifetime."

"Any kids?"

"No. We tried, but I don't think I'd be as good an uncle if I did."

Becca glanced at Charlie as she moved fries onto her plate. "Are you married? Kids?"

"A husband and a baby."

Steve smiled. "How old?"

"Little girl. Destiny. She just turned six."

"Too great."

Becca nodded. "I saw her at the carnival. She's gorgeous."

"Thanks." his head tilted. "You weren't..."

"I trailed Cowboy the entire time, and was right beside you for your conversations with him …and the kid's parting quip."

"Damn. One infiltrator *is* worth a thousand soldiers."

~*~

Jaime covered her phone with her blanket as she lay in bed, then opened a group text to Faith, Ben, and Kye and pressed keys. *Major Madison was the one who had me captured. They brought me to her office and we both watched them capture Karma But she told me something almost as bad ..they have surveillance vid of us at the restaurant next to Field Ops and then at the cargo ship parking lot!*

DAMN!

She told you that?

Why aren't they arresting us?

We have to tell G and P !

And C ..he needs to know that befor he visits the base tomorrow

We don't have his number

Yeah but it aint like he can do anything.

Why don't we hav his number? He has a secret phone too doesn't

he?

Yeah but only P texts him

Well we need to be able to too

ToToo is spelled Tutu

Kye ...do you ever stop being an idiot?

I tried once. booorrrriiinnnngg

Did any of you think of anything yet?

This is just like the last time when we had no idea how to ...

Yeah it is ...and it sucks! ...again!

But its so much fun working together

...Wired guy is officially weird guy!

Don't talk to our leader like that

He's my PITA little brother 1ˢᵗ

No Im not ...Im your leader!!!!!!

...we're DOOMED

GUYS! Did U hear what I said first?! They KNOW we did something! They got us on video!

I want a copy so I can show my grandkids! It was R finest hr!

You're an idiot

They aint getting their $ back!

I'm telling them I spent it!

The money? ...You're not worried about jail ..you're worried about the money?

I aint worried about either

And I'm worried enough for all of us!

Oh relax. We're kids We aint going to jail

You don't know that

That doesn't make me feel any better

Good night team

You're an idiot too

Chapter Thirteen
Unkept Secrets

Charlie turned from his workstation as the metal door blind clanged. "Good morning."

"Good morning." Mitch detoured to the coffee maker and filled his mug, then glanced around the room. "Where are we starting?"

Charlie leaned back and slid his hands through his hair. "Shall we go get a coffee?"

Mitch huffed as he noticed Charlie's full cup. "Too chilly." He waved, "Better idea." then led him from the Control room to the bomb shelter door. He unlocked it without a word and did a doubletake as Charlie raised a finger, then disappeared into his office. He reappeared moments later with a handful of military blankets, and smiled as Mitch held the door open.

It sealed with a screech as Mitch pulled it, and both continued down the concrete steps in silence. Mitch flicked the light switch and scanned the dimly lit expanse. "This is lovely."

"I won't tell you about the places I've been that make this look homey."

"Thanks. At least it's warmer than the picnic area."

Charlie chuckled. "And some military aholes think we're club med."

"What?"

"Nothing. Just some Army and Marine shit on the web." Charlie dropped the blankets on a metal table as Mitch walked to a far wall and flipped light switches. He kicked a dead cockroach into a web. "No bugs down here that don't predate humans."

Charlie snorted as he broke cobwebs with his hand. "We need airmen down here, pronto."

"Good idea. I think I will." Mitch brushed the webs off a metal chair, then nodded with mock-approval as he surveyed the room. "A picture here …a throw rug there ..and this may be our winter home."

"Climate or nuclear?" Charlie huffed as he reached for a chair. "We're both in a mood."

"Yeah. That was a hell of a message last night. They darted and kidnapped her?"

"Yep." He removed a second stacked chair and broke the cobwebs with his shoe. "I think I'd have to go ballistic on somebody."

"Easier said than done. How do you physically strike back without costing yourself more than you cost the scum abusing you?" Mitch stared at the floor. "All these people want is a normal life. Hell, they even want a normal life for harmless aliens." He shook his head. "I can't believe the military would do something so blatant again."

"It worked. They hooked the fish."

Mitch met Charlie's stare, then pointed as he walked to the chairs. "When the airmen are done …a lava lamp there and a little beer fridge over there, and we're spending time down here."

Charlie sat. "You know, rescuing Karma isn't going to be possible. About the only thing our government is damn near perfect at, is learning from its mistakes."

"Yeah, but it's hard to be ever-vigilant, and we need to jump when they get distracted." Mitch leaned back and covered his eyes with his forearm. "Or they move her first, and we never get the opportunity."

"Out of all the people I know, you're absolutely the last person I thought I'd be discussing sedition with."

"We're not planning a coup, but we do need a plan. Do we have one?"

"I have to buy you a phone and hook you into the group."

Mitch lifted his forearm off his eyes. "Who besides the four kids?"

"The aunt and uncle."

He shook his head. "One hell of an elite force."

Charlie pointed. "Don't make fun. They kicked your ass once."

"If I remember, weren't you the highest ranking member of my team?"

"Hey, I'm only a civilian contractor."

"Yeah, that's all you are." Mitch stood and covered his chair with a blanket. "Do we have a plan?"

"I'm heading to the commissary at lunch."

Mitch fought his grin. "Grocery shopping?"

"I have to buy a beer fridge."

"I like your priorities, but see if you can bring back a fish, too."

Charlie glanced around the room. "Why? This place doesn't smell bad enough?"

~ * ~

"And what are the criteria for thesis sentences?" Ms. Krupinski glanced at the ringing phone on her desk, then raised her finger. She lifted the phone and listened. "Jaime, you're wanted in the office. Bring your things."

She whispered to Nina as she slid her notebook into her backpack. "Send me a picture of your notes?"

"Sure."

She entered the administration office, and Ms. Tomlin motioned to the principal's closed door. "You can go in."

She inhaled and entered, then shut the door behind her as a silver-haired officer stood and extended his hand. "Hi, Jaime. I'm Police Chief Joe Craven and it's great to meet you."

She hesitated. "Nice to meet you too?"

Principal Jessica smiled as she pulled a chair from under the office table. "Come join us. Do you want anything to drink?"

Her eyes widened as she reached for a chair. "No thanks."

Chief Craven folded his hands on the table. "You're not in trouble. I'm here because I can't let yesterday's events wait until the end of school, to be discussed."

"I understand."

Jessica patted her hand. "And I'm involved because you're one of mine, and I need to know what you went through and how to handle any reaction you have."

"Thanks, but really …I'm more alright than even I understand."

"Do you mind if I record our conversation?"

Jaime's brows rose. "Will I be in trouble for anything I say?"

"You're the victim, young lady. On my watch, victims are guilty of nothing."

"Then yes, it's fine."

"Thanks." He removed a small device from his thick leather belt and placed it on the table. "First, let's discuss what happened to you." He adjusted a notepad and lifted a pen.

Her smile disappeared as she concentrated. "Faith, Ben, Kye and I just split, and I was in our back alley, and next thing I know, I'm waking up in a military hospital."

"Do you have any idea why?"

"I was told, because a Major Madison wanted to …wanted something from me."

Chief Craven looked up after writing. "What did she want?"

"Me to help her catch someone."

"The Teacher?"

"Yes …Karma." Jaime smiled at Jessica. "Not a teacher, teacher …at least we don't think so. We really don't know actually. We never met

306

her." She faced Chief Craven. "They consider her a terrorist, but she's not. She just doesn't like how the military has been treating the four of us, and she kind of did some things that pissed them off when she helped us."

"And they took you against your will?"

"Yeah. And I have the black and blue mark on my leg to prove it."

Chief Craven's eyes rose. "You've been physically injured?"

"Not bad. I've had worse, playing soccer," She glanced at Jessica before refocusing on the chief. "...but the bruise is pretty impressive."

"Do you know how they gave you the bruise?"

"The dart they shot me with."

He exhaled as he paused. "I need a picture of your injury. Are you okay with that?"

She shrugged. "Sure."

He opened his cell phone after raising his finger, then dialed. "Sergeant, I need a female officer with an evidence camera at Fallwater High School, immediately." He ended the call and lowered the phone. "Can we discuss Karma for a bit?"

"Sure."

"Would you tell me what she did that makes the military consider her a terrorist, and why she did it? Where were the four of you, that she felt the need to come to your rescue?"

"We were taken against our will to a facility, and they interrogated and threatened us with prison and wouldn't let us sleep that night. We have no idea how she knew, but she contacted them and told them to release us. When they didn't, she started blowing up their cars until they released us."

"And why were you being interrogated?"

"Because we took something back, that they took from us."

"And what was that?"

Jaime glanced at Jessica before turning to Chief Craven. "An alien spaceship, with alien life on it. It crashed in my back yard a week before last summer vacation started, and the four of us were helping it when the military discovered it. They took it, and we were sure they would harm the life in it, so we took it back and helped it fly away …and that kind of pissed them off."

Jessica gasped, and Jaime patted her hand. "That's the secret we're still hoping everyone lets die …but it doesn't look like that's happening anytime soon."

He continued jotting notes. "How sure are you, it was an actual alien spaceship and there was alien life on it?"

"The second one waved back every time we waved at it, during the rescue. Then it showed us pictures of the rescue and the celebration on their planet, when it came back. We think it was their way of thanking us for saving their astronauts' lives."

Chief Craven asterisked the note before looking up . "Where was this second ship during your rescue?"

"Floating invisible, over our heads, watching."

"How did you know it was there?"

"It gave us the power to see it."

"Where are both ships now?"

"We succeeded, and they both went home after our rescue."

He drew a line on his notepad after writing a quick note. "We got slightly off-topic. Let's refocus on Karma. How do you know the cars blowing up were her doing?"

"She was communicating with the military when they had us, telling them they needed to let us go, or there'd be consequences. Then things started blowing up, and they let us go. But then they decided they wanted to catch her, and that's why they captured me. They figured she'd reappear …and she did." Jaime sighed. "And they captured her."

"So they have her now?"

"Yeah. I watched them shoot her …probably with the same thing they shot me. And I watched her fall to the ground, then get carried away."

"Where did you watch this from?"

"Major Madison's office window, on base." She leaned forward. "Are you going to do anything to help her? She really isn't a terrorist and she kind of saved our lives."

He nodded and smiled, "I'm sorry." and continued nodding as he pointed to the recording device. "I'm not privy to say. Can I assume the military is now done with you four?"

"No."

He looked up. "May I ask why?"

"We're not in trouble?"

"No, you're really not." Chief Craven smiled. "So what would be the reason the military isn't done with you four?"

"They think we have more of the thing that helped us help the aliens escape."

"Do you?"

"No. The alien ship showed us it needed the stuff. It was this clear jelly stuff. It spilled from the crashed ship, but the ship stuck out a straw thing and sucked some off a blanket, so we figured it needed it, so we filled a mason jar and fed it to them."

"Where was this substance, that you had access to it?"

"There was a puddle beside the crashed ship."

"And you don't have any more?"

"We don't need it. The aliens needed it …and it was theirs." Jaime shrugged.

The office door opened after a knock. "A female officer is here."

"Thank you, Selina." Jessica refocused on Jaime as she raised her coffee. "But you really did help a crashed alien ship recover and fly away?"

Jaime turned. "Please don't spread it around. …The military…"

Jessica reached for her hand. "I'm so impressed!"

"The military isn't."

Chief Craven inhaled. "They think you took it from them. Did you?"

"Yeah, but we had it first and it isn't theirs anyway. Why do they think it's theirs? The aliens are obviously highly intelligent ...more intelligent than us. They fly here from who knows where ...and they were friendly and grateful. They showed us our faces in their sky, with fireworks around us, when they came back."

Jessica snickered. "I love this!"

"We're not loving it as much anymore."

Chief Craven eyed her. "Would you not have saved them if you knew the aftermath?"

Jaime sighed. "We probably still would. We saved lives. Not human lives, but intelligent being, lives ...without hurting anyone. And Karma saved our lives without hurting anyone too, and she deserves better than to be treated like a terrorist because she stopped our interrogation."

Chief Craven dropped his pen after jotting a note. "You should consider being a civil rights lawyer, young lady. Because that was a very heartfelt and compelling closing argument."

She frowned. "The military doesn't think so."

~ * ~

Ben held his backpack straps and bounced on his toes trying to keep warm as he waited outside the school's side entrance doors, then smiled as Jaime appeared. "Are you gonna tell us about yesterday?"

"Sure, but I'm pretty tired. I feel like I was drugged or something."

He looked down. "I'm sorry."

"Why?" She patted his cheek. "You don't have anything to be sorry about."

"Yeah I do. I didn't protect you."

Her eyes widened as she stared at him. "You mean that, don't you."

His brows rose. "Yeah I mean that."

Jaime inhaled in response to his sincerity, then peered in the thin entrance door window to hide her remaining reaction. "Where are they?"

"At their lockers, probably."

He turned toward the pathway home after Faith and Kye appeared, then noticed Jaime limp down the concrete steps. "How's your leg?"

"Big ass black and blue mark."

He watched Faith and Kye walk ahead as they crossed the parking lot, then whispered as he stepped close to her. "Can we have a meeting about everything?"

"We kinda have to, don't we?"

He scrunched his nose after eyeing the other two. "Can you call it?"

She glanced at him. "Nope. The leader needs to."

"But we're all the same."

She smiled at him. "Well?"

He inhaled as he zipped his jacket. "Guys, can we have a meeting?"

Kye turned, then fell in step with him. "Sure. Buddy. Where?"

Jaime raised her hand. "My room."

"I'll text mom where we are."

He glanced at Faith and smiled.

They walked silently into the house, and Kye shut Jaime's bedroom door as she set the stereo volume.

"So what happened?" Faith eyed Jaime after they gathered in a circle on the floor.

Jaime breathed deep. "I was just looking around, and then I don't remember a thing until I woke up in a hospital room. But the weird thing about the hospital was the noise outside. There was a constant rumble of airplanes. Then they told me I was at the Air Base, and I wasn't in trouble, but Major Madison wanted to see me."

"What did she want?"

She frowned at Faith. "To catch Karma."

Ben sat up. "How'd they do it?"

"They dropped a whole planeload of that white powder on the area where a new explosion happened ...and there she was in the middle of the dust-covered street."

311

Kye grinned. "She blew up more stuff?"

Jaime nodded. "Then I heard a pop, like a gun …and she dropped to the ground."

Faith's eyes widened. "You saw it?"

"Yeah. The major and I were looking out her office window, and let me tell you; it was like she knew exactly what was going to happen."

"And the major didn't want you for anything else?"

"Nope. She told me before they caught her, that's all I was there for, and I threatened her with kidnapping charges and everything else, and she told me they got permission to capture me. Oh, and they know about our rescue."

"Bullshit."

She faced Kye. "They have video surveillance tapes from when Becca and Steve picked us up at the restaurant next to Field Op's, then video of their cars in the cargo ship parking lot."

"Then why aren't they arresting us or something?"

Ben sat up after glancing at Kye. "And why didn't they arrest you while you were there?"

"The only thing I can figure is, we didn't break any laws saving that ship, but Karma did when she blew up their cars. They're calling her a terrorist."

Ben nodded. "The police chief told us."

"When?"

"We called them when we realized you were kidnapped, and they searched the alley and arrested four guys, hiding."

"Did one of them shoot me?"

"We're guessing."

"They must have been waiting for one of us to be alone, because we rode around when I got your text, and you were gone that fast."

Jaime stared at them. "So what are we doing next?"

"Do we tell the world what happened?" Faith sat up. "Tell the principal she can give us the award she talked about, and then share our story when she does?"

"I think we might want to leave out the military part."

She nodded at Ben before eyeing Faith. "The principal part kind of happened today."

"What do you mean?"

"She called me into her office and the Police Chief was there, and he asked me a bunch of questions."

"Does that ruin the Invizibles' secret existence?"

"Nope. I worded it so nothing was given away."

Faith covered her face with both hands. "God, I wish this was over."

Kye grimaced. "I don't want no frigging award. I'd rather do something ourselves and stay a secret."

Ben pressed his fingers through his hair as he knelt on the carpet. "What can we do ourselves?"

"You know the adults aren't going to do anything, so I think we should go to the base and see if we can."

Faith covered her eyes and laid back. "Man, I thought it'd be longer than this before we did something moronic again."

"We don't have to do anything. We can just look around to see if anything can be done."

"But we don't even know if Karma is still there, and we may not be able to find out even while we're there."

Kye stretched his arms toward the ceiling. "Yeah, yeah, yeah. Everybody's thinking, and nobody's doing."

"It's not an either-or, Kye. Thinking before doing, is actually a good idea."

"Okay. Let's think." He put his finger on his chin as he smiled at Faith. "Do we visit the base?"

"Are we thinking about ignoring the adults completely?" Jaime covered her mouth and yawned.

"Do you remember the first thing we decided when we helped the ship?"

Ben nodded at him. "Don't get adults involved."

Kye pressed his finger into the carpet. "Or we end up right here."

"So we're not letting the adults know if we do anything?"

Faith sat up. "Aunt Kitt and Uncle Steve really were there for us."

"I have a feeling they'll try to stop us this time." Jaime frowned. "And won't be so willing to keep the secrets from our parents."

"And mom really will ground us until we're twenty-one."

"Not if we screw up big-time. If we end up in military prison, she won't be able to ground us."

"Oh yeah." Jaime smacked Kye's shoulder. "That solves that problem."

He leaned forward and lowered his voice. "We have a choice. Karma is in trouble because she saved us, so we already should be in jail or something ...so trying to save her is the right thing to do on two levels."

Faith sighed. "But we really didn't do anything wrong, so technically she really didn't have to."

"But she didn't know that and she saved us, and I want to return the favor, and the adults aren't going to help. In fact, they're probably gonna stop us."

Ben waved his arm at Kye. "And punish us for life."

"So look ...all I'm suggesting is we go take a look. Spend a Saturday there, instead of the mall." He eyed them. "Okay? ...We back to voting"

Ben energized as he thrust his hand out. "Just like old times."

"Yeah ...June was a century ago." Faith eyed everyone's thumbs and shook her head. "I knew it."

Ben watched her hand. "What's your vote?"

"It doesn't matter now, does it."

Kye motioned to her hand. "We're going but you need to vote."

"No I don't."

Jaime's voice softened. "Are you coming?"

"Of course I'm coming."

"All right!" Ben thrust his arms up as he leaned back. "The Invizibles are back in business!"

"Scream it a little louder, genius. The surveillance devices across the street may not have heard you."

"Sorry."

Faith eyed the ceiling as she placed her hand on her forehead. "That, he whispers."

He glanced at her, then the others. "Are we telling Charlie, or asking him to help?"

"We didn't go there first, last time. Let's use the same plan. We're not doing anything yet, so we don't need to bother any adults yet."

Faith squinted as she shook her head. "That sounded like the right option, last time. How come it doesn't sound so good this time?"

"Because it isn't, unless this remains just a reconnaissance mission, like when Ben ran to the C-one-thirty before we rescued the ship. Agreed?" Jaime glanced at each friend.

"Agreed …unless we get an opportunity too good to pass up."

Faith smirked at Ben. "Yeah …cause that's how real life works."

~ * ~

The desk sergeant presented papers as Chief Craven entered the lobby. "Here's your messages."

He leafed through. "Anything significant?"

"The Air Force major called a few times."

"How funny. She was about to be my first call. Anything else happening?"

"Normal day, normal crap. How was your school meeting?"

315

"Informative, and not good. There's more to this bullshit than the military is sharing, and it's all I can do right now not to have a heart attack on them."

"Really."

The chief nodded and frowned. "They're overstepping their boundaries, big-time."

The sergeant pointed to the lobby counter. "Grab yourself a coffee before you get settled. I just made a pot."

"Good idea." He placed his filled mug on his desk and removed the call slips from his pocket as he sat, then reread his meeting notes before dialing the major's number.

"Major Madison's office."

"It's Fallwater Police Chief Craven. Put me through."

"Yes, sir."

He pressed the phone speaker and re-cradled the receiver as the call forwarded.

"Major Madison."

"Hello, Major."

"Hello, Chief. Can I have my personnel released by phone, or do I have to visit?"

"Now, there's an offer I'd be foolish to refuse."

"I'm kind of busy at the moment, though. Is there any way we can do it by phone?"

"None, actually. The four are being charged with felony kidnapping."

"You're kidding."

"Then why aren't you laughing?"

"To be truthful, it's not very funny."

He stared at the phone. "Kidnapping almost always isn't."

"You're serious."

"Like the heart-attack I'm about to have all over you. Are you actively and currently holding a United States citizen against her will?"

"I don't feel the need to answer that question."

"I will add obstruction of justice to your six felony kidnapping counts, and I'm issuing a warrant for your arrest, as soon as we're done this call. You can come surrender voluntarily, or you will be apprehended at your residence or workplace."

"I had permission from…"

"Stop. You have the right to remain silent, and anything you say can and will be used against you in a court of law. You have the right to an attorney. If you cannot afford one, one will be provided. Do you understand your rights?"

"Come on, Chief."

"Do you understand?"

"Yes."

He inhaled. "Do you wish to continue this conversation?"

"Jesus, Chief. I'll talk to you until you understand I had permission from higher powers than you understand."

He raised his coffee. "Who?"

"Political and military authority."

"I'm sure you know, but not sure you appreciate the difference between the legislative and judiciary branches of our government, Major."

"I recognize all I need to know, Chief."

He rubbed his forehead and inhaled. "Do you understand you don't have the authority to kidnap anyone, regardless of who gave you permission?"

"Do you understand, certain people of authority have the power to execute other basic laws, when national security is at stake?"

He stared at the phone and smiled. "Ah …the difference between the two branches of government. I am sworn to uphold the law, and protect the citizens in my jurisdiction. Others decide when exceptions are permissible."

"And they have, so are you really going to cause the red tape hassle you're currently suggesting?"

He eyed the phone. "Do you appreciate the protection our citizens own, by birthright?"

"I don't appreciate your lack of cooperation, Chief."

"And I don't appreciate your blatant disregard for communal law, Major. Nor do I appreciate the way you've trivialized my investigative acumen."

"What do you mean?"

"I secured a sworn statement from your most recently released abductee, and it includes an eye-witness account of your latest abduction. Your arrest is pending, and I suggest you use your connections as quickly and thoroughly as possible."

"And this isn't open for discussion?"

"Active arrest warrants rarely are."

"And my soldiers?"

"…Remain in my custody on felony kidnapping charges, until they're arraigned and bail is posted."

~ * ~

Becca twitched as her second phone vibrated in her back pocket, and Steve smiled as he cut the end off a brussels sprout. "Your ass is beeping. Are you getting ready to back up?"

She fought her smile as she waved the cooking tongs. "If I didn't think you'd enjoy it, I'd beat you with these."

He laughed. "Don't burn the chicken."

Her brows rose. "Seriously? …Just get the phone. My hands are greasy."

He dried his hands, then reached in her back pocket, and she eyed the ceiling. "Just take it out already."

"I thought I'd enjoy the moment."

"No. You just don't want to help me."

He swiped the phone open. "I don't mind cutting veggies when you ask."

"Why do I still have to ask?" She glanced at him as she flipped a cutlet. "Is it Charlie's reconnaissance report?"

He tapped the screen and began reading. "Yeah."

"Don't sound so thrilled."

"It says he drove around the base and visited a few friends. And there are traps laid out at a few different locations."

"What kind of traps?" She opened the oven and placed the cooked chicken on a platter.

"Diatomaceous earth surrounds certain buildings, and the video surveillance is extensive at those locations." He raised his stare. "Have you texted the kids since we were together?"

"No." The pan sizzled as she lowered another breaded cutlet into the oil. "I'm trying to discourage their next action."

He placed the phone on the counter and lifted the next sprout. "Are you sending this email to their secret phones?"

"I don't want to."

"It isn't a point of wanting to. I think we have to."

"We can't go against Taylor's wishes."

"If we don't, we leave the kids vulnerable by not counseling them, and that's foolish. They know Charlie is supposed to report. Do you really think they're not going to do something, just because she forbade it, or we don't help?"

She wiped the splattered grease off the stove face. "But we'd be enabling them."

"I disagree. We're not their enabler. Their initiative enables them. We're their counsel."

"But you know they may misinterpret our actions, and I can't go against my sister."

He rinsed the trimmed sprouts. "Am I using the small cookie tray?"

"Use the toaster-oven pan. Coat them with olive oil, garlic powder, salt, and pepper, and add a few red pepper flakes if you want."

He removed the spices from the cabinet. "I think just the opposite. If we keep the relationship as strong as it is now, we get to advise them not to act, as we share the report."

"Why do the opposing opinions seem both right and wrong?"

"Because they are." He grinned. "Life isn't black or white."

She offered a derisive sneer.

He chuckled. "Okay …except for our skin colors. …Better?"

She grinned. "It isn't often we get to exclude it."

"Welcome to modern existence." He kissed her after slipping the tray into the small oven. "See. I can cook."

"Sure you can." She motioned with the tongs in her hand. "Set the table and get drinks."

"Do you want ice tea?"

"Yeah."

He reached in the cabinet. "So, what are we doing?"

She glared at him. "Eating dinner."

He filled both glasses. "You know damn right well I meant after dinner."

"Let me think about it." She placed the oven platter on the table.

"We win the kids over again, *and* get to tell them, take no action." He scooped sprouts onto her plate.

"You have no intention of letting me think about it, do you."

"What's to think about? They need counsel and we need to keep our connection and influence."

She placed a cutlet on his plate. "I swear, if they do something, I'm going to be furious."

"No you're not. Pass the salt." He glanced at her as he took it. "Our love for them is close to perfect. It's also non-judgmental."

"Don't you dare tell them that."

"It's obvious enough, no one has to tell them, but we do have to keep proving it."

~ * ~

Major Madison glanced into the antiseptic medical prep room before continuing along the cold basement hall, and stepped back as the large metal door swung open. "Hi, Colonel. You wanted to see me?"

"Yes. I wanted to talk to you before we start."

She extended her hand. "Do you prefer Doctor or Colonel?"

"Either is fine, Major." He released the door and it clicked shut behind him. "The interrogation team is setting up inside and I wanted to share some preliminary information."

"Is she still sedated?"

He referenced his clipboard after adjusting his white lab coat. "She's at the end of the cycle and we have roughly forty minutes before her next medication, so we'll be working with her at her most lucid, but that won't be anything close to fully cognizant. It's one of the reasons I summoned you. You understand, the sodium thiopental is not infallible. It just reduces the tendency to lie, and the results today may be less than you hope. Her cognitive state may also affect the truth serum, and we have to monitor the dose carefully. It can cause cardiac arrhythmia or even diaphragm paralysis." He smiled apologetically. "...Death."

"I've been briefed, Colonel." She stepped against the hallway wall as an attendant passed. "Is there any sign of her physical being, since her capture?"

"None whatsoever, Major. She's definitely here physically, but we only see her due to our use of external measures. She was completely undetectable when we washed the white material off, and is currently detectable only because of the aerosol powder."

"Does she exhibit any signs of unusual abilities?"

"Nothing yet, though she's been sedated and in physical restraints since we captured her, and we believe these led-lined concrete walls aren't conducive to any mental aptitude projection." He glanced at the reinforced metal door leading to the unusual hospital room. "We can't determine how she caused the incidences she's credited for. She has nothing incendiary on her person, nor did she at capture, so we're being overly cautious."

She motioned to the ceiling. "It's why a second team will be monitoring remotely."

The doctor paused as another attendant passed. "Has there been any determination, regarding a schedule for weaning her completely off the medication?"

"I haven't received word yet, but what would the timeline entail?"

"We can begin the weaning process at any point, and she would be fully cognizant within five to seven hours of her last dosage, though a medical assistant with the ability to re-anesthetize her, will be available and will accompany anyone entering the room."

She eyed the door. "Is the anesthetist there now?"

"Yes." He glanced at his clipboard. "How long will our subject be on base?"

"Indefinitely. Our permission to move her has been temporarily rescinded until we begin formal processing."

"Why are we hesitating?"

"Reporting reasons." Her gaze narrowed. "The process isn't as simple, or cut and dried as we'd like, but we're more interested in her abilities, than anything else."

"Still, my expertise would suggest we move her to a more accommodating facility as soon as possible, and let them handle the information extraction."

"It would be my preference also, Colonel. I'm sorry neither of us can make that happen." She smiled politely. "In the meantime, is there something we can put on her that would allow us to detect her if by chance she has the ability to disappear when she awakens fully?"

"You mean like a homebound criminal's ankle cuff?"

"Yes. Exactly."

"I don't have one at my disposal, but I'm sure you can secure one."

She swiped her phone open and keyed a message, and he watched her finish before continuing. "Are you going in to see her?"

"I have no need to visit her, Doctor. She's in capable hands."

He shook his head. "I know I wouldn't want to be her."

Her phone signaled an incoming message, and she swiped it open, then raised her stare. "Thank you for the information, Doctor. I'll keep you informed as to her departure schedule, as soon as it's received."

"Thank you, Major."

She rode the elevator three floors, and Lieutenant Jeffries greeted her as the doors opened. "I was just coming to get you, Major. There's a message for you from General Avory."

"Alright. Go back to the group and I'll share any new information after the interrogation."

She closed her office door, then tabbed to her email program and clicked on the message marked urgent. She smiled at the last two sentences, then lifted her phone and dialed.

"Fallwater police, desk sergeant Gallagher speaking."

"It's Major Madison, Sergeant. Is Chief Craven available?"

"Hold a moment."

She heard the call connect. "This is Chief Craven."

"Hello, Chief."

"Hello, Major. What can I do for you?"

She continued composing an email. "I took your advice to heart, and would like to know if you'd release my personnel, with receipt of the electronic copies of our pardons, or should I have the original copies hand-delivered in an hour?"

"And who pardoned you?"

"We were military thorough. They're signed by the governor and a federal judge ...to cover all state and federal charges."

"Have you forwarded the electronic copies?"

She clicked the computer button. "I just hit *send*. May I send a vehicle for the four, or will you need time to process their release?"

"Send a car. They'll be ready when it gets here."

She leaned back as she eyed the phone. "Have you received the documents?"

"Yeah. Please send the originals by certified mail."

"The driver will hand-deliver them when he comes for my associates."

"I'd like to say it was a pleasure interacting with you, but I'm not that polite or dishonest."

She smiled. "Then we're more alike than you wish, Chief. But I appreciate your loyalty to your constituents."

"Likewise, Major."

"Oh! I almost forgot. We'll be formally charging the person in custody with domestic terrorism, and prosecuting her. She is no longer your concern, and you'll be receiving written documentation accordingly."

"Understood, Major."

"Has anyone reported a missing person in the vicinity of the alley?"

"Not that I'm aware. Why?"

She glanced at the incident file on her desk. "I was just wondering if I can put a name to our anonymous friend." She ended the call after the resulting silence, then sent a note to General Avory before joining the group huddled in the conference room, watching the interrogation.

Captain Griziani sat forward as the questioning ended. "That was disappointing."

"Extracting information is a gradual process, Griz."

"Yeah, but they treated her like a friend, and she's not."

"She isn't a twenty-five year-old murderer, either."

"I think it's all an act." Cowboy placed his fists on the table. "She had no problem getting on base and she's three for three, coming into our territory and wreaking havoc."

"We'll get payback. We own her now."

"True, but why did they let her take so long to answer. What the hell was that about?"

"She's still drugged and the doctor informed me, the control agent and truth serum will be interacting until she's weaned off the agent. It's a process, Lieutenant. We'll get our information."

"Any new word on the rest of the process, Major?"

She nodded as they faced her. "Our associates will be on their way home shortly, and we're prosecuting her as a terrorist."

"Excellent!"

"Congratulations."

~ * ~

Chichi began barking as she jumped off the sofa and ran to the door, and Kye glanced at Jaime, then waited a moment before rising from the loveseat. "I got it."

He held the dog back with his foot as he opened the door. "Since when do you knock and not just come in?"

"It was the two of us."

Faith nudged them apart and walked ahead. "I should still be sleeping."

Ben knelt and greeted the dog. "I told you the work hours suck."

"Hi, bestie." Jaime smiled as Faith appeared behind the loveseat.

"Hi, girlfriend." She plopped on the sofa and hugged a pillow. "Why are we doing this again?"

"Because we're the Invizibles, and it's what we do." Kye grabbed a pillow off the loveseat and laid on the carpet.

"Yeah. We're so bad-ass, we need to bum a ride from a friend."

Jaime tapped Faith's leg. "We're giving him gas money."

Kye chuckled. "That makes it far less pathetic."

"What time is TJ coming?"

Jaime glanced at her phone. "He said he'd pick us up at ten."

"I'm so glad there's an away basketball game."

"I'm not. We stay home if we couldn't conjure an excuse." Faith tossed her pillow at Ben. "What'd you tell mom we're doing after?"

He turned from the sliding glass door. "I told her we're going to a pizza restaurant, then the mall with everyone."

"And she bought it?"

"Kind of. She made me swear."

Jaime glanced at her phone. "Everyone got gel?"

"Yeah."

"Second phones?"

Kye patted his pocket. "Where's TJ dropping us off?"

"I went on a street-view map. There's buildings and strip stores all along the road leading to the base. We'll pick one when we get there."

"Who's picking us up when we're done?" Kye tossed Faith's pillow on the sofa.

"Uncle Steve."

Jaime sat up. "He knows?"

Ben nodded as he turned from the sliding glass door. "I asked after he sent my other phone a text with Charlie's report."

"Why are you just telling us now?"

He shrugged. "Because we probably wouldn't be going?"

Faith huffed. "And why not?"

"Charlie said the place is boobytrapped like they're waiting for us."

Kye slapped his thigh. "I frigging love it! They know we're coming to rescue her."

Faith sat up and pointed. "No we're not! We're going to scout the place, and that's all…or I swear…"

"Oh relax." Jaime's phone pinged. "Guys. TJ is here."

Ben raised his fist as everyone stood. "Invizibles unite!"

"What a nerd." Faith shook her head as she followed everyone outside.

Kye squinted and raised his hand, blocking the sun as he approached the driver window. "Hey, TJ."

"Kyle."

Jaime smiled after sitting in the front seat. "Thanks for the lift."

"Thanks for the beer…I mean gas money."

Ben waited for Faith to move toward Kye in the back seat, then climbed in beside her. "This is our official seating arrangement."

Faith nudged him. "You really do think too much."

He raised his hands and grinned. "What? What's wrong with that?"

"Nothing." Jaime stared at Faith before smiling at Ben. "Nothing at all."

"Would you rather Jaime sit between us?"

Faith waved a finger. "Unacceptable."

TJ shook his head and smiled. "You four crack me the hell up. I never saw anybody like you."

"What?"

"You guys give each other more shit than anyone I know, yet you're inseparable."

"But I have to hang with them. Who else would be friends with these three?"

Jaime snorted as she faced Kye. "Oh yeah …you're the prize."

TJ pounded the steering wheel with his palm as he laughed. "See what I mean?"

They listened to music as they drove and Jaime broke the extended silence. "Can we talk about our business to each other, in front of you?"

"Hell yeah. I can be Kato. Just don't say anything too revealing. I like my plausible deniability."

"Who?"

"What?"

He glanced at Ben, "Your bad-ass black-belt limo driver." then smiled at Faith through the rearview mirror. "Saying I don't know anything, and really meaning it."

"When did you come up with that?"

"You never heard that from a criminal TV show?"

Ben sat up. "You know karate?"

"Hell no ...but I ain't Kato either, so I'm good."

"You're the frigging best, TJ."

"Yeah, and I'd miss you lunatics if anything happens to you ...so be careful for whatever you're about to do."

Jaime pointed. "That store looks like a good spot. See if you can pull around back."

He turned into the parking lot and stopped by a dumpster behind the building. "Is this good?"

"Perfect, TJ. Thanks." Jaime handed him his money as their car doors opened. "And you took a drive, and nothing more."

"Who the hell is gonna ask me where I was?" He shoved the money in his pocket. "Go have fun and come back in one piece."

They slipped behind the overfilled dumpster and disappeared after TJ drove out of sight, then walked to the intersecting street and turned toward the guard shack in the distance. Jaime raised her invisible phones. "Everything on silent."

Faith squinted as an armed guard stepped from the white shack and greeted an entering car. "I hate seeing people with guns."

"I was here." Ben swiped his phone open and checked the volume. "I had a dream about this place."

Faith grabbed his arm. "When?!"

"Last night."

Her eyes widened. "So did I!"

"No, I'm serious."

Jaime stopped. "Holy shit. So did I." She pointed ahead. "There's going to be a wide, black building that has a little navy blue front awning, a strange walkway around it, and a raised round patch of grass with a flag pole in the middle of its parking lot, and..."

Faith covered her mouth. "And a really wide street behind it with buildings on both sides and trees in the middle strip, and Karma is in the square glass one on the left."

Kye motioned to Jaime. "Bullshit. You were here just the other day."

"Yeah, but I didn't leave this way, and I was unconscious when I came ...remember?"

"And I wasn't here." Faith pointed. "If that building is there, I'm gonna freak a little."

"Then you're gonna freak a little. The only thing I remember about my visit, was the building I was in. That's where Madison's office is, but on a side without buildings across from it."

Ben hopped. "No, guys. Our dreams are a good thing, especially if Karma is trying to talk to us. I want to talk to her."

"Can we keep going?" Kye waved them on and began walking. "So she's asking us to rescue her, or trying to help us rescue her?"

Ben shook his head. "Nope. That ain't the message I got." He placed his hand on the top of his head. "She wants us to stay away."

"And just leave her with these aholes?"

Jaime raised a translucent hand. "Time to be silent, until we pass the guards."

Ben raised his second phone. "If you want, we can text."

Faith waved a finger. "No. Did you see the video of that lady walk into the fountain at the mall while she texted? They might notice us if we trip or something."

Kye grinned. "That video is hilarious."

She eyed Jaime as she gestured with her head. "He's like trying to talk to a cement wall."

"Concrete." Ben's eyes widened as they stared. "What? Don't you remember?"

"What she's trying to say is, we can't pay attention and text, so let's just shut up and get past the guys with guns."

They walked the last forty yards in silence, then took turns sliding between the guard shack and white wooden drop gate, before carefully walking away.

Jaime turned and gauged the distance between them and the guards. "I think I had a dream about something talking to me too."

Faith squinted. "Me too. Not really a dream. Kind of a dream, but different. It's like, we say goodbye to each other, almost the same time I wake, and it's real."

Ben stared at her. "That's freaky."

"You're both talking to things while you sleep?" Kye smirked. "Yep. You're gone."

"Kye…"

Jaime smiled at Ben. "No. It's alright. I mean, it's a little freaky now that I realize it, but it doesn't seem like they're bad or anything."

"Who do you think they are?" He fell in step with her. "The aliens? Karma?"

"I have no idea."

"Just the same." Jaime nudged Faith. "Don't tell anyone else."

Faith glanced behind them as they walked along the edge of the road. "Guys, be careful. Cars can't see us."

"Should we cut across the field? It'd be shorter."

"No, and look out for traps on the grass and stuff."

Kye laughed. "You think they set trip wires for us?"

She frowned. "Just look out for stuff, will you?"

He pretended to stumble, then shielded his head with his hands. "Oh no! Bombers!"

"Ow!" He started hopping as she kicked his calf.

"You deserve it." She stopped as the buildings came into view. "Okay, my dream is really starting to freak me out."

Ben pointed to the dust-covered ground as they approached. "Be careful where you're stepping. Don't leave footprints. *C* mentioned video cameras and dust from Karma's capture."

Jaime led them to the first building's back parking lot, then sat on the curb facing the divided street. "What could we possibly do here? There's dust all over the ground, and surveillance cameras on every building corner, and I bet you need an ID to open every door."

Kye raised a finger. "I got it. Let's wait for them to carry her out on a forklift, and we'll cover her with a box, then switch her with a mannequin."

"That's brilliant!" Ben fist-bumped him.

Jaime sighed. "Why couldn't I have a normal brother?"

Faith leaned against her shoulder as they sat together. "There's no such thing."

Ben pointed to the square office building. "Want to go look in the windows?"

"No. Too much dust on the ground and too many cameras. Getting caught ain't gonna help Karma."

Kye raised his hands to his head as he stared at the building. "There's nothing we can do, is there."

Ben rested his hand on Kye's shoulder. "Maybe we just haven't thought of it yet."

He frowned as he stared. "Or maybe we're in way over our heads and there's nothing we can do."

"This was a complete waste of time." Faith stood and sighed. "And the dumbest thing we did so far."

"Look at the bright side." Kye wrapped his arm around her shoulder. "We'll probably do a lot dumber shit in the future."

Jaime's shoulders drooped as she stared at the road. "Some superheroes we are."

Kye straightened. "Are you kidding? I know a superhero god who got so defeated, he turned into a fat candy-eating drunk video-gamer couch potato." He turned to the group. "Okay. We're smaller, weaker, have fewer powers, and less tools and resources than any superheroes we know." He grinned. "So we ain't doin' *that* bad."

"We're pathetic."

He raised a finger. "It could always be worse."

Jaime glanced at him after staring at the building. "You're so comforting."

Ben hopped as he displayed his secret phone. "Should I call Steve to come pick us up?"

"Sure."

He keyed a text. "Guys. We can still try to think of something."

"Sure." Jaime brushed the back of her pants as she led them away.

They walked in silence until Kye turned and stared at the building complex. "I'm not okay leaving her, without trying to rescue her."

"Maybe we could get better prepared to do things in the future."

"Like what?" He glanced at Ben, then refocused on the buildings.

"I was thinking we should all take karate lessons or some kind of martial arts."

"I could do that." Kye turned and began walking. "Especially if we do it together."

Jaime raised a finger to her lips. "Time to be silent, guys."

They stepped around the liftgate and past the guard shack, and Faith covered her mouth as Kye silently kissed his thumb and pressed it to his ass as they walked away.

Ben glanced at the distance between them and the guards, then turned to the sisters. "So what do you think? Are you in?"

"On what?" Jaime zipped her jacket as the wind picked up.

"Learning martial arts together?"

"Yeah, and one of us can learn to use a whip."

Faith raised her hand. "He wasn't a superhero, but I volunteer for that."

"Think anybody will make us a shield?"

"No, but dad has a nice three-pound one-hand sledge-hammer. I'll ask him if we can borrow it."

Jaime grinned. "But are we worthy?"

Ben pulled a pretend bow, then released it. "Don't forget bow and arrow shooting."

"I thought of it, but where would we get the fancy arrows?" Kye laughed, then winked at Faith. "…and now that I think of it, the whip may come in handy for a whole 'nuther reason."

Faith snickered. "No. Those kinds of whips are a lot shorter."

Ben scrunched his nose as he ran his fingers through the side of his hair. "You guys are sick."

Kye pointed at him. "No judging."

Chapter Fourteen
Nocturnal Conveyance

Commander Lacey knocked on the office door frame. "Good morning, Aidan."

He smiled as he peered above his computer screen. "Good morning, Don."

"You keep long hours, my friend." He adjusted a guest chair and placed his briefcase next to it.

"I enjoy working when there's work to be done. Especially morning hours." Aidan rose from his desk and lifted his laptop. "Please sit here."

"Some would insist, it's still night." Don glanced at his watch, then waved him back down. "Sit. I'm okay with a guest chair."

"But I'm not, Commander. We all have our idiosyncrasies, and one of mine is honoring rank." He slid his computer onto the table.

"Then we'll sit as equals and I'll secure you two nicer guest chairs." Don removed a document from his briefcase. "A lot's been happening on the surface. Have you heard any good rumors lately?"

Aidan smiled. "One of my other idiosyncrasies is, I have the ability to narrow my focus to suit my psyche, and I currently don't care what's happing in a world that removed me from it."

Don chuckled. "I'm telling you anyway." He shuffled through the report. "Your predecessor executed a failed raid in Fallwater, and then captured one of the adolescents, which led to her and four others being charged with a few felonies. But they also captured the person they believe destroyed the vehicles and your house. She's being charged with domestic terrorism." Don raised his stare. "You really don't care, do you."

"If you were suddenly unceremoniously expelled from all you worked for, would you give a shit what happened to the place or the people in it?"

"I never thought about it." He inhaled. "But I can see what the argument means to you, so let's move on to a different subject. How is our super-soldier project proceeding?"

"Excellent. The two soldiers have been selected, and have been in training."

"Who are they?"

"Both are special op's. One from the Marines and one is Army. Both have undergone minor operations and now have subcutaneous tracking devices tied to three offline computers, but neither has experienced invisibility, though they're instructed daily on the different aspects of its properties."

"Who's the lead?"

"The marine, for the single reason, he's smaller. Otherwise their physical, mental, and emotional talents are identical."

"Then why the smaller of the two?"

"In case he has to experience a place where the larger agent won't fit."

"And strength?"

Aidan opened a file. "Human strength?"

Don spread his open hands.

Aidan perused the document. "It ranks twenty-third on the qualities by priority list, and is insignificant."

"Really. Why so low?"

"On a world scale, two of the top three fighting armies are people who would be categorized as diminutive. Size and strength count for…" Aidan searched the document. "One point four six percent of cumulative attributes." He smiled as he raised his stare. "Next to nothing."

"What's the highest ranking quality?"

"Mental intellectual, physical, or emotional? We've categorized them by psychological domain."

"I like your attention to detail." Don jotted a quick note. "Is there anything to see?"

"Sure." Aidan closed his laptop. "Let's take a ride down to their training facility."

"I'd like that." Don stood and waved his arm. "Lead the way."

They exited the lab and Don sat in Aidan's vehicle. "Any updates on the aunt and uncle's surveillance assignment?"

"Everything is proceeding without issue. We've secured their garage frequency, and have been monitoring and recording not only their daily routines, but the neighborhood routines as well." Aidan keyed in his six-digit code as their cart entered the elevator. "The uncle's movements are constant. Like clockwork. The aunt is a little more erratic, but she has days which are routine enough to allow us an uneventful penetration." He inched the cart forward as the elevator slowed. "Do we have a contingency plan for being discovered?"

"It'll look like a neighborhood robbery." Don's voice softened. "And if necessary, I'll use my connections to get criminal charges dropped."

"I'll request assistance if needed." Aidan pulled the cart forward and turned right as the door opened.

"With recent events though, I suggest we delay any action. I'd like things to reach normal activity levels for at least a few weeks before we act. Normality creates natural gaps in vigilance."

Aidan parked, then connected the machine to a charger. "My counterargument is, we're more likely to find our prize, the sooner we search, and if our mission is noticed, surface people will probably get blamed."

Don smiled as he followed Aidan into the complex. "I like your change in allegiance."

Aidan pointed as they walked inside the suite. "Instruction rooms …workout rooms. The only time the two leave this specific suite during their work hours is when they distance run."

"What's their regimen?"

"Cross-training roughly two hours a day, martial arts until their endurance is pushed to its limits, strict diets throughout the day and roughly six hours of instruction mixed with independent study …everything from survival to technology. The program rotates every day, so I'm not sure exactly what they're doing at the moment. If you give me a moment, I'll figure out when they're returning."

Don glanced at his watch. "Don't worry about it. I have a meeting in half an hour. We'll catch up with them, another time." He peeked into a side room. "Who are their instructors?"

"A few have been recruited from outside, but the majority have been recruited from this facility."

He nodded as he turned toward the exit. "We do have talent here."

~*~

"Any strange dreams last night?" Ben zipped his jacket as he reached the sidewalk.

Kye adjusted his backpack and smiled. "Good morning to you too."

"Seriously."

"No." Kye studied him. "You?"

He hopped, trying to keep warm. "Yeah."

"Are you serious?" Kye rubbed his hands together before turning to the school. "C'mon."

He pulled his hoodie strings tight. "I want to wait for them."

Kye stepped away. "It's too cold to stand here. We'll meet them at the door."

Ben hesitated. "I don't want to talk with anyone around."

Kye stopped and turned. "You like her. She likes you. It's weird but I get it."

"It was weird."

"Finally, you agree." Kye squinted as he started bouncing. "Wait. What's weird?"

"The dreams." Ben turned as he heard his front door open.

"Why?" Kye huffed a breath and watched the vapor dissipate in the cold morning air. "Were they about Karma?"

"Yeah."

"Do you remember any of them?"

Ben squinted. "Yeah. Kind of."

"Why do you think they're not just normal dreams?"

He gestured to Faith as she shut the front door. "Their dreams."

Kye faced her as she walked closer. "Did you have any crazy dreams last night?"

"Oh, yeah." She tightened the scarf around her neck. "Did you?"

Kye turned toward the school. "You're all just screwing with me."

Ben stepped next to her as Jaime approached. "Karma?"

She nudged him and nodded.

"Hi." Jaime's eyes darted between them. "What's new?"

Kye pointed. "They're totally screwing with me."

She smirked. "I'm sure you deserve it."

Ben turned after stepping next to Kye. "Anything interesting about last night?"

She fell in step with Faith. "I'm still trying to process it. Why …you guys too?"

Ben nodded. "Oh, yeah."

"Big time." Faith pulled her scarf over her mouth.

Kye smiled as he shook his head. "Bullshit."

"I think I have to touch the gel."

Ben's eyes widened as he spun and stared at Faith. "No! Not happening."

"But I think I'll be able to do things if I do."

"But you can't. You won't be normal. It doesn't wash off."

"Didn't everyone warn us about touching it?" Jaime shook her head as she reached for Faith's arm. "Please don't."

"Then we have to think of something."

"Why is that so important now?"

The school door clicked open and they filed in. "Can we keep talking about this?"

Faith smiled at Ben. "Sure."

"Breakfast in the caf after we go to our lockers?"

"I could eat." Kye grinned. "Or am I no longer included since nothing is whispering to me."

"Are you jealous the voices in my head only talk to me?"

Faith snickered at Jaime. "Are you channeling him?"

"I'm as funny as him." Jaime turned down a different hall.

Kye straightened and called after her as she walked away. "You're taking that away from me too?"

Ben hesitated at the next hallway intersection. "See you in three."

Jaime slid her tray on the table as Kye sat across from her. "So what are we discussing?"

"Our dreams?" Faith opened her juice container. "Were either of you told what your special abilities would be?"

"I know what mine is." Kye grinned as he unwrapped his breakfast muffin. "I have the power of cute butt-ness!" He stood and turned from the table then bent over and arched his hips. "Hiya!"

Ben covered his mouth as he coughed. "That'll scare the shit out of anybody!"

Jaime dropped her muffin. "It made me want to barf."

"Can we get serious?"

"Boring." Kye pounded the table as he sat.

Faith smirked at him before facing Ben. "Abilities?"

He squinted. "Diversion …confusion …mental clutter?"

She faced Jaime.

"Fire and fury. You?"

Faith's eyes narrowed. "Influence and persuasion."

"Not very impressive. One fart and I wipe you all out." Kye leaned sideways. *Pfffft!* "Hiya!"

Faith fought her grin. "You really are a pig."

Jaime tapped her arm. "Did you get any other messages?"

"Guys, we have to get to class." Ben pointed at the cafeteria wall clock. "The bell is going to ring in like three minutes."

"Yeah." Faith glanced at her phone, then pointed as she stood. "After school meeting. Write ideas."

…And don't forget the varsity basketball game tonight against the Spartans. Come out and show your school spirit. Game time is seven o'clock. Have a fantastic Fallwater day, my fellow Phantoms. See you at the game.

Ben turned toward his locker as the day-ending announcements concluded, and finished adding books to his backpack.

"Ben?"

He glanced toward the soft voice as he shut it. "Hi."

Jacquelin slid her fingers through her thick curly hair. "Do you want to be on the freshman hall decorating committee?"

He hesitated as he flung the backpack over his shoulder.

"It'll be fun."

He glanced at the hallway behind her, then exhaled. "Sure."

"Our first meeting is in Mackenzy's room after school tomorrow."

"Okay."

She smiled as she clutched her books against her chest. "See you there."

"Okay." He scanned the hall as she walked away, then hurried toward the gym hallway exit.

"Bro!"

He stopped and smiled as Kye approached. "Hey."

"Are you being serious with me?" Kye adjusted his backpack on his shoulder as they fell in step. "You really think something's talking to you in your sleep?"

They turned toward the exit. "I wouldn't believe it either, except for our sisters' dreams."

Kye frowned. "When you talk to them again, can you tell them I exist?"

"Tell who?"

"Whoever you're talking to in the dreams?"

"I'm not talking. I'm only listening." He smiled as Jaime approached. "Hi."

She smiled at Ben then faced Kye. "What's wrong? ...Don't like your pathetic superpower anymore?"

He pointed at her. "Be careful! I'll sit on you and unleash my fury!"

She grabbed her throat as her head swayed back. "Ugh ...make me gag."

Faith nudged Jaime's shoulder as she walked up. "What's going on?"

"Kye's being disgusting."

"So ... nothing new?" She hid her grin as she led them down the steps and across the parking lot. "Anyone think of anything?"

Kye zipped his coat. "I want to know who's talking to you."

"Why? Are you going to file a complaint with the superhero union?"

Faith glanced at the brothers, then refocused on Jaime. "Who do you think it is?"

"Maybe he got demoted to sidekick!" Ben pulled the draw-strings on his hoodie. "Can we walk faster?"

Kye stopped walking. "That ain't funny."

"Whose house are we meeting at?"

"My room." Faith angled across the neighbor's lawn, heading to their garage, then led everyone through the family room and up the stairs. She placed her phone on the end table, then plopped on the bed. "Okay. Where do we start?"

"Can you all explain what you're all talking about, with these dreams you're having?"

Ben fought his grin as he sat on the carpet. "You mean, how you became a sidekick?"

"Man, that's the second time you sold me out as fast as possible."

He straightened. "When did I ever sell you out?"

Kye leaned forward and whispered, "Her."

He leaned away. "You can't count that 'cause you'd do the same thing."

"Guys …I don't care what you're discussing, but let's get something done."

Kye stared at Jaime after nudging a stuffed penguin with his foot. "Seriously, I want to know what you're all talking about, with the dreaming shit."

Faith hugged her pillow as she sat against the headboard. "It's been going on for days, for me."

"Who is it, do you know?"

"I don't really know. It seems like it's Karma when it starts, but then I seem to get introduced to someone or something else, and the conversation changes."

Kye opened his hands. "To what …another language?"

"No." Her eyes narrowed. "No language."

"So the conversation ends?"

She shook her head. "No. It just changes."

"I don't think I have that part. I just have Karma, then I get this nice feeling after it ends. Then I don't remember anything."

Ben sat up and nodded at Jaime. "Me too."

Faith leaned forward and shook her head. "Oh, no. There's a whole other part."

"But it starts out as Karma?"

"I think so." She glanced at Kye, then faced Jaime. "Is that who you think it is?"

Ben motioned to Faith. "Is she asking for help, or teaching us how to help her?"

"No …at least I don't think so."

Kye rubbed his face. "Man, this is messed up."

"I don't know." Faith smiled. "I get the opposite feeling."

"Well, what do you think it is?"

She turned to Jaime. "Karma introducing us to the aliens."

Ben jolted up. "Do you think?!"

Faith nodded. "I really do."

"Why?" He waved a finger at Jaime. "And why aren't we getting that part?"

Kye sighed. "Why ain't I getting any of it?"

"And the aliens are talking to you?" Ben's eyes widened. "What are they saying to you?"

"Well …it ain't that easy." She squinted. "They're not using words."

Kye's eyes narrowed. "How are they talking to you without using words?"

"I don't know how to explain it, but they are."

"What are they talking to you about?"

"First, I get an elation …a gratitude that's intense, for helping and saving them."

"Okay. That may be what I feel."

She smiled at Jaime. "Then I get a complicated set of curiosity questions … stuff about us like, why are we so different but so close, and why did we immediately help them."

"Different?"

"Male and female or dark and light skin color different?"

"They don't say. They just notice our differences and are amazed that it doesn't affect our friendships. I even had a vision of Uncle Steve and Aunt Kitt's difference, and how they live together."

Jaime laughed. "It's gotta be skin color if they don't find anything different about our parents."

"Are they upset by it?"

"Just the opposite. They love that we can look so opposite yet be so friendly with each other."

Ben thrust his fist up. "They *are* advanced!"

"What else? Anything else?"

"I wanna frigging talk to them!"

Ben snickered. "You can't now. You're only a sidekick."

Kye's eyes widened. "Do you remember when we met and became friends? …Me sticking up for you at recess when those idiots were making fun of you? And I was willing to fight every one of them for you?"

Ben sighed. "Yeah. I think about it a lot actually. But you know I'm just completely screwing with you, don't you?"

Kye tilted his head and raised his brows. "Then the next time you have the dream …tell them I'm one of you?"

"Damn. You did that for him?"

Kye eyed Jaime. "I'd do that for anybody …wouldn't you?"

Faith raised her open hand. "Relax. I don't see them separating you from us. Maybe it's just you."

Kye frowned as he leaned back. "Oh, that's much better."

"Just concentrate when you go to bed. Tell them you want to talk to them too."

"Do you think?"

"They're highly intelligent beings. I think you can."

Jaime waved a finger between her and Ben. "And we don't have the level of communication Faith has."

He sat up. "I wonder what my super-power is!"

Jaime shook her head. "Wonderful."

"Guys …it's why I think I have to touch the gel."

"No, you can't!" Ben inhaled. "I can't lose you."

"Holy shit, Ben." Jaime blinked repeatedly, fighting back tears.

"Then we have to think of something."

Jaime raised her fingers. "Our nails."

"Nail polish again?" Kye sat on his hands. "We're not painting our nails."

"No …but if we let them grow a little, we can touch the tips to the gel, then cut the nail and become normal again."

"That's too much like touching our skin."

"Maybe, but it also may be the next best thing and allow us to explore a little deeper."

Jaime caressed her ponytail. "Or we could touch our hair, then wrap it in something and cut the ends off later."

"I vote fingernails." Ben raised his hand. "It's a little easier."

Kye pulled on his short hair. "Especially for me, but I have a better idea. If fingernails work …so do toenails."

Jaime gave him a limp-wristed wave. "So you're okay with a pedi but not a mani?"

"What?"

Ben's gaze narrowed as he glanced at her. "We have to cover the tip we touch with a band-aide or something, or else everything we touch disappears."

"Dad makes his own band-aids and they don't come off for days. He uses a piece of napkin and wraps it in electrical tape when he cuts himself at work."

"That's pretty brilliant."

Kye scanned the room. "We have to try this out."

"Do you mean, touch the gel before we sleep and try to talk to them?"

"I meant, do it together and try to talk to each other, but that works too."

"We have to be careful. Mom and dad can't catch us doing it or we'll have more problems than we could want."

"They're not the only ones who can't catch us."

Faith pouted as she eyed her friends. "How did we get here? I thought all this was supposed to be over, and we were just going to live happy normal lives."

Kye laid back on the carpet and chuckled. "Well you thought wrong."

She scowled at him. "I know. And this is going places I don't want to go."

Ben sat up. "We haven't even discussed everything."

Faith sighed as she rubbed her face. "And what did we miss?"

"Karma?" Kye eyed them each in turn. "You're all talking to her?"

Ben leaned against the dresser. "I'm just listening."

"Then what's she saying?"

"She's talking about future abilities but nothing about being rescued."

"Should we though?"

Jaime eyed the window as a cloud darkened the room. "We should if we could but we can't so we won't."

Ben smacked his thigh. "That's excellent!"

"Maybe we'll be able to after we get our powers."

"Abilities, Kye …and we don't have them yet. And in this reality, when you get bombarded with radiation, you just die. You don't turn green and get super-powers."

Faith patted Jaime's hand. "I'm not sure we have to rescue her."

"I wish we could though."

She eyed Ben. "We all wish we could, but you don't understand. Think about some of the things she's done …and now she contacting us, but not to ask us to rescue her?"

"But are you sure she's not? Maybe she is and we're not getting the message."

Ben smirked. "Man, there ain't nothing cut and dried about our superheroness."

Kye raised his brows and stared at him. "Superheroness?"

Ben shrugged before refocusing on Faith. "So are we just touching the gel before we go to bed tonight?"

Her head tilted. "Time to vote?"

Ben raised his hand. "That's what I vote for."

Jaime glanced at Faith before nodding. "Us too."

"Alright! Finally a superhero assignment I can get into!" Kye lifted his leg. *Pfft!*

Jaime covered her mouth as Ben and Faith snickered. "We're doomed."

~*~

General Avory dialed Captain Harris's phone and waited for the connection. "I'm here, Captain, but can't seem to get buzzed in, or reach anyone else by phone. Is the emergency, ongoing?"

"Sir, I'll be right there to explain." Cowboy saluted as he opened the door. "Welcome, sir. Thank you for coming."

"What's going on, Captain?"

"Something has happened to the unit, General. I'm not quite sure what the actual cause is, but I've concluded I'm the only one not affected."

He motioned Harris to lead. "Have you formed a preliminary theory, with regard to the cause?"

"The only thing I can think of, is our guest." Harris opened the door leading to the office cubicles. "Please view for yourself, General." He turned to the open office space. "Attention!"

The general scratched his head as everyone remained seated while giving no indication they heard or understood the command. He strolled through an aisle as the personnel in each cubicle offered no acknowledgment, then stopped at a desk as the occupant laughed at a phone video. "Do you know who I am, soldier?"

"Hi! Are you new?" He raised his phone "You gotta see this! It's a riot!"

The general inhaled as he faced Cowboy. "Is Major Madison available?"

"She's in her office."

"…Other officers?"

"In their offices."

The general gestured toward the hallway. "Were they informed of my visit?"

"To the best of my ability, General. Everyone seems to be affected but me."

"Isn't our prisoner sedated?"

"Yes but we wean her off the medication every few hours, so we can interrogate her."

"Completely?" He followed Cowboy along the corridor.

"No, but enough so she's lucid."

"And you think this is her doing?"

"I can only assume, General."

"And you feel no ill effects?"

"I seem to be the only one, General." Cowboy knocked on the open office door. "Major, General Avory is here."

She glanced up and smiled. "Oh hi, General."

"Come to attention, Major."

She glanced up from her phone. "But I'm almost done this level and I'll get free coins." She displayed the brightly colored game on her phone. "Did you ever play this? It's so much fun!"

General Avory slid his hand over the back of his neck as he turned to Cowboy. "Have you visited the prisoner in the course of this discovery?"

"Yes. The personnel administering to her are exhibiting the same unusual behavior."

"Do we have a prisoner transport …a caged van?"

"Yes, sir."

"Make sure she's drugged good, then get her away from the complex as quickly as possible, and measure the effect." He motioned to the major's computer. "And have the wifi killed until everyone's back to normal. We don't need any security breaches."

"Yes, sir. Can I requisition two MPs?"

"Do what's necessary, Captain, to make sure she's good and secured. My permission is your order."

"Where should I take her?"

"An off-site bomb shelter until I can make permanent transportation arrangements." The general turned from Major Madison's doorway. "Let's see if we can confine her abilities until we deliver her to her next hosts. What's the closest off-base facility with a bomb shelter?"

Harris frowned. "Field Ops Two-Eleven."

"Make it happen, soldier."

"Yes, sir."

General Avory stopped at an unoccupied open office. "Meanwhile, I'll get someone here who can keep an eye on things."

Harris hurried to his office and dialed.

"Base logistics. Sergeant Ireland."

"Sergeant, this is Captain Harris. I need two MPs and a prisoner van by the basement doors of the Intel building in fifteen minutes. We have a prisoner to transport."

"Yes, sir. Destination?"

"Field Operations building two-eleven."

"Do you wish me to inform them?"

"Yes. Tell them we'll be temporarily housing one person in their bomb shelter as further transportation arrangements are made."

"…Any other messages, sir?"

"Yeah. Tell them, Captain Cowboy Harris will be the accompanying lead officer, and we'll notify them of an ETA."

~*~

Charlie spun in his chair. "Who?"

"You heard me."

He jolted up from his workstation and pointed to the back of the building. "Coffee time."

Mitch filled his mug, then followed him out the back door, and Charlie turned as the door clicked shut. "This ain't funny."

"I'm serious."

Charlie began circling the picnic tables. "Why would they bring her here?"

"No idea. Maybe Harris will tell us."

"Harris who?" Charlie stopped in his tracks. "Not…"

"Did I tell you the story gets better?"

"No. You didn't!" Charlie leaned on the picnic table. "Somehow you missed that bit of information."

"Are you sure?" Mitch fought his smirk. "I can't see not mentioning it."

"Are you screwing with me? You're screwing with me, right?"

"Would I screw with you?"

Charlie pointed. "Yes. Yes you would!"

351

"What are you so worried about?"

Charlie lifted his coffee mug. "There is nothing good that can come from this visit."

"Stop. We're not going to do anything."

"I won't do anything but eat some of my soul."

Mitch sipped his coffee. "Promise?"

"Did you have anything to do with this?"

"Yeah. I called and told them we miss their company, and invited them for morning tea."

"Very funny." Charlie pointed to the back of the building. "Do you realize that if anything happens while she's here …anything at all… we're both going to military prison for the rest of our lives?"

"Yeah …if we live that long. And that's why we have to make sure nothing happens."

"Why are you joking? This is not good."

Mitch sat at the picnic table and gripped his warm coffee mug. "Two MPs are guarding her, and they're our witnesses."

"I hope nobody finds out we had her and did nothing."

"I hope nobody finds out we had her and did something."

Charlie pointed at him. "Don't make me laugh. I wanna be pissed." He squinted. "Why here?"

"The bomb shelter. The only thing I can guess is, she started doing things, so they're burying her as deep and far away as conveniently possible."

Charlie's eyes widened. "I have to make sure the shelter is all neat and clean. Where's the shelter door key?"

"On the keyring in my middle drawer. It's larger than the other keys."

"I need something from my car."

Mitch raised his stare as he lifted his coffee. "I don't need details."

"See you inside." Charlie grabbed his mug and hurried along the path to the parking lot.

~*~

"Ben." Faith quietly knocked on the bedroom door. "Ben. Wake up."

"Hold on. I'm not *dressed*."

He opened the door an inch. "What?"

"I got a message."

"From who?" He opened it further and stepped back. "What kind of message?"

"I think from Karma. I think I have to stay home today so I can help her."

He sat on his bed and clipped his toenail after removing the bandage. "Help who do what?"

"Help Karma, but I'm confused about how."

"Just you? What does she need help with, that all of us can't help?" He slipped the toe bandage and clipping in a plastic bag, then slid it in a drawer. "I don't want you to help without the rest of us. We do this together so we can help each other in case something happens."

"No, you don't understand. I have to stay in gel contact so I can communicate …so I can relay messages to others who are helping her."

"Others are helping her too?"

"I got a message last night asking if I could relay messages."

"Why you?"

She grinned. "I'm developing the power of persuasion. I think I can help her convince people to help her."

"Wait. What powers am I getting?"

"Never mind that. You have to go downstairs and tell mom I'm throwing up in the bathroom."

He grinned. "Persuade me."

She pointed to the bedroom door as she clenched her teeth. "Go downstairs and tell mom I'm sick and have to stay home from school, or I'll beat you to a pulp."

He hopped off the bed. "I like it! Very persuasive."

"Idiot."

He slipped his arm in his robe as he headed for the stairs. "I love you too."

He knocked on her bedroom door after running back upstairs. "It's me."

"Come in."

"Mom said it's okay, and told me not to get too close to you. She doesn't want whatever bug you're dealing with, to be a household event."

"Is she coming up?"

He stepped against the inside of her bedroom door. "She said, since it's your first missed day this year, just to tell you to take it easy and hopefully it's just a twenty-four hour bug."

"I'm faking, genius." She shook her head. "Can you remember five minutes ago? Me mentioning Karma contacting me?"

"Not by phone, right?"

"No. Last night while I was touching the gel. Do you hear a third of what I say?" She sighed, then pointed to his toe. "Did you get any messages last night?"

He smiled after glancing down. "Yeah. Kind of. ...Things about you."

"I contacted you?"

"No. It was more like, you were in my dreams."

"More than one?"

"Yeah. Nothing special happened, but you were the main person, like I was only thinking about you."

"This is so weird."

Ben frowned. "Tell me about it. But it's kind of cool too, don't you think?"

"I'll tell you how great this is, about a year or two after we don't do this anymore."

He displayed his phone. "You need to text us too, so we know what's going on."

She wrapped her robe tighter as she sat on the bed. "Then you need to bring your other phone and tell S and B they need to bring theirs too."

He swiped his phone screen and she hit his forearm. "No. We don't want our texts recorded. Tell them on your way to school."

"And text us if you need something or if there's a way we can help."

She pressed her fingers through her hair. "I think I got this."

He gripped the door handle. "You think you can really share messages with people you don't know?"

"It's more than that, but don't worry about it. Just tell *S* and *B* what's happening and I'll fill you all in when you get home. And I'm texting Melisa and Fahima, and telling them to give you any paper assignments. So look for them between classes."

Chapter Fifteen
Disenchanting Decrees

Cowboy stepped against the corridor wall as a medic pushed a gurney into the room. "Be careful. We still haven't gotten the information we want from her."

"Understood, sir."

He eyed the second medic as he followed the gurney into the room. "Is she fully sedated?"

The woman in the white lab coat lowered her phone, then gestured toward a used needle resting next to the sink. "We gave her enough to kill her."

Harris's eyes narrowed as the medic raised her phone and covered her grin. "Okay ...drop that for a minute and help them load her into the transport."

He studied Karma's limp body as the medics transferred her to the gurney, then followed them along the corridor and through the outer doors. He leaned between the van's open back doors and scanned the cage enclosure as they prepared to slide her inside. "Strap her down good."

"You bet, Sarge." The gurney's wheels collapsed as they slid her inside.

The two approaching MPs saluted. "Good morning, sir."

"Good morning gentlemen. Are you familiar with Field Operations Building Two-Eleven and the proposed route?"

"Yes, sir."

"You'll also be standing guard for as long as she's away from this facility, or until formally relieved of duty."

"Understood sir."

He locked the back doors after the medics exited. "Let's get going."

"Do you want to ride up front, sir?"

"I'd rather sit where I can keep an eye on the prisoner." He glanced into the back cage as he slid to the middle of the back passenger seat.

"We were told not to use the highway."

"Good idea." He eyed the traffic as they exited the base. "Does your navigator have an ETA?"

"Yes, sir." The MP pressed two buttons. "One hour and twenty minutes, sir."

"I'm calling our destination." He opened his phone and dialed.

"Field Op's. Captain Cooper."

"Good morning, Captain. This is Captain Harris. Have you been informed of our impending visit?"

"I have."

"Our ETA is roughly eighty minutes. We want access through a bay door and we want it shut as soon as we pull in."

"You got it, partner."

"Captain Harris …partner."

"Sure it is. Is there anything else we can do for you, to make your stay as pleasant as possible?"

He adjusted the phone. "If I think of something, I'll share."

"We can't wait. See you soon …partner."

~*~

Faith's concentration broke and she shivered as the edge of the damp bedsheet sent a chill through her. She lifted her phone off the nightstand, opened a group text, and pressed keys. *Guys ..she's not at the base anymore*

How do U know?

Are you in contact?

Im exhausted and soaked

In what?

Sweat

Why? Are U really sick?

Im concentrating

R U in vis

What do U think

Is she alright?

What pd is it?

2nd

She needs gel

Is that the msg?

Why? isn't she like perm invis?

How? We dont have a car

1 of the msgs

omg ..do U think she's still covered in dust or something so they
can see her?

OMG Yes.

What other msg

Im trying to let those helping her know she's ready

Where would we give it to her? Where is she?

Gotta go. I need to ask

Who?

Who do U think?

She dabbed more gel on the tip of her longest fingernail and rebandaged it, then pulled her comforter over her head and shut her eyes. *Karma ...Karma ...help me help you. Where are you? How can I get you gel?*

She concentrated as pictures of past incidents flashed in her mind, then a vivid image of the Field Ops building lingered. She suddenly felt the cerebral ability to move closer to the building, and her breathing increased. *Are you inside? Are you here?*

She drifted toward the gray metal side door and her vision narrowed to its number-lock, then the side of the building came into focus as her damp hair sent a chill through her. She shivered as she envisioned gliding along the sidewalk toward the back entrance, then the middle bay door resonated as she approached and the motion startled her enough to disrupt her trance.

She inhaled, then gasped as her phone vibrated.

Tape an inv bag onto the back fence-gate for when you contact them! Whoevers rescuing her can drive her gel.

She inhaled slowly as she wiped the perspiration from her forehead, then hit reply. *I think she's going to Field Ops*

Our Field Ops?

She pressed buttons. *Guys ..dont text me until I text U again*

Sorry ..bag on the post - bye

Faith shivered under the damp sheets, then sighed as she failed to recreate her previous vision, and decided to tape the gel bag to the fence. She rose and hurried to the bathroom, then started the shower and as she stepped into the steaming hot water, a silent message pierced her consciousness. She quickly dried off, then hurried to her phone and dialed.

"Hi, precious! How've you been?"

"Hi, Aunt Kitt. I've been better."

"What wrong?"

"I have to do the second most important thing I've ever done in my life, but I can't do it without help."

"By yourself?" Becca's voice lowered. "What are you trying to do?"

"Save another life."

Becca broke the short silence. "Haven't you saved enough lives?"

"There isn't a quota."

"I love you, dear, but there comes a time when you four should disengage."

"But you said you'd always be there for me …for us."

"That doesn't mean I would agree with every decision. Sometimes it's necessary for me to say no, for your own good."

"Do you love me?"

Becca's voice softened with dejection. "Don't. That's not fair."

"I have to. A life hangs in the balance and I'm going to do something to save it. You can help, or you can hope the next person I ask cares enough to not cost me my life as I try to save another. I have about the time it'll take me to get there, to do what I have to do, so wish me luck!"

"To quote a person I adore, who is making me cry right now …I hate you."

Faith sighed into the phone. "I love you too, Aunt Kitt. How long before you're here?"

"I've been driving to you since you answered my second question."

"Please hurry. We're going to be real close to missing her."

"Where do we have to go?"

She wrapped her blanket around her shoulders. "Field Ops."

"Our Field Ops? Why?"

"Karma is there and needs gel."

"I don't have any on me. Ours is home."

She opened her closet door and reached for a boot box. "I have enough for the three of us."

"Your mother can never find out about this, do you understand?"

"Aunt Kitt …there's a whole lot, my mother needs to never find out."

"Oh, that's comforting. So …is what we're doing dangerous, or just stupid?"

She smiled. "Don't laugh at my hair when you see it. I'm not straightening it. I'm supposed to be home sick today."

"Oh my god, I can't wait to see it! I love your hair long and natural! I bet you're beautiful!"

She moved her phone then pulled the blanket tighter. "I just remembered …you won't see it. I have to be inviz."

"Aww."

"How long before you're here?"

"Fifteen minutes, maybe …if I don't get pulled over."

"I'll be waiting by the garage, but it won't look like I'm there. Pull in the drive."

~*~

"Watch out!"

The MP braced himself against the dashboard as the driver swerved away from an oncoming car, then cut his front wheels in the opposite direction to avoid the roadside ditch, and the front passenger tire popped under the pressure. He skidded to a stop as the car behind them honked and swerved around them. "Damn!"

The passenger MP wiped his forehead. "Damn, nothing! That was impressive!"

The driver eyed the rearview mirror, "Are you alright, sir?"

"I'm fine. Are you two?"

"Fine, sir."

The driver inched the van to the embankment. "Sorry for the delay in plans, sir."

"Don't be. Any landing you can walk away from, is a good one."

"Sir?"

"Nothing." He opened his side door. "Flashback from a previous life."

"Please feel free to stay inside as we fix this, sir."

He stepped from the van. "We all deviate from the norm when it's called for, and I've learned not to underestimate unexpected circumstances."

"Sir?"

"I'll keep watch. I don't trust this at all." He walked behind the van, to the edge of the trees lining the road and unclipped his sidearm.

"Should we check the prisoner?"

"Look inside. Is she still strapped to the gurney, lying motionless?"

The MP turned after shading his eyes against the rear window. "Yes, sir."

"Then she's good."

Cowboy eyed each passing car as the MPs changed the tire; occasionally turning to the woods as motions or noises gained his attention. A slowing truck caught his eye and he stared as it pulled onto the shoulder. He scanned the woods then stepped back and drew his firearm as the commercial vehicle stopped.

The driver peered over the windshield after leaning out the door. "Hey, gentlemen. Need any help?"

Harris unholstered his weapon, then pointed it to the ground as he gripped it with both hands. "No! Do *not* step away from your vehicle!"

The guy raised his arms as he stood between the cab and open door. "Damn, dude. I was only offering assistance."

Cowboy glanced at the MPs. "We don't need help. Leave!"

"See ya." The driver disappeared inside the cab, then backed up a distance before driving wide around their van.

He stared at every passing vehicle on the desolate road until an MP broke the brisk intense boredom. "We're finished, sir." The soldier wiped his hands on a rag as his associate inserted the tire iron into its slot.

Cowboy scanned the roadside trees before clipping the holster strap over his gun. "Then let's get gone."

~*~

Charlie stood in the doorway entrance and tapped his wristwatch. "They're late."

Mitch smiled as he turned from his computer screen. "Relax. Only good things can happen if they don't make it."

He frowned. "Do you think?"

Mitch rested his arms on the desk. "Hell no. But I like the way it sounded."

"What's up with you?" Charlie pointed to a guest chair.

Mitch nodded and motioned toward it. "I've adopted a new way of dealing with things I can't control." He raised an eyebrow. " ...and I see you have too."

Charlie sighed. "I know her final destination. I've seen it."

"Do I really need to know?"

Charlie rubbed his face. "You really don't need to know, but..."

Mitch extended his hand. "Then stop there, 'cause I really don't want to know."

"It isn't pretty, and she's not some foreign terrorist."

He rested his elbows on the desk and his chin on his fists. "I don't know what to tell you."

"Damn, Mitch. Should I get..." He removed an invisible something from his pocket, and dangled it. "...and be ...out to lunch, when they get here?"

"No. So far, she's been able to do more than we've been able to explain. This little trip may be more than what we see."

"What if it's her attempt to get help?"

"If she can go this far, you doubt the rest of the journey?" His brows rose. "Let's trust the process."

Charlie's eyes narrowed. "Are you throwing my words back in my face?"

He fought his smirk. "What can I say? You've taught me well."

Charlie fidgeted in the chair. "I'm not really built for inaction."

"Right now, our best action is inaction. Let's be visible and present when our guests arrive and show them whose side we're on."

Charlie shook his head. "Visible and present is fine, but I wouldn't advise showing them what side we're on."

~*~

Faith tightened the scarf around her neck and opened the car door as Becca stopped in the driveway. "Hi, Aunt Kitt."

"Hi, precious." Becca reached across the console as she backed out. "It's still the weirdest thing."

Faith offered a scratchy cackle as she cradled Becca's hand. "I'm here. It's me."

"You sound a little worse for wear. Are you sick?"

"No. It's just been an intense morning."

Becca smiled. "Another something you'd like to hide from your mother?"

"Oh yeah."

She sighed. "Then maybe it's best I don't know too."

"It really is." Faith reached across the middle console and caressed Becca's forearm. "But I have to do something while we drive, that has to do with what I can't tell you. Please don't think it's weird."

Faith's gasp broke the hour's silence, and Becca reached across the console and grabbed her invisible arm. "Are you alright?"

Faith hopped in her seat and smiled. "I think so."

"What's happening?"

She recognized the road. "Don't drive close! Cameras."

"Whose?"

"Surveillance cameras. Park somewhere and we'll walk, but I may run ahead."

"I'll try to keep up." Becca's eyes narrowed as she glanced at the seemingly empty passenger seat. "Am I getting inviz too?"

"Only if you're coming inside with me, but you don't have to."

"Then I have to find a good parking spot. You're not going in that building alone."

"Yay!"

She parked under a tree on a quiet side street. "Phone on silent."

Faith snapped out of her trance. "You're going to see me in a minute, and once you do, we're silent until we're vis again." She placed an invisible plastic bag in Becca's hand.

"Understood." She slid down the driver seat then manipulated the bags before disappearing. "Oh, I do love your hair! Why is your finger bandaged?"

She opened the car door. "To protect me from the gel and the gel from everything I touch."

"Why? Aren't you just using a bag?" Becca shut her door and the car chirped. "More things I don't want to know?"

"There's another I have to explain." They hurried along the sidewalk toward the main road. "I can communicate with Karma. It's how I know she's here and needs gel to escape, so please don't text me unless it prevents danger. I need to be in contact with her until I know she's got what she needs."

Becca followed as they entered the building's parking lot. "Okay. I'll just be our eyes and ears."

Faith hurried along the building and an instant vision pierced her consciousness as she passed before the second garage. *Yes ...I'm here.* She stopped and placed her hands on the brown metal door.

Welcome, child.

Hello, teacher. She closed her eyes and concentrated. *It's an honor to help you.*

You are a joy.

Where do you want me?

I hoped we could meet outside but the loading will take place inside this bay.

Where are you now?

The basement bomb shelter.

Where should I meet you?

Between the shelter door and the van.

A vision of the plant adorning the corridor corner flashed into focus as she began walking toward the rear entrance. *Then I'm coming inside.*

Tell me when you're secure and I'll have Cowboy call his associates. Meanwhile, would you like to converse?

Yes! May I ask questions?

Sweet Angel ...a teacher yearns for engaged students.

A thrill passed through her. *I love that you're my teacher.*

And I have so much to share.

May I ask my first question?

...Child ...always.

Will you communicate with Kye too?

I do! He's a sound sleeper.

Oh thank god!

How have you four managed to become so close?

She pressed the four-digit code into the rear door lock, then slowly pulled it open. *I don't think we question it.*

Perfect answer!

We're very grateful for you saving our lives.

As our distant friends are grateful to you! They call you ...Angels.

You can talk to them!?

Communicate. They don't use words and only feel sounds, and we're just learning how to share thoughts.

Faith raised her open hand toward Becca before following the corridor past the inside bay doors. *Why you and not us? Is it because you touched the gel?*

That's part of the more complicated answer.

Will we be able to someday?

It's one of the things I hope to help you accomplish but most of your future abilities will be based solely on your desire to learn. A teacher's ability weighs less than most students understand.

Faith inhaled. *How can I feel you and talk to you so easily?*

Because you sincerely want to connect with others. You have great empathy.

She stared at the Control Room door as she passed. *It's not just you?*

It's mostly you, angel. Remember the teacher's rule.

Do you need me to help beyond sharing the gel? She stepped behind the corridor plant.

No, child. All that's necessary has been put in motion. Our friend is about to call the base and get my release permission.

I'm behind the plant in the hallway.

Be patient and don't be afraid of my appearance. The spray powder is the tool they use to see me. I also look unconscious. I'm not.

Cowboy stepped from the guest office with the phone to his ear. "Yes, sir." He pointed to the MPs. "Load the prisoner."

The guards came to attention as Mitch approached from his office and unlocked the shelter door. "Safe trip, gentlemen."

The two MPs disappeared down the steps as Captain Harris walked toward the door, and he stood guard until the gurney appeared in the doorway. Faith covered her mouth and glanced toward Becca, standing at the intersection leading to the inside bay doors.

Your presence is strong, child! You will develop impressive abilities.

The MPs lowered the gurney's wheels as they exited the shelter and the mechanism clicked in place on the corridor floor.

It hurts to see you like this. Are you sure I can't help?

I've recruited Cowboy to assist me. He'll be more than sufficient for the task.

She covered her mouth and held the bag, ready to place it in Karma's hand as they wheeled the gurney toward her.

"Go easy around the corner. I don't want any mishaps."

"Yes, sir."

...That was for you, child. All will be fine.

Karma's opposite arm dropped off the far side of the gurney as they reached the corner, and as the MPs focused on the minor diversion, Faith slipped the invisible unsealed gel bag in Karma's closest hand.

Thank you, beautiful child.

I'm honored to help, teacher.

The MP secured her arm in the body strap before resuming their journey toward the inside bay door.

When will we talk again?

In a few days, child.

She watched the procession pass the Control Room door. *May I ask why you refer to me as ...child?*

It's just my endearment. Is it okay?

Oh, yes! Like we call you, teacher! She hurried to the intersecting corridor as she lost sight of the gurney.

Yes.

Her eyes widened as the communication ended, and she noticed Becca beyond the bay doors. She raised her thumb and watched Becca silently clap, then inhaled as she heard a window blind rattle. She hurried to Becca as Charlie turned the hallway corner then disappeared inside the middle bay, and Faith quickly turned to her. "Wait here."

She hurried to the Control Room and drew a smiley face on a workstation notepad, then removed her phone and typed. *Is Charlie still in the bay?*

Her phone lit. *Yes. What are you doing?!*

She hit the reply and typed, *Be there in a sec* ...then hurried out the door and turned the corridor corner as the middle bay door opened and Charlie suddenly appeared.

She backpedaled slowly and stood against the wall until he passed, then hurried silently to Becca before grabbing her hand and heading to the back exit.

Charlie glanced at the notepad on his desk as he sat, then pulled his arm back. "Damn!" He lifted it and ran to Mitch's office, then grabbed the doorframe and turned inside as he raised the pad. "How do you like this?"

Mitch smiled. "It isn't Kilroy, but it's not bad. Is that what you did while our visitors were here?"

"Not exactly." He grinned. "Guess again."

"Did your child draw it?"

"Still wrong."

Mitch turned from his computer and reached for his coffee. "I give up."

"It wasn't here when I left the Control Room, to open and shut the outside bay door."

"You drew it when you got back? ...Even more impressive, knowing it didn't take you an hour."

He smirked. "I didn't draw it at all."

Mitch straightened in his chair as he fought his grin. "Oh, bullshit. ...Some ghost drew it?"

Charlie nodded, then displayed his secret phone. "Do we want to know?"

Mitch's eyes widened. "No. ...Did you leave anything downstairs that needs cleaning up?"

"Maybe."

Mitch pointed. "Go clean up the basement."

Charlie glanced at the hallway. "By myself?"

"Besides our guest, you were the last one down there."

"But it's dark and buggy down there."

"Alright, you big baby..." Mitch exhaled, then reached for his coffee as he stood. "...I'll go with you."

~*~

Cowboy opened his phone as the van exited the Field Ops parking lot, then accessed a previous call and hit send.

"General Avory speaking."

"It's Captain Harris, sir. We're on our way back."

"Major Madison has resumed charge, Captain, and everything seems to be back to normal. Communicate with her."

"Yes, General. I'll call her now."

"Your stay at Field Ops was uneventful?"

"Yes, sir."

"Excellent. I won't be here when you return, but the prisoner's formal transfer has been initiated."

"That's good news, sir." He heard the click and immediately dialed.

"Major Madison."

"Welcome back, Major."

"...Captain. ...Is our prisoner on her way?"

"Yes."

"...Uneventful trip?"

"Not quite, Major. A minor incident on the way, but an uneventful stay."

"Your ETA?"

"Roughly seventy-five minutes."

"Do you know when her last shot was?"

"Right before we left. I walked in on the medic just after she finished the injection."

"Did you note the time?"

"It should be in the medical logs, Major." He covered his ear with his open hand as they approached a freight train rumbling across an overpass.

371

"It isn't."

He studied his watch. "Roughly three hours ago. We're well within safe parameters."

"Okay. I was concerned when I discovered we had no formal record."

"I understand, Major, but so far, she seems well sedated."

"That's good news. ...Call when you reach the base."

"Are we returning her to the same room?"

"No. Drive her directly to hangar five at the end of runway egress four-*R*-two and lock her in the maintenance office. A nurse, custodian, and two MPs will meet you there. Tell your MPs they're relieved when the prisoner is secured, then visit me when you return to our building."

"Yes, ma'am." Cowboy ended the call and pocketed his phone, then studied the mile markers on the secluded tree-lined road. He discreetly clipped the second seatbelt across his chest, then braced himself as the mile marker approached.

The driver slammed on the brakes until the van came to a screeching halt as they passed the marker, then both MPs slouched forward as he quickly unbuckled, stretched over the middle console, and threw the van into park. Two cars performed screeching U-turns as he unlocked the rear door and an off-road vehicle appeared at the edge of the woods as he climbed inside and unstrapped the invisible prisoner.

"Hello, Cowboy."

"Hello, Rachel. It's good to see you."

"I'm sorry I look such a mess, but I'm so glad you're the one rescuing me." She fussed with her hair. "I owe you my life."

He grinned. "This is payback for saving mine, but you can owe me a dinner date if you want."

"I'd like that very much." She slid her hand down his cheek. "Please come collect when we're both home safe."

"How ...where?"

372

She stepped away from the gurney and paused in front of him. "You'll have a note from me with a number on it when you return to our country."

He took her hand and helped her exit the van. "...Incentive to stay alive."

"Please come home safely."

He waved her toward the off-road vehicle as she continued holding his hand. "I wish you a safe journey home."

"Thank you, brave soldier." She glanced back at him as she hurried to the waiting vehicle, then watched her associates remove a life-size powdered mannequin from a car trunk and carry it to the van. She slipped into the jumpsuit the driver handed her, and strapped on the helmet, then sat behind him and wrapped her arms around his waist.

The driver lifted his helmet visor. "Are you ready?"

"Not yet. I need confirmation."

The others hurried to their cars as Cowboy locked the van's rear door, then sat behind the MPs and signaled out the window.

She tapped the driver's arm. "I've seen enough."

"Yes, ma'am." He revved the four-by-four's engine before releasing the clutch and turning into the woods.

Cowboy reached forward and put the van in drive, then buckled his seatbelt before jolting both front seats. "Damn! I can't believe you avoided another accident! You know the deer population is too large when you see them crossing roads in the middle of the day."

The driver's head snapped back, and he pressed the brake as the van drifted forward.

He placed his hand on the driver's shoulder. "Did you hit your head?"

He gripped the steering wheel. "I don't think so."

"That was a hell of a jolt! I didn't realize this thing could stop so fast." Harris placed his hand on the other MP's shoulder. "Are you alright?"

The MP adjusted his helmet. "That buck was on us in a shot!"

Cowboy grabbed both front headrests. "I wish I had my shotgun. He was at least a ten pointer."

"I can't believe we didn't hit him." The driver looked in the rearview mirror. "Are you okay, sir?"

"A little worse for the jolt, but I'm fine." He rubbed his chest, then turned and examined the gurney. "It seems, she is too. If she only knew what she slept through today."

"She's okay, sir?"

"It doesn't look like she moved. Are you alright, soldier? Can you resume, or would you like a relief driver?"

"I'm fine, sir. I just need a moment to re-orient."

"No problem. And nice driving, soldier. You saved us twice."

"My pleasure, sir."

Cowboy patted the front seat headrests. "Alright. That's enough excitement for the day. Let's get the hell home."

~*~

Becca dropped her plastic gel bag in the cup holder, then shut her car door. "Oh, that was so exciting! And you guys were in there overnight? Where did you hide?"

"Everywhere." Faith suddenly appeared next to her after her door shut. "And forgive me, but I'm not feeling your thrill."

"But you did it! You saved her!" She started the car and pulled onto the road.

"We didn't save her. We only gave her gel." She opened a plastic bag. "And I'd rather be in school, worried about a test or something."

Becca lifted the invisible gel bag from the cup holder. "Put this with yours."

"Keep it." Faith removed another visible plastic bag from her pocket and placed the gel bag inside, then handed it to Becca. "We have more."

"You're a reluctant hero, which makes your accomplishments that much more commendable!" Becca tucked the bag in her door compartment.

She smirked. "Yeah …hooray for me."

"The emotional crash after the high." Becca reached across the console and caressed her forearm. "I get it, but it sure feels good when the deed is done."

"Yeah, but I don't want an exciting life. I just want to be a dancer." She glanced at the dashboard clock and gasped. "And I have to be home in bed before mom gets home, or I'm grounded for the rest of my life!"

Becca signaled right, then entered the highway onramp. "Don't sell the calling short. It comes with more goodwill than you think."

"Aren't you the one who wasn't sure I should do this today?"

"Yeah …and you showed me how important it is to do the right thing whenever you can." She set the car on cruise-control and released a relaxing exhale. "But I wouldn't mind a little more time between hero experiences."

Faith swiped her phone screen. "Do you mind if I text everyone?"

Becca glanced at her. "On that phone?"

Faith gasped, then switched phones. "See!? I'm so not built for this."

"Yet you're perfect at it." Becca smiled.

She opened a group text and keyed a message. *P and I did it*

She's safe?!

No idea

How R we gonna know?

She said she'd contact me in a few days. She pressed send, then continued typing. *Oh …B   …she said she talks to U but youre a sound sleeper!*

YYYESSS!!!

you talked to her?

Kind of

?

Faith smiled as she typed. *I can talk to her when we're close …W/O Speaking!*

!!!COOL!!!

'W'ierdo

U love ME

Is she nice?

…very!

R U on your way home?

Yeah but can U all hang at our hse and leave the garage door open in case mom beats me home?

Sure!

We got your back Dancer girl!

~*~

The MP stood by the gurney, at the hangar door. "What do we do, sir?"

Cowboy raised a finger, then pressed phone keys and waited for the connection.

"Major Madison."

He stared into the expansive hangar. "Major, we're at the maintenance office, but there's a problem."

"What's going on? Is she resisting?"

"No."

"Is she secured?"

"No." He turned and scanned the cargo planes parked along the tarmac. "She's not here."

"Explain."

"I don't know what to tell you. We loaded her. There are three witnesses."

"And?"

"We don't have her, and a powdered mannequin is strapped to the gurney."

"Are you sure you loaded her?"

"Positive."

"I'll message forensics immediately. Tell them I want a thorough scientific evaluation of everything." She turned to her computer and began typing. "Are you sure you unloaded her?"

"Positive. We got a flat on the way, but we left her locked in the cage and I stood guard as the MPs changed the tire. None of us left the van, and we had reason to replace her arm in a gurney strap as we reloaded her, and the difference in what we felt and saw, and what we now feel, is impossible to mistake. We didn't stop …wait …we stopped on the way home but only for a second. No doors opened and she was locked in the cage."

"Was the van locked while at Field Ops?"

"Yes, and we didn't unload until we were inside a closed bay, and the two MPs never left their posts. Major, I swear nothing happened and after questioning the MPs, swear we all believe nothing went wrong and there was no window for a possible escape or rescue."

Mia sighed into the phone. "That didn't stop us from losing our first prize, either."

Her secret phone beeped in her drawer and she looked down. "I have an urgent message, Captain. Instruct the forensic agents, then visit my office as soon as possible."

"Yes, ma'am."

She ended the call, then removed the secret phone from her drawer and read the text. *Thank you for the ride home.*

She stared at the message before keying the reply. *My pleasure. Feel free to visit again.*

I visited you this time. You visit me next time.

377

Her eyes narrowed as she contemplated the message, then smiled and typed. *I'd like that.*

I'll arrange it. Wear layers. The room you'll be staying in is rather chilly this time of year.

She inhaled, then slid her fingertips over her eyebrows. *And if I decide not to come?*

That wouldn't be very gracious ...besides ...I insist.

Cowboy knocked on the office doorframe and Major Madison glanced at the wall clock. "Why the delay?"

"The MP's and I went to internal and wrote incident reports."

"Individual or collaborated?"

"Individual."

She stood before gesturing to the office table. "Why at internal?"

"To remove any suspicion of complicity."

"I'm sorry you took that initiative, Captain."

He pulled a chair from under the table. "I thought it would be best for all involved."

"You thought it would be best for you as the lead officer." She sat facing him. "But everyone doesn't need to know the specifics of our interactions with certain individuals. Did anyone interview you or the MPs?"

"No."

Her brow furrowed as her head tilted. "No one asked you who you were transporting?"

"No, ma'am."

She leaned forward and rested both forearms on the table. "Please refrain from individual initiative from now on."

"Yes, Major."

"You'll be writing me a comprehensive statement after this interview but first, share a detailed explanation of what you believe transpired, from your departure to your return."

She raised her stare after he reported. "Now concentrate on the two driving incidents."

"Sure, Major. Like I said, an oncoming car drifted into our lane, and the driver successfully swerved to miss it, then veered in the opposite direction to avoid the roadside ditch and the front passenger tire popped during the maneuver. We exited and I stood guard at the edge of the roadside woods while they changed the flat. The prisoner cage was never opened and there was no incident as they changed the flat. Then we continued on our way."

"Nothing approached the vehicle and you never lost consciousness?"

His gaze widened. "A post and rail truck pulled behind the van and stopped a distance back, but I exposed my sidearm and immediately threatened the driver …and he quickly got back in and drove away."

"The second travel incident?"

"A ten-point buck darted across the road…" He swiped his hand in front of his shoulders. "…and the driver slammed the breaks and we skidded to a halt. I don't know how we missed it, but after a quick pause, we continued without ever leaving the vehicle."

"Did you note the mile marker, during either incident?"

"No, but the tire skids were pretty significant. I bet we could drive the road and find them." His eyes narrowed. "Do you think there's something about the spot?"

"Probably not. …Alright, Captain. That'll be all for now."

She stood and he immediately stood. "You'll have the written statement shortly."

"Go over it multiple times before submitting." She stepped behind her desk and reached for the computer mouse. "I want the smallest details."

"Yes, ma'am." He pushed the chair under the table, then stepped to the door. "Should I ride the road and report mile markers?"

"I'll let you know." She waited until he disappeared, then opened the base directory and dialed.

"Security Forces office. Sergeant Nasir."

"This is Major Madison at Intel. Two soldiers from your unit just returned after a short mission to Field Operations building two-eleven with a Captain Harris, and I need to meet with them immediately."

"Yes, ma'am. Shall I send them to you?"

"No. I'll visit you in roughly the time it takes to cross the base. Have them present, along with two additional corpsmen. They'll be retracing their trip after I interview them."

"Yes, ma'am."

~*~

Faith unbuckled then kissed Becca's cheek as she stopped in the driveway. "Love you, but I gotta go!"

"I love you too, precious. Hurry!"

Ben sat up as the inside garage door opened. "You made it!"

"I ain't in bed yet." She waved at Jaime and Kye as she rushed around the family room coffee table. "Hi."

"Hi, *BF*."

Ben motioned to them, "We'll slow mom down when she comes in." then pointed as she passed. "I like your hair."

"So do I." Kye grinned at Jaime.

"Thanks." Faith disappeared around the hallway corner. "You're the second and third person who said that today." She hurried up the stairs. "Wait five minutes then come in my room."

Kye knocked minutes later. "Are you decent?"

"Yes."

"Bummer." He opened Faith's bedroom door. "Your mom just pulled up."

Ben followed, pumping his fist as Jaime shut the bedroom door. "Our second mission...accomplished!"

"Yell a little louder. Maybe mom didn't hear you."

"This is too cool! We saved her!" He jumped on the bed and hugged her, and she squirmed. "Get off me, you weirdo."

"Hello!? Are you both up there?"

Ben hopped off the bed and opened the door. "Hi, Mom. Yeah ...and so is Jaime and Kye."

"How's your sister?"

"Still ugly but not as sick." He turned and grinned, then ducked a flying stuffed panda.

"Benjamin! ...I'll call up when dinner's ready."

"Okay." He shut the door and leaned against it. "What's Karma like?"

Faith smiled. "She's wonderful."

"You saw her?"

"And talked to her?"

She nodded at both brothers. "Yeah. I could hear her in my head, but we didn't speak. And she answered my questions, so she heard me too."

"That's awesome! Do you think we'll ever be able to?"

Jaime leaned against the dresser. "How does she do it?"

"She told me it's how the aliens communicate. They don't speak or hear."

"She talks to the aliens?"

"She said it's difficult, but she's learning. Oh! They call us angels for saving them."

Kye raised a fist. "I love it!"

"I wanna talk to them!" Ben flipped the panda to Kye.

"So do I." He flipped it back. "She said I have powers, right?"

"Yes, Kye."

He laid back with his arms raised. "I bet they teach us stuff!"

"…They know English?" Jaime reached for a pillow.

"She said she'd teach us." She faced Jaime. "I don't know."

"I wonder if they studied it or something." Ben stood and hopped in a circle. "Oh my god, we're going to talk to aliens someday!"

Jaime smiled. "And Karma's going to be our teacher?"

Faith nodded. "That's what she said."

"We need to learn and practice, and we need to sign up for martial arts classes." Ben spread his arms. "Superheroes!"

Faith laid back and covered her eyes. "I can't believe this is our lives."

"Are you crazy? This is fantastic!" Ben jabbed and kicked an imaginary foe. "We're gonna be legit superheroes."

Faith shook her head. "Yeah …sure we are. …Saving who and doing what?"

Kye grinned. "Okay, so we don't know all the details."

"Are you kidding? We're already two and oh!" Ben karate chopped and back kicked another fictitious foe.

"What else did she say?" Jaime sat at the foot of the bed and hugged a pillow.

"I don't remember. I was really scared and just wanted to get her the gel."

"How'd you get it to her?"

"She told me to hand it to her at the corner where the hallway plant is, so I did when she passed." Faith energized. "She made Cowboy say something for me!"

"Oh, I wanna learn that."

Jaime pointed to Kye. "No hurting anyone with our powers!"

Faith raised her hand to her forehead. "They're not powers …just abilities."

Ben sat on the carpet, then leaned back and raised his arm. "This is bad-ass!"

"Did you see Mitch or Charlie?"

She nodded at Jaime. "Just Charlie when he closed the garage door after they left."

"Is she going to contact us? …Let us know she escaped and is safe?"

"She said she would in a few days."

"This is awesome."

Jaime smiled at Ben. "And just a little freaky."

Kye stood. "Okay …freaky and awesome."

"Guys! Dinner! Faith, are you eating?"

She opened the door as the others stood. "Yeah, mom. We're coming."

Jaime led them to the kitchen. "Hi, Mom M."

"Hi." She continued setting the table. "What are you doing here?"

"We came to visit a sick friend."

She chuckled, then tapped the back of Kye's head. "You're the funniest person I know."

"Thank you. Thank you very much."

"…But you now know you're all going to be sick, right?"

"Nah …we'll be fine. We're immune or we'd have already gotten it. Half the school's been sick."

"Wonderful."

"We're heading home for dinner…" Kye inhaled and eyed the kitchen. "…Unless you got something better."

She fought her grin. "Goodnight Kyle."

"Kyle?" He covered his chest and staggered. "Damn. What did I do?"

"Nothing unusual." She patted his cheek as she shook her head. "Thanks for checking on my child."

"No problem, Mrs. McCloud."

Chapter Sixteen
Operative Sanction

Aidan glanced at his watch as Commander Lacey's chauffeured electric cart approached, and Don smiled as it stopped. "Good morning, Aidan. Am I late?"

Aidan chuckled. "No, Commander. We're both early. I'm just curious, how their first mission went."

"I understand." He lifted his briefcase and stepped from the vehicle. "So am I."

Aidan keyed in his code, then held the suite door. "After you, Commander."

They entered the meeting room and set their computers on the conference table. "Shall we hunt for a coffee pot, General?"

"It's been a while since I was called that."

Don led them from the room and glanced twice into the kitchenette, "Found it." then turned as he entered. "Your retirement wasn't ceremonious but your career still reached the level of success all soldiers desire, and hopefully your new career has helped your transition."

"I've come to grips with the end of my career." He opened the coffee canister, placed the filter packet in the machine, and flipped the illuminated switch. "And yes, the new beginning has helped. I'm hesitant to think about the end, with any other subsequent scenario."

Don leaned against the counter. "It's my pleasure to be part of your successful transition and my good fortune to have you lead this endeavor."

"I can't tell you how grateful I am." Aidan reached for the coffee pot as it finished brewing, and filled both mugs. "But there is one additional thing regarding the transition, I'd like to request."

Don led him toward the conference room. "…Which is?"

"I'd like to order our surveillance team to look for any signs of the young McCloud boy's participation in the original rescue, and if we find concrete proof he was involved, I'd like his pending commitment to the Academy, rescinded."

"And if there's no empirical proof?"

"I'll concede to the benefit of the doubt, but allegiance to our duty is foremost to me, and his involvement would indicate a weakness in that trait."

Don placed his mug on the conference table and adjusted his chair. "It could be argued, his participation is before any expected or requested allegiance, and shows a level of reasoning that involves deeper intellectual reflection."

"Or he's just following others' leads."

The commander unlocked his laptop. "I'll relent to your reasoning, but if he can't be explicitly identified, I think the Air Force would benefit from someone with his character and initiative."

Aidan removed a folder and notebook from his briefcase. "And I'll concede to that argument if no proof exists."

"I'm noticing, your allegiance is your prize characteristic." Don smiled as he raised his coffee.

"Thank you for the acknowledgment, Commander."

The conference door swung open. "Commander …Aidan …welcome."

"Hello, Colonel." Aidan smiled and nodded as Dosh, Jocilyn, and Nong joined him at the conference table.

Commander Lacey folded his hands by his laptop as the remaining people finished taking places around the table. "Let's share quick introductions." He gestured to his colleague.

"Colonel Bram Delvin. Mission training and execution leader."

"Aidan Dimitri, project team leader." He gestured toward his associates.

Dosh gestured to his two colleagues. "We're the advanced planning, logistics, and analysis team. I'm Doshmere Davis."

"Jocilyn Quarters."

"Nong Nuyen." He turned to the next associate.

"Kayla Cassidy. Engineering, technology and supply."

"Trevor Chayse. Tech department."

"Lieutenant Raphael Faviola. Communications."

"Lieutenant Gil Tyler. Travel coordination, procurement, and logistics."

Colonel Delvin gestured to the two remaining attendants. "And last but certainly not least, our two operatives, Narmer and Sobe`."

"Welcome, everyone." Aidan removed papers from his folder and passed them. "As you can see by the agenda, this meeting will be an open forum, to discuss any and all matters relating to the implementation of the greatest secret weapon our military has ever initiated. An undetectable infiltration device capable of things previously only imagined. We're about to initiate the means to adjust human history as we so please."

Aidan pulled another paper from his folder. "First …the results of the communication mission Narmer and Sobe` undertook. You're all aware, they've been circling the globe to test all levels of communication and tracking." He noted every confirming nod, "Excellent." then placed the report on the conference table. "Our communication and GPS tracking tests were a complete success. We have an ongoing, real-time secured connection with our operatives, from the highest mountains to the deepest ravines, in some of the most remote places on earth."

He referenced the agenda. "Item two. Regular meetings like this will occur as deemed necessary, when these operatives are active. Their assignments will be fluid, so constant analysis and adjustment to their and our needs are our only focus, and everyone in this room now has a new primary assignment. We serve them first, foremost and immediately, in any relevant capacity."

He handed out additional papers. "You are here to witness and participate in the formal initiation of Project Tarnhelm."

"Norse mythology."

Aidan nodded at Dosh. "Yes …but instead of a helmet, we have an alien substance that will render our operative invisible and undetectable." He turned to the two soldiers. "Please stand. …Narmer and Sobe` …you who have given up your true identities and adopted the names of ancient Pharaohs … Are you prepared to make the final and binding commitment to this mission?"

Sobe` glanced at his peer, then came to attention. "We have one new request, sir."

Commander Lacey moved his laptop and folded his hands on the table. "Please share."

Narmer stood at attention. "Sir …we request that we both be made invisible and perform duties as a single inseparable unit."

"Interesting." Don turned to Aidan as he stood. "Let's speak alone for a moment."

Aidan followed the commander, then paused at the door. "I want an undiscussed written evaluation of the plusses and minuses of this deviation from everyone present, while we're gone."

Don turned as he entered an adjoining office. "Your first opinion?"

Aidan stood by the door after shutting it. "I'm pleased with the commitment they've made to each other, and the loyalty they're already showing each other."

"Agreed." Don paused. "Initial concern?"

"There are now more variables and we don't know how this will affect their communication abilities. Your concern?"

"The request shows more allegiance to each other than to us."

"That's a two-edged sword."

Don sat behind the desk. "My concern is ...who wields it."

"That would rest on our ability to choose the right soldiers."

"Do you trust your vetting abilities?"

Aidan nodded. "I stake my military success on it."

"Then let's trust our instincts."

"Agreed. ...I'll retrieve everyone else's concerns." Aidan stepped from the office and opened the conference room door, then circled the table, collecting papers. "These are not for open discussion. This is an exercise in real-time open-ended analysis. No one's opinion is a group concern until it is deemed significant enough to be elevated to that level." He collected the last pages, then opened the door. "We'll return shortly."

He presented the papers as he re-entered the office and Don looked up after reading silently. "All positive and no concern."

Aidan shook his head. "None."

He placed his hand on the notes pile. "This shows me, everyone is willing to adjust to the needs of our two operatives, but do I detect your hesitation?"

"It's not a hesitation, Commander. It's more of a technical glitch."

Don folded his hands on the desk. "Which is?"

"We have very little invisibility material. I'm concerned, splitting it between them may affect its properties."

"Ahh ...the cause, effect circle." Don rose from the desk chair. "It's time for the process solution to eliminate the obstacle preventing its existence."

They re-entered the conference room and Aidan faced the soldiers. "Your request is unanimously supported, but only you can grant your final demand. We don't believe we have enough of the substance to afford you both an adequate portion, so your first mission …if you wish to proceed …is to procure more material."

"Is there potentially more material available, sir?"

"Yes, and we have reason to believe we know where it can be found. It already was your next mission, but now you have additional incentive toward success. If you obtain more material, the initial portion will go toward fulfilling your request."

"Then we wish to proceed, sir."

Aidan joined his hands behind his back. "Are there any additional stipulations you wish to present?"

They came to attention. "No, sir."

The commander stood. "Narmer …Sobe` …Are you prepared to make the final and binding commitment to this mission?"

"Yes, sir."

"Do you accept the consequences of your decision, today and in the future?"

"Yes, sir."

"Are you prepared for the ramifications of indefinite invisibility?"

"Yes, sir."

"Do you continue to swear allegiance to your superiors and our cause?"

"Yes, sir."

"Do either of you have any last trepidations?"

"No, sir."

The commander nodded. "You have both proven worthy of our expectations, on all measurable counts and are hereby formally promoted to the rank of colonel, and will receive combat differential indefinitely. …Thank you for your commitment, and congratulations!"

Quiet applause filled the room and as it subsided, Trevor turned to Aidan. "May I?"

"Absolutely."

"In honor of the moment, the tech department has a few gifts for you." He reached into his briefcase. "We like to create things in our spare time, and we've made some unique items for your missions. We've invented a carbon fiber tool system that is integrated into your work jumpsuits, including the soles of your boots. They also act as protection when in place. Details will be provided during your training process. But our biggest gift to you, are these." He unfolded goggles. "They allow silent communication, not unlike the late Stephen Hawking's glasses, but instead of translating into audible language, they convert to text, readable in a drop-down screen in the upper left lens quadrant. They also have internet access, motion recording, and photo-taking capabilities. Instructions are pending, per your schedule, and software suggestions are always welcome."

"Impressive. Please share my kudos with the tech department."

"Will do, Commander."

Aidan removed three folders from his briefcase. "The details of your first assignment." He slid two folders across the table. "For security purposes, certain assignments and their details will be kept from certain members of the team. Please know, it isn't our preference. We're a team, and no one knows that or appreciates it more than leadership. You've heard what the assignment is and we know, every one of you can extrapolate and understand why the particulars must remain the knowledge of as few as possible. So on that note, the meeting is adjourned. You'll be notified of future meetings as events dictate and your excusal from your previous activity will have already been sanctioned. Thank you for your participation today. All but Narmer, Sobe`, and my team are dismissed."

Aidan waited for the door to shut behind the last associate, then opened the second folder. "Narmer, Sobe` ...Jocilyn, Nong, and Dosh will be your FARO connection for the foreseeable future. In task, they'll be referred to as HQ. Narmer, your inoculation will take place at oh-nine-hundred today. Otherwise, your next three days will be spent studying the particulars of your first assignment. We'll have a daily mock extraction, mainly to verify and become familiar with the technology connections, and when you arrive at the location, preparation will also include a preliminary drive-by of the Mantua residence, hereby designated as location-zero. The address is included."

He removed papers from his folder and displayed them. "We have façade photos, construction blueprints, and access inside but no permission to enter the location. We'll have two teams tracking the residents while they're away and can share the more likely places you'll find your…our prize. Sobe`, for this exercise, since only Narmer will be initially inoculated, you'll be the delivery, stealth communication, and extraction system."

Aidan removed additional documents from his folder. "…What our prize will look like… Captain Devereux of our emergency recovery department, experienced the gel's visual properties while temporarily invisible and has shared an extensive report. It's enclosed, but we'll also have a miniscule amount left after your injection, so you'll both be able to study it since its properties allow its effects to manifest through indirect as well as direct contact. If we must guess, we believe the location residents carry it in a protective pouch or bag, as they alternate between visible and invisible during their undertakings. Our forensic studies department has researched where such an item or items would most likely be placed or hidden in a residence, and that report is included."

He set his computer aside and leaned forward. "We're expecting a simple and uneventful search and extraction. We want you in and out as quickly as possible. Narmer will have updates and support from an entire team, but his information will be shared using silent means, from Sobe` only, who will be nearby in the transport vehicle. Indirect communication will include, informants monitoring the residents' real-time locations, as well as your video eyes and ears here at HQ."

He slipped the remaining reports into the folder. "We've prepared for this operation for roughly a month, so if all remains consistent, there should be no surprises. Do not disturb anything inside the residence. We want no one to see signs of our visit. We expect you'll have roughly two to three hours inside but if an abort message is received, do so without hesitation. You will have no engagements on this first mission, and that's an order."

"Yes, sir."

Aidan nodded. "The more I think about it, the more I like an invisible team. Both of you searching would be twice as efficient."

"We agree, sir."

"Study. Know the inside of the residence like you've lived there for years. Contact our suite if you have any questions or trepidations." He studied his watch. "We are roughly one-hundred hours from execution."

~*~

Major Madison's instant message pop up appeared and she tabbed to the open program. *Meeting in General Avory's conference room at sixteen-hundred hours. Gather and bring all Fallwater files.*

She glanced at the wall clock then typed, *Received* before opening the drawer and noticing the special phone. She raised it after placing the file on her desk, then hid it under the remaining files before pressing her office phone's speaker button.

"Captain Griziani."

"Griz, I've just received orders to collect all Fallwater notes and files."

"From who? For what?"

"From Avory's office. I'll let you know for what, when I return. Meanwhile, collect everyone's information and bring it to me."

"Yes, ma'am."

He walked into her office with an armful of folders as she loaded her briefcase. "This is everyone's. Do you need anything else?"

"Not at the moment."

He placed them on her desk. "This is a strange request."

She paused loading the files into a nylon carry-all. "Nothing about this entire encounter has been anything but strange."

"I've never been asked to relinquish files on a case before."

She paused again. "I won't ask if you made copies of anything before bringing me these." She inhaled as he stood, silently staring forward. "We'll speculate further when I get back."

"The entire team?"

She slid the remaining files in the bag. "Let's you and I have a pre-meeting first."

He stepped aside as she lifted both bags. "I'll wait for you."

"I have no idea how long I'll be."

He followed her toward the exit, then stopped at his office. "It's all good. I have no plans for the evening."

"Then I'll see you when I return." She crossed the divided road, then entered an adjoining building.

"Welcome, Major."

"Hello, Lieutenant." She opened the conference room door, then placed the files and her briefcase on a chair as General Avory appeared.

"Hello, Major."

She stood at attention. "General Avory … General Mahir." Her eyes widened as two unfamiliar officers entered.

"This is Lieutenants Bonilla and Perez."

She nodded. "Nice to meet you."

"Relax, Major. This isn't an inquiry."

"Please forgive me, Generals. The request is somewhat confusing and has caused concern."

"There's nothing to be concerned about." Avory waved his hand. "Please sit."

She glanced at her carry-all, then adjusted the chair.

"Are they the files?"

"Yes, sir."

General Mahir eyed the lieutenants as they typed on their laptops. "Nothing copied, I hope?"

"Not that I'm aware of."

"I ask because we're no longer engaged with, nor will we have any future engagement with anyone or anything regarding the Fallwater incident."

"But General …if we continue engagement, we'll eventually get everything we're pursuing."

"That's no longer your concern. You handled everything we requested, creatively, and we're pleased with your efforts."

Her eyes narrowed.

"Yes, that includes all aspects of the assignment." General Mahir nodded to Lieutenant Bonilla, then gestured to the files.

"We don't hold the unfortunate circumstances against you."

"I feel very confident we could re-apprehend her." She watched the lieutenant gather the files.

"That's no longer our concern, Major."

The Lieutenant lifted the carry-all. "I'll bring this right back."

General Mahir waited for the lieutenant to move away. "And we would like you to refocus on our intended military mission …the continued efforts against our actual foreign enemies."

Avory leaned forward. "We've spent enough time and resources on this endeavor, don't you think?"

She watched the lieutenant leave the room, then refocused, "If that's what you think, General, then it's what I think."

"Well stated, Major. Yes …it is what we think."

She eyed them. "And if contact is somehow re-initiated?"

"Direct it immediately to me, Major, and have no personal reply."

She inhaled. "Yes, sir."

General Mahir smiled. "You're a good soldier, Major, and we appreciate you not asking for an explanation, but you're also advanced enough to be privy to one. This edict comes from above and responsibility has been transferred, but by no means is our Fallwater business over. This group's participation however …has ended."

"Understood, Ma'am."

"Any other questions, Major?"

"No, sir."

"Excellent."

"We really do appreciate your efforts to accomplish this task."

"I'm sorry I wasn't more successful."

"We consider your freedom to engage, limited, and you outperformed our expectations, given those limitations." General Avory stood. "Don't concern yourself with the incidentals. You went above and beyond, as our records will show."

~*~

A pop-up notice appeared on Aidan's computer and he tabbed to the instant-messenger program. *We're about to start.*

He clicked into the reply box. *Thanks, Nong. I'm tuned in and listening.* He tabbed to the closed-captioned audio program and sat back.

"Transport one requesting permission to initialize."

"You have authorization."

"Roger, command. We're at drop point."

"Test communication signals."

"Operative."

"Commence separation."

"Copy."

"Mobile one, confirm arrival."

Narmer broke the extended silence. "At residence zero gate. No obstructions. We're at physical go point."

"Test video signals."

"Cameras on."

"This is HQ. We have dual video, command."

"Test silent signal. Mobile two, report on your tracking signal."

"Affirmative. Resident one's car is parked at his workplace and he is inside the building."

"Mobile three?"

"Affirmative. Resident two is twenty minutes out, in transit toward her work office. Expected arrival, thirteen minutes."

"Mobile units two and three, report every change. Transport one, report on each com signal."

"This is transport one. I have all four signals. Mobile one is live and now silent. We are at the gate with communications go."

"HQ, report."

"We have two-way with transport one and dual video."

"Diversion one, GPS locates you at start point. Confirm."

"Affirmative, command."

"Mobile one, are we a go?"

"Transport one for M one. Affirmative, command."

"Execute."

The yellow and green moving van crawled along the street, and Becca and Steve's garage door rose as it began passing the residence, then at twenty inches, began lowering.

"We have breach."

"Copy, transport one."

"Mobile three reporting. Resident two has parked and is entering her workplace."

Sobe' reclined in the driver seat and watched Narmer enter the residence's interior as his glasses received the video feed from Narmer's special optics. He watched Narmer pass through the inside garage door, then head directly to the master bedroom and begin his methodical search.

Command broke the extended silence. "We are at T plus thirty minutes. Resume silence."

"Transport, we have a possible variance."

Sobe` signaled Narmer to freeze. "What do you see, HQ?"

"The plastic bag, top dresser drawer, upper left below the envelope and papers. Please expose further."

Narmer revealed the bag, then focused the camera and his glasses on it.

Jocilyn whispered into her headset. "Anomaly confirmed. We have prize one."

"Copy and confirmed, HQ. This is transport one. *M* one has obtained prize one at *T* plus thirty-seven minutes. We have also narrowed the search parameters."

"Copy, transport."

Command broke the next silence. "Coming up on *T* plus sixty minutes. Countdown commencing. Mobile one status?"

"Copy, command. M one is in room three."

"Copy, transport."

"This is mobile three. Resident two is approaching her car."

"Report movement direction."

"…Resident two is mobile …and turning east"

"Abort readiness, level three."

"Roger, command."

"Variance."

Sobe` froze Narmer. "Please identify, HQ."

"Resident two has turned north but on an alternate route. Thirty-four minutes to residence zero."

"Abort readiness, level two."

"Copy, command. HQ?"

"Trundle bed middle drawer. Revisit."

Narmer slid the drawer open.

"Irregular shaped grocery bag."

Narmer untied the plastic handles and removed smaller plastic bags before focusing the dual video transmitters.

"Multiple Anomalies."

"Bingo."

"Well done, Dosh."

"Transport one reporting acquisitions two through nine at T plus seventy-four minutes."

"Do we have confirm?"

"Yes, command. Request extraction process initiate."

"Freeze. We have a reassessment variable."

"Expound."

"Hold."

Nong covered his mouthpiece. "Returning prize one would most likely delay discovery."

"Agreed."

Jocilyn looked up from her computer screen. "Do we need permission?"

"I'll request." Dosh typed an instant message.

"Status update requested."

Jocilyn uncovered her mouthpiece. "Decision in three minutes, transport one. Signal M one to extract all prize twos, and return to prize one location."

Dosh read the incoming instant message. "Return prize one, as found."

"Copy, HQ."

"Can he identify amounts? If identical packaging, return smallest quantity if possible."

"Understood." Sobe` silently communicated, then watched Narmer complete the task. "Requesting a second extraction initiation."

"Affirmative, transport. Initiate abort sequence."

"Extraction initiated."

The moving van approached from the opposite direction, and slowed as it ground into a lower gear before continuing its journey. The garage door began rising as the van blocked visual access, then reversed direction at twenty inches.

"Mobile three reporting. Resident two has parked at an unknown residence, twenty-two minutes from point zero."

"Transport one reporting. We have extraction."

"Copy transport one. Confirm rendezvous and recovery."

"Transport at recovery zone. Mobile one approaching"

"*T* plus ninety-seven minutes."

"Recovery complete. Transport returning."

"Mobile two disengaging."

"Mobile three disengaging."

"Excellent, team. Time to get gone. See you all at home."

www.ingramcontent.com/pod-product-compliance
Lightning Source LLC
Chambersburg PA
CBHW071152250626
47159CB00001B/68